A Leaf of Faith

BOOK 2 IN THE MESSENGERS AND THIEVES SERIES

J. Suthern Hicks

DEDICATION

To the One who loved us before even time began.

Inquires can be made by contacting the author at HumbleEntertainment@yahoo.com
Editor: Keith Gordon
Cover Design and Illustrations: Tatiana Minina
A Shophar So Good Book: www.shopharsogood.com

ISBN: 0-9970778-4-0
ISBN-13: 978-0-9970778-4-1

ACKNOWLEDGMENT

To my mom, for teaching me how to save and live frugally which has been a huge part of creating the resources that have allowed me to spend time with a little red fox, talking insects, and worlds I could only dream of visiting. To all my Christian brothers and sisters who have given me their time, support, and conviction—thank you.

A Leaf of Faith

CONTENTS

CONTENTS

Author's Note

The following pages contain no risqué situations or foul language. The *Messengers and Thieves* series is a safe haven for everyone. Even though the genre is primarily fantasy, the adventures the characters face are not too unlike our own. We are all messengers to some degree, yet we all must live in a fallen, imperfect world.

> *"But how can they call on him to save them unless they believe in him? And how can they believe in him if they have never heard about him? And how can they hear about him unless someone tells them? And how will anyone go and tell them without being sent? That is why scriptures say, 'How beautiful are the feet of messengers who bring good news!'" Romans 10:14-15 NLT*

Chapter 1

RUMORS

Everyone in the woods had heard the rumors. Something was amiss with the house beside the giant hickory tree. In fact, all the woods of Garland County seemed to be affected by a mysterious and malevolent force that had begun to creep down in the ground, up into the trees, and through the very air. Even though many of the local inhabitants ignored the signs, there was no denying that a spiritual battle was brewing.

Sticky, an insect—known as a walking stick, was one of the inhabitants that knew something was wrong. He made sure that no one could claim ignorance of any rumored matter, especially one as important as the current times seemed to indicate. After overhearing the robins chirping about the strange wind currents, Sticky wasted no time disseminating the ominous news to anyone willing to listen—and to many who were not. Of course, as gossips often do, he added a bit of panache to the robin's story, which sounded even more grandiose with the persnickety bug's pretentious British accent. With much flair, he proclaimed that the strange winds surrounding their fair county were spawned by the wings of evil spirits.

Sticky first shared his version of the evil winds with his flying friend, Dauber, the ever-loyal dirt dauber. When it was his turn to spread the questionable tidings, Dauber, much like Sticky, took it upon himself to embellish the story even further. The evil gusts were now reported to have emanated from outside of the known universe, from a fantastical world that had no name but was instinctively known to exist by all in the animal kingdom.

Gossip spreads rather quickly when delivered via airmail. And the usually unpopular dirt dauber enjoyed the newfound attention that sharing such important—if not questionable—news awarded him. Embellishing was just one of many bad habits Dauber had picked up from his friend, the walking stick.

Soon everyone in the woods began discussing the rumors. To instigate or spread unsubstantiated tales should never be advocated by judicious individuals, but there is one thing about rumors that often gets overlooked by those who rightly advise against them: there is the possibility they might just prove true. In the case of the ominous winds stirring over the house beside the giant hickory tree, the growing concern was indeed warranted.

Few knew exactly why the potentially evil winds had come to Garland County, but many had an inkling of the way in which they came. Somehow the currents had sneaked their way into the woods with the return of Seth and Melissa, the brother and sister who had somehow survived the journey of recognition in the other realm. All the critters in the woods were so happy to see that the teens made it back home safely that they did not stop to consider something otherworldly had slipped in with them.

According to the wise ones, known as the Terra Two, Melissa and Seth had passed the test of the "hardened hearts" in the other world and would continue their calling to discover the Great Creator. If they had not attained at least an inkling of faith, they would have simply been unfortunate additions to the ever-growing list of missing persons. It is not that all who go missing have no faith, however. In fact, only a select few are even chosen for a journey like the one that the siblings endured.

The Terra Two were considered to be the most prophetic elders in the woods, and their names were quite hard to pronounce by those outside their species. Most would identify them as turtles, but they were actually terrapenes.

The Terra Two knew the successful return of the teens would not come without a cost. They also knew the truth about the wind but would not make any public proclamations until the right time. Even the Council of Three applied pressure in order to get information out of the Terrapenes, but they kept mum. The Council of Three had influence and power, but the Terra Two had wisdom. Wisdom almost always beats out power in the long run. The two also had a terrific sense of humor, which did nothing but frustrate the Council. The Terrapenes and the Council of Three did not always get along, but their influence helped maintain much-needed balance in the woods.

The strange weather would have eventually had everyone talking, regardless of Dauber and Sticky's impatience to share their own take on it. But the worrisome news might not have been what an outsider would have expected. The rumors circulated about how exceptionally *good*, not bad, the weather had been.

In fact, the weather had been so good that many whisperings suggested God might be intervening in order to squash whatever evil might have come back with Seth and Melissa. Evil cannot grow in the light; it thrives in darkness. Perhaps the critters in the woods were overreacting and there was nothing to fear. Even so, the Terra Two's silence on the matter did not help to quell their suspicions.

Fox was perhaps the most concerned of all. She had asked her faithful friends Sticky and Dauber to be on the lookout for anything out of the ordinary around the house and under the hickory. She would snoop around as much as possible, but a red fox stands out a lot more than a small insect. She did her best to seek out any possible intruders under the cover of night, but she knew the people of the house would become much too curious seeing her kind so boldly traipsing around their territory. Sticky, with his spider-like legs attached to his distinctly stick-like body, and Dauber, with his translucent wings, could go almost anywhere undetected.

With or without the help of the wise ones, these three friends were determined to stop anyone, or anything, from destroying the woods of Garland County. The red fox knew very well what kind of hidden evil lurked in the darkness. Unlike the others, she had been to the other world. She was instrumental in helping guide Melissa through many perils on the young girl's journey of discovering the great creation. Fox understood better than anyone the importance of working together and maintaining a sense of hope and faith.

Melissa was Fox's first and only human friend. She hoped that someday Melissa would return to the little house under the hickory tree and they could go on more amazing adventures. There was only one problem: Melissa remembered nothing from her journey. When she and her brother returned from the other world, they had no recollection of anything, including her new friendship. Fox knew that if the rumors were even remotely true, it would be vital to join forces with the humans.

While Fox anticipated that Melissa and her brother would return to the woods soon, she was not about to waste time twiddling her paws. Fox was nothing if not industrious. That is why she had ventured so close to the house a few days before Thanksgiving. She met Dauber and Sticky to discuss a plan. They were determined to figure out why the weather was behaving so strangely.

Dauber hung upside down under the eve of the garage, the perfect spot to signal Fox that it was safe to cross the road. Fox hunkered patiently behind the mailbox and the expired iris plants. Sticky signaled to Dauber that the little old lady was at the dining table. Everyone in the woods knew that the best time to gather near the house was during feeding times. Humans loved their food and would not be distracted easily. The three unlikely detectives would have at least thirty minutes to coordinate their next steps.

"Are you daft? What took you so long?" asked an irate Sticky, his British accent thicker than usual. "I have been motioning to you for at least five minutes straight!"

"Sorry, I must have dozed off," said Dauber. "This fall air makes me so sleepy."

"Never mind, you two," said Fox. "We only have about twenty minutes left before the human finishes her meal. Give me your reports."

Both Dauber and Sticky began speaking simultaneously. Sticky's antennae flickered excitedly, and Dauber's wings stuttered and fluttered. Fox, while appreciating their enthusiasm, could not make out anything they were saying.

"Calm down," she said. "One at a time, please."

"The family is coming back—"

Dauber interrupted, "And I heard that the Terra Two won't—"

"Who cares about the Terra Two?" said Sticky. "We already know they won't divulge—"

"Look, the point is that the young ones are returning. They will be here in two days' time!"

"Perfect!" Fox proclaimed. "I'll make sure the news is disseminated through the proper channels."

"Do you think Melissa will remember?" asked Dauber.

"I do hope so, but that's neither here nor there. We will find a way to remind her of the important things, should her memory fail," said Fox.

"Well," said Sticky, "I hate to be the one to remind us all that everything, and I mean everything, rests with these two children. She must remember or we are all doomed! The world is doomed."

"Such a pessimist!" added Dauber.

"She will remember," Fox promised. "And they are not exactly the children our parents and grandparents saw years ago. They are adolescents now."

"Adolescents? Never heard such a word."

"That's because your kind spend all of theirs in the mud," said Sticky.

"They are young adults now," Fox explained. "Quite capable of making most of their own decisions."

This made Dauber happy. "Well, that's great. Maybe we can all start working together now instead of sneaking around in the background."

"Perhaps," said Fox. "But for now, we shall stay safely under cover. Let's get ready for their arrival, shall we?"

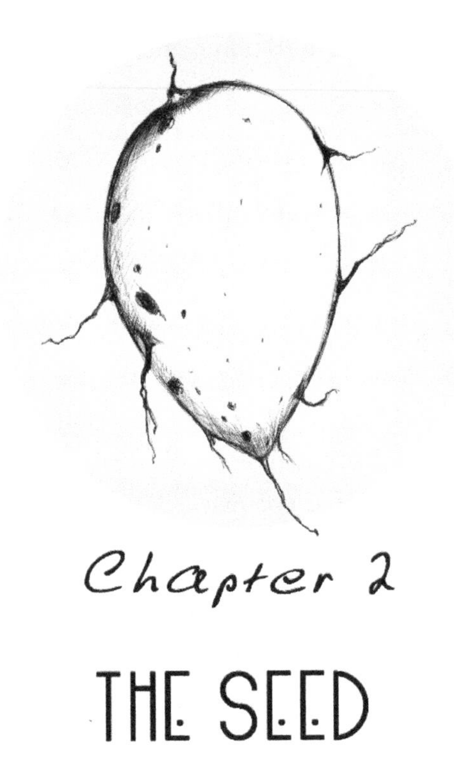

Chapter 2

THE SEED

(August, three months earlier)

This had been one of the best seasons for gardening Garland County had seen in decades. The unusually cooperative weather had not allowed a frost in late spring, or *early* spring for that matter. The previous three years had seen most folks planting their gardens as late as April—and often for a second time, after their first attempt had been wiped out due to freezing temperatures.

Last year happened to be one of the absolute worst seasons Azora had seen in all her eighty-plus years of living. The almanac suggested an early planting, but sure enough, a freeze came and killed most of the young seedlings across the entire county. Azora and her son, Henry, had just planted a second time when hail fell in early May, crushing all hopes for a mid-season harvest. The third planting was no charm, either. The weather seemed to cooperate at first, but then the rains came and did not let up for two straight weeks. With no sun and too much water, they were lucky to get enough fresh vegetables to eat, let alone leftovers to can.

To Azora, a sun-deprived, water-logged tomato plant was akin to a dog that needed to be put down for distemper. Not a pretty sight. No one ever said growing food in the South was easy. Unlike out West where lemon and orange trees rarely feel temperatures below forty and strawberries are constantly fanned by ocean breezes, farmers in the South require perfect timing and lots of prayer. Even if blessed with ideal weather, the perpetual struggle to keep varmints from eating the fruits of one's labor overwhelmed even the most experienced gardener. Nothing about farming in the South had ever been easy.

Nevertheless, planting, growing, and cultivating was a labor of love for those who dared put forth the effort. The results, in fact, could curl the toes of even the most discerning of palates. Nothing tasted better than a tree-ripened peach grown south of the Mason-Dixon Line. All other peaches were simply imposters. Those lucky enough to have visited the South at harvest time know this to be fact, but very few of them could appreciate all the hard work that went into getting the sweet reward.

This year was different.

The harvest would be remembered not for its quality of fruits and vegetables, although truly superb, but for the ease at which they grew. No frost. No floods. No sunless days. No hail. No heat waves. No windstorms or tornadoes. No, this was the year that would live on in the cupboards, pantries, and storm cellars of all the gardeners and their beneficiaries for years to come. This season's peach preserves, blackberry jam, green beans, black-eyed peas, and canned tomatoes delighted like no other in recent memory.

Henry and Azora's experience had been no different. They had grown the sweetest corn, the juiciest blackberries, and the most robust tomatoes ever. Azora could not find enough mason jars to can everything, so they ate fresh vegetables every day for a month. They filled the freezer with zip-locked bags of black-eyed peas and lima beans. Every shelf of the pantry had jars of colorful peaches, figs, and plum jelly stacked two high. They were also able to give away lots of produce to the townies—folks in the city with no room or inclination to grow their own gardens.

Azora was too euphoric to realize how worn out she had become from all the extra work of picking and storing the over-abundant harvest.

Yet, there was one singular exception to the superb growing season. Azora seemed quite perplexed when she looked down at the lifeless bucket of dirt before her. Not even a weed found its way into the perfect combination of mulch, fertilizer, and compost. A few months earlier Azora used the bucket to plant a pit that her granddaughter had given her, but it did not germinate.

Azora had promised not to plant it until Melissa returned for the Thanksgiving holiday, but she would have been a fool to pass up such a splendid growing season. She simply had to take advantage of the good weather. She felt sure her granddaughter would be excited to see the sapling when she returned for her next visit.

Azora had a green thumb and could grow anything, even if she did not know the exact specimen, which in this case she did not. She had taken the seed to the Master Gardener's club in town and everyone agreed it must be some sort of tree.

"This seed is one of the biggest I've ever seen. I suspect it was dropped by a very large bird migrating from some tropical island," said Dorothy, the president of the club and self-proclaimed expert on all things, living or otherwise. She was no more knowledgeable than Azora, but the consensus held that it was from a tree.

"Well, I'm not wastin' any more time waterin' and takin' care of this thing, whatever it might be. Must have been a bad seed," Azora mumbled out loud. She picked up the bucket. "A total waste of space and good dirt. I could have planted a late pepper in here." Azora did not like waste, but more than that she did not like to be defeated. She would, at some point, have to tell her grandchild that she failed. The seed, if that's what it was, had refused to take advantage of Azora's hospitality and God's good weather.

How very disappointing, she thought. This was an opportunity to have sparked an interest in Melissa to take up gardening. Azora grumbled to herself as she carried the bucket. Her intent had been to take the bucket to the greenhouse and reuse the dirt for one of her winter flowers, but she got distracted by the side door of the garage standing wide open. Instead of freeing her hands to close the door, she absentmindedly carried the bucket of dirt into the garage with her.

"I don't remember comin' through this door the last few days. I wonder if one of those meddlesome opossums pushed it open." Azora placed the bucket of dirt in the corner behind the side door to free up her hands to investigate.

The garage had no windows, making it perpetually pitch black. She blindly felt her way to the door of the old Plymouth Duster. She sat in the driver's seat, felt around for the garage door remote, and pushed the button. She had asked her son a half dozen times to grease the chain, but the door squeaked and rattled like a band of kids dragging tin cans behind bicycles.

Now that the garage was fully illuminated, Azora carefully stepped out of the car and looked around for anything scurrying about on the ground or hanging from the rafters. She methodically made her way to each corner, poking at everything along the way with an old broom handle she had found. There was nothing alive in the garage except a cantankerous old woman. Azora clapped her hands loudly in one final attempt to prove the garage free of any four-legged varmints. When no creatures emerged from the shadows, she gave up looking and sat back down in the driver's seat of the old Plymouth. She pushed the remote once again and the garage door clattered and squealed.

The pitch black returned as she sat quietly catching her breath. Carrying dirt and hunting opossums was hard on her tired old body. She had almost dozed off before something furry tickled her neck. After reaching back to feel what it was, she immediately did what one should never do in the dark with a wild animal pressed against their flesh. She screamed. Her arms flailed and her short legs convulsed. All the commotion caused the unidentified beast to conjure up the deepest, most terrible growl.

In her haste to escape, Azora's chest hit the steering wheel, blowing the Duster's horn for what seemed an eternity. The trapped and terrified animal reacted by letting out an ear-piercing screech of its own. In a futile attempt to escape, the furry creature leaped from the back seat to the front windshield. It rebounded off the glass and landed squarely in Azora's lap. This caused the elderly grandmother of ten to instinctively push up out of the seat, striking her head on the roof. On the way down, quite by accident, Azora again laid heavy on the horn.

With all of the windows rolled up, each attempt to get away from the horn-honking human was met with cold hard thuds against the glass. Azora, in her most composed moment of the ordeal, reached for the door handle—but she felt nothing. She then suffered a momentary paralysis. Her panic was fueled by the many stories she had heard of similar encounters with frightened animals. Ironically, the two occupants of the Plymouth Duster wanted the same thing—nothing more than a quick escape—even though each would swear that the other had every intention of inflicting bodily harm.

"Oh, dear Lord, please see fit to get me out of here in one piece." Just as she finished her earnest plea, she recalled that she had never closed the car door, which was the very reason she could not find the door handle. Fortunately for Azora, the beast had beaten itself practically unconscious, allowing her to make a clean getaway. Once clear of the car, she quickly made it to the side door.

The terrorized grandmother ran like a track star at the Olympics. She made it all the way to the house and never looked back. The bucket of dirt, which started the whole series of events in the first place, would not be seen again for months to come.

Chapter 3

GREEN BEANS, LETTERS, AND LEAVES

(The Present)

Dear Grandma, this is just a short note to remind you that we are going to be at your house the Wednesday before Thanksgiving. I can't wait to see you. I'm now reading the book of Acts which I heard was actually a letter, not a book at all. So, I guess I'm really reading the letter of Acts. Anyway, getting through the Old Testament was surely a testament to my resolve. You can't believe how hard that was. Well, I guess you can since you've read the whole Bible yourself. Do you think if I skipped over all those lists of names in the Old Testament that I can still say I read the whole Bible? That is after I read the rest of the New Testament, of course. I really want to tell Seth that I have read the entire thing from start to finish. Surely no one expects a teenager to read all those names. I can't even pronounce most of them. Well, I love you and miss you, but will see you soon.

Love Melissa.

PS, did you plant the seed yet?

Like many of her generation, Azora preferred letters over phone calls. Melissa's most recent correspondence had been read not less than four times in as many days. The stamp off the envelope was immediately placed in her scrapbook which always had dedicated sections for stamps from the grandchildren. This latest addition had special meaning because of the contents it delivered. Melissa, for the first time, expressed a genuine interest in reading the whole Bible.

Azora's life pursuit focused on ensuring her family would come to know Jesus. During the last couple of years, she began to think her life's pursuit had become a dying wish. She saw no progress. However, something changed after the children's last visit. She began receiving profound questions from her youngest granddaughter.

Melissa had been known to write the occasional letter over the years, often under the duress of her mother, but they usually contained little substance. At most she wrote a simple birthday greeting or a polite acknowledgment of a gift. But lately her letters inquired about subjects like the age of the Bible, its authors, and the apostles. This made Azora a very happy proselytizer.

The Bashams—comprised of Melissa, her brother Seth, their father Patrick and Azora's daughter, Bethany—were tough nuts to crack. But unlike her other grandchildren, who were all grown and scattered across the country, she still had time to influence the Basham kids.

Azora loved everyone in her family, even if they were unwilling to see things her way. But that did not stop her from ardently blaming Patrick for Seth and Melissa's theological confusion. Little love was lost between Patrick and his mother-in-law. If anyone stumbled into hell, Patrick would surely be there to greet them—or so Azora had been heard to say on more than one occasion.

But with Melissa's letters came hope and good news. Azora's prayers were being answered, and she had never been more excited for the future of the Basham children. The challenges, however, were still very evident. Never before had Azora been asked so many questions. First it was Seth with his questions about science and the days of Genesis, and now Melissa was asking about who wrote the Bible. Azora sent words of encouragement, but good, solid answers were harder to come by.

Azora took the questions to her pastor from time to time, but he was a busy man with a large congregation. She even considered taking a computer class down at the local senior center so she could "learn the internet," as she called it. Truth be told, Azora was a little nervous about Melissa and Seth's next visit. What if they asked questions and she did not have the answers? No one really expected an old lady to know much science, but everyone expects an old country Christian woman to know her Bible. "What have I gotten myself into?" Azora wondered aloud.

The last time Azora read the Bible all the way through was seven presidents ago. Her last attempt at the Book of Revelation was when President Reagan was shot. The best she did these days was to read a verse or two while following along with the Sunday sermon. But the last three months were different. Melissa had inspired Azora to start reading again. She even got a study Bible from her church. She would read a chapter or two and then read the commentaries at the end. She got all sorts of new insights from her most recent endeavors.

Perhaps this is why her pastor called the Bible the "Living Word." The words were the same but her understanding of them had become richer. Her current circumstances gave the Bible a new relevance. Some verses stood out more and others simply faded into the background. Job, for example, was once a character that she found hard to identify with but now he seemed more like a peer. Coping with psoriasis of the scalp, barnacles sprouting up on her skin, root canals, and gout helped Azora understand Job's tribulations.

Azora's pastor assured her that Melissa would not expect her to have all the answers. More than likely, the two of them would find common ground on which to discuss questions and find answers together. He also reminded her of the scripture that states iron sharpens iron. To talk about God will always be a blessing if the parties involved are open to learn and grow.

As Azora nestled into her old leather recliner, she contemplated the possibilities of biblical discussions with her youngest grandchild. She had no more scrunched and squirmed into a comfortable position when she remembered the canning still needing to get done before the family arrived. Her son Henry, who owned the house they both lived in, was away on business. Had he finished snapping the green beans before he left, Azora would not be a day behind. Azora absolutely despised stringing and snapping the beans. She would have waited for the kids to help, but nothing ever got done with a house full of company—but that was just as a visit should be, free of work and full of sharing good times and memories.

Azora gently folded Melissa's letter and reluctantly rose out of her chair. She placed the letter in the top drawer of the old secretary's desk, then she grabbed the big brown paper bag of green beans and sat back down to break them into thirds. There was not much snap left in the beans. She should have frozen them, instead of just refrigerating, right after they were picked. Better late than never, Azora thought.

There were barely enough beans to cover the bottom of the bowl before Azora's eyes closed and her head dropped. Not much would get done before her first catnap of the day.

In no time at all, Azora dreamed. She was on a dark and dreary road. She walked while holding a spade in one hand and a shovel in the other. Every few steps she looked down into her apron pocket to make sure no seeds had fallen out. They were precious seeds, and she must get them planted. Her walk turned into a slow jog—making it more difficult to hold on to her garden tools. She heard birds angrily squawking high above, sounding as though they might attack her. She quickened her pace out of fear, never taking her eyes off the precious seeds.

"Where am I going?" Azora spoke in her sleep. "I've got to find the sun. The sun must be close." Before long, Azora ran at full speed. She noticed that she had dropped her tools along the way, but she did not dare stop to go back for them. The birds were louder and closer, causing her to run faster and faster. Then the birds sounded as if they were only a few feet away. "Squawk … squawk … squawk …"

The birds swooped down violently towards her. Azora prayed as she ran, but the birds kept up their assault. They were relentless. She knew she must protect the seeds. There were more birds now, many different kinds and of all colors and sizes. She looked down at her apron and gasped as she noticed two small sparrows clawing at her apron pocket. She did not have time to shoo them away before the claws of a large black crow came bearing straight down over her head.

The last squawk woke Azora. She lifted her head and widened her eyes as much as possible. She used the back of her hand to wipe the perspiration from her forehead. She took a deep breath in an attempt to slow her breathing. Then she heard a knock on the door. "Those weren't birds, just my unconscious tellin' me someone was knockin' on the door. For land's sake Azora, get up and answer the door!"

Azora slowly lifted herself out of the recliner and pulled her blouse down over her waistline, which was always a little larger than it should be this time of the year. Azora yelled towards the front door. "Just a second, I'm a comin'" She could not think of who would be calling. She did not expect anyone. Perhaps the postman had a package that would not fit in the box.

"It's alright, take your time. It's just me, Jimmy."

Jimmy? What was he doing there? She opened the door and there he stood with a big grin, holding a rake and a pair of worn leather gloves.

"Hi there, Azora. I just wanted to ask where you wanted the leaves."

"What leaves?"

"Oh, didn't your son tell you? He asked me to rake the yard today. It should be the last time it needs to be done this year."

"What's with the big puss on your face?"

"What do you mean?"

"You know if you go around smilin' like that, everyone will think you're up to somethin'. There's nothin' happy about rakin' leaves."

"Oh, I'm sorry about that. I'm not up to anything. I guess I was just happy to see you."

"Happy to see me? Why?"

"I don't know. It's been a while and I like you."

Azora, without saying a word, walked past Jimmy and went to the corner of the house. She pointed towards the garage and said, "Over there on that side of the garage is a compost pile. It's where we put all the leaves. Be careful not to disturb the worms. We don't turn it over—we just let it sit there and rot. They tell you on the news that you got to turn the compost over and spray water on it but that's all a bunch of hogwash. God takes care of all the decomposition. There's nothin' that takes less work than a pile of rottin' leaves."

"Yes, ma'am. I'll be careful not to disturb the worms."

"Well, what's that supposed to mean?"

"Excuse me?"

"Are you trying to make fun of me? That's what that big puss on your face is all about, isn't it? Well, you can just watch your manners is all I have to say."

"But I wasn't making fun … That wasn't my intention at all … I'm sorry if you thought—"

"Oh, quit frettin' about it. I'm just in a bad mood. Had some kind of outlandish dream right before you knocked on the door. I guess it's a good thing you woke me up. No tellin' what would have happened next."

"Next?'

"In the dream. Listen, since you're here, I could use a little extra help. As I recollect, the last time my grandkids were in town you were able to relate to em' pretty well with all your fancy talk. Melissa has got a new batch of questions about the Bible. Might take a bit of your time, but my son still pays you by the hour, don't he?"

"Yes, ma'am."

"Well, you help me come up with some good answers, and it'll be the easiest pay you'll make all week. Meet me out under the willow tree. I need to put on some warmer clothes. You want anything to drink? I can make us some iced tea."

"No thanks. I'm fine."

Azora walked slowly to the front door and turned back to look at Jimmy before entering. "Well, what are you waitin' for? I'll be changed and down on the bench before you get through the back gate." With that she turned and closed the door behind her. Jimmy stood frozen for a second, shaking his head and wondering what she wanted to talk about this time. He hoped it would turn out better than their previous discussions.

During their last conversation, Azora accused him of leading a cult. Jimmy had spent the last several years studying science, specifically astronomy, in order to get a better understanding of the connection between faith and science. Although he absolutely believed in the essentials of the Christian faith, some people, like Azora, thought his views were somewhat heretical. However, he knew, even if Azora did not yet understand, that they agreed on who Jesus was. He hoped the rest would become clearer in time.

Chapter 4

EDUCATING AZORA

Five minutes had passed with no sight of Azora. Jimmy was tempted to start raking the yard while he waited. It was hard for him to sit idle, and he detested wasting time. He was only known for having a calm demeanor because he had always fought against letting anyone see his impatience. Azora, on the other hand, wore her impatience like a badge of honor, and if he was not ready for her when she arrived, he would surely face her wrath.

In the few months he had been doing yard work for Henry, this was the most agitated he had seen Azora. Yes, she was always a little ornery, but never as grumpy as this. After five long minutes of watching clouds roll by, his impatience got the better of him. He started back towards the truck to get his rake, but before he made it, he heard Azora yelling like an Indian squaw fighting a black bear.

"Whoooa! Stop right there! Where ya goin'? Good Lord have mercy on my soul! I can't take a couple of seconds to put on some warm clothes to keep myself from catching a cold without you runnin' off?' Well, if my generation had been so flighty, we would all be speaking German today!

German!"

Grumpy was an understatement. She was downright intolerable. Jimmy knew there was no sense in trying to explain that he was just going for the rake. He walked over to Azora and held out his arm for her.

"What's that for?" asked Azora.

"What?"

"Sticking your arm out like that?"

"I just thought you might like to hold onto it as we walked down—"

"What do you think I do when you're not here? Crawl on my hands and knees? I don't need any help walkin'! Thank you kindly."

Jimmy bit his lip and walked slowly beside Azora, not saying a word. He felt sure nothing he said or did would be construed as anything other than combative or suspicious. Heck, he could not even smile without getting his head bitten off. He certainly did not know how he was supposed to contribute to any kind of conversation, but he knew if he said nothing or shortened his responses, she might light up like a Roman candle.

It was a no-win situation for him. Even though Azora thought he was still getting paid, he did not think it fair to charge her son for conversation rather than doing actual yard work. The beautiful November day had turned into an arduous act of biding his time. If he was lucky, he would be sweating and covered in bits of fall leaves before the end of the hour. He never thought he would prefer his least favorite yard work over visiting with a senior citizen.

Azora abruptly broke the silence. "Sit."

Jimmy obliged without saying a word. In fact, neither of them said anything for at least a full minute. A minute is a long time while sitting awkwardly as a guest of someone you do not know very well. It is even longer when sitting outside in the chilly air. For his part, Jimmy just wanted to get the visit over with. The interaction was not going to end well, not with Azora acting like the tail end of a scorpion.

Jimmy muttered a little silent prayer to himself. "Please God, help me to be a blessing to this woman. Whatever I can be, whatever I can offer, your will be done."

"Well, this is a little ridiculous, isn't it?" said Azora.

"What's that?"

"It's not often I sit out here this time of the year. Not really the prettiest spot on the planet, is it? Sitting under a tree that has lost most of its leaves. Skinny little branches sticking around like the whiskers of an old mountain lion that's lost its pride."

"Oh, I don't know. I was just thinking how beautiful the silhouette is. Feels like the old tree is baring her soul."

"Hmm, maybe. But thank God for the pine trees, right?"

"Yes, yes. Thank God for the evergreens. I do love the change of season though, from the hot humid air of summer to the crisp chill of fall with the pungent smell of leaves cascading all around."

"You sure have an old soul," she told him.

Jimmy never thought about it before, but she was probably right. Having grown up an only child with few friends, he found it easier to talk to older people. He had only known Azora for a few months, but they had already sparred over several controversial subjects.

Jimmy broke off a tiny branch that was hanging between him and Azora. "Yeah, now that you mention it, I think I always have been a little older than my years."

"I never did thank you for what you did last spring, did I?"

"What was that?"

"Talkin' to my grandchildren about God. I might not understand how the Bible and science are mixed together, but it sure sparked a fire under Melissa and Seth. Melissa has been readin' the Good Book ever since she left, and I hear Seth has been studyin' religion as well."

"That's great to hear. But it probably didn't have much to do with me. God works in mysterious ways. What about you? Have you given some thought to our conversations?"

"Thought, yes, but I'm an old woman and it's goin' to take a lot to get me to change my mind."

"But you don't still think I'm a member of some cult, do you?"

"The jury is still out on that one."

"You know that I believe in all the essentials, just like you, right?"

"Essentials?"

"Yes, I believe that there is one God who created everything, that his Son, Jesus, also being God, died for our sins and completed His work and atonement on the cross. I also believe that He physically rose from the dead. Salvation only comes through Jesus, and if we accept Him for who

He said He was and is, then we shall be forgiven, and our home will be eternally with Him in heaven. The Bible is the inspired word of God, written by the Holy Spirit with the hands of Godly men—"

Azora interrupted, "The younger generation makes everything so much more complicated than we did. Back in my day, we would just say we were Christian and that was that. Nowadays you got to give a whole presentation and hours and hours of discussion to follow."

"Well, yes, I guess you're right. But you know there is a devil and he loves to convolute the message of Christ. There are a lot of false religions out there and false gods. Seems to me that many of these false religions try to emulate Christ as close as possible without actually being the real Christ, and that makes for a lot of explaining about what we really believe and who we say Christ really is."

"Well, I think it just opens up a whole can of worms, if you ask me."

"What do you mean?"

"Melissa, for one, has been writin' me letters and askin' all kinds of questions."

"Like what?"

"Well, first she asked me who wrote the Bible. I always thought God wrote the Bible, but really, he didn't. People wrote the Bible. So, I thought some more, and of course, the Holy Spirit inspired the Bible, right?"

"Yes."

"Then she writes and asks me how do we know that we didn't lose a lot of the Bible or that it's been mistranslated all these years and some other such nonsense."

"I understand your frustration, Azora, but she's not speaking nonsense, really. Those are good questions and there are good solid answers to them. They're not new questions."

"Well, they're new to me."

Jimmy smiled as he thought of what to say next. The conversation was going much better than he had expected. Maybe it was because Azora was not her usual self. Who would have thought that a bad mood could actually help a conversation go better? At least with Azora, anyway. She was confused and frustrated, and this made her unsteady. She might not have needed to grab his arm to walk, but she certainly was leaning on his wisdom to help her think.

Perhaps wisdom was the wrong word. Maybe Jimmy was too young, at twenty-four, to be wise, but he was intelligent, and more than that he was industrious. Jimmy was willing to work to find answers and he had spent the better part of the last three years exploring those answers. Azora was not too proud to recognize this fact.

They spent the next hour discussing things like how the Bible was translated over the years, who canonized the Bible, when the first letters of the Bible were written, and on and on and on. And to Jimmy's amazement, with no discussion of the Big Bang or the creation of the universe, Azora did not accuse him of being a cultist.

She asked him to visit when the grandchildren arrived. Since Jimmy was a little short on family, they decided he would come for Thanksgiving dinner. That would give Jimmy a few days to brush up on some Bible facts.

But for the next few hours, he would be using a rake to rustle up some material for the compost pile. Fall had its beauty, but like most good things, there was a price to pay. Raking leaves would always remain one of Jimmy's most detestable chores, but it was just as good for the body as exercising in the gym. No matter what the chores entailed, working in the yard helped to give his mind a break after spending so much time on computers and in books.

Chapter 5

PATRICK

Melissa, as usual, was the first to make it to the front door. She rang the bell a few times, and when no one answered, she let herself in. She quickly darted into the living room expecting to find her grandmother napping in her favorite chair. When the recliner proved to be empty, she ran to the kitchen, and then to the bedroom. No luck. Upon entering the hallway for the second time, she noticed that the bathroom door was closed. Melissa lightly rapped on the door. "Grandma? Are you in there?"

"Yes, child, I'll be right out. Just had to tinkle."

Melissa chuckled. "Tinkle. That's such a funny word, Grandma."

"Yes, but oh-so-fittingly descriptive of the moment."

"I'm going to grab some lemonade out of the fridge, is that okay?"

"Of course, sweetheart. There are some chips in the cupboard next to the stove if you want a snack. Did you help your mom and brother bring in the bags?"

"Yeah, we have all the food and stuff. But Dad came with us and he can help."

Azora's excitement to see the family quickly turned to dread. No one mentioned that Patrick was coming. How this fact could have been completely overlooked perturbed Azora. The last time she saw Patrick he had ended up with a hamburger patty on his face. How it got there would live on in Basham and Fray family folklore forever. Some like to joke that it fell from the sky courtesy of hamburger fairies. Others think for sure that one of the small children flung it playfully and quite by accident struck Mr. Basham in the snout. Only two people really know what happened on that warm July day ten years ago—Mr. Patrick Basham and Mrs. Azora Fray. The two had never been within one hundred miles of each other since.

Azora sat back down on the toilet just in case her bowels were affected by Melissa's revelation. The news of one Patrick Basham joining the family in the country for Thanksgiving might just cause the well to run dry from repeated flushing by a very irritated mother-in-law.

Melissa grabbed a bag of potato chips and sat down in front of the television. She picked up the remote and proceeded to change channels every two seconds. Melissa had recently turned seventeen and, despite her poor eating habits, maintained a healthy physique and a clear complexion. No one really talked about it (or perhaps some did not notice) but her complexion had spontaneously cleared during her last visit to the country when she and her brother mysteriously disappeared for almost 36 hours. Upon their return, both of them had noticeable changes.

The gentleman callers seemed to have increased just as spontaneously, much to the chagrin of Mr. Basham. A good thing for dad, however, was that Melissa had lost all interest in boys. She had traded her flirtatious habits for a new love of reading and studying. Her parents were beyond pleased with the turnaround. It was this change of behavior that kept them from inquiring more deeply about the strange circumstances of the visit last spring.

Melissa's mom stood at the front door holding a fully prepared twenty-pound turkey in a roasting pan. Plastic grocery bags dangled precariously from both wrists. Bethany naturally thought Melissa would have either left the door open or come back to help with the load. She thought wrong. Bethany attempted to push the door open with her backside, but it was securely closed. What she really wanted to do was drop everything on the ground and just leave it for someone else to clean up.

Unfortunately, Thanksgiving dinner without a turkey would probably bother her more than anyone else. She briefly blamed herself for trying to carry the roasting pan and two bags at the same time—something she would have scolded her kids for doing. Her arms began to give under the weight, and she could not set the turkey down without help. She looked back towards the garage, but no one was in sight. With no other obvious option, she bent down and used her nose to ring the doorbell. She immediately felt liquid dripping down her arm and onto her leg.

Melissa opened the door, and instead of helping her, she looked down at her mother's pants and asked, "What's that?"

"That would be turkey drippings, dear. And thanks for leaving the door open—or better yet, grabbing a few things on your way to the house." Exasperated, Bethany hurriedly pushed past Melissa and moved as quickly as possible to the kitchen. Melissa followed closely behind. "How did you get turkey juice all over you?"

Bethany awkwardly sat everything onto the counter while answering Melissa's question. "My hands were full, Melissa. There was no one to help me. The door was closed and I had to lean over to ring the bell with my nose. When I did, some of the juice ran out of the pan and onto the only pair of pants I brought with me! Any more questions?"

"Gosh, you don't have to get all huffy. I was just asking."

Bethany took a deep breath and went to wash her hands. Melissa retreated back to the living room. She felt guilty for not helping, but did not see any benefit in making excuses, not that she had one.

Once Bethany finished washing the grease from her hands and arms, she unpacked the grocery bags. Her pants would have to wait until later. She sat two pies on the counter and put a dozen deviled eggs and some celery stuffed with cream cheese into the refrigerator.

Melissa shouted from the living room, "Hey, Mom?"

"Yes, Melissa."

"Why did you only bring one pair of pants?"

Bethany sighed and shook her head. "Have you seen your grandmother?"

"Yeah, she's in the bathroom having a tinkle. Hey, Mom?"

"What?"

"Why did you try to carry everything in one trip? You're always yelling at me and Seth for doing that."

Bethany grabbed the counter with both hands, looked up towards the ceiling, and pleaded, "Dear God, please get me through this weekend without killing anyone."

Azora entered the kitchen just in time to hear the end of Bethany's cry for help. She switched on the light and asked, "Who you talkin' to?"

"Oh, hi Mother. I was just mumbling to myself. How are you?" Bethany released her grip on the counter and gave her mother a warm embrace which was received with less than the expected enthusiasm.

"Melissa said that Patrick was joining us, is that true?"

"I thought I told you. Is that going to be a problem?"

"Of course not, dear. It's just good to know these things in order to prepare the right amount of food. That's all."

"But I told you I was handling all the food. Everything is pretty much cooked. All we need to do is warm it up."

The front door burst open with Patrick and Seth. "Hey Grandma, Dad fixed your squeaky garage door," Seth yelled loud enough to be heard in every room of the house. He lowered the volume when he found everyone in the kitchen. "Hi, Grandma." Seth gave his grandmother a hug and then nervously pushed the hair out of his eyes.

Last spring, Seth looked like the epitome of a fresh-faced college freshman. Seven months later, he resembled a man lost in the wilderness for a few months. His light brown, wavy hair fell past his shoulders, and it appeared not to have been washed in weeks. He was fifteen pounds lighter, and his once bright-blue eyes looked tired and red. Azora was quite taken aback at how her once overly confident grandson appeared.

"Dear Lord! Seth, you look like you either have a bad cold or you've joined one of them rock bands? What on earth has happened to you?" Subtlety was not one of Azora's strong suits.

Melissa, who had followed everyone else into the kitchen, chimed in, "He's depressed, Grandma, although he won't admit it. No one will admit it."

Bethany immediately came to her son's defense. "He is not depressed, Melissa. Seth is in college now and everyone in college experiments with their look."

"Okay, so he's experimenting with looking depressed," Melissa said. "What's so wrong with being depressed? It happens to everyone. He'll get over it."

"Shut up, Melissa. I'm not depressed! Gosh."

"You shut up!" exclaimed Melissa. She put her hand over her mouth, feigning an apology. "Oh sorry, I didn't mean to be harsh. I wouldn't want to push you over the edge or anything."

"Melissa, don't start a quarrel. This is a quarrel-free weekend," said Bethany.

Patrick had worked his way slowly into the dining room, just outside of the kitchen. He thought this was the perfect time to make his presence known. "Where should I put the bags?" The only one not opposed to the children arguing on this trip was their dad. It took the attention away from him and made it easier to avoid saying anything to his mother-in-law. Besides, kids fought all the time–it was normal.

Azora responded, "You and Beth can stay in Henry's room, I guess. Just try not to touch anything and make sure you leave it exactly as you found it. You know how Henry dislikes people going through his things."

Without saying another word, Patrick made his way through the small dining room adjacent to the kitchen. He briefly glanced over to acknowledge Azora, but she had her back to him. He almost made it to the hallway before his wife spotted him.

"Well, aren't you going to at least say hello?" Bethany asked.

Patrick stopped, took one step backward, and pivoted on one foot until he was facing Azora, who had also turned around. "Of course. Hello, Grandma." He knew Azora vehemently disliked being called grandma by anyone other than her grandchildren, but it slipped out anyway. He could not take it back, and he wanted to kick himself for starting off on the wrong foot. This was going to be a rough weekend.

"Hello, Patrick. I'm glad you could make it. It was quite a shock—I mean surprise—that you decided to join us. It's been so long since I've seen you."

"Yes, well, after what happened last spring, I thought I should come along and make sure everyone stayed safe."

"What is that supposed to mean?" Azora quipped. Of course, everyone knew what it meant. Last spring, the kids disappeared. The police were involved and half the town was out scouring the woods before Jimmy found the siblings sitting in a tree. The police report called it an animal encounter in which the two youths had to scurry up a tree for safety.

"Well, Azora, I would like my children's faces to remain off milk cartons this year. We only have a little over a month to go, is that alright with you?"

Azora boiled over and she wished she had something to throw at him, like ground beef, but instead she inhaled and exhaled slowly. Needless to say, everyone else was on pins and needles. There was a quiet understanding among the family that the two of them did not get along, but it was an entirely different matter to witness it in person.

"Are you insinuatin' that it was my fault that the children were attacked by wild animals?" Azora demanded.

Bethany interrupted, "Patrick, why don't you take the bags to the back bedroom? Melissa and Seth, take your things and put them in the office, Mom and I will start warming things up for dinner."

"I dunno, feels like everything already got heated to me," said Melissa.

"Melissa, go! Now!" said Bethany.

"Alright, alright. I'm just trying to lighten the situation." Melissa went back into the living room and turned off the television. She grabbed her overnight bag which she had left sitting by the front door. Bethany gave Melissa a very hard stare as she passed the kitchen on the way to the guest room. Melissa shrugged her shoulders and mouthed that she was sorry. She then tugged on Seth's shirt to get him to follow her.

Seth pulled back from Melissa and said to his mom, "I'm not sleeping in the same room with her."

"You can have the couch in the living room," said Bethany. "I just want all of your things put up and out of the way for dinner. We'll be ready to eat at six. That gives you a couple of hours to take a nap or whatever."

Seth and Melissa retreated to their Uncle Henry's office, which also acted as a guest room, while Azora and Bethany sorted things out in the kitchen. The usual custom on a holiday was to eat around two or three, but since they drove up on Thanksgiving Day, instead of the day before, dinner would also be supper. No one seemed to mind. It just pushed leftovers to the next day instead of the same night.

Patrick considered going into the kitchen to see if his help was needed, but instead he quietly made his way back into the living room where he started to doze off in the old leather recliner. The six-hour drive to the country was not tiring, but the thought of spending the holiday with Azora was exhausting.

Chapter 6

THANKSGIVING

The house wren on the Audubon Society bird clock tweeted, which meant it was six o'clock.

No one besides Azora paid any heed to the clock that had now been an annoying fixture for over twenty years. Henry had once tried to sell it without his mom's knowledge at one of his garage sales, but she discovered it and grabbed it out of the hands of a little girl. Henry found some solace from the strange looks it got from first-time visitors. Peggy was able to ignore it by attributing the tweets to actual birds rather than to a battery-operated timekeeper. The various grandchildren once had their favorite chirps when it was still a novelty, but the ones who still visited could not be bothered anymore. Azora, unlike the others, adored each distinctive hourly tweet.

No cook worth her salt wanted guests to experience a lukewarm meal, and so Azora and Bethany began hollering "dinner's ready" five minutes prior to the house wren's six o'clock announcement. It always seemed, at least to Bethany, that an hour before a meal everyone was chomping at the bit, but when it was ready, the only way to get people to the table required nothing short of physical force.

Azora opened the oven to see if the brown and serve rolls were brown and ready to be served. Hot rolls were always the last thing to make it out to the table. To live up to their name, at the very least, they had to melt margarine. Azora did not want to fail at the one job she was given so even though the rolls were brown, she closed the oven door so they would stay warm until the guests were seated.

After placing a gravy boat on the table, Bethany set off to corral the family. She tapped on the office door and then peeked inside. Melissa was reading, a newly acquired habit that her parents very much appreciated. "Melissa, dinner is ready. Your grandmother and I have been calling you for at least five minutes. Where's your brother?"

"He's in the bathroom, probably."

Bethany turned to the door opposite the office and knocked gently. "Seth? Are you in there?"

"Yes, I'm almost done. I'll be out in a second."

Upon walking back down the hall, Bethany could have kicked herself. She should have gone to the living room to get Patrick first. If Azora beat her to it, there would not be much to be thankful for this Thanksgiving. She practically ran the rest of the way to her husband all the while visualizing her mom chastising Patrick for being late to the table. Patrick did not react well to being treated like a child, even when he acted like one.

As she rounded the corner, Bethany saw her mother still in the kitchen, staring into the oven. She let out a sigh of relief. She walked the rest of the way to the living room and crept up behind the Barcalounger where her husband was napping. She lightly kissed him on the cheek and whispered into his ear, "Dinner's ready."

Patrick reluctantly opened his eyes and stretched his arms. "Thanks, honey. Is there anything I can do to help?"

"No, everything is on the table. We're ready to eat."

Just as Bethany turned back towards the kitchen, there was a knock on the front door. She had forgotten that Jimmy was coming for dinner. It was not like her to blank on such details, but the whole visit had her a little on edge.

"I've got it," Bethany yelled to anyone who might have heard the knocking.

She opened the door and gave Jimmy a welcoming hug. The two had forged a bond during the family's last visit to the country. It was as if they had known each other for years, yet it had only been months. No one ever really discussed what had happened in the spring, but Jimmy's help in finding Seth and Melissa would forever form a bond of trust between Jimmy and the family.

Bethany stepped back, looked Jimmy up and down, and said, "Wow, I've never seen you in anything but blue jeans and a Stetson hat! You didn't have to get all gussied up just for us."

"Well, thanks, it's nice to put on somethin' a little fancy for a change," said Jimmy, who was wearing gray dress slacks and a dark blue sweater over a white oxford.

"Jimmy, I would like for you to meet my husband, Patrick." Bethany waved her husband over. "Patrick, this is the young man that was responsible for finding our kids. He looked everywhere, which is more than I can say for the authorities."

Jimmy shrugged, trying to appear as humble as possible. "It was nothing, really. I know these woods like the back of my hand. I was gonna help do whatever I could."

Melissa had made her way to the dining room but high-tailed it to the front door after hearing Jimmy's voice.

Patrick snapped his fingers as if remembering who Jimmy was and walked over to shake his hand. "Oh, you're that astronomer that Melissa keeps talking about."

Melissa, mortified at her dad's mentioning, exclaimed, "Ugh! Dad, he's not an astronomer. I keep telling you that. He just studies astronomy at school and stuff. Gosh!"

"Well, let's just say we've heard an awful lot about you these last few months, young man," said Patrick.

"Oh, my gosh! Are you for real right now, Dad? I can't tell you anything!"

"Patrick, why don't you go help mom in the kitchen?" Bethany patted her husband lightly on the back. "I'm sure she's wondering what's taking us so long."

"I thought dinner was already ready. What's left to do?" asked Patrick.

"I don't know who's worse, you or the children. Yes, dinner is ready.

Why don't we all go take our places at the table?"

"Hey, I'm willing to do whatever you want. I just thought—"

Bethany interrupted her husband and pointed towards the dining room, "That way." Patrick shrugged and began walking, followed by his wife. Melissa trailed behind but not after glancing back at Jimmy, who was more or less clueless about Melissa's schoolgirl crush.

Azora had finally managed to get all the rolls wrangled into the warming basket and onto the table. The rolls would be warm enough to melt margarine, but it was unlikely that they would have a chance given that they were burned to a crisp. Unlike Bethany, Azora rarely looked frazzled during family events and festivities. She was a take-it-or-leave it kind of lady. She had always been poor, and there were not many options in the way of hospitality. What she had on hand would just have to be good enough. It was iced tea or water. Margarine, no butter. Paper napkins. No matter the occasion, the number of people, or how special the event.

Bethany's generation, on the other hand, had more second-guessing to do. Should she have fried the turkey instead of roasting it? Should she have used fresh green beans for the casserole instead of frozen? Maybe Jimmy preferred wheat rolls instead of white rolls. Just one new guest was enough to make her jump around like a fish out of water. No one could say that Bethany did not care about making others feel comfortable and appreciated.

"Well, lookie here!" Azora exclaimed as Jimmy walked into the kitchen. "It's the Cuban cowboy without his hat and gloves. Don't you look pretty! You sit right there at the head of the table?" Azora did not waste the opportunity to use Jimmy as a means to belittle her son-in-law. "It's nice to have a strong man that knows how to carve a turkey sitting at the head of the table."

Patrick knew that this trip would be hard, and he had promised his wife to be on his best behavior, but Azora had a way of catching him off guard. It was all he could do not to grab the carving knife and plunge it into Azora's prized antique table.

"Well, actually, I'm sure Mr. Basham would be much better at carving the turkey," said Jimmy.

"You would be surprised, Jimmy," Azora replied. "City folk don't know their way around the kitchen. They order out, ya know."

Thankfully Seth walked in at just the perfect time to diffuse the already dicey conversation. "Hi, Jimmy." Seth leaned over to shake Jimmy's hand before sitting next to his father at the table.

"Hi, Seth. How have you been?"

Seth himself was not prepared to answer that question to anyone's satisfaction, especially his own. The last few months had not been good to him and while everyone else avoided asking Seth personal questions, Jimmy had not been clued in. Seth remained silent. Patrick raised his eyebrows, Bethany glanced in the other direction, and Melissa let out a gentle cough.

"Who would like to pass the blessing?" Bethany finally asked.

"Patrick?" asked Azora.

Everyone knew Patrick never said grace. He was a devout atheist and despised participating in religious traditions—or superstitions, as he called them. He took little issue with other people's choices in the matter, but it was not something he himself believed in. He knew Azora was just goading him, and he was not about to let her win. So, for the first time ever, in her presence, he bowed his head and clasped his hands together.

Azora gasped.

"Dear supreme being, thank you for this food that I bought and paid for. We ask that it passes easily from one place to another. Amen."

Azora quickly cleared her throat and proceeded to place her paper napkin with the cartoon turkey across her lap. But the napkin did not want to cooperate, and her agitated attempts to open it only caused it to rip in half. Azora was beside herself. That would be the last time she would ask her son-in-law to pray. She had never known anyone so ornery.

Bethany grimaced as she handed the carving knife to Jimmy, who was not taken aback by the family dynamics. Every family had them. He sliced the turkey. He had hoped to avoid the patriarchal tradition, but he was afraid if he did not take the knife quickly, Azora might find another use for it.

Melissa was the first to pass her plate. "I'll take just the white meat, if you don't mind, Jimmy."

"Not a problem, Melissa." One by one, dinner plates and various dishes were passed around until everyone was satisfied. Bethany had prepared all the major fare the night before: turkey and dressing, sweet potato casserole, and a green bean casserole. Bethany was an excellent cook, but the sweet potatoes were her specialty. Her secret ingredients were a touch of orange juice and a wee bit of mashed apricots.

The family was most grateful that Azora had stuck to the easier additions like the brown-and-serve rolls and corn. Even so, the corn was oddly charred. Jimmy could not fathom how one could burn boiled corn.

It was true that Azora was not a good cook, something of which she was blindly unaware. No one ever said anything when she was younger, and now that she was older, what would have been the point?

"Wow, who made the corn? I'm not sure a horse could penetrate these hard, shriveled up kernels," said Patrick.

Bethany quickly changed the subject. "Jimmy, Melissa has been doing a lot of reading since we were last here. I think the Bible is her favorite new book."

"Yes, I'm up to the part where Malachi is trying to tell all the people to straighten up and turn back to God," said Melissa.

"Wow, you're already on the last book of the Old Testament. Good for you," said Jimmy.

"Yeah, there's some gnarly stuff going on in there. I mean for real. I can't wait to get to Jesus."

"That's interesting, because if I remember correctly, the book of Malachi is actually foreshadowing the coming of Christ. Is that right, Azora?" asked Jimmy.

"Well, I don't know about all that, but I do know that God was wantin' His people to start actin' right. Like not treatin' the womenfolk so bad." Azora glanced in Patrick's direction.

"What are you looking at me for? I treat my wife with the utmost respect."

"Yes, you do, Patrick. No one is saying otherwise," said Bethany. Patrick rolled his eyes. It was obvious to him that no one else noticed Azora's behavior towards him.

"I asked Grandma in one of my letters last month if it was okay to skip over all those long names and stuff in Chronicles," Melissa said. "I mean, I can't pronounce them and I won't remember them anyway. But can I still say I have read the entire Bible if I skip over the really super boring stuff?"

"Personally, I think it is fine," Jimmy replied. "Besides, most believers read the Bible many times in their lives."

"Well, we know that's not true," said Patrick. "Most of you people never even read it once. I bet Melissa here has read more than most of the Christians twice her age. And she just started."

"I can't really disagree with you there, Mr. Basham. I will say, though, that the real issue is that a lot of folks who call themselves Christian aren't really Christian."

"What do you mean?" asked Bethany.

"A Christian isn't born being a Christian. Just because your mom or dad say they are Christians, or just because you go to church, doesn't make you one. Christianity is not only a conscious decision—it's also your life, a way of living, everything."

"There again, a bunch of hypocrites if you ask me," said Patrick.

"I don't recall anyone here askin' ya," said Azora.

Patrick could not help himself. He stared his mother-in-law down and said, "Seth, would you pass the burnt-and-serve rolls, please?"

Bethany nudged her husband under the table as Seth passed the rolls.

"Actually, Mr. Basham has a valid point, Azora," said Jimmy. "Again, there are a lot of folks who say they are Christian but don't know the first thing about what that really means. And yes, even some of the ones who do know still can be hypocritical at times."

"I'll give you credit, young man," Patrick said. "You may believe in a fairytale, but at least you're honest."

"I try to be realistic and truthful, but of course I don't think it's a fairytale. It may be miraculous, unexpected, and amazing, but a fairytale? Nah, too much evidence to substantiate the Bible's claims."

Seth set down his fork and looked up for the first time since dinner began. "I've been doing some reading myself. And it seems to me all the stuff I have read is science fiction."

"Yes, yes, like father like son. He's not so gullible." Patrick winked at Seth as he grabbed the sweet potatoes for a second helping.

"Dad, Seth has not been reading the Bible," Melissa said. "He's been reading some of the other religious books."

"That's true," said Seth. "One of them actually states that the universe rests on the back of a turtle."

"Craziness," said Patrick.

"And one of them was written by a dude who found some gold plates engraved with a language that only he could interpret. I think he had to stick his head in a bag or a hat to decipher it."

Bethany wanted to divert the conversation to more neutral topics, but the best she could do at the moment was food-related. "Would you like some more turkey, Mom? There's plenty of dark meat left."

"Don't mind if I do. Stab me that big piece off the leg right there would you dear?" Azora passed her plate to Melissa who in turn held it up for her mom.

The interruption did not derail Patrick. "See what I mean. All religions are just based on craziness. Some guy sticks his head in a hat and comes out with all the truths of the universe."

Seth added, "I read part of another holy book that I think is one of the most dominant religions in the world—not sure, but I think so. Anyway, the founder of that one was as corrupt as they come. His wife told him to tell everyone that his epileptic fits were revelations from God. I read somewhere that he married a nine-year-old girl."

Bethany, shocked, responded, "That wasn't anything to do with Christianity, I hope."

Seth reassured her, "No, Mom. I haven't really started researching the Bible, yet."

"The point here is that all of these books were written by men," said Patrick. "And they've changed so much throughout history, so how can anyone even be sure they contain the original text? We can't. It's been handed down generation after generation with so many changes according to what the culture at the time found helpful or necessary."

"Oh please," said Azora. "You don't know what you're talkin' about! You haven't even read the Bible, let alone figured out how it came to be and who wrote it. You're about as knowledgeable as a dog on a squirrel!"

"What is that supposed to mean? I suppose I'm not allowed to have my own opinion."

Jimmy responded, "It's not really a matter of opinion, Mr. Basham. Pardon me for saying, but there is actually a lot of manuscript evidence that the Bible is very much the same today as when it was first written. And unlike most all other books of antiquity, the Gospels were written as early as thirty to sixty years after the death of Jesus Christ by people who actually saw Jesus. And the Dead Sea Scrolls, for one example, laid to rest the same argument about the Old Testament."

"What is this, are you all ganging up on me? Corner the atheist at dinner and fire all rounds!" exclaimed Patrick.

"I don't recall you even bein' invited to dinner," said Azora.

"Mom, of course Patrick would be coming with us for Thanksgiving dinner," Bethany protested. "What did you expect?"

"Well, who is he being thankful to if not God?" asked Azora.

"I didn't mean to start an argument," said Jimmy. "I was simply addressing a larger question. A lot of folks, even Christians, don't realize the amount of evidence that exists in support of a trustworthy, accurate Judeo-Christian text."

"I guess evidence can be slanted in favor of one position or the other," said Patrick.

"I suppose," said Jimmy, "but that doesn't mean the evidence is any less credible. Perhaps the interpretation must be scrutinized just as carefully as the evidence."

"Dad, have you even looked at any of the evidence?" asked Melissa.

"I suppose you're on his side?"

"Actually, I can form my own analysis and opinions. I do think Jimmy has probably studied this more than either you or me. I'm willing to be open."

"Of course, you are," said Patrick. He stabbed another piece of turkey as if it were about to leap off the plate and run. He looked at Seth and asked, "What do you think, son?"

Seth looked up, somewhat surprised at the open-ended question and not really prepared to give an answer.

Bethany chimed in, "Why don't we table the discussion until after dinner. Surely there are more pleasant conversations to be had."

"Jimmy, why don't you explain to Dad how the Bible and the Big Bang agree with one another," said Melissa.

"Melissa, that's not exactly changing the subject," said Bethany.

"Imagine that, not bein' able to discuss the Bible at Thanksgivin'. Perhaps the Gestapo would like to suggest a topic of conversation to *his* liking," said Azora, looking directly at Patrick.

"What difference would that possibly make? Nothing I say could possibly pass approval by the notorious nun," said Patrick.

Azora clenched her fist tight around her fork, unable to think of another comeback. Melissa wanted to giggle but thought better of it. Seth was still trying to formulate an answer to his dad's question.

It was Bethany that finally broke the silence. "Jimmy, has my brother been keeping you busy around the house here?"

"Not too much to do now that fall is here."

"What other work do you do?" asked Bethany.

"Well, college is keeping me pretty busy, so I'm glad to have a little more free time to study. Mostly I just do whatever handyman work comes around through word of mouth."

"Jimmy can do almost anything—plumbing, electrical, you name it," said Azora, who had finally released her death grip on the utensil. She had taken a moment to pray silently and repent of her actions. Prayer was the only proven method of lowering her blood pressure when Patrick was around. He may not have believed in God, but God was the only reason he did not have a fork sticking in him.

Jimmy turned to Seth and asked, "How about you? You've been a little quiet. How's college been treatin' ya?"

Everyone at the table went silent again. Melissa glanced at Seth and then quickly back to her mom. Patrick shrugged his shoulders and started back to work on his next plate of turkey. Bethany bit her lower lip and nervously cleared her throat. Azora was not sure what the awkwardness was about, but she had a feeling this conversation was not going to go any better than religion.

Seth finally spoke, "Yeah, well, not so good."

"What do you mean by that, Seth?" asked Azora.

"He's more than likely going to lose his scholarship for next semester," said Melissa.

"You don't know what you're talking about, Melissa, so just be quiet!" Seth shouted.

"Let's just say that Seth needs to get his grades up," said Patrick. "Substantially."

"Why don't we let the boy speak for himself," said Azora.

'It's alright, Grandma. It's true. I just sorta had a little setback this semester. That's all. I'll do better next year."

"If he doesn't, he's going to have to learn some plumbing and electrical himself or figure out a way to pay for his tuition," said Patrick.

Bethany said, "You know, people are allowed to have struggles, Patrick. We are not all perfect."

"Don't you worry about a thing, Seth. You'll bounce back like a hickory nut off a tin roof. Our side of the family has always been very capable of living up to the task at hand."

"Thanks, Grandma. I appreciate the vote of confidence. I just had a minor setback. I'm better now."

Melissa, perhaps more than anyone, knew that Seth's problems started last spring when the two of them got lost in the woods. Neither Melissa nor Seth could remember many details of what had happened, and no one pressed them for answers. Seth confided in her that he had started seeing a counselor at school, and he did seem to be getting better.

As the dinner guests began to get full, the conversation became less controversial. A peaceful calm came over everyone. It was as if the awareness of Seth's struggles brought everyone into one accord. No matter their religious perspective, or their thoughts about one another, there was much to be thankful about on this day.

Little did any of them know that the winds, outside the small house next to the big hickory tree, were beginning to stir. Wind storms were not common in the month of November, but a storm was indeed brewing.

Chapter 7

MEMORIES

Melissa said, "This book of law shall not depart out of thy mouth; but thou shall meditate therein day and night, that though mayest observe to do according to all that is written therein: for then thou shall make thy way prosperous, and then thou shalt have good success."

"What is that from?" asked Seth.

"Joshua, Chapter 1, verse 8. I memorized it. It's the old King James Version, isn't it super cool? That thou mayest, therin, shalt—so retro." Melissa sat on the living floor next to Seth who was still under the covers on the sofa.

"Good for you," said Seth.

It was very early in the morning. Not that long ago, Seth would have been irritated by his sister disturbing his morning slumber, but like most other things in life at the moment, he felt differently. He welcomed her company.

"Dude, you've gotta start reading the Bible. It's giving me so much inspiration," said Melissa.

"Anything that gets you out of bed before sunrise must indeed be inspiring."

"I'm serious. Are you done reading the other so-called holy books yet?" Melissa began to do sit-ups. Exercise was the newest addition to her ever-growing list of ways to improve herself.

"Of course not. I mean I haven't had time to read that much with school and all. But what I have read is pretty weak. They all lose credibility in the first few chapters."

"Okay, then why not just jump into the Bible next?"

"It's pretty easy for you, you're just in high school. College is a lot more demanding."

Melissa sat up and looked Seth in the eyes. "You made a promise. *We* made a promise to do this, Seth. What could be more important than learning about our eternal destiny?"

"It only affects our eternal destiny if it's true."

"Not so. Either way, you could argue, it affects us. If the Bible turns out not to be true, then that most definitely has consequences as well."

"I'll give you that one." Seth, once a very confident teenager—perhaps overly so—had become substantially more vulnerable in recent months, especially where his sister was concerned. Since he graduated high school last year, he had grown to almost six feet tall. He was still quite strong, from his days on the wrestling team, but his heart had softened and his demeanor had become more graceful. His sister enjoyed this new side of her brother. She always knew he would protect and defend her, but now she knew he respected her as well. Their relationship was blossoming into something neither of them could have foreseen.

"Jimmy is coming over tomorrow. He's bringing his canoe. I thought we could all go on the lake."

"It has been unusually warm this time of the year, huh? But I don't know about taking a canoe on the lake. I, for one, don't feel like rowing that much."

"He has a trolling motor. We won't need to work a whole lot. Please come with us."

"Dad won't let you go unless I come along, right?"

"Honestly, that's not my reason for asking you. I just think it would be fun if we all went. I'm going to ask Mom and Grandma to come too."

"You really think Grandma is going to go on a canoe in November?

The water is freezing!"

"Yeah, Mom probably won't come either, but it's still nice to ask. I did promise that you and I would pick and shell the rest of the purple hull peas before we went, though."

"It's November, there's nothing left in the garden."

"Apparently there is this year. There can't be much left though. They won't take long."

"I don't mind shelling the peas. That's fine. I'm just not sure about taking another extended trip into the woods this year."

"We aren't going into the woods. We are going on the lake. Besides, Jimmy will be with us. It won't be the same if you don't come."

"Either this whole Bible reading thing is changing you or age is taking its toll. It's weird seeing you be so nice," Seth smiled at his sister and added, "Okay, sure, I'll go."

"Great! I'm so excited."

"I bet you are." Seth asked one more question as Melissa headed back to bed for a few more hours of sleep, "Why that verse?"

"Huh?"

"Why did you pick that verse to memorize?"

"Oh. Well, I figured that if I'm going to learn this stuff, I might as well start committing it to memory—like the verse says, 'This book of law shall not depart out of thy mouth.' I can't help but think having it memorized will come in handy someday."

"You already believe, don't you? I mean really believe."

"You know, that's an interesting question." Melissa paused to twirl her hair around her finger. "I know that it's true. I don't even know how or why I know. I just know. So yes, I guess you're right. But just because I believe that the Bible is true doesn't mean I understand what it all means. I'm sorta like you, I guess, still looking for answers."

A few minutes after Melissa went back to bed, Seth got dressed. He went into the bathroom and splashed cold water on his face. He forgot to get a clean towel, however, and he briefly considered dripping his way to the linen closet but instead opted to use the slightly soiled bright yellow hand towel hanging next to the sink. He pressed the cloth to his face and inhaled. The scent of his grandmother's towel, something similar to dust and old perfume, gave him comfort. Some things never change.

His thoughts quickly turned to the lake. He hoped for a relaxing, fun day. But his hope was not enough to overcome the sinking feeling that something was amiss in Garland County. Was it that the weather was so unusually warm? Or did his unease have more to do with venturing out into the woods for the first time since his and Melissa's misadventure last spring?

Perhaps a walk with the sunrise would help calm his nerves and clear his mind.

He buttoned the shirt over his tee. Even though it was warm, it was early in the morning and a chill was in the air. Everyone else was still sound asleep, including Melissa, no doubt. Seth put on his shoes and quietly let himself out the back door. He turned the knob so it would not click upon closing. It was not a thoughtful gesture; he simply did not want to be bothered by anyone who might be awoken by the noise. He needed a few moments in the fresh air, under the trees, to gather his thoughts. He needed time alone.

He stepped onto the back porch at precisely the right moment. The sun had just begun to peek over the hill and through the trees. Many of the trees still had leaves on them even though the beautiful oranges and reds of fall had mostly turned to brown. There were plenty of leaves on the ground as well, but a sufficient number still clung to their branches, causing the sunrise to be partially obscured.

Seth walked down the old wooden steps onto the worn trail made by his uncle and grandmother. The path reminded him of the cattle trails his grandfather used to follow on the old farm when he and Seth would count the pregnant heifers. He loved visiting the farm and wished he had gotten to spend more time with his dad's parents like most of his cousins, but they had died when Seth was only seven. They were full-time farmers with big gardens, usually forty head of cattle or more, chickens, barns—the works.

Seth walked past the worn trail, past the garden surrounded by chicken wire, past the old willow his grandmother loved to sit under. Before he knew it, he had wandered all the way to the creek. He had caught many a crawdad in that creek. His favorite method was bacon securely fastened to rope on a stick. Crawdads love pork, and they hold on just long enough to be lifted up and flung onto the creek bank. His mom sometimes complained that the bait cost more than the catch.

Seth looked up and realized he had missed what he came out to see—the sunrise. No worries, he told himself. There were plenty more of those to come. As he began to walk beside the creek, it occurred to him that there was a good amount of water flowing. That would mean the lake level was probably high enough to tool around through some of the less explored coves. The coves were difficult to traverse when water levels were low.

"Hello there, young feller."

Seth thought he had heard someone speaking. It sounded like the voice of an older man. But he looked around and of course, there was no one to be seen. Who would be out here in the middle of nowhere, he thought.

"My name is Bumpy."

Seth looked around, but again saw no one. He did, however, notice a rather large leaf sticking out of his pocket. His grandmother always said finding a leaf in your pocket was good luck. But the leaf, and the luck it might bring, would need to wait. Where did that voice come from? Seth found a small boulder next to the creek bank. He placed his right foot inside a crevice and grabbed onto a small protrusion to pull himself up to the top. He could see quite far from this vantage point, but he still couldn't see anyone.

He sat, inhaled the crisp, clean air, and drank in all the beauty. The voice, he ascertained, was simply in his head. But the babbling creek was real, and it sounded as sweet as ever. The wind gently blew, causing some of the crisp leaves to fall from the trees. The ones that would not let go of their branches made rustling noises as they tickled one another. Yes, this is what he needed: peace, quiet, serenity, and sanity.

"You can just call me Bump," said the old voice.

"Man, I just can't win for losin'," said Seth.

"What do you mean?"

"If you're in my head, I'm a nut bag. If you're hiding behind some tree, there's no place on planet Earth I can find peace and quiet."

"Well, you're in luck," said the voice cheerily. "I am neither in your head nor behind a tree. I used to hang on one, though."

The voice was very close. In fact, so close that Seth was left with no option but to conclude he was hearing things. The sound was practically emanating out of his chest. "Please, just leave me alone."

"You know how that old wives' tale began?" asked the voice.

"What's that?"

"That finding a leaf in your pocket is lucky. Pull me out and I'll tell you."

Seth took a deep breath. He looked up into the sky and sighed. Then he took the leaf out. The leaf was brown and perfectly intact. Seth knew it was an oak leaf, but the exact variety of oak, he was not sure. With the stem between his pointer and thumb, he speedily twirled the leaf around several times.

"Whoa, partner, I'm not as spry as I used to be. Slow it down there, will ya?" requested the leaf.

Seth complied. "It's gonna be another one of those trips to Grandma's house, isn't it?"

"Yes, sir. Indeedy it is." said the leaf.

"This happened last time, didn't it?"

"Well, yes. Yes, it did there, young feller."

Seth stared intently at the leaf.

"Would you mind turning me around? I can see better from the other side," said the leaf.

Seth complied and brought the leaf closer to his face. He squinted and examined the leaf up and down. Slowly it began to morph, not into another shape, but rather a face of sorts. The leaf literally came to life right before Seth's eyes. Its natural structure mimicked four limbs and a head. It sort of looked like a little person with a tail—the tail being the stem, of course.

The top part of the leaf nodded yes, as if thanking Seth. "There, now we can see each other noggin to noggin. Much better."

"Wow, I remember. I remember that turtle who talked to me last time I was here in the woods. How could I have forgotten that?" Seth asked, more to himself than to the leaf.

"Terrapene, not turtle, as he constantly reminds everyone. He's too big for his britches, if you ask me. He would have been here today, but he had to bury himself for winter." The leaf paused for a moment and then said, "You're a tricky one for our kind."

"Terrapene. That's right. He hates being called a turtle, pesky little thing. But what do you mean I'm a hard one?"

"You, youngin', are what we supernatural ones call an in-betweener.

You don't recognize miracles, you demonstrate very little faith, and you're stubborn as all get out. It's quite rare, your kind—folks who can hear and see some of us, but not all of us. It'll be talked about for many years to come."

"Why did I not remember the turtle until just now? And what else happened last spring that I forgot about?" asked Seth.

"It'll come back to you soon enough. I'm just thankful I caught you in a contemplative state of vulnerability."

"I don't even know what that means. But I'm not gonna freak out this time."

"Good. Because we have a lot to talk about. A lot to *do*, really."

"Okay, slow your roll, Mr. Leaf. I may not freak out, but I most definitely want to avoid the crazy train."

"I hear you loud and clear there, partner. Let's start over. My name's Bumpy. It's due to that bug that bit me when I was young. It healed, but left a bump right there on my left leg."

"I see it. I didn't know leaves had legs."

"We don't have legs, really. It just makes it easier for you to relate to me during our time together. I'm from a black oak tree. You passed it about a hundred yards back. Old, old tree, been around for hundreds of years. You climbed it once when you were just a young whippersnapper."

"How would you know that?"

"The tree told me, of course."

"Oh, I thought maybe you were reincarnated or something."

"Ha! There's no such thing. Appointed once to live and once to die. That's true even for us leaves."

"Well, aren't you dead now? You're all brown and detached from your host."

"Gee, thanks. Do I really look all that bad?"

"No, I'm just sayin', if you ain't dead now, when are you dead?"

"You're a real charmer, aren't ya?" The leaf rolled his eyes, none too happy with the current topic of conversation. "I'll have you know I've got plenty of good days before me. Don't you be worryin' about that."

"Fine. What do you want with me?"

"Right to the point, I like that. I'm here to take you and your sister on a bit of a journey. There will also be a third human joining us, if everything goes as planned."

"A journey to where?" asked Seth.

"To the place you have already been … only somewhere different."

"That's not vague at all."

"We're goin' to the Spring Tower by way of the Water Gate. Course I've never been there myself, but I've been told the way by some trustworthy folk. I hear it's an amazing place. And don't you worry none—as you start rememberin' the other world, it will begin to make more sense. But first we need to go collect our other travelers."

Little dots of perspiration appeared on Seth's forehead. His arms bristled with goose-bumps and his breathing became more laborious. Bumpy could sense that Seth was beginning to remember things from his trip to the other world. He had hoped the memories would not have returned until they were well on their way, but the lucky leaf's luck had run out. He had to do something to distract Seth or it might be impossible to convince him of the importance of the task before them.

Seth's past experiences with creatures that should not speak, and worlds that should not exist, almost killed him. The journey took him from being a confident straight-A student to an insecure college kid on the verge of losing his scholarship. In the span of twenty-four hours, he went from knowing everything to knowing nothing at all.

Bumpy had to distract Seth from his worrisome memories. He looked up at the trees towering overhead and then he rubbed his little leaf-hands together. This was no easy task because he was not as limber as he was when he was green, but there was still a little elasticity in him yet.

As soon as he rubbed his hands together, what must have been a thousand leaves fell from the sky all at once. But they did not just lazily cascade to the ground. No. These leaves had purpose, and every movement they made was a delight to the eyes. Seth looked up and was immediately mesmerized.

The orange leaves joined with the red leaves to paint an abstract flow of color amidst their mostly brown comrades. Seth and Bumpy were witnessing a live, moving work of art. The leaves undulated with the wind and their varying shades of burnt sienna and raw umber intermingled to create ever-changing displays of beauty. Just when it appeared to be over and the leaves almost touched the ground, another gust of wind lifted them back up into the air.

The delightful distraction worked. Seth's unpleasant memories retreated into the recesses of his mind, and they were replaced with a smile. It would not be long until they returned, of course, but not until Bumpy had everything well under control. Bumpy and Seth, with a little help from friends and family, were about to embark on the most important journey of their lifetimes.

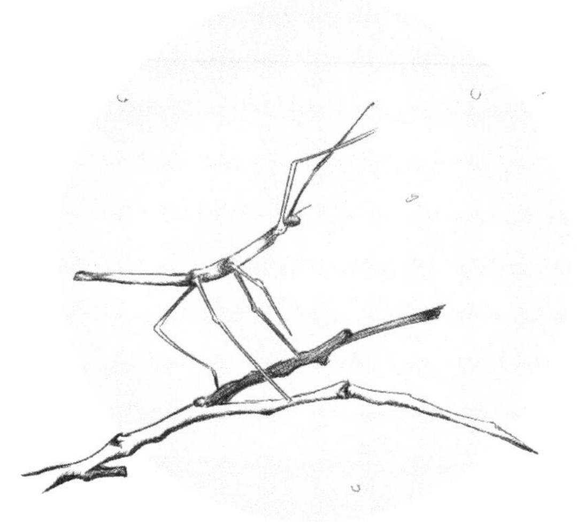

Chapter 8

The Long Journey Across the Yard

Sticky was completely breathless. He rested on the iron rail that the humans held onto when they walked down the steps. He gasped for air as he looked ahead to determine how much farther there was to go, then he became distracted by an aromatic rosebush. Just a few more feet and he could have eaten while he rested. Rosebushes were his favorite.

As it was, he would have to nibble as he walked if he was ever going to make it to Dauber's and back home again before nightfall. He would have spent the night at Dauber's, but Dauber's wife gave him the heebie-jeebies. Dauber said she only ate spiders, not walking sticks, but Sticky preferred not to take any chances.

Dauber did a flyby earlier in the day to ask Sticky over for tea. Sticky would have declined such a long journey if the air had been chilly, but his limbs remained quite limber in the uncharacteristically warm autumn air.

Of course, there would not really be any tea—Sticky did not even know what tea was, exactly. He often saw humans on the British television shows drinking it out of dainty porcelain cups. Oh, how he longed to travel to England someday, but it was quite a challenge to simply make it across the yard.

Even after an extended break, Sticky could not seem to catch his breath. He was exhausted, but he recalled the words of Winston Churchill: "If you're going through hell, keep going." Truth be told, Sticky had become quite lazy in his old age and a simple stroll seemed like a battle of the wills. At two years, he was considered elderly for his species and he rarely traveled beyond the main house anymore.

After another short hike, he finally made it to his most favorite place in the known universe, the thorny yellow rosebush. Sticky said a quick prayer, giving thanks to the creator of rosebushes. He took his first bite. He was in heaven. All of a sudden, he heard the melody of birds singing in the distant trees. The sun seemed to brighten as he rolled a tasty green leaf around in his tiny mouth. He intended to only take a nibble, but he ended up leaving a trail of unsightly bite marks the whole way through. No matter, he thought, it would not be long before the humans pruned it for winter, erasing any indication he had ever been there. Thankfully, these particular humans did not spray the plants with poison. He had lost many friends and family to such an awful and curious phenomenon.

After a few more delicious bites of the last leaves of the season, Sticky had to decide whether to walk along the ground or along the wood planks of the garage. On the ground there was a chance of confronting a hungry lizard, so he opted for the safety of the garage. He licked the last bit of gooey green mesophyll off his legs—not wasting a drop. He felt as though his stomach might explode and momentarily regretted his gluttony as he walked.

As it turned out, Sticky's overindulgence gave him just enough added energy to continue marching onward. Dauber and his wife were building nests under the weathervane. He estimated about another fifteen minutes before his arrival. It was indeed a beautiful day to travel, and he was thankful that he would have the chance to say a final farewell to his best friend.

He paused below the rain gutter at the edge of the roof. He really should have walked around, but instead he chose to reach his front legs up over the slippery gutter, hoping there would be something to grab onto with his tiny grippers. Traversing along plants and other rough surfaces was a breeze, but man-made obstacles could be tricky.

Fortunately, he found a little crimp on the tip of the gutter that he could grip and hoist himself over. With his foreleg securely gripped, he lifted his second leg off the wood and was almost home free until he caught something out of the corner of his eye. Something was coming straight for him. He could not quite make it out, but it looked poised for an attack. Sticky nervously lost his balance. His foreleg came loose and with his other foreleg not yet attached, he was only holding on with his back legs. His front body was being pulled down by gravity, and the pressure on his back legs was almost too much to bear. Sticky's life flashed before his eyes. He was about to fall to his death.

"Whoa, hold on there, buddy," said Dauber. Dauber landed on the gutter and quickly took hold of one of Sticky's forelegs as they flailed in the air. This helped stabilize the shaky walking stick.

"You scared the living daylights out of me, old chap!" Sticky cried. "That was a bit dodgy. Are you trying to knock me off?"

"Oh, please, don't be so overly dramatic. I've got you big boy. Just take your other leg there and pull yourself up. Hurry up now, I can't hold onto you forever. Seems like you've put on some weight since I last saw you—this morning."

Sticky secured his other leg on the gutter and, as Dauber pulled, the determined stick used all of his strength to hoist himself up and over the slippery metal. He was now safely on the roof. The rough shingles felt good on his toes as he walked.

"Come on, we're almost there. Just a bit this way," said Dauber. Sticky walked along the roof while Dauber hovered slightly above him.

"I thought I would never get here."

"Why on earth would you try to go over the water channel? You could have just come around the long way."

"I'll have you know I am completely knackered. Not all of us have wings to carry us quickly from one place to the next."

"Knackered? I assume that's something you learned from that electric squawk box of the humans."

"Yes, yes, I suppose we can't all have the depth of language as I have acquired from the benefit of being so close to such a cultural phen... as the telly."

"You do know that attitude and your fake accent are highly annoying to most everyone around here, right?"

"Of course, it is. Most of the folks around here have just enough intelligence to open their mouths to eat, but little more—P.G. Wodehouse."

Dauber shot back with a quote of his own, "Quotation is a serviceable substitute for wit—Oscar Wilde."

"Well, well, well ... touché. Someone has been doing a little listening in themselves, haven't they?"

"I used to overhear things when we were spying on the house last spring. I thought that quote might come in handy."

"And so, it did. Bravo, old chap, bravo."

They finally arrived at the weathervane. Sticky marveled at Wanda's meticulous architecture. Dauber's wife was quite the builder. She, all by herself, had constructed a three-inch-by-one-inch cylinder mud house for her offspring. There would be only one egg for this little house and it would be packed with spiders for the baby to live on until it was time to emerge in the spring.

Sticky crawled under the eave in order to avoid the sun, which was now directly overhead. Wanda had chosen the most ideal place for her nursery, right under the top corner eave of the garage and above the metal cross bar used to secure the vane. Hidden from wind and rain, the little baby dauber would remain completely safe until time to fly away.

"Where's Wanda, Dauber?"

"Don't worry, she'll be gone for a while. You really should relax, though. No dauber that I know of has ever harmed a walking stick. In fact, if you look on the top of the iron bar next to the hut, she left you a little leaf to snack on."

There was no way Sticky was about to eat anything Wanda had touched. As far as he knew, she might have injected it with her poison in order to subdue him and cram him into that tiny mud tomb. He was not about to become baby food for Dauber and Wanda's next generation.

"How absolutely sweet of her. But to be honest, I already had dinner."

"Suit yourself. But she didn't do anything to it."

"What? Why, what on earth do you mean? I assumed nothing of the ort."

"Yeah, yeah, whatever. I can read your mind at this point, Sticky. Listen, I asked you over here today for your advice and maybe for your help."

"Absolutely, you're my best mate. I'll do anything that I can to help."

"This is my ninth cycle, and I have been blessed with such a long life. The things I have been a part of—being asked to help the Council of Three with their plan to overcome the Prince of the Air, and of course my friendship with you—have been nothing short of amazing for a creature of my kind. But I have a wish to see the fruit of our labor."

"What are you saying?"

"I know it's almost unheard of ..." Dauber paused to look around to make sure no one was listening in. "I want to go to the other realm with the young humans. They're going back, you know. I want to help them stop the evil one from invading our woods. If we don't stop him, the future of our kind and that of the humans will be in dire jeopardy."

"This all sounds quite dodgy. Are you talking about going into this other spiritual realm and fighting alongside the humans?"

"Exactly."

"It's not up to such insignificant beings as us to face the spiritual forces of evil. Just because we know of the spiritual realms and can see the evil more clearly than the humans, does not give us the right to intercede. It's up to the will of the Creator on how the battle between good and evil will transpire. You can't just go to the heavenly realms on your own accord."

"But why not? I thought the whole purpose of our meddling in the human's affairs was to lead them to an understanding of what it means to have faith and to perhaps be strengthened by that very faith to fight the battle to come? Why can't my own faith carry me to the places I wish to go?"

"Yes, but we are merely the chorus in the grandest of operas. We, my friend, were only needed for the first act. Our meddling, as you call it, was a success. It was because of us that the young girl and boy even opened their hearts to the possibility that God exists. We helped spark their curiosity, but I'm afraid our parts are over. In fact, I agreed to make this journey today to say one final farewell, my dearest and most loyal comrade."

"One final farewell? What do you mean?"

"It's ironic, really. We both are at the end of our cycles, you in your ninth and me in my twenty-third."

"Just how many cycles do you have left, Sticky?"

"I have heard of distant relatives living up to twenty-eight or thirty-cycles, but the average is twenty-four."

The two friends sat silently, contemplating the reality that was upon them. The end of both of their lives was near, and it was time to say goodbye. Dauber's right wing fluttered a bit, revealing an innate sadness—not for his own natural demise, but that of his friend. He had been so busy thinking about how to say goodbye that he did not realize Sticky was facing the same fate.

"Why don't you join me?" asked Dauber.

"For what?"

"I want to do great things for the Creator before I die. It's my heart's desire to help the humans love Him as much as we do. I truly believe that's why God even created us—for them. He made everything for the humans. If God loves the humans that much, shouldn't we love them too? But so many of them just can't see it. They don't know His love, and the evil one will stop at nothing to make sure they never do. We can help them, Sticky. I have the faith to get there. If you would only believe with me, we could help them together."

"Yes, I believe we must have faith to do any great thing, but it must also be the Creator's will."

"How do you think Fox was able to go to the other realm with the girl and boy? She has a love for the humans and there is no denying she loves the Creator. Her relentless faith has propelled her to greater things than anyone I have ever known in these woods."

"Yes, but it was obviously God's will." Sticky paused to seriously contemplate Dauber's proposition. "Supposing it is the will of the Creator, what exactly did you have in mind? How would you get there and what would you do upon arriving?"

"I was able to get away from Wanda the other day, and I followed the boy out into the woods—all the way to the creek."

"Yes?"

"I overheard him speaking to a leaf."

"A leaf, you say?"

"Yes, a leaf!"

"Imagine that. The Creator is so amazing. To think He would use a leaf to speak to the boy. A leaf. How perfectly stupendous." Sticky grimaced a bit as he reflected on his last meal.

"Well, it wasn't all that stupendous, I assure you. You and I could accomplish much more than a leaf! I use them to rest on and you make meals out of them."

"You see, that's what you fail to understand. It's not about what we simple creatures or a leaf can accomplish. The Creator doesn't *need* any of us to fulfill His plan, old chap."

"Simple? Ha! Ounce per ounce I'm one of the strongest creatures in the world."

"Oh, blimey! I didn't mean to insult you. Now get on with what it was you wanted to tell me."

"The brown leaf told the boy that he would be going back to the other realm again."

"You don't say? When?"

"Tomorrow."

"And I suppose you have some shenanigans in mind?"

"Like you said before: if the Creator wills it, it will be. Shenanigans or not."

"That doesn't mean you have permission to go around doing as you please. What would the world be like if everyone just went around doing as they pleased?"

"That's precisely what the world does, Sticky. You have to go out there and grab what you want and that's what I intend on doing."

"But we are not to be of the world. We are not slaves to unscrupulous behaviors. We are to act according to what is good and right."

"I have thought much about this and I have prayed. I'm convinced it's both good and right that we go."

"So, what is it you want to do?"

"I want to stow away with the boy and girl until they get to the other realm. I want to help stop the Prince of the Air from getting a stronghold here that will forever threaten the humans."

"You're just one little dirt dauber. How do you plan on stopping such a powerful evil?"

"I can fly. The humans can't fly. Imagine all that I could do to help. I would be masterful at reconnaissance in any realm, just as I am in this one.

"It's too dangerous and if you were called to go, you would know it. You wouldn't need to stow away. You already have made a big enough impact right here at home. You're the bee's knees, old chap."

"I appreciate the kind words, but I have nothing to lose. At most I've only got another cycle or two left. I'm going to go with them tomorrow, and I'm going to do what I can with my last remaining breath to help our world. To make a better future for the little one inside that mud house as well as the humans."

Sticky walked over to Dauber, gently patted his head, and put a leg around him.

"Well, I for one think you are a complete nutter! But I see your mind is made up."

"Won't you join me? When we make it to the other realm, imagine the possibilities. We can help finish what we started."

"I don't think so, Dauber. I'm old and just not able to get around as well as I used to. It took me almost half the day to get across the yard, you see?"

"I could help you. We could do it together."

"I would just slow everyone down. Besides, maybe I'll beat the odds and be the oldest living walking stick ever to have lived."

Just as Sticky finished his last word, he looked up to see Wanda flying directly at him. He screamed with fright, which for a walking stick was nothing more than an odd clicking noise. He cowered and covered his face. Wanda landed a few centimeters away. She had a mouthful of mud, so before speaking she had to add it to the almost-complete nursery.

Wanda spit the mud onto her work in progress and tapped it into shape with her leg. Sticky lifted his head to peek at her whereabouts. Dauber was too amused to say anything. Just when Sticky seemed to ease up a bit, Wanda quickly snapped her head towards him and shouted, "BOO!" Sticky fainted. All six of his legs collapsed at the exact same time and he laid sprawled out, unconscious. Dauber laughed so hard that the noise alone revived his friend.

Sticky ended up sleeping over at Wanda and Dauber's place that night. He was simply too weak to make it home. Wanda was even nice enough to bring him a rosebush leaf, which Sticky had no choice but to eat. The nourishment helped to calm his nerves and the three of them actually ended up having a very nice time. Sticky was surprised to hear how much he and Wanda had in common. They both liked to listen to the crickets sing, they both counted fireflies, and they both had a bad habit of eating way too much. He began to appreciate her, and the two would soon become very good friends.

Chapter 9

Canoes and Coves

About a third of the canoe stuck out of the old Ford. It slid from one side to the other every time the pickup took a slight turn. Seth wondered why Jimmy had not secured it better. Melissa never even noticed the canoe. She was overjoyed to be sitting in the middle of the bench seat, discussing the meaning of life with Jimmy.

Seth was surprised that his parents let them go, considering that Melissa obviously had a crush on Jimmy. He reasoned that his mom and dad must have been concerned about them getting lost again—something Jimmy would not let happen. Or perhaps they knew that they could trust his sister in any situation. There was no denying that everyone had noticed a change in Melissa. In the last three months she had become a serious student, no longer talked about boys incessantly, and even did the dishes without being told. In a lot of ways, Melissa was earning the respect and trust that came with maturity. This trip was surely a result of that trust.

Jimmy exited off the main street and turned onto an obscure dirt road. The canoe slid to the left, as did Melissa. Seth never noticed this turnoff before, but there were many different coves in which to launch a boat. Lake Ouachita (pronounced wah-shi-tah) had almost 700 miles of shoreline.

Very little sunlight filtered through the thick canopy of trees. The shade made it seem as though they were entering another world, far away from the bright sunny one they had just left back on the main road. Tree limbs scraped the top of the cab as the three travelers slowly wound their way around sharp curves and small dips. The skinny dirt road worked its way down a gentle sloping hillside until it abruptly came to an end. Jimmy turned off the truck while simultaneously opening the driver's side door. He stepped out and looked around as if surveying an old familiar place that he had not seen in years.

"We'll have to carry the boat the rest of the way down," said Jimmy. "Thankfully it's not that heavy and it's not that far."

Not that heavy? Seth knew that the seventeen-footer weighed much more than its modern lightweight counterparts made from fiberglass or aluminum. Another thing Seth knew was that there was no trail down to the water. Apparently, they were going to lug this wooden behemoth directly through the thick undergrowth and gnarly vines. But rather than comment negatively, Seth held his tongue.

Melissa, quickly assessing the situation, was not concerned. Two strong men were not going to ask a girl to help them carry something as heavy as a boat.

Jimmy looked at Melissa and said, "The two of us will take the ends. You can support the middle."

So much for chivalry. Seth was beginning to like this guy.

"Where are we, anyway?" asked Melissa.

Jimmy responded, "I thought since the water level was so high, we might check out some of the more obscure coves. This one is about as obscure as they get. If we're lucky, we might spot some freshwater jellyfish."

"Did you plan on going snorkeling? Cause if so, I didn't bring a wetsuit," said Seth.

"No snorkeling," Jimmy chuckled. "On warm sunny days they come to the surface in groups. I've only seen them once for myself. But it's pretty cool, something to definitely watch for."

Jimmy slid the canoe over the back tailgate letting one end rest on the ground. He then moved to the end of the boat that was sticking up and lifted it off the truck. Seth took notice and immediately grabbed the end that was on the ground.

"Melissa, it looks like Seth and I got this. Will you grab the oars in the back of the truck?"

"Absolutely," answered Melissa.

"Seth, we're gonna lift the boat over our heads, like this." Jimmy turned the canoe upside down with Seth's help. They both stuck their heads underneath. "Just watch the ground and follow me. Like I said, it's not that far to the water."

Seth was surprised at the weight of the three-person canoe. While it was not exactly as light as a feather, it was not as heavy as he had first assumed.

Jimmy led the way off the dirt road and into the woods. His choice seemed random to the siblings. There was no trail or any other indication of a path, but he obviously knew which way to go—which was down.

Meanwhile, Melissa fumbled the four long oars three times before finally balancing them well enough to bang them into the first tree she encountered. But she fought the temptation to utter sounds of frustration; she did not want the boys to think her unable to maneuver in the wild.

Although Seth could not see anything other than his feet, he heard all the clamoring and he enjoyed every second of his sister's struggle.

For the first time in a long time, Seth showed more confidence and skill than his younger sister. He attributed this to the recovery of his memories with the help of Bumpy. He finally knew the cause of the unease and fear that had held him captive for the last few months. Bumpy the leaf had assured him more answers were still to come.

Seth recalled that on his last trip to his grandmother's house, he had been tricked into going to a fantastical world full of strange creatures and important choices. Bumpy insisted that he had not been tricked but rather went willingly.

Seth disagreed.

Bumpy reminded Seth that he and his sister agreed to accept the rarest of invitations: an invitation extended by the very Creator of the universe Himself. They were offered the opportunity to witness how time, matter, and the universe itself came into existence. The journey to the beginning of time was to not only answer questions, but to build faith.

Seth remembered things differently. He did indeed remember being shown how the universe came into being, but something went terribly wrong. Supposedly, because of their unbelief—even after having witnessed the miracle of creation itself, he and Melissa were abandoned in a strange world. They had to endure many trials and tribulations in order to make it back home. Seth would write details about the ordeal when time allowed, but suffice it to say, the biggest doubter of God himself, Seth, had discovered a few reasons to believe. And while not totally convinced, he promised his sister that he would spend the next year in pursuit of God.

Bumpy had informed Seth that they would be going back to the other realm, but this time they would need to be equipped with a stronger faith—something that Seth was still in short supply. A strong faith, as Bumpy foretold, would help Seth and his sister to reveal long-lost good news that had been hidden from the other realm for thousands of years. Countless souls were dependent on them being triumphant. Seth did not fully understand what Bumpy meant, or how such things could happen, but he liked the idea that he had an important role to play. He even imagined he might someday become a hero.

"We're almost there, y'all," Jimmy shouted in a slow southern drawl. Although Jimmy was of Cuban ancestry, he was born and raised in the deep South and no one would mistake him for anything other than a true Southerner. Except maybe those from the South, who often asked where he was from—probably due to his olive complexion.

Melissa spotted the blue water glistening between all the trees. Seth, of course, could not see anything but leaves, dirt, and the tops of his shoes. The boat was beginning to get heavy and he could not wait to set it down. His arms ached and the jolts from running into branches and trees were becoming increasingly annoying. At least there were no bugs this time of the year to bother him.

"It's amazing," said Melissa. She had been on this lake many times, and it was always beautiful. Natural and pristine, this was one of the cleanest lakes in the United States. Situated in a national forest, no houses, buildings, or commercial entities were allowed anywhere near the lake, other than a couple of commercial boat docks.

Lake Ouachita was the result of damming the Ouachita River, and many other creeks and streams fed into the lake as well. Nothing but trees adorned the shoreline for miles and miles. Even the least observant visitor could spot the occasional bald eagle flying overhead, or huge catfish trolling the shallow shoreline in search of food.

"Let's set the boat down here," said Jimmy. Seth, following Jimmy, lifted the boat up over his head and gingerly brought it back down on the sandy shore. He looked around, taking in the beauty and enjoying the silence. There were no crickets chirping, katydids singing, or frogs croaking. Most of the bugs and other critters had already packed up in preparation for winter.

"Bumpy!" exclaimed Seth.

"Yeah, sorry, for the rough hike. That's the price we have to pay for beauty," said Jimmy.

Seth was not referring to the hike but rather Bumpy the leaf, which he left in his backpack back in the pickup.

"I forgot my backpack. I need to run back to the truck," said Seth.

"How are you going to find your way? Your head was stuck under the boat the whole way down here," said Melissa.

"I'll get it," said Jimmy.

"Do you really need it, Seth? We're not going to be gone that long," added Melissa.

"Yes, I brought along a little surprise for you guys. Believe me, you're gonna want to see it."

Jimmy, already on his way, looked back and said, "It's not a problem, I'll be back in a few minutes." He disappeared into the woods as Melissa took a seat on the edge of the canoe.

"Why don't you set the oars down?" asked Seth.

"Oh, yeah. I guess I could. Where should I put them?

"Just lay them in the boat."

Taking Seth's advice, Melissa turned her body just enough to slide the oars into the canoe's cavity. "So, what's the surprise?"

"It wouldn't exactly be a surprise if I told you."

"Whatever." Melissa struggled to appear uninterested. "It's so quiet."

"Time of the year—starting to get cold,"

"I suppose. But, it's *really* quiet." Melissa took her backpack off her shoulder and unzipped it. She took a book out and began to leaf through the pages.

Seth agreed. "Wow, even the water is so still. Not a ripple. I might expect it to be like that in the early morning, but not this time of day."

"Listen to this." Melissa began to read from the book she had just retrieved. "He made the storm be still, and then the waves of the sea were hushed. Then they were glad that the waters were quiet, and he brought them to their desired haven."

"More Bible verses?"

"It's a Psalm. I just opened to that page and it was the first verse I came to."

"What does it mean?"

"I don't know exactly, but it reminds me of when Jesus quieted the sea for the disciples in the boat. The waves were crashing and the storm seemed like it was going to sink them. When the disciples cried out to Jesus, He quieted the waves and all was well."

"Interesting."

"Well, there's no storm here now."

"But there was. The last time we were here. There was a huge storm."

"What are you talking about? There wasn't a storm the last time we visited Grandma."

"Yes, there most certainly was. Don't you remember?"

"Oh my …" Melissa stood up and faced Seth. "You remember, don't you?

"With the help of a new friend, I remember most of it. Do you?"

"Yes. Most."

"Why didn't you tell me?"

Melissa paused, she wanted to choose her words carefully. She assumed that her memories had come back sooner because she accepted that God was real and she believed that God had protected them in the other realm. She knew Seth still had doubts. "It seemed so crazy, unreal. I planned on talking to you about it, when the time was right."

"Believe me, we are going to talk about it."

"When did you remember?"

"Like you, things started coming back in pieces." Seth's first memory of what happened in the other realm came to him right before a big exam, which he failed miserably. "I guess I just repressed most of it. But when I went for a walk yesterday, down by the creek where the big boulders are, I bumped into someone."

"Way out there? That's odd."

"That's an understatement. If I told you who—or should I say what—it was, you would never believe me. Anyway, everything came back. And I understand why I didn't want to remember. A lot of it was pretty terrifying. But I think the verse you just read is a good omen, though."

"Why is that?"

"Because I'm fairly sure that we are about to find our way back to wherever it was we were last time, and I for one wouldn't be going voluntarily if I didn't have some reassurances."

"Fox!"

"Huh?"

Something Seth said had jarred Melissa's memory of an adorable red fox that not only became a trusted friend, but also helped save her life. "I know she's out there somewhere. This is my chance to find her. She's the one that helped me find you, and if it weren't for her, we would never have made it back home." Melissa paused and then continued, "Reassurances? What do you mean by that?"

"Quit skipping around and try to focus for a minute." Seth took a deep breath. "This thing that helped me get my memories back reassured me that something greater than ourselves is on our side. He said we have an important mission."

"Seth Basham, are you startin' to get a little faith?"

"I'm open, sis. There's got to be something out there bigger than me, us, than what we can see."

"I do declare! This is going to be a very fun day indeed."

Chapter 10

The Incident

There was only one bathroom in the house. If the children had not gone out on the lake or had the women stayed home instead of visiting distant relatives, it would have been inconvenient to lay the new tile. The tacky 1970s linoleum had made its last offense if Patrick had his way. He planned to lay the tile in the afternoon and then grout it on Sunday, while everyone was in church. He knew his brother-in-law would never get around to doing it himself, and quite frankly it gave Patrick an excuse to avoid all the holiday hoopla.

Patrick thought ahead and brought his wet-saw from home and some other equipment to make the job easier. The floor was less than fifty square feet and it would not take long to complete. Bethany had mentioned seeing ceramic tile stacked in the garage for the last five years, and she mentioned it after every visit to her mother's house. He was not sure if Bethany was hinting at him to do it or was just making small talk, but either way he was pretty sure it would earn him bonus points.

Since everyone else was gone, the elderly man next door offered to help Patrick. It was a job Patrick could do by himself, but he felt sorry for the older gentleman. He looked lonely and bored.

"How come you didn't have dinner with us yesterday, Earl?" asked Patrick.

Earl was a widower. His wife of fifty years had passed away eight years prior. She was everything to Earl. On the day of her funeral, his son-in-law coerced him to sign all that he owned over to his daughter. In his grief and with a trusting heart, he did what his only remaining family requested. It was not long before they took over all of his savings and sold his house and property. The son-in-law spent the next few years buying boats, cars, land, and even bought a fast-food franchise, which failed miserably. Earl was left with nothing but a promise that they would take care of him. They did build him a tiny one-bedroom house next to theirs—so they could collect and deposit his retirement checks into their own account.

As it was, his daughter and only grandchild rarely spoke to him unless they wanted him to pay for something out of his meager monthly allotment. The son-in-law was worse. He forced Earl to work in the yard, would never take him on family trips, and would not allow him to have a phone. All of the neighbors found the family to be creepy. Controlling, that was what Azora and Henry called them. The grandson was in his thirties but still lived at home, never dated, and rarely ventured far from the house. Needless to say, they were a peculiar bunch.

Patrick was secretly grateful for Earl and his odd family. It was this family he often cited as the reason he could not accept Christianity. How could a family that professed to be so Christian, attend church every Sunday, and write Bible verses on their chicken coop treat their poor old father so terribly?

Earl had taken the cord of the wet saw into the garage to plug it in. On his way back out, he responded to Patrick's question, "I thought maybe my daughter might have asked me to come to their house for dinner."

Patrick knew it was a long shot. But he also knew that Earl loved his family dearly and would never give up any chance to be with them, even if it meant spending Thanksgiving alone. "Did they even bring you leftovers?"

"No, I don't reckon they had any."

"Well, we have plenty. I'll make sure Beth sends some over your way when she gets home. Would you mind grabbing the garden hose for me? I need to attach it to the wet saw here."

"That's a mighty fancy cuttin' machine there. What's the water fer?"

"It helps keep the blade cool. It's a diamond blade, makes smoother cuts and it's more precise."

"What er' ya gonna tile?"

"The bathroom floor."

"I can't wait to see this. Does Henry know you're about to tile his bathroom floor?"

"I'm sure he won't mind. He's had the tile sitting around for years." Patrick went into the garage to retrieve the first box of tiles.

"Yup, you're right about that. Seen it in the garage there myself. Wondered what it was fer." Earl turned and headed to the house to retrieve the water hose.

Patrick exited the garage and set the tiles in between two sawhorses. "I guess you heard what happened to the kids the last time they were here."

"Say what?"

Patrick raised his voice, "The incident this spring with the children, did you hear about it?"

"Who didn't hear about it? I do declare that's been the talk around here ever since April. My daughter even came over a couple of times to see if I had heard anything."

"Really? What did she want to know?"

"First, she wanted to know if they was runnin' away from home. Then word got out Seth was havin' problems in school."

"How in the world do people around here know anything about Seth's school?"

"Don't ask me. Word gets around, ya know. She heard he was actin' kind of queer."

"Queer?"

"Yes sir, you know, strange in the head."

"Well, wouldn't Margret be happy about that. More of her kind to relate to. Well, you can tell your daughter that Seth is just fine. And to mind her own business."

Earl finally managed to get the water hose untangled and stretched out far enough to reach the saw, which was now sitting on the sawhorses. "Where didja want this attached?"

"Right here." Patrick took the hose and twisted it onto the machine. "What have you heard?"

"'Bout what?"

"The kids. The incident."

"What could I hear, I only see the few neighbors around here and they don't know much."

"Well, they must be saying something."

"The only interestin' thing I heard was that somethin' similar happened to Jimmy when he was about the same age as your youngins'."

"Jimmy? You mean the gardener?"

"Yes, sir. He disappeared for a couple of days and it was all a big mystery. But there wasn't much fuss 'cause he had a bit of a checkered past. Folks just figured he was misbehavin'."

Patrick, who had begun marking the tile to be cut, looked up at Earl. "What kind of past?"

"Oh, it ain't nothin' fer you to fret over. He's a good kid. Just teenage stuff."

"Man, it's always the religious ones you've got to keep an eye on."

"You think so?"

"Yes, I do. Tell me, what happened to him?"

"From what I hear tell, Jimmy came back claimin' not to remember a thing. Didn't your youngins say the same thing?"

"Did it happen here, in Garland County? Was it the same place where Seth and Melissa were found?"

"I don't reckon I know all the details. You'd have to ask him yerself. But I will say this—things started gettin' all cattywampus around here after that."

"What do you mean?"

"The animals started actin' peculiar, for starters."

Patrick ignored this last comment and mumbled under his breath, "Great, I sent my kids off to spend the day with a hooligan."

"Come on now, Pat. Jimmy is a good young man. He straightened himself out. Give em' a chance."

"Hand me that measuring tape there, would ya?"

"But frankly, if I may ask," Earl went on, "why didya allow them kids to go off in the woods again after what happened last time? I figured you'd wanna keep a good eye on 'em."

"It's important to get back up on the horse after you fall off. Seth needs to build up his self-confidence. Besides, from what everyone says,

Jimmy knows this place better than just about anyone. I thought the kids would be in good hands—at least until I heard what you had to say."

"I reckon you're correct, about gittin' back up on the horse, that is. Can't run around the world worryin' about everything that might go wrong."

Patrick knew Earl was right. It sounded like something he might say to Bethany. Patrick used the back of his hand to wipe a bit of perspiration from his forehead as he changed the topic of conversation. "Man, it's almost hot today. What's the temperature?"

"Radio said it was s'posed to git up to around eighty degrees."

"Wow. Eighty on November 26th. That's got to be some kind of record." Patrick unfolded a piece of paper that had the measurements for the tile. He stuck one corner of the paper under the box of tiles so it would not blow away. He then took the pencil from his back pocket and with his measuring tape in hand began to mark the first cuts.

Earl, always self-conscious about being in the way, began to walk to the back of the garage. Earl's little guest house was only a few yards away from Henry and Azora's, and there was a nicely worn path from his front door to the Fray home. "Well, if you need me, give a holler. I best be gittin' back over to the house."

"What's going on at the house?"

"Nothin' much—just want to be there in case the kids come over. They might need me for somethin' or other. Besides, I need to git all them hickory nuts picked up off of the yard."

"Hickory nuts?" Patrick knew, by the way Bethany and the kids spoke, that there was little chance Earl would be getting any visits from his family. The only time they came over was to put him to work or complain about something he did wrong.

"Yeah. Ray don't like them hickory nuts hittin' the lawnmower blades. They're just about as hard as rocks, ya know."

Ray was Earl's son-in-law, and he always made sure that Earl had some useless task to do. In the summer Earl had to go down to the creek to fetch water because Ray didn't want him using the well water on his roses. The well had never gone dry, and there was no indication it ever would, but to Ray, making an elderly man carry buckets of water up a hill seemed like a reasonable expectation. To the neighbors, it bordered on elder abuse.

"Alright then. I'll be sure and have Beth wrap up some food for you."

"Don't go to no trouble."

"No trouble at all, Earl."

Earl slowly walked to the back of the garage and disappeared out of sight right after shouting goodbye.

Patrick thought about his own dad, regretting not spending more time with him before he passed. He was never really close to his own father, but he was thankful that their relationship resembled nothing of the one next door. Earl was a very nice man and he did not deserve the sad lonely life his only family in the world afforded him.

Chapter 11

Through the Water Gate

Although Jimmy had not been gone that long, Melissa had already managed to situate herself on the bottom of the boat between two life preservers. Her left leg dangled over the edge, and the position did not look comfortable, but it was obvious she had claimed the spot that would not allow her to row.

Seth was skipping rocks on the glassy water a few feet down from where the boat rested. He quickly turned around upon hearing footsteps crunching through the leaves.

Jimmy had returned with Seth's backpack. "What was so important that you had to have this?" He tossed it to Seth.

"Since you asked," Seth placed the backpack on the ground and unzipped the middle compartment. He lifted a quart-sized mason jar into the air and held it there.

"You didn't need to bring any food, I picked up some sandwiches and stuff at the Sunshine gas station," said Jimmy.

At this point, Melissa sat up and began to maneuver her body off the floor and onto the middle seat of the boat. "I brought granola bars."

"That's great, because I didn't bring any food." Seth lowered the jar to the front of his face. The lid had "blackberry preserves" and a date he could not quite make out written on the top. He looked at his grandmother's old canning jar as if it had gold in it. He unscrewed the two-piece lid then carefully reached inside. He angled the jar until it was almost upside down and gingerly pulled out some tissue paper. He never took his gaze off the contents as he set the jar on the ground. With wide eyes, he gingerly unfolded the white tissue paper.

Melissa was so taken by her brother's fixation that she lost her balance and tipped the canoe over. She fell and hit her caboose on the hard dirt. She was more embarrassed than hurt, but she could not help but rub her sore behind. She quickly sat up, folded her arms, and acted like the whole clumsy event never happened. She skipped a few beats before looking over in Jimmy's direction. Jimmy still watched Seth and acted like he never saw Melissa's accident.

Seth had now completely unwrapped the fragile contents of the tissue paper. Jimmy and Melissa glanced at one another before moving over to get a closer look. Surely this thing that had so much importance was not what it looked to be—a leaf!

"Melissa, Jimmy, I would like you both to meet Bumpy."

A few seconds passed. Jimmy spoke first. "What else is in the backpack?"

"No, really, this is what I wanted you both to see. It's amazing. It explains everything. I mean I thought I was going crazy and then I realized, because of this leaf, that I am perfectly sane." Seth stood up to share his newfound revelation. He walked over to Melissa and held the leaf up to her face. "Can you imagine my relief? Here I am thinking that I totally went insane getting lost in the woods, remembering bits and pieces about some other strange universe—and then I find this magical leaf."

Jimmy glanced at Melissa and then back at Seth. "Okay. You found a magic leaf. What does it do exactly?"

Seth, quite elated, laughed and turned to hold the leaf for Jimmy to get a closer look. "Why ask me? Why don't you ask Bumpy?"

"Bumpy?" asked Melissa.

"Yes, I told you, that's his name."

"How do you know what his name is?" asked Melissa.

"Well, because he told me of course. How else could I have known what his name is? Unless maybe some other leaf told me, but then why would another leaf need to tell me when he can just tell me himself?"

"How do you know it's a he?"

"Seriously, Melissa, this is what you ask when I hold a leaf that has all the answers to the universe right in front of your face? Ask him something. Anything."

"Sure, okay." Melissa paused to consider her options. She did not want to say something that might upset her brother. This was the most joyful she had seen him in quite some time. Even though she was worried, she did not want to seem doubtful of his claims. "Hi, Bumpy. Where did you and my brother meet?"

Seth interrupted, "Oh my gosh, really? Where did you and my brother meet? Wow. Alright, Jimmy, why don't you give it a go?"

"Can I hold it?"

"No, I don't think that would be appropriate. Bumpy came to me after all. Just ask your question."

Melissa nodded for Jimmy to oblige her brother. "Well, what does a person ask a leaf anyway?"

"Never mind, if you two can't see the importance of this, just forget it."

"I'm sorry," said Jimmy. "So, Bumpy, how did you come to be able to speak?"

After a few moments with no response from the leaf, Seth became agitated. "Well, he obviously doesn't like the two of you. Let me talk to him." Seth twirled the leaf in front of him until he found that the bump was facing the right direction. "You see that bump there?" Seth asked his sister and Jimmy. "That's how Bumpy got his name." He looked at the leaf in his hand. "Hi Bumpy. Sorry for these two doubters. Anyway, here we are at the lake, just like you said would happen. We are all here, Jimmy, me and my sister. Now what do we do?"

There was still no response by the leaf. Seth shook his head in frustration. "See what you two have done? He must not trust you two. Otherwise, I'm sure he would speak. Well, there's nothing I can do to change that. I just met him yesterday. It's not like I know what turns him off and on. But one of you, or maybe both of you, are a turn off!"

"Gee, so sorry to hear that, brother. I'm sure Bumpy has a good reason not to speak."

Jimmy, playing along with Melissa, said, "Yes, I'm sure he'll speak up when it's the right time.'

"Oh yeah, exactly," said Seth. "He's probably reserving his energy. He is pretty old, after all."

"Of course, that's got to be it," said Melissa.

"I'll just put him here in my shirt pocket. And when he's ready, he'll let us know."

Jimmy was not sure what to make of Seth's leaf, but because of his own past experiences in the woods of Garland County, he chose not to make much of it. He also figured that Seth might just be playing a practical joke and he did not want to spoil the fun. "Great, now that that's all settled, let's put these life preservers on and get the boat in the water."

"By the way, where is the trolling motor?" asked Seth.

"What do we need a trolling motor for? The water is calm and there are three of us. We'll manage just fine.'

Seth looked at Melissa and rolled his eyes. She shrugged her shoulders as if she never said anything to the contrary. Jimmy took hold of the canoe and sat it right side up. Seth and Melissa retrieved the life vests that had fallen on the ground and proceeded to put them on. After Melissa had secured the third buckle on her vest, she noticed there was not another vest for Jimmy.

"Where's yours?"

"Oh, I don't need one. We are going to stay close to the shore anyway."

Seth began to immediately unbuckle his preserver, "If you're not wearing one, I'm not either."

"Yeah, like you said, we are not going that far out." Melissa also began taking her vest off.

"I take it you two are good swimmers."

"Absolutely," said Melissa. "We spent a lot of summers coming to this lake as kids."

"Alright, Seth doesn't have to wear a vest if he doesn't want to because he's over eighteen. But sorry, you're going to have to keep yours on, Melissa."

"This is the opposite of fair!" said Melissa.

"The exact opposite," mocked Seth.

Melissa put her arms back through the life vest while Seth and Jimmy each took an end of the boat and placed it in the water.

"I'll take the back and you can take the front, Seth. Jump in and I'll push us off after Melissa gets in."

Melissa put on her vest but either forgot or intentionally neglected to buckle it up. She walked over to the boat and just before getting in looked back at the woods behind them. She was not sure what prompted her to take that look. Was it the thought that she might never see this spot again, or did she hope to see Fox peeking out behind a tree? Now that most of her memories had returned about her last trip into the woods, it was those of Fox that she cherished the most. Without the help of the red fox, she might not have survived. She and Fox had a bond that surpassed most of her human friendships.

Melissa climbed in and took the middle bench. Jimmy positioned the boat as far in the water as possible without having to get wet when he jumped aboard. He pushed off the shore and made it aboard without so much as getting a drop on him. Melissa was surprised by his graceful agility. As they coasted freely out into the middle of the cove, each one of them grabbed an oar.

The cove, like most coves on Lake Ouachita, was not that wide or deep. It was perhaps less than one football field across and even less in length. Jimmy began rowing first. The boat glided effortlessly on the water.

"We're going to head north around this bend and then east for a bit. The sun will be mostly in front of us, but it shouldn't get too warm until about noon," said Jimmy.

Seth began to row. With no current pushing or pulling their canoe, it was easy enough with only two of them doing the work. Seth looked around, admiring the beauty around them. The fall colors were more easily seen out on the lake, and the reflection of the tree line in the calm water made it look as though there were two beautiful woods to explore. This was arguably the most gorgeous time of the year to be in the South.

The colorful leaves on the trees reminded Seth of the leaf in his pocket. Why had Bumpy refused to speak? Was it something Seth had done? Did he say something wrong? Seth would not allow any negative thoughts about his own sanity to enter his mind. He had to hang onto what he knew was true. He had not imagined a talking leaf—the leaf was alive and it was real.

"Shhh, be really quiet and look up there at that tree on the right." Jimmy pointed to an unusually tall pine that stood several yards from the shoreline. Seth immediately ceased rowing as he and his sister looked up. The quiet tone and serious inflection of Jimmy's voice indicated there was something very special to be witnessed.

"There's a bald eagle perched at the very top," whispered Jimmy.

"I see it. Wow, how majestic," said Melissa.

"I see it too," said Seth. "It's so big. Even that high up it looks huge."

"Do you think it cares that we are down here?" Melissa asked.

"She's aware of us, but I don't think she views us as a threat. Otherwise, she would have flown away already."

"How do you know it's a girl?" asked Melissa.

"I don't. But I do know that it can live up to almost thirty years. And male or female, it prefers to mate for life."

Jimmy continued to row as Seth and Melissa stared up into the trees. It was not every day that one had an opportunity to see such an amazing creature. When Seth finally returned his oar to the water, he must have been a little too loud because the eagle took flight. Rather than retreating back into the woods, the huge bird with the white-feathered crown gracefully soared over the three watchful souls below. She opened her wings wider than Seth was tall. The grand bird floated effortlessly in the warm autumn air, circling once and then flapping her great wings to lift higher and higher. It was as if she had no fear and perhaps took just as much delight in the boat and its passengers than they did in her. Finally, she flapped harder until she reached the other side of the lake and disappeared into the trees.

As pretty as the scenery was, Melissa had gotten quite bored. It was the third cove they had ventured into with nothing more than the same old trees and dirt shores. Yes, there were plenty of little things to notice—little brim surfacing around the boat looking for food, an occasional bass or carp flopping around in the water, and a paddling duck or two—but nothing like a great eagle or freshwater jellyfish to entertain them. What was worse, the sun was overhead and beating directly down upon them. It was much hotter than it should have been for this time of the year, and Melissa was getting increasingly uncomfortable.

"Okay, I don't care what anyone says," said Melissa. "I'm taking this vest off. I'm burning up. If the water wasn't so cold, I'd jump in to cool off."

"What do I care, take it off," said Seth. "It's not like were floating down the rapids of the Buffalo River."

Jimmy responded, "Fine, Seth, you can jump in after her if she falls in." Jimmy was not too much older than the siblings and did not want to act too parental, but when it came to safety, he felt a little scolding was warranted.

Melissa proceeded to undo the bright orange foam vest that engulfed her midsection but only managed to get the straps tangled up. She could not help but think if Jimmy had invested in more fashionable vests, his passengers might not be so opposed to wearing them.

Seth noticed something in the water and excitedly yelled, "Did y'all see that?" He pointed in front of the canoe.

"What was it?" asked Jimmy.

"Help me row out to the middle of the cove. There's something in the water."

Jimmy shook his head. "How could you see something in the water that far from the boat?"

"I don't know. Maybe it's the sun playing tricks. Let's go look."

Jimmy and Seth both rowed with a little more vigor than they had earlier in the day. The three of them were excited to finally have something different to investigate. Even if it was just the sun playing tricks with the water, it ignited their imaginations and gave the moment added purpose.

Seth pointed in the direction he wanted to go. It was back towards the opening of the cove—directly in the middle. About five minutes earlier they had just rowed all the way back to the creek that fed into it. After a short debate whether to attempt venturing into the creek a ways, Melissa objected on the grounds that there were too many low-hanging branches—and that surely meant spider webs and tree snakes. The boys were annoyed, but they reluctantly agreed to head back.

Seth took his oar out of the water. "Here. Stop rowing. It was right about here."

"What is it you saw, exactly?" asked Jimmy.

"I saw a light in the water."

"A light?" asked Melissa. "How could you see a light in the middle of the day? Are you sure you didn't just see the sun beaming through the clouds into the water?"

"What clouds? Besides, this was different. It was a golden color and it was glowing. It's hard to explain." Seth maneuvered his oar in the water to keep the boat situated around the area in question.

Jimmy placed his oar in the boat and leaned over the side to peer into the water. "It's super clear. I can't see anything."

"Can you see the bottom?" asked Seth.

"Of course not, it's gotta be at least thirty feet deep here."

Seth nodded, "Too bad it's November. If it was summer, we could just dive in and look."

"Yeah right, like I'm getting into some strange illuminating water! Not a chance." Melissa stood up to get a better look, causing the canoe to tip severely. She immediately sat back down, clutching the side. "Oh my gosh, that was close. My heart is about to beat out of my chest."

"Way to go, Melissa. Dump us all into the cold water why don't you!" said Seth.

"I still can't see anything. What do y'all say we head over to one of the little islands to eat lunch and then we can head back home?" Jimmy proposed.

"Sounds good to me," said Melissa. "But first I've gotta get this vest off. I'm getting claustrophobic in this thing." Because the vest was so tight and ill-fitting, Melissa had a hard time getting her arm through the opening. The bottom belt got stuck, so she yanked hard in an effort to pull it over the top of her head. In frustration—and without thinking—she quickly stood up.

"Uhg! Can someone please help me with this thing?" The canoe rocked, and Seth stood to help keep his sister from falling over. He was able to maintain both his balance as well as his sister's, and he then proceeded to help her pull the life vest over her head. At first it was stuck, but after he gave it one more tug, it came off with an unexpected jerk and made him lose his balance. The canoe rocked even harder. Jimmy tried to counterbalance but it was too late. Seth lost his balance and fell backward out of the canoe, which caused the boat to rock even more. Melissa screamed when she realized she too was going overboard. As Melissa's weight crashed into the side of the canoe, there was no way for Jimmy to keep it from capsizing. All three fell into the cold water.

The unusually warm autumn air had no effect on the temperature of the lake, which was filled from northern streams. The water was so cold it felt like someone had punched Seth in the stomach. He could not stop himself from sinking deeper and deeper as his limbs numbed to the chilling shock. He took refuge in the fact that his body's natural buoyancy would eventually bring him back to the surface. But what should have been mere seconds seemed like an eternity.

Melissa fell backward into the water, and she had never felt anything so shocking in her life. All she could think about was how unbearably cold it was. Her whole body tensed up as she sank faster and deeper than she even thought possible. She was unable to use her arms and legs to propel herself back towards the surface. Her limbs were stiff and useless. All she could do was hope for a miracle. Everything around her was dark and confusing. Her last thought was the regret of taking her life jacket off. If only she had that life jacket, she would eventually find her way back to the surface despite losing her senses.

Jimmy's reaction was immediate and without any thought. Although he too fell deeper into the water than he would have imagined possible, he immediately used his legs and arms to kick and pull upwards toward the light. He shot out of the water like a bullet and used his momentum to pull himself up on top of the canoe, which was now upside down in the water. Everything happened so fast that it took him a moment to get his bearings. Where were Seth and Melissa? They fell in before he did. They should be up to the surface already. He panicked. He did not know what to do. He had never been in any situation like this before. They must have gone into shock with the cold water, but how could he save both of them? He had no choice but to dive back into the water. As he dove, he prayed for God's help.

Chapter 12

THE TABLE

Seth shot up and out of the water first. He took a deep breath while pushing the hair off his forehead. He trod water as he tried to get his bearings. Melissa quickly followed after Seth, popping up just a few feet away from her brother. His face was the first thing she saw after she caught her breath. Relief enveloped her as she swam towards him.

"What happened? Where's the canoe?" asked Melissa between breaths.

"I don't know. Do you see Jimmy?" The teens treaded in place, keeping their heads above water while scanning the area around them. After a few seconds they heard a splash about ten feet away. It was Jimmy. He finally made it to the surface.

Jimmy looked at the two teens and loudly proclaimed, "Thank God. I thought I lost you two." He swam in their direction. "That was the scariest thing that has ever happened to me. I've never had to save one drowning person, let alone two at the same time!"

"Did the canoe sink?" asked Seth.

"You couldn't sink ol' Gloria if you tried."

"Gloria?" asked a breathless Melissa. She was getting tired from her efforts to stay above water.

"That's the name of my canoe."

"So, where is she? Where's Gloria?" asked Seth.

Jimmy responded, "I have a more important question."

"Can it wait till we get to shore? These clothes aren't great for swimming and I'm getting really worn out," said Melissa.

"Of course, let's go. The shore's not far. But one thing, did y'all notice the water?"

"What about it?" asked Seth.

Jimmy answered, "It's warm."

Melissa had already started swimming to shore, but stopped long enough to say, "I just thought I had gotten used to it, but I guess you're right. We should have hypothermia by now."

"That's right. When I hit the water all I remember is how insanely cold it was," said Seth.

"Me, too," added Melissa.

Jimmy waved them on as he too headed for dry land. "Come on, let's get to shore. We can count our blessings as we dry out." Jimmy led the way, and they followed closely. All three were good swimmers, but being fully dressed—with shoes no less—made it much more difficult.

Jimmy made it to shore and looked back to see if the siblings needed assistance. They were doing just fine and were not that far behind him. Jimmy sat on the soft sandy ground and took a few deep breaths. He untied his shoes and managed to empty the water from one before Seth made it to shore.

Seth walked out of the water and then immediately sprawled out on the ground, breathing heavily. Melissa, right behind him, walked slowly out of the lake, her clothes heavy. She shook her arms and legs like a dog after a bath. She turned to look back at the lake and scanned the entire horizon, looking for the canoe.

"It must have sunk, I can't see it anywhere," she said.

"I don't see how that's possible," Jimmy said, "but I guess you're right, where else could it be?" He paused. "Too bad. That was a good boat."

Seth changed the subject. "So, what's up with the warm water? Did our adrenaline kick in or what?"

"I don't know, maybe," answered Jimmy.

Melissa sat down on a large flat rock to wring out her hair. "Well, how do we get back to the truck from here?"

"Not a problem. We just follow the shoreline. We didn't go that far," said Jimmy.

While the guys were still scanning the lake, Melissa took notice of their surroundings. "Hey guys, look behind you."

"What is it?" asked Jimmy as he turned around.

Seth also turned to look. "Oh. This is pretty weird. I don't like the look of this at all."

Confusion descended on Jimmy. "I don't get it. Where are we? This isn't the same cove we rowed into."

Melissa nodded in agreement. "I don't think this is the same lake we fell into, or the same woods we came out of … I remember this place. I've been here before."

"What are you talking about?" asked Jimmy.

Melissa pointed farther offshore. "Look at those trees—they're all dead. They've been dead for ages. Like they died and then froze in time. In fact, there is not one living thing except—" Melissa was interrupted by a barking animal.

Everyone looked to see where it was coming from, but Melissa was the first one to see it. It was Fox, and she was standing about thirty feet away along the tree line.

"Fox?" said Melissa.

The fox immediately started yapping. She then lowered the front half of her body much the way a cat would just before pouncing on a mouse. She quickly jumped up on all fours and began running towards her long-lost friend. She was so excited that her yaps actually became squeals. Fox could not contain her joy. Before anyone had time to react, Fox had reached Melissa and instead of stopping, she literally jumped in the air as Melissa instinctively raised her arms to catch her furry friend.

"You are real, I knew it! I just knew it. And you're alive, Fox! You're alive! I thought I had lost you in the Lake of Entitlement. I remember being so worried that you might have drowned."

Fox tried to speak, but she could not stop licking Melissa all over her face. Every word she spoke just came out mumbled. Still, she kept licking and mumbling.

"Aren't you going to introduce us to your friend, Melissa?" asked Seth.

While still holding the red fox, Melissa quickly moved her head to avoid the fox's tongue so she could answer her brother. "Seth, Jimmy, this is Fox. I met her when we were here last time. In these same woods as a matter of fact. Isn't that right, Fox?"

Fox answered, "Yes, yes, these woods. This was where I met my very first human friend."

Melissa set Fox on the ground. Fox immediately rolled on her back for Melissa to rub her belly.

Melissa looked at Seth and asked, "Can you hear her speak?"

"Yes, I can. Thank God. I was so mad that you could understand everyone last time and I couldn't. It wasn't fair!"

"What about you, Jimmy?"

"Loud and clear. And I've been here before too. Long time ago. It was quite an experience and one that I had hoped not to repeat."

Fox heard Seth sneeze and she ran up to him and said, "May God bless you."

"That wasn't me."

Fox backed away and tilted her head in a curious fashion when she saw Seth's front pocket move. Seth looked down at his chest and instantly remembered that's where he had put Bumpy. Bumpy sneezed again. Seth took his thumb and pulled the pocket open to get a better look.

Bumpy pulled himself halfway out of the pocket with his top two lateral veins, which he used as his arms. "I don't do well in damp places," he said.

"A talking leaf!" exclaimed Jimmy. "It is a leaf, isn't it? Well, that's a first."

"And a sneezing leaf, too, I might add," said Fox, who had moved back towards Seth in hopes of getting a good sniff.

"You two didn't believe me. See, I was telling the truth," said Seth, beaming. "This is Bumpy, everyone."

Bumpy looked around and said, "Alrighty then. It looks like we made it to the Dead Woods. Good job everyone."

Seth looked down at Bumpy. "If this is where you wanted us to go, why didn't you just say so? Maybe you could have saved us from almost drowning."

"Nothing can get you to the other side but faith and sacrifice," said Bumpy. "I planted the seed of what could happen and you believed, so it seems."

Jimmy walked over to Seth and bent down to get a better view of the leaf hanging halfway out of his pocket. "So now that we are here, do you know what we are supposed to do?"

"Do? What makes you think you are to *do* anything, young feller?" said Bumpy.

"What do you mean by that?" asked Melissa.

"I reckon you yourselves are the doin' and the rest is the result of that," said Bumpy.

Seth raised his eyebrows and said, "I have no idea what that's supposed to mean."

"Don't you worry none about that, partner. We'll all figure it out together. Suffice it to say that a lot of what we were supposed to do has been accomplished just by us showin' up here. Now would you kindly pull me out of this here soggy pocket so I can get dried off?"

Seth complied and gently lifted him out with his right hand. He then grabbed Bumpy's stem and quickly twirled him around.

"Whoa! I'll dry off fast enough without you turning me into a twister!" exclaimed Bumpy.

"Sorry, I thought it might help speed it up."

"How would you like it if someone picked you up and spun you around like a pinwheel?"

Fox stood on her hind feet and turned in circles—imitating the leaf. Suddenly a gust of air lifted Bumpy out of Seth's hand. Bumpy glided over the fox. Every time Fox tried to touch the leaf with her paw, Bumpy would go higher, just out of reach, and then come back down to repeat the whole process over again. Melissa chuckled. Jimmy smiled. It took Seth a little longer to realize they were playing.

It was not until the wind currents brought the playful pair to a large wooden structure that things got a little more serious. The structure turned out to be a table that sat at the edge of the Dead Woods. The fellow travelers joined Fox and Bumpy to get a closer look at the odd find. The table was beautifully polished and in surprisingly perfect condition considering it was outdoors. One by one, the travelers came and stood directly around the table.

"Why in the world is this thing just sitting out here in the middle of nowhere?" asked Seth.

"Look," Jimmy said as he pointed behind the table, which was long enough to seat a hundred people. Jimmy was pointing at a trail that led straight into the woods. It was wide, smooth, and free of impediments. It seemed obvious to everyone that it was the way to go. But any discussion of the trail would be tabled for a while.

"This table, it's amazing," said Melissa. She looked down at the gleaming wood and right before her eyes appeared the most delectable collection of sweets. There were chocolate cakes, cobblers of every variety, sweet rolls, pecan pies, cheesecakes in every flavor imaginable, cookies, and much more.

"I've never seen anything like it," agreed Seth, but instead of sugar-filled treats, he saw gold bowls filled with emeralds and pearls. There were bars of gold, and stacks of round coins. There were even diamonds and all kinds of precious stones. The treasure on the table must have been worth millions in Seth's estimation.

Jimmy was also mesmerized as he looked at the table. He saw ancient books and writings. He looked closer and saw the names of Nicolaus Copernicus and Galileo Galilei, among others. He ran his fingers along ancient refractors and antique telescopes. He opened the closest book in front of him. "This is an original writing of Edwin Hubble. It's got his signature right here."

Melissa began to laugh. "I thought Hubble was an astronomer, not a baker."

Seth, not taking his eyes off the table, said, "Well, whatever he did, he made a lot of money doing it, but why leave it just sitting out here like this for anyone to steal."

"What money?" asked Melissa.

"What are you talking about?" asked Jimmy.

"There's nothing at all on the table," said Fox, who had to keep jumping up to get a better look.

Bumpy, like Fox, saw nothing on the table. He even slid on the surface of the shiny wood all the way to the other end to prove his point. But no one noticed. He returned back in front of the others to find them all still transfixed. "This is obviously an illusion. Fox is correct, there's nothing at all on the table."

"Nonsense," said Melissa. "It's right there in front of me. I can see it. She picked up a beautiful blueberry cupcake and scooped a bit of the light blue icing off with her finger. "What do you think this is?"

No one saw anything on Melissa's finger but Melissa.

Jimmy was the first of the three to take a step back from the table to gather his thoughts. "We are all seeing different things. Why would there be amazing desserts, all perfect and fresh, out here in the air and the sun? They would be ruined in no time."

"You may be right," said Seth, "but just on the micro possibility that any of this is real, I could be—we could be beyond filthy rich for the rest of our lives."

"Oh no, this is bad," said Fox. "It's already started right from the get-go. These terrible woods..."

Jimmy ran his fingers along one of the beautiful brass telescopes. It was cold to the touch and the metal felt rich. "Fox and Bumpy are right. This is not why we are here; this is a distraction. We should just go past this to the trail behind this table. That's what we are supposed to do."

"Well, you guys go right ahead. I for one am taking as much of this treasure back home as possible." Seth opened the main compartment of his backpack. "I'll fill this and all my pockets and keep diving in that water till my head pops up in the cold water of Lake Ouachita. Do you know what I could do with this much money back home? Maybe God wants me to have this so I can buy food for the poor and houses for the homeless. I might even be called to send Bibles to places where they are forbidden. I would be a fool not to make the most of this."

Jimmy said, "Stop. Before you do anything, let's just pray."

"Good idea," said Melissa.

"Yes, yes, very good idea," said Fox, who had already assumed the position with her head down, paws crossed, and eyes closed.

Melissa, who still saw all of the beautiful food on the table, thought better of tasting it. She recalled her time in the Land of Indulgences and knew that not much of this world was as it seemed. "Seth, you and I both know nothing is quite what it appears to be here. We need to stick together and figure this out."

"Fine, pray," said Seth. Everyone bowed their heads as Jimmy prayed. He asked God for guidance and he also asked God for forgiveness. He thanked Him for whatever plan He had for them and prayed for the wisdom to make the right choices. He prayed about a lot of other things, too.

Seth, looking up, continued to stare at this bounty, paying no attention to anyone else—or to the prayer. He slowly opened his backpack and quietly scooped up a large pile of gems, a bar of gold, and a few shiny jewels—all of which he had no idea their variety or value. He paid extra attention to one particular item: a very large pearl. It was the size of a baseball. He found a special spot for it in a side compartment, which he managed to quietly zip closed before Melissa or Jimmy noticed.

After they finished praying, Jimmy continued to examine the items on the table. He could not help himself. He knew he would not take anything, but he was ashamed for wanting to.

Fox followed along behind Melissa, who had walked about seven yards south of the table of illusions. She had spotted another trail that was much narrower than the other. There were rotting logs along the path and a lot of dried-up undergrowth. It was obvious not many people traveled this way.

"This is the way," Melissa told Fox.

"How do you know?" asked Fox.

"I'm not sure exactly. But something tells me this is the way. I just know it."

"I believe you," said Fox. "But how are you going to convince the others to come with us?"

"They'll come."

Melissa and Fox both looked back at the others. Jimmy was exploring the other trailhead. Bumpy was nowhere to be seen, or perhaps he was just too small to see from such a distance. Seth looked like he was tossing an invisible salad with his fingers. But if they could have seen through the eyes of Seth, they would have seen the gold coins cascading through his fingers like water.

"What on earth is he doing?" asked Fox.

"He's about to give up a fortune, that's what he's doing." Melissa and Fox walked back. She knew the path to take, and she was convinced they would all be going together.

Chapter 13

CIRCLE OF REPETITION

The dirt trail was so narrow that two people could not walk side by side. They formed a single-file line with Jimmy leading the way. Melissa thought that Jimmy was a natural-born leader. Seth was completely egoless in allowing him to take point because Jimmy was a few years older—at least that's what he kept telling himself. Truth be told, Seth was still apprehensive and he was glad to have someone willing to take the lead. He felt responsible for taking care of his little sister, and to be honest, Jimmy took some of the pressure off. Seth knew that Jimmy would always have his back.

The way was not always easy. At points a yellow-grayish moss covered the entire forest floor, making it difficult to know if they were still following the trail. Making matters worse, the tree limbs were thick and tangled even though they had no leaves, which prevented much light from reaching the forest floor. But despite the obvious challenges, the travelers somehow managed to always reconnect with the trail.

Though such a concept as time might have been questionable in this world behind the Water Gate, everyone felt as though they had been walking for hours—except for Bumpy, who was comfortably tucked away in Seth's front pocket. Bumpy would never tell the others, but he was scared of the dark woods. His woods were full of life and color, unlike this place which was dark and full of colorless shadows. Thankfully, the warm confines of Seth's pocket provided a sense of safety.

Fox, with four legs instead of two, was only half as tired as the rest of the party. She was still overly excited to be with her human friend again, and she pranced, hopped, and at times practically danced ahead of the slow-moving ensemble. Every once in a while, she would dig at the trunk of a tree in search of a snack. She was not hungry, just opportunistic. As an expert tracker, she was also on the lookout for markings of possible inhabitants. Whenever she ventured out in front of Jimmy, it would not be long before she came right back to Melissa's side. She loved the way Melissa smelled; like flowers in the spring air. The smell of the Dead Woods, on the other hand, lived up to its name.

"Why a leaf?" asked Jimmy out of nowhere.

"Are you asking me?" inquired Bumpy, who had lifted himself partway up by resting his arms on the rim of Seth's pocket

"I'm asking anyone, really. But I guess you'd be privy to the best answer."

"I'm not unlike the rest of you in that I'm a created thing. I suppose the only difference is that I don't have to wonder about my Creator. My whole existence represents a full season of His glory. Born in the spring. Then full of vibrant life in the summer. A change of color—and sentiment, I might add—in the fall. Followed by the inevitability of death in the winter. And the most perplexing thing of all: I exist because of His love for you, His greatest creation."

Jimmy replied, "Romans 1:20 talks about how people cannot have an excuse not to know God, because His creation is all around them. I think I understand what you mean, Bumpy. Even something as simple as a little leaf communicates the absolute glory of our Creator."

"Yes, sir! Indeedy it does. I am but an ordinary leaf. Yet even as simple as I and my kind might be, your kind still doesn't understand who deserves the praise for it all."

"I'm sure by that you mean *me*," said Seth.

Fox, who had trotted several yards in front of the rest of the group, came bounding back, yapping. "Oopsy-daisy."

"What's wrong, Fox?" asked Melissa.

"I'm very afraid that we have been going around in circles," said Fox.

"Oh, no. That's not good," said Seth.

"I agree there, partner," said Bumpy. "This place is very dark. All these trees and not one leaf to be found. We need to find our way out of here, and quick!"

"What we need is to find a place to rest. Everyone is tired," said Jimmy. Seth nodded in agreement and quickly found a soft mound of moss to sit upon.

"Get up! We can't rest here. That's what this place wants," said Melissa. The urgency and conviction in Melissa's voice caused Seth to reluctantly get back up to his feet. He brushed the dirt from his pants and leaned against a tree, waiting for a group consensus on what to do next.

"Yes, yes, Melissa is quite right. Sleep means certain death here," added Fox.

"Surely it won't hurt just to rest our feet for a few moments," said Jimmy.

"That moss may look harmless," said Melissa, "but it consumes anything that falls by the wayside. And there is something in the air here that brings on sleep. Trust me, I've been here, and I learned my lesson. We keep moving."

"Moving is good, moving is great, but move where is the question of late," said Fox.

"The fox is right," said Bumpy. "We need a plan. Roaming around in circles is getting us nowhere."

Seth said, "Well, while y'all figure out a plan, I'm gonna see if any food made it with us from home. I could use a boost of energy." He lifted the backpack off his shoulders. While he began unzipping the backpack, Melissa walked over to Fox and scratched her behind the ears.

Melissa bent down eye-to-eye with Fox and said, "We need to go back to the Land of Indulgences."

"No, we mustn't go back there," said Fox. "We'll never make it out alive."

Jimmy noticed that Fox, for the first time, appeared nervous. It was quite a contrast from the seemingly carefree creature who had, up to this point, only displayed an aptitude for friendship and play. "You've been before, I take it," said Jimmy.

"I should say yes, she and we have been before, but that's neither here nor there as we shall not be going back again," assured Fox.

"Fox, we know the secret to the Land of Indulgences," said Melissa. "The old tree has no power over us. But I'm afraid we have no choice. We must go and talk to Willow. She is the only one I know that can tell us what we must do, what we are here for."

"Willow?" asked Bumpy.

Melissa responded, "Yes, Willow. You would very much like her, Bumpy. She is the absolute most beautiful tree I have ever seen. Her leaves make wonderful music. You really must meet her, and I'm sure she would love to make your acquaintance as well."

"Yes, Willow is our friend," said Fox. "But that's neither here nor there because she resides on the other side of a very bad land."

Seth was unconvinced. He asked, "What makes you think this Willow has the answers we need?"

Jimmy sided with Seth, "Might there be another way or someone else who could help?"

"Melissa is right," Bumpy declared. "We can't keep wanderin' around in circles. I think we should set out to find the place she speaks of and if we think of some other course along the way, we can consider it."

Seth, still digging around in his backpack, had yet to find anything edible. He unzipped another pocket and something quickly flew out. It buzzed around Seth's head, and in a panic, Seth stood up and swatted at the bug with both hands. He walked backward while trying to shoo the creature away from him, but he only managed to trip over a tree root. He fell hard onto the ground, squealing like a little girl flailing her arms all about.

Fox tilted her head and looked quizzically at Seth. She then yapped, "Stop! That's Dauber." Fox ran over to Seth and attempted to calm him down by placing both her front paws on his chest. She then looked up into the air and said, "Dauber, what are you doing here and how—"

Dauber buzzed over to Fox and hovered around her head. "I overheard the leaf talking to the boy in the woods and I stowed away in his backpack. Voila! I'm here. Now where is here, exactly?"

"We are in the Dead Woods and you're quite fortunate you didn't get squashed in the boy's pack," said Fox.

"Fox, who are you talking to?" asked Melissa.

"I'm sorry. Let me introduce you. Everyone, this is Dauber. He's a dirt dauber."

"A bug? You have a pet bug?" asked Seth as he sat up.

"Pet! Bug! How dare he insult me twice in one sentence," said Dauber. He then landed directly on Fox's nose and with a very serious expression on his face looked directly into her eyes and asked, "These humans can understand you? You can speak to them?"

"You betcha!" said Fox as she trotted over to Melissa. "Dauber, this is Melissa." Fox nudged Melissa with her nose and then looked over at Seth, who was slowly getting up to retrieve his backpack. "That one on the ground over there is her brother, Seth, which you surely already knew. Over there is the tallest one, like a tree. His name is Jimmy. The leaf is Bumpy, isn't he swell? But you surely know him already as well."

Dauber acknowledged Fox, but while Fox could hear Dauber quite clearly (as she had acute hearing), everyone else but Bumpy (as he had superior senses as well) only heard an indistinct buzzing noise.

"Is the wasp thingy actually talking to you?" asked Melissa.

"Wasp! Really? If I'm going to be continually insulted by these humans, I'll just buzz off!"

"Where would you go, Dauber? Just be patient and allow everyone to get to know you," said Fox.

Melissa said, "I'm really sorry, Mr. Dauber. Our ears can't hear your words, but if you have something important to say, I'm sure Fox will let us know."

Seth, no longer listening to the others, pulled a candy bar out of his backpack and exclaimed, "I have food, thank you God!"

Melissa, standing within arm's reach of her brother, quickly yanked the candy bar from Seth's hand. "I have an idea."

"What are you doing? That's mine."

"You'll do just fine without it. None of us are hungry here. I don't know why exactly, but we don't need to eat or drink in this place. But I know someone here who does need to eat."

"Who?" asked Fox.

"An ugly old vulture," Melissa began to whisper. "In fact, I bet she and her friend are watching us from above right now. Don't look up. I have an idea." She motioned for them to huddle closer together as she explained how Screech and Gawker, the vultures, might be able to help them find their way out of the Dead Woods. She told everyone that the two birds were familiar with the trails but also quite untrustworthy. She explained in detail what had happened to her and what the vultures did the last time she was in the Dead Woods.

After Melissa had finished filling them in, Jimmy whispered to Dauber, who was still resting on Fox's nose. "How high and far can you fly? Can you find these two birds, Mr. Dauber?"

Dauber answered and Fox repeated, "He assures you that he is the fastest dirt dauber in Garland County."

"That should be plenty fast," said Jimmy. He instructed Dauber, with the help of Fox, to fly up to the forest canopy, find the birds, and spy on them.

With the help of Dauber, Jimmy and the others had hoped to know the exact whereabouts and intentions of the vultures at all times. Dauber was more than excited to be assigned his very first mission in the other world. He only wished that Sticky was there to help.

He casually flew away, meandering here and there until he was out of sight. He did not want to be too obvious with his flight plan, just in case the vultures were watching. While Dauber was on his secret mission, the others stayed huddled together and formed a plan. They were going to trap the birds in order to get the information necessary to find their way out of the Dead Woods—and, hopefully, eventually, get to Willow.

"Go see what it is," demanded Screech.

"It's nothing," said Gawker.

The two vultures had been following the travelers for quite some time, but it was not until the youngest male dropped something that they really became interested. Neither of them had ever smelled anything like it before. Their neglected taste buds suddenly started to perk up and stand at attention. Not once, at least since the two vultures had taken up residence in the Dead Woods, had such an aroma permeated the forest floor. The dark rectangular four-inch bar was undoubtedly delicious. Gawker wanted it all for herself.

Gawker, skinnier and less attractive than her homely companion, had hoped Screech would continue following the creatures from the other world so she could have the sweet-smelling delectable all to herself. But no such luck was to be had.

"Fine, you stay here and I'll go see what it is," said Screech. Neither of them trusted the other.

Gawker unfolded her wing until it blocked Screech's ability to fly off the branch. "No, that wouldn't be right, now would it? Let's just glide down together. Once we are on those lower branches, we can get a better look."

The two large scavengers knew there was something delicious on the ground waiting for them. They also knew nothing came without a price in the Dead Woods. They had been in this place a long time and were not easily fooled—but food was scarce, and with their stomachs growling, it was just a matter of time before they succumbed to their desires, no matter the cost. They were so hungry they would not even allow themselves to consider the possibility of a trap.

They watched each other closely as they let go of their perch at the exact same time. Screech was out of shape and could not maneuver as quickly as most vultures. Fortunately for him, his companion was missing many feathers, which hindered her ability to fly. Screech was also the more cunning of the two and often got the most of what little food the woods offered.

Once they reached the next branch, Screech looked over at Gawker and said, "Lower still, wouldn't you agree?"

"Yes, the smell is devilishly exciting, is it not?"

They landed on the next branch down, one eye on the other and one eye on the prize.

"I can only imagine it tastes greater than what the gods themselves dine upon," said Screech.

"The crunch more satisfying than the bones of the recently deceased, I'm certain," added Gawker.

"Really? I sense that the texture is smoother and creamier than the best blood wine," said Screech, salivating.

There was one more branch beneath them. They looked at one

another, then at the food waiting for them on the forest floor, and back at each other again. They both knew that there was little hope in sharing the prize, as it was rather small. It was obvious, by this point, that the winner would take all. Both fluttered, without taking their eyes off the other, to the last remaining branch between them and their next meal.

"You haven't beaten me to a meal in eons," said Screech.

"Then why are you so worried this time?"

"I'm not worried."

"Indeed, you are. Otherwise, you would already be devouring the prize," said Gawker with a more confident tone.

"Oh, alright, fine! You're right." Screech lowered his long neck in an attempt to appear even more pathetic than he already was. "I have an ingrown feather on my right wing. It's not only slowing me down but it hurts so terribly much. Every time I raise my wing, I feel the teeth of a mighty dragon clamping down upon it."

Unbeknownst to Screech, Gawker was just as wise as he was in the ways of the Dead Woods. She knew the challenges that came with survival, and she could compete with the most skilled hunters. There was, however, a reason she was thinner than her companion. There was an explanation for her bald patches, and justification for her slower ability of flight. Gawker had a heart. Yet she could never reveal her capacity to love or care for others, not in these woods. She always found a way to come in second when second would help a friend in need.

"Well," said Gawker, "I guess you ..." Before Gawker could finish her sentence, Screech released his hold on the branch, and he dropped like a missile towards his next dinner. He had decided on his way down that he would leave a morsel for Gawker. He was not completely without scruples, after all.

Gawker followed quickly after Screech but knew she did not have a chance. She would have been happy with half, but Screech rarely left anything other than scraps. What she did not know, however, was that neither she nor Screech would be eating anytime soon. When they touched their feet upon the ground, less than a foot away from the object of their desires, they were immediately surrounded by the travelers from the other world.

It was a trap. They should have known.

With the quick and agile fox bearing down upon them, there was no hope for escape. "How did you miss this large orchestration of deception!" Screech demanded of Gawker.

"*Me*? I'm not as capable as the great Screech! If *you* missed it, surely *I* would not have seen it coming," she said, almost convincingly.

The two birds were backed into a corner with two large trees blocking their escape. Fox was crouched in an offensive position to the right, baring her teeth. On the left, Seth and Melissa stood with legs spread and arms stretched. Screech and Gawker felt capable of evading the humans, but they did not want to take a chance with the red fox—she looked more than capable of jumping high into the air, and her teeth looked sharp.

Jimmy, between the Fox and the siblings, opened his hands to show he had no weapons. He approached the frightened birds. "There's no need to worry. We mean you no harm. All we want is a little help."

"Yes, just directions, really," offered Seth.

"And we'll even let you have the candy bar after we get what we need," added Melissa sympathetically.

"Oh my," said Gawker. "It's the girl with the blue eyes."

"You remember me," responded Melissa.

"You look different, your hair is golden now, but yes. Those blue eyes, how could I forget those?" Gawker swallowed hard.

"Yes, it's me, and these are all my friends. We need your help."

"And in return?" asked Screech.

"In return we won't roast you over a fire," said Seth.

"Ha! Start a fire here and we'll all go up in flames. What is it you want?" demanded Screech.

Jimmy moved in a little closer to the birds. "We noticed, with the help of our fox here, that we have been going around in circles. We can't seem to find our way."

"We need to get to the Land of Indulgences," added Melissa.

The vultures shrieked.

"Why would anyone purposely want to venture into the Land of Indulgences?" said Screech as he boldly waddled up to Melissa. He was no longer scared since he knew they needed information from him.

Fox quickly jumped in front of Melissa, blocking Screech. She was strikingly confident as she said, "We have nothing to fear. My friend and I have been to this land and we made it out alive and well."

Melissa was surprised at Fox's change of mind from when she first proposed going back into the Land of Indulgences. As for the birds, they seemed to be in utter shock. Screech nodded at Gawker to come closer. He whispered something in her ear. They both stared at Melissa from head-to-toe, then did the same to Fox.

"What are you misfits up to?" asked Bumpy, still tucked safely in Seth's front pocket. The two birds shrieked again, louder than before. Screech carefully waddled over to Seth and flapped his wings and rose up off the ground just high enough to get a better look into his pocket. This caused quite a stir as Fox jumped to stop his flight, Jimmy moved to the left, and Melissa blocked passageway to the right. They realized their concern was unwarranted when Screech simply landed back on the ground. He stood frozen in thought.

"Well, what is it?" an irritated Bumpy asked.

Gawker looked directly at Screech, as if no one else were there, and said, "It can't be."

"Yet, it is," said Screech. Screech and Gawker were obviously overwhelmed with emotion. They fluttered nervously as they paced in circles, thinking of what to say or do.

The travelers began to get jumpy as well. Fox stood on her toes, ready to pounce. Jimmy knew that if the large birds of prey decided to take flight, there was little chance of stopping them. They might be able to grab one, but not both. Bumpy, not being able to see everything that was happening on the ground, lifted himself out of Seth's pocket. A gentle breeze scooped him up, and now, in flight, he was able to see everything much better.

Unfortunately, the birds became more excited at the sight of the falling leaf and both began flapping their large wings, which caused the air around Bumpy to get unpredictably turbulent. Bumpy was tossed around like a boat in a storm. The air became thicker and thicker with dust after each flap of their wings. Bumpy tried hard to right himself, but it was hard to see and even harder to predict the currents. He was spinning out of control.

Fox began yapping excitedly. Melissa tried to calm her down to no avail. Fox stood on her hind feet and attempted to pounce on Screech, but the bird was too quick. Jimmy waved his arms up and down to confuse the birds; he did not want them to escape. In the meantime, Seth kept his sights on Bumpy, who was now at the will of the ever-changing gusts. Seth was worried about Bumpy, and he had good reason to be.

While Screech and Gawker's original intention may not have been to flee, all of the commotion made the prospect of escape the only sensible option. Ingrown feather or not, Screech flapped his powerful wings and quickly cleared all of the hands, arms, claws, and paws below. He shot straight up into the air until he was out of sight.

Gawker was not so lucky. Jimmy had decided early on that if the birds tried to flee, he would go after the weaker of the two, which to him appeared to be Gawker. Before she could even raise her wings to lift off of the ground, Jimmy sprang into action. As the dirt kicked up behind him, he swooped her up in his arms like a baseball player sliding into home plate. Before she knew it, he was holding her wings tightly against his body. She tried to peck at him with her gnarly beak, but Jimmy was a country boy and he knew how to handle wildlife. She was not going anywhere anytime soon.

Unbeknownst to the others, as Bumpy was being tossed around in all of the upheaval, one of Screech's wings struck him and pushed him off the trail. Bumpy had never felt such pain before—not even when that bug bit him when he was young—but a piece of Bumpy broke off when Screech struck him, and it felt like a thousand needles sticking him all at once. There was no time to make an assessment of the damage. Bumpy was quickly headed towards a perilous landing on the deadly smothering moss. He was hurting and unable to control his trajectory. In debilitating pain, he sank closer and closer to the waiting moss below. As small as he was, he knew he would not have long before the moss completely consumed him.

With Screech now high above them on the dead limbs, and Gawker securely bound by Jimmy, the dust slowly began to settle. Melissa had both her arms around Fox, who was still panting from all the excitement. Seth was frantically searching for Bumpy. He remembered what Melissa had said about the moss and how it consumed anything that touched it for too long. Once the others realized Bumpy was missing, they too scanned the area. They moved around carefully, just in case Bumpy might be underfoot.

"Does anyone see him?" asked Seth.

"Not I," said Fox.

"Sorry, I didn't see which direction he went," said Jimmy. "I was too focused on catching this nasty bird—who stinks to the high heavens I might add." Gawker squawked in reaction to Jimmy's insult.

"Shhh, everyone be quiet," said Melissa. Everyone immediately stopped what they were doing. This forest was strangely silent. There was little life to make much noise. It only took a moment before they heard a muffled voice.

Fox gingerly followed the unintelligible sounds until it took her about ten yards off the trail. The muffled sounds abruptly stopped, but not before Fox located the approximate area from which they originated. She then sniffed her way around on the squishy grayish-yellow moss until her nose caught the scent of something familiar. She yapped for the others to come over.

"Is it him?" asked Melissa.

"Under there. Something is under there," said Fox as she pawed at the ground.

Seth dropped to his knees and slowly began poking at the vampire moss with his fingers, at times separating it enough to see below the surface. He lifted up a chunk and lying directly beneath was something brown. He removed more of the invasive moss, and to his relief he saw the little brown leaf. It was Bumpy. He carefully picked at the moss one piece at a time. He lifted each clump between his thumb and pointer finger until his friend was completely exposed. He gently put four of his fingers underneath Bumpy and slowly lifted him up and out of the life-depleting sponge.

"Why isn't he saying anything? Is he alive?" asked Melissa.

"Oh no, he's missing part of his leg. It broke off," said Seth

As everyone was attending to Bumpy, the part of his lower left leg, the size of a kernel of corn, landed several feet away underneath a large corpse of a tree. Quite inconspicuously, a scraggly thin root began to creep towards the missing bit of leaf. The root sprouted several tentacles, and each one of the newly sprouted tentacles spawned their own set of even smaller, thinner tentacles. It was only a matter of seconds before the piece of Bumpy's leg was completely consumed. And without anyone noticing, the roots from the tree towering overhead disappeared back under the moss and dirt from which they came.

There was still no response from Bumpy. It was as if the life had been sucked right out of him.

"There is a place with restoring streams," said Gawker. "I've heard tell that it brings life back to all who drink of it."

"Where is this stream?" Seth asked desperately. It had been a long time since Seth had shown much interest in anything. Melissa was surprised to see his attachment to the leaf.

Gawker replied, "It matters not where it is, because you all are caught in the most ancient part of the Dead Woods. The path of repetition."

"We have been here before and we have all gotten out," said Melissa. "Even Jimmy has been here before and you made it out. Right, Jimmy?"

"Yes, a long time ago. I found myself here, and yes, I was able to leave."

Gawker squawked, "Tis true you might have been in the Dead Woods. The blue-eyed girl and the fox, for sure I have seen before. But you were not in this particular part of the woods. It is most unfortunate to have arrived in this area."

"There must be a way out," said Seth, who was still holding the lifeless leaf in the palm of his hand. "After all, you must come and go."

"Yes, we come here to feast on those that die on the trail of repetition. None before you have ever even realized the trail goes in circles. Screech said it was the fox that is different than the rest. Never before has something as clever as she been in this part of the forest. But knowing does not change the going."

"Listen here, if you don't fly above and lead us out of here, I'll personally wring your skinny, ugly neck!" exclaimed Seth.

"Calm down, Seth," said Jimmy. "Threats probably aren't going to help us here. But I know God would not have put us in this situation if there wasn't a good reason. I also know, for the same reason, there is a way out. Do you have a name, bird?"

"My name is Gawker."

"Think hard, Gawker. You know this place better than anyone. What's the one thing that is different in this place? What's the one unique thing that stands out from all the rest? Think. There must be something no one else has noticed before."

Melissa, who had only moments earlier retrieved the candy bar that caused all the problems in the first place, waived it under Gawker's nostrils. "I bet you have never tasted anything as delicious as this. Wouldn't you like to have this all to yourself? I happen to know for a fact that it tastes even better than eyeballs."

"Even blue eyes?" asked Gawker as she tried to push herself out of Jimmy's arms to get closer to the candy.

"Yes, even blue eyes," assured Melissa.

"I'm sorry, but I just can't think of anything. Perhaps if I had a bite of the food, it would give me the energy to think harder," said Gawker as she licked her beak in anticipation of feasting on the thing that tasted better than eyes of blue.

"I know what it is," said Seth.

"How could you possibly know," asked Jimmy.

"Think about it. I'm more familiar with this path than any of you, including the vultures. I've been going around in circles my whole life. This is my path, and it's my path to change," said Seth.

"That sounds pretty profound. Okay, so what do we do?"

"This path is a lie. What is the opposite of a lie?"

"Truth," yapped Fox.

"That's right." With his free hand, Seth rubbed the top of Fox's head. "We get off the path. We get out of the darkness and go towards the light."

"Wow, brother, that sounds awfully poetic, but what does it mean?"

"What's different between us and everyone else that's been here?" Seth waited for an answer, but none came. "The bird told us. No one else knew they were going in circles. The only reason we knew is because of Fox. That's the only difference. We know. We simply stop going in circles."

Jimmy shook his head. "But obviously we wouldn't know we were going in circles. This place is deceptive. Any direction we go, we might still be stuck in the pattern of this evil place."

"These trees here were once living, right? What did they need in order to live? Dirt, light, and water. Look up. Those branches are so tightly interwoven they've blocked most of the light from penetrating. If we can climb to the top and follow the thickest branches and trees, it will lead us to where the water is."

"That's just mere conjecture, brother. There's no way of knowing for sure."

"You're exactly right, and that's where I get off this path that I've been on."

"What are you saying?" asked Jimmy.

"Bumpy told me before any of this began that I had something to learn. He called me an in-betweener—someone who has little faith. But he said it was odd that I could still hear him, that I could glimpse part of the supernatural."

"Okay…" said Jimmy.

"I know that you have faith, Jimmy, and so does my sister, even if it's a baby faith. Fox has faith, Bumpy has faith, and that wasp, wherever he is, has faith. I'm the only one that doesn't have any faith. But that's all about to change because I'm getting us out of here. I have faith that the God all of you believe in will help me lead us out of here."

"Well, it couldn't hurt to try," said Melissa.

"Gawker, the water that fed these woods, does it connect to the restoring stream that you mentioned, the water that could save Bumpy?" asked Seth.

"Yes, the waters are the same. But we haven't flown over that way in many eons. Life is not something my kind desire. It is death that suits us best."

"Give her the candy, Melissa," said Seth.

Gawker gasped, "But I did not help you."

Seth smiled and moved closer to Gawker, who was still held captive in Jimmy's arms. "Perhaps not, but who knows, maybe you did. I don't think you are as bad as you appear. Maybe all you need is a few more friends, and you can count me as your first."

Gawker, unable to stop herself, immediately began to sob. She cried so hard that she could not catch her breath. This surprised everyone. Jimmy let go of his grip on her and gently rubbed her balding, prickly back. Fox came over and nuzzled Gawker's beak, and before Fox knew it, she was crying too. After this, there was no hope for Melissa, who also began to sniffle. It was all Seth could do to maintain his composure. He had no idea such a simple gesture would mean so much.

"Human friends are the bestest friends ever," said Fox.

"Foxes make pretty good companions too," said Melissa.

Gawker, in between sniffles, managed to say, "Am I really your friend?"

"Absolutely," smiled Seth.

"Why don't you eat the candy, it's pretty tasty. I'm sure you will like it," said Jimmy, still petting Gawker's prickly feathers.

"I'll take it and share it with Screech."

"Even though he left you?" asked Melissa.

"He's really not as bad as he seems. Besides, when you all leave, he's all I've got left."

"Well, the way things are going, we might be back again before you know it," said Melissa.

"Gawker, may I ask where the strongest and tallest tree is? One that can get us to the top of the canopy?" asked Seth.

"Any tree will do, I should think," said Gawker. "The one next to you is an impressive specimen."

"Well, that'll be the one we take, then."

"Wait, how do you suppose Fox is going to climb a tree?" asked Melissa.

Seth answered Melissa as he gently placed Bumpy into his shirt pocket. Fox was not much larger than a house cat and much smaller than a typical yard dog. Seth unzipped the largest compartment of his backpack and tore it open as far it would go. It looked large enough to accommodate Fox. After asking Fox to try it out while they were still on the ground, he made a few more adjustments with the straps to make sure she would fit securely without falling out.

"Let's try her out on my back," said Seth. Seth pulled the modified pack over his arms and Jimmy lifted Fox up while Melissa held the pocket open. Fox tucked her back legs up, rounding out her lower half so she could fit comfortably. She put one of her front legs under a strap. While it was not the most advantageous position, facing neither forward nor backward but sideways, it was comfortable enough as long as the journey was not too far.

"Not too shabby, if I say so myself," said Seth.

"Well, we should really be on our way," said Jimmy. "You all go ahead and I'll follow up in the rear."

"Before you go, there is something I should tell you all," said Gawker.

"What is it?"' asked Melissa.

"The reason that Screech and I were so shocked to see the girl and the fox is because of what happened after the last time they were here."

"Yes?" said Melissa.

"It is true that Screech and I go nowhere but the Dead Woods, but we hear things from those that come from other places, such as yourselves."

"And?" asked Jimmy.

"The Lake of Entitlement is full of water once again, and perhaps even the restoring streams are flowing again," said Gawker.

"We know about the Lake of Entitlement, don't we, Fox?" said Melissa.

"Do we ever," said Fox.

Gawker flapped her wings just enough to carry her in front of Melissa, "But that's not the part that concerns me. The rumors are that a war is spilling from our world out into your world. I know not much of anything, so what I hear and what I say must be verified before acceptance."

"What kind of war?" asked Jimmy.

"The evil here is weakening, but evil does not simply disappear. Where has the evil gone? That is what one must ask. Perhaps you brought goodness to this world, but what does that mean for yours?"

"You mean that the better things get here, the worse they get in our world?" asked Seth.

"I have not the capacity to mean anything. I'm only repeating what has been told by others. But if what they say is true, if you do make it back to the place you are from, be wary and be watchful. Look around you now, because this may be your future."

"I have one more question, if you would be so kind. Why the reaction to Bumpy, the leaf? Why did you and your friend freak out when you first saw him?"

"The prophets said that when the leaves return, the battle begins. We don't know what the battle is, but the prophets have never been wrong."

"But Bumpy is just one leaf. He's not even attached to a tree anymore. He said he was in his last season of life."

Gawker replied, "There has not been a leaf of his kind, the kind that grows from the roots of the trees, for longer than the prophets themselves have been alive. It must mean something."

After a lively discussion, no one was quite sure what to make of the new information. Even if they knew what it meant, there was little they could do about it. Their first task was to find their way out of the Dead Woods.

"Thank you again, Gawker. We wish you well," said Melissa. "I think I can speak for all of us when I say that we are all your friends now."

"And I you. Now I must find Screech. He will be most pleased to partake of this meal you have so kindly given to me."

Just as Gawker was about to take flight, there was a loud, horrible squawk, as if a bird had just been shot. While everyone looked around to see where the noise came from, Dauber buzzed up to Fox, giggling.

"Dauber, where have you been all this time?" asked Fox.

"I was obeying instructions and spying on the birds. When the fat one flew away, I stayed under cover and followed along behind him. Then when I saw the skinny one about to fly away, I figured my job was done so I gave the nasty bird a big ol' sting right in the caboose."

Fox laughed along with Gawker, as they were the only ones who could hear Dauber. Fox would share the story with the others as they journeyed up the tree to the top of the forest. She was sure they would all get a chuckle out of it as well.

"Welcome back, Dauber. Shall we get going everyone?" said Seth as he began to climb the tree with Fox on his back. Gawker said her goodbyes, and with the candy bar securely in her talons, she flew up to her recently stung companion. Melissa followed after Seth with Jimmy not far behind.

Before joining the others, Dauber stopped for just a moment on the end of a branch. He had to clean his leg from the nasty vulture excretions that rubbed off on him when he gave Screech the what-for. He never noticed what was on the branch only centimeters away. A sprout began to emerge. There was only one, and it was tiny, but it was green and it would soon be a leaf. Losing a part of himself may have been painful for Bumpy, but it was just enough nourishment to spark life back into the Dead Woods.

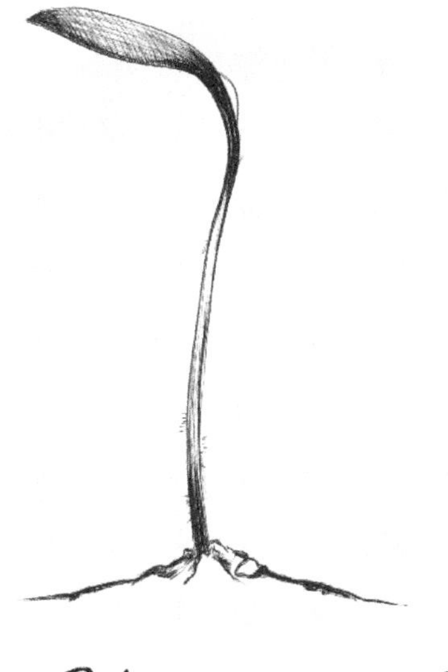

Chapter 14

SOMETHING'S AMISS BACK HOME

Garland County was rich with history and interesting people. The first inhabitants were thought to be the Natchitoches, who along with other indigenous peoples utilized the healing powers of the hot springs thousands of years before the first European-American settlers arrived. The water was the subject of legend among several Native American tribes.

President Thomas Jefferson requested exploration of the area in 1804, and almost thirty years later a portion of the hot springs was preserved by the federal government as an area for recreation, the first time this had ever been done. It was not long before a successful spa town emerged with illegal gambling, speakeasies, and gangsters. Al Capone was known to be a frequent visitor. All kinds of notorious stories arose during those days, many of them true.

There was no place more storied along the road to Azora and Henry's house than the old Harris place. When Seth and Melissa were younger, they would investigate the old dilapidated house and overgrown grounds with much-adrenalized excitement. To a child, the abandoned house was a place to explore. To everyone else, it was an eyesore. Azora had passed the house so many times that she rarely paid it much attention. To Bethany, however, the house had developed new meaning after searching the grounds with Jimmy last spring when her children went missing.

"When are they going to demolish that monstrosity?" Bethany asked as she and Azora passed by the old Harris place. She really did not mean to ask the question out loud, but she did and her mother was bound to answer.

"I kinda like it just the way it is. It has history, tells a story."

Bethany was surprised by her mother's brevity, but after the day they had had, she did not want to invite further conversation. The better part of the morning and afternoon had been spent visiting first and second cousins not seen or heard from since Bethany was a teenager. As usual, Azora did most of the talking by dominating the conversations with stories that Bethany had heard many times before. The cousins seemed happy to hear the old tales, or perhaps they were just being polite. Bethany would have preferred to listen to her cousins speak.

As they rounded the last corner, they saw Patrick and Earl in the front yard. Patrick was sweeping the walkway and Earl stood nearby holding a dustpan.

"I hope he didn't leave a big mess for me to clean up," said Azora as she craned her neck to get a better look.

The garage door was open but Bethany pulled in slowly in order to give her husband enough time to wave her down in case he wanted her to park outside until he was finished.

"Good Lord have mercy, Beth. You drive slower than a moth in a jar of molasses," said Azora.

Bethany did not have the energy to explain. She just nodded in acknowledgment, which any onlooker would have read as defeat. She was exhausted and could not wait to take a nap. She managed to pull all the way into the garage without any further critiques from her mother.

Azora squinted her eyes, looking at a shelf in front of the car. "Why in the world did your husband put all those boxes there?"

Bethany turned the motor off, but before she could get the keys out of the ignition Azora reminded her of the parking brake. Why she felt it necessary to use the parking brake in the garage was beyond Bethany. "You will need to ask Patrick about the boxes, mom."

"No. It was nice of him to do all that work for Henry. I reckon I shouldn't be complainin' none," said Azora. "I'll just ask Earl or Jimmy to cart em' off on garbage day."

"That's a good idea, mom."

Patrick had worked his way around to the back of the garage with the broom. "I was beginning to think you ladies were never coming back."

Bethany shut the car door and walked to the rear of the car and gave her husband a kiss on the cheek. "I would have gladly tiled the bathroom floor and let you escort Mom around to all the relatives," she whispered.

"Well, it looks pretty good, if I say so myself. I'll have to wait until the morning to grout it, but that won't take too long. On second thought, maybe I should have Seth finish it up." Patrick looked over at Azora who was still sitting in the passenger's seat. "Do you need some help there, Azora?"

"What do you plan to do with all those empty boxes?" asked Azora.

"Whatever you would like," answered Patrick.

"Oh, I suppose we could put them in the compost. Are they all cardboard?" She already knew the answer to her question, but asking it allowed her more time to finally get her seat belt undone. Her fingers were not quite as nimble as they once were, and the extra pounds around her belly made it hard to locate things below the waist.

Bethany rolled her eyes, shrugged her shoulders, and mouthed "sorry" to her husband before saying hello to Earl. Earl adored Bethany. Most people liked Bethany, but no one was as isolated and lonely as Earl. "How do you do there, Beth. It sure is mighty nice to see you again so soon. Don't reckon I ever remember you a comin' for two visits so close together like this."

"It was the children, they insisted on coming back for Thanksgiving. But I must admit it's nice being in the country during the holidays. How are you doing?"

"Fair to middlin', I s'pose."

"I guess that's good, right? Mom tells us your kids have you picking up all the hickory nuts in the yard, that's bound to be good exercise."

"Exercise!" exclaimed Azora as she finally managed to drag herself out of the car. "It's elder abuse if you ask me. That son-in-law of yours should be put in jail for how he treats you." Azora leaned against the car door to catch her breath, closing it in the process.

It suddenly occurred to Patrick that he deserved better treatment from his own in-law. There was nothing she could hold against him, especially compared to the nasty son-in-law next door. Ray Ratcliffe was the notorious neighbor that treated his father-in-law worse than trash on the street. Anyone who knew Earl knew how despicable Ratcliffe was. It was not that Earl badmouthed him; in fact, Earl rarely had a foul word to say. He simply shared stories about his day, not even realizing the audaciousness of his daughter's husband.

Last year, while splitting wood, Ratcliffe had Earl positioning the wood. He ended up smashing the elder man's finger. No one took Earl to the hospital to have his hand x-rayed. According to Earl, it still hurt. The only reason the neighbors did not report Earl's family to the authorities is because they would have surely placed him in a nursing home. At least the Ratcliffes provided housing, food, and necessities. With the neighbors keeping an eye out, the Ratcliffes never pushed the envelope too far, it seemed.

Azora yelled in Patrick's direction, "Don't worry about them boxes. I'll have Jimmy cut em' up and place em' around the seedlings next spring. Might help if there's a late frost." As she made her way around to the side door of the garage, she noticed a bucket of dirt. "Oh, my word, I plum forgot about you."

"What's that mom?" asked Bethany from the other end of the garage.

Azora placed one hand on the wooden workbench behind the five-gallon bucket of dirt so she could bend down to get a better look. She froze and her eyes opened wide. She lowered herself as far as she could until her head was mere inches from the top of the bucket. She squeezed her eyes as hard as she could and shook her head. When she looked down, there it was. Right before her, smack dab in the middle of the bucket of compost, was a sprout. Two tiny green leaves pushing up into the cold dark garage.

"Well, I declare! It's a miracle," exclaimed Azora.

By this time Bethany, Patrick, and Earl had all joined Azora at the front of the garage. They were intrigued at what could possibly have Azora looking so perplexed. Earl stood behind Azora, hands in his overalls, bent slightly at the waist and leaning to the left in order to get a better view of what Azora might be looking at. Bethany stood in front of the table and peered over the top. Patrick stood in the middle of the other two, with the best view.

"Is there a problem, Azora?" asked Patrick. He got no immediate answer. Azora, now on her knees, with both hands clasped around the top of the bucket, just knelt in silence, staring at the dirt.

"Mom, are you alright?" asked Bethany.

"Y'all s'pose she had a spell or somethin'?" inquired Earl.

"Well, she's still breathing and her eyes are wide open," said Patrick.

"Mom! What is it?" asked Bethany again.

Azora lifted her hand towards Patrick, without taking her eyes off the bucket. "Here, help me up, will ya?"

Patrick complied and gently gave support as she rose to her feet. Azora, still not taking her eyes off the bucket, pulled her blouse down over her waist and then rubbed her eyes. "Y'all see what I see?"

"Yes, we see a bucket of dirt," said Bethany.

"You don't see that little seedling in there?" asked Azora, finally breaking her gaze to look up at Bethany.

"Yes, I see it. So, what," said Bethany. "What's the big deal?"

"Help me outside, I need some fresh air," said Azora.

Bethany looked at Patrick and shrugged. Earl awkwardly backed out of the side door and held it open, which was not necessary as the door had already been open the entire time. Patrick, still holding his mother-in-law's hand, escorted her outside to a lawn chair.

Azora sat with her head tilted, deep in thought. She looked as though she were contemplating the meaning of life. Bethany thought that her current pose should be immortalized in bronze as the elderly version of Rodin's "The Thinker."

"Patrick, will you please set that bucket out here in the sun where I can get a better look at it?" asked Azora.

Patrick was one step ahead of the request and just needed orders for where to set it down. He placed it on the grass directly in front of Azora. The three of them stood while Azora remained seated.

"Do you mind sharing what the big deal is, Mom?"

"That there," Azora said as she pointed an accusatory finger at the dirt, "is a sprout from a seed Melissa gave me last spring."

"And?" asked Bethany.

"Well, it's growing."

"We all see that. Isn't that what it's supposed to do?" asked Bethany.

"You would think," said Azora. "If there's one thing I can count on in this world, it's my God-given ability to grow things."

"Bethany has always said you have a green thumb," said Patrick.

"Well, I put the best compost, dirt, and fertilizer I ever had in that bucket, and then I placed it in a greenhouse with the ideal amount of humidity and light. Watered it just enough to sprout a seed."

"And voila! You succeeded once again," said Bethany.

"I remember carryin' that there bucket down to the greenhouse for you back in the spring. How'd it git all the way up here to the garage?" asked Earl.

"I drug it up here myself. It was my only defeat the whole season," said Azora.

"Defeat?" asked Bethany.

"Yes. With the best growing season in the history of Garland County, the most ideal circumstances, and all the love and care I'd ever given, that seed just would not sprout."

"I guess you were wrong, it did grow," said Patrick.

"Yes, indeed it did. That saplin' is no more than a couple days old."

"So, it's a late bloomer," said Patrick.

Azora shook her head. "It's been in the garage with no light and no water for about three months now."

"That's not possible," said Bethany. "Maybe Henry watered it."

"I doubt that. Besides, that garage don't get a lick of light. It's pretty much shut up all year long. So even if he was a watteirn' it, a plant needs light to grow."

"I don't see what the big deal is," said Patrick. "It's growing. Who cares? Somehow it got some water and some light—or else it's a miracle. I thought you loved miracles, Azora. Just be glad the thing didn't tarnish your good record."

"Now what are you going to do with it?" Earl asked.

Azora continued to contemplate. "Well, I'm not even sure what it is, to tell you the truth. We think it's a tree of some sort."

"Well, no matter. It's gonna have to spend a year or two in that there bucket before you set it loose out in the real world. Might as well just find a good place to park it for a spell."

"Should I just put it back in the garage?" asked Patrick.

"No," responded Azora.

"The greenhouse, then," suggested Patrick.

"No," Azora repeated.

Bethany put her hand on her mother's shoulder. "Well, I wouldn't leave it outside in the winter. Might get too cold for it."

Azora agreed. "Put it in my room."

"Your room? The only window in your room is almost completed shaded by the hickory tree," said Bethany.

"Well, it did alright in the garage. Maybe it don't like too much light."

"Alright, your room it is," said Patrick.

"Help me up, Beth, would ya? I need to go and fetch a saucer to catch the water."

"I can get it, Mom. Where is it?"

"There's a few big ones to the right of the greenhouse door. I appreciate it, Beth."

Patrick carried the bucket with its strange inhabitant into the house as Bethany made her way to the greenhouse. Azora and Earl remained seated in the lawn chairs. Although Earl often got on her nerves with his simple ways and repeated excuses for his family's odd (and often questionable) treatment of him, she appreciated having someone around who needed a little love. He was one of the sweetest men she had ever known, and he deserved so much better than what the Ratcliffes offered. He was a blessing to Azora, if for no other reason than that he gave her a chance to exercise God's love for others.

"Earl, why don't you have dinner with me and the kids tonight?"

"Oh, I don't know. My daughter might come over and want me to eat with them."

"Earl, when was the last time that happened?"

"It's been a while, I reckon. I s'pose I could come over for a bit."

"Good, it's settled then. The grandkids will be happy to hear some of your nutty jokes."

"They like my jokes, do they?"

"Of course, they do. They're city kids. We're like ol' country relics to them. Curiosities. Glimpses into the past, the way things used to be."

"Humph! I'm a curiosity. Ain't that somethin?"

"Yes, it is, Earl."

Earl looked towards the house and said, "Mighty strange about that plant, don't you think?"

"Mighty strange indeed."

Chapter 15

A Tight Squeeze

Climbing a tree in the Dead Woods was as easy as climbing stairs. The trees were as old as time itself, with thick branches seemingly made of iron. Even after being dead for a thousand years, a single limb was sturdy enough to support a whole horde of travelers.

Seth took hold of the next branch and lifted himself up. The wood was smooth to the touch; all of the bark had long been erased by the elements. He admired the ancientness of this place. It made him feel small, like a child. He recalled the many fun times he had roaming the woods and climbing trees when he was younger. But these colossal towers dwarfed those back home.

Melissa yelled up to Seth, who was a few branches ahead of her, "Remember that fort dad built for us in the old pine tree in our backyard?"

"Fort? You mean the four-by-four quarter-inch plywood with the three-foot-high safety rail? Not exactly a fort." The magnificent specimen he was currently scaling would have supported multiple forts with hanging bridges to connect them. He and his friends would have undoubtedly spent more time in the trees than on the ground had they discovered this forest.

Seth grabbed the next limb and hoisted himself up, careful not to jostle Fox, who was resting comfortably in his backpack.

"Can you see the top yet?" asked Jimmy, who was bringing up the rear.

Seth sat down and steadied himself in order to get a better view of what the rest of the climb had in store. If he were to compare it to a high-rise building, there appeared to be at least three or four more stories until they reached the top of the canopy. Seth knew this would be daunting news to Melissa, so he decided to lie. "It's not far at all. I can see it from here."

"Thank God," said Melissa. "I'm not in the greatest shape for climbing trees. Remind me to start exercising more when we get home!"

"You should have stayed on the water polo team, sis." Seth was very athletic and always encouraged his sister to play sports, but she was never much of a joiner.

Dauber could have flown all the way to the top and returned with a report already, but instead chose the laziest route possible, hitching a ride on Seth's backpack with Fox. He only wished Fox was awake so he would have someone to talk to. How anyone could fall asleep in such an awkward position, at the bottom of a bag on a human's back, was beyond Dauber. He did enjoy listening to the banter of the others, however. In the short time he had been with them, he could tell that Melissa once had a crush on Jimmy, but she had either outgrown it or was trying to hide it. It may come as a surprise, but dirt daubers are wise in the ways of love.

The travelers huffed and puffed as they pulled and pushed their way towards the top of the Dead Woods. Melissa began to doubt her brother's assertion that the top was close. Her arms were growing weary and she was unsure how much further she could go. The last thing she wanted was for the men to think her weak. Coddling was for little girls, not someone as independent as Melissa, so she did not complain—although she, like Dauber, did wish that Fox was not snoozing. She could have used some encouragement.

Despite Melissa's best efforts to appear nimble, Jimmy noticed that she was slowing down. He kept an eye on her and followed as closely behind her as possible. She even stepped on his hand a time or two, but he wanted to be close in case she stumbled.

"Maybe we should stop and rest here for a while," suggested Jimmy.

"No need for that," said Seth. "It's just a few more limbs and we're there."

"Whew! Thank you, Jesus." Melissa, in her eagerness to see the top, quickly reached up for the next branch, but she failed to get a good grip with either her foot or her hand. Before she knew it, she started to slip.

She felt helpless as she tried to grab hold of something, but it was too late. She was going to fall, and there was nothing she could do about it. How stupid, she thought. Why had she not been more careful? She was able to slow herself down by leaning to the right and grabbing the trunk of the tree. The tree was much too big and her arms would never reach around, but at least she could dig in with her fingernails as she slid downward. By some miracle, Jimmy was right there to grab her arm. She felt his strength as he firmly took her life in his hands. She was no longer sliding down but rather hanging, feet dangling, with nothing below her but certain death.

"Don't worry, I got ya!"

"Please pull me up, I'm losing my grip!" shouted Melissa.

Jimmy's grip was steadfast, but he obliged by quickly hoisting Melissa to the safety of his branch. The two of them sat, catching their breath. It would take Melissa a few moments to calm her nerves. Her heart was racing.

"What's going on down there?" Seth shouted from above. Melissa and Jimmy laughed.

"Nothing brother, dear. How much farther?"

"Oh, you'll be happy to know that we have arrived."

"Excellent," exclaimed Jimmy.

"There's just one thing," said Seth.

"Yes," inquired Melissa.

"Does anyone have an idea of how to get through these branches? I didn't stop to think that the reason the forest floor is so dark is because the tree limbs have grown together to form a barrier. There's no way through them—unless of course someone brought an ax along with them."

"Maybe I can find a spot to squeeze through," offered Fox, who had only moments ago awakened from her nap.

Seth responded, "That's all well and good, our fine friend, but what then? The rest of us would not be able to follow."

"I have an idea," said Jimmy.

"We're all ears," said Seth.

"We passed a large hole in the tree about three-fourths of the way up. It was large enough for all of us to climb into. One at a time, of course."

"And how does that solve anything? Do you suppose we just spend the night in the tree and figure it out in the morning?"

"If the tree is hollow all the way through, perhaps we can follow the hole out to the top."

"So instead of going around the trees, we go *through* the trees. Literally," said Seth.

"Quite literally," said Melissa.

"Literally, quite, quite literally," echoed Fox.

"I vote that Fox's friend Dauber go check it out first," said Jimmy.

Melissa playfully punched Jimmy in the shoulder. "That's a great idea, Jimmy. You are so clever."

"Jimmy is like a fox, clever as clever can be," said Fox.

"Yes, I think Melissa might agree with you there, Fox," said Seth with a smirk. "Foxy Jimmy."

"Shut up, Seth!" exclaimed Melissa. Melissa glanced over at Jimmy, hoping he was not paying attention to her brother. Unfortunately, he caught every word and gave a wink like Prince Charming.

Melissa's face was turning a bright shade of pink. She was starting to wish she had fallen all the way to the ground. It was true that last March she had developed something of a crush on Jimmy, but it did not take long for her to realize that he was too old for her. It was nothing more than a momentary sense of admiration. It happened to girls her age all of the time, but she had quickly become too old for school girl infatuations. Life had presented more serious issues to contemplate of late.

"Dauber is on his way to where the hollow tree leads," said Fox. "But first, if it is even hollow, we shall see."

"Well, rather than wait here, let's climb back down to the opening and be ready in case Dauber returns with good news," said Jimmy.

"That's smart. Either way, we are going to have to figure out another way other than this one," said Seth.

Jimmy began the descent first, followed by Melissa and then Seth. Fox pressed down on the zipper of Seth's backpack with her paw to open it a little more. She stuck her head out and looked down to get a better view of the action. She had snoozed through most of the journey up the tree, but now that things were starting to get exciting, she did not want to miss a beat.

Unfortunately for Fox, there was not much to see. She spent more time ducking back into the backpack to avoid getting struck by branches than doing anything else. It seemed to her that Seth had forgotten all about his precious cargo.

Dauber had entered the tree long before Jimmy made it down to the hole. By the time Seth had joined Melissa and Jimmy on the limb directly in front of the large opening, it occurred to Jimmy that Dauber should have been back already. How long could it take to fly less than a hundred feet?

"Do you think we'll find the living stream that Gawker told us about?" Melissa asked Jimmy. "What if we don't find it in time to save Bumpy?"

"I don't know," Jimmy replied. "This place is so strange. I am certain, however, that whether or not we find the living stream, God wants us to look for it."

Seth said, "That's an odd conclusion. Why would God have us look for something that doesn't exist?"

"Just because we don't find it, if by chance we don't, doesn't mean it doesn't exist."

"It just means we didn't find it," offered Melissa.

"Exactly," said Jimmy.

"What would be the point then?" asked Seth.

"I love those who love me, and those who diligently seek me will find me," said Melissa.

"That's a proverb, right?" asked Jimmy.

"Yes, Proverbs. Chapter 8, I forget the verse number."

"Wait, are we looking for some water or for God?"

"You tell us," said Jimmy.

"As for me, I know we are going to find the living stream," said Melissa.

Fox yapped, "Melissa knows, she is full of faith, this I know."

"Thank you, Fox."

"What happens if we don't find the stream?" asked Seth. "Does that mean God, as you understand him, is not real?"

"Like Jimmy said, the stream is there whether we find it or not. Same goes for God. I just happen to think, in this case, we are going to find it, that's all," said Melissa.

"Okay, fine, but if we do find it, it doesn't mean it is from God. And if we don't, it doesn't mean it's not. There's really no proof either way."

"What if the waters bring Bumpy back to life, what then?" asked Jimmy.

"We'll cross that bridge when we come to it," said Seth.

Fox pushed up out of the backpack and put her chin on Seth's shoulder. "Is there going to be a bridge over the water?"

"I have to admit, Melissa, this fox is adorable," said Seth as he reached up and scratched Fox on the head. Fox began to enthusiastically lick Seth all over his face. Seth laughed and tried to move his face away from the gregarious fox, but he could not avoid her kisses. Melissa and Jimmy could not help but laugh as well.

Fox suddenly stopped when she saw Dauber fly out of the large hole in the tree. "He's back. He's back."

"What's the news?" asked Jimmy.

"Yes, ask him what he saw," added Seth.

Fox's ears perked up and pointed toward Dauber as he explained everything. "Dauber says that the tree leads all the way to the top. He says it's very bright up there."

"What took him so long?" asked Jimmy.

"Oh, he said he got a little lost after exploring on top and couldn't find the tree right away."

"How did he find the tree after getting lost?" asked Melissa.

Fox listened as Dauber answered. "He just followed the laughter," said Fox.

"I guess laughter is good medicine after all," said Jimmy. "Shall I go first?"

"Sure, I'll go after Melissa," said Seth.

"Alrighty then, here we go."

Jimmy took hold of both sides of the large entryway and peered inside. He looked up and then down. He then sat on the rim and stepped inside. The tree was solid up to this point. There was not much light to speak of, and it would undoubtedly be dark until they neared the top. "How are y'all with dark cramped spaces?"

"How cramped? Is there enough room for me with Fox on my back?"

"I don't know. Maybe we should rig something up. Why don't we undo all the straps and tie her to your belt? That way the backpack can hang a little below you and won't take up as much space," said Jimmy.

"Great idea. Melissa, why don't you go first while Jimmy and I figure this out? We won't be too far behind."

"Okay. Let me be the guinea pig. I got this," said Melissa with confidence. She stepped around Jimmy, holding onto his shoulders for support. She stepped into the tree and felt around for a way to climb up. "Oh, this is going to be easier than I thought. There are lots of places for our hands and feet to go." Melissa wasted no time at all before she started to climb. She continued talking to the boys but they could not understand much as her voice echoed and began to trail off.

"Give me your belt, Seth," said Jimmy. He took off his own belt and attached it to Seth's, then looped it through the backpack and pulled it tight, making sure it was secure.

"Perfect," said Seth. "Now I'll just attach her to a belt loop and she'll hang a foot or so below me."

"You go next and I'll follow behind. If something happens, I'll be there to catch her."

Fox did not like the sound of that. She scowled and whimpered before ducking deep down into the bag.

"It'll be okay, Fox. We won't let anything happen to you," assured Jimmy.

With that, Seth entered the tree and began his climb. Jimmy held onto Fox until Seth was far enough up for her to hang freely. Jimmy gave the Dead Forest one long, final look before he said a quick prayer. Then he too entered the dark musty tree.

With the travelers gone, the forest went back to the way it was before: quiet and lonely. If there had been any living creature there to notice, however, the travelers did leave something behind. It was more than a green leaf emerging where none had been for thousands of years. It was what some might call hope. Hope that there was something more, even for a place as dead as this.

Chapter 16

ATOP THE CANOPY

Melissa was the first to arrive atop the canopy, if you did not count Dauber who had already been there and back. She pushed herself up from what now looked like a stump protruding from the underside of a woven basket. Limbs were intertwined together, creating an almost solid surface that continued on for as far as her eyes could see. She stepped out onto what would become the ground beneath her feet. It was not perfectly flat or smooth, but walking on it would not prove too difficult if speed was not a concern. She walked out a few yards to see how far it stretched.

Once out of the tree, Melissa had forgotten all about Dauber—as well as everybody else for that matter. She was mesmerized. She had never seen or imagined anything like this before.

Melissa's fixation on the wonderfully rich and textured path before her was interrupted by Fox squeezing between her legs. Melissa broke her gaze and bent down to pet her friend. Fox nuzzled Melissa's face and the two sat down, welcoming the familiar affection in an unfamiliar place.

Fox had no problem adjusting to the craggy, weathered terrain. Her mom had taught her how to run with grace and agility on all kinds of surfaces. She might not have been able to climb a tree, but this new path would be as easy as pouncing on a mouse under a blanket of snow.

Seth had ventured a few steps away from the hollow tree, but it was not just the ground that caught his attention—it was what floated above. Several feet over his head was a thick layer of fog. A bright light was able to penetrate through the cloud-like substance, or perhaps it was the fog itself that caused the illumination. Seth could not be sure. He was also unsure of why it all seemed so eerily beautiful. To Seth, the woody ground resembled that of a beach littered with various kinds of driftwood, which contrasted nicely with the iridescent softness of the brilliant fog floating above.

This place should not have been beautiful. It should have been scary. It reminded Seth of a painting he saw in a book once. He could not remember the name of the painter, but he would never forget the name of the painting: "The Young Martyr." The martyr was an angelic woman floating lifeless in a dark pool of water with mysterious figures looking on. The painting may have been arguably beautiful to some, but it was undoubtedly haunting to most everyone else.

Jimmy was the last to arrive atop the canopy. He too took a moment to drink in the view, but he refused to let anyone know he was surprised by what he saw. He walked over to Melissa and gently put his hand on her shoulder. As calm as he tried to appear, Jimmy spoke with a sense of urgency that Melissa had not heard from him before. "Call your brother over here. We need to pray."

"What's wrong?"

"I don't know exactly. But I had a vision many years ago. This place reminds me of that."

"What happened in your vision?"

"I didn't exactly know it was a vision until now. It was a dream I had a couple of years ago. I just remember seeing this place, and in each direction I looked, there was something different."

"What are you talking about?" asked Seth, walking towards them.

"Jimmy had a dream about this place," Melissa explained.

"Well, I'm not sure if it was this place or what, but it seems familiar," said Jimmy.

"Didn't you say you had been here before?" asked Seth.

"Here, but not here. I, um … I was in the Dead Woods, like below what we just came from, but I … I got scared. I couldn't move. I couldn't do anything. So, I just prayed and begged God to help me. I didn't even really believe in God at the time. But he was real. He showed me the way out. And I never looked back."

"Okay, but what does that have to do with your dream or vision or whatever it was?" asked Seth.

"Before I came here, the first time, I had woken up from a vision that more or less told me what was going to happen. I knew the vision was different from an ordinary dream, and then when it started to really happen, I ran from it. I'm ashamed to say that I was too scared to trust that God was telling me something. And I think that's why you all are here now. To finish what I couldn't."

Melissa asked, "What makes you think it wasn't always supposed to happen this way? Maybe we were meant to be here together, to help one another."

"What else did you see in the dream?" asked Seth.

"I saw the Dead Woods, and then a place that looked like this—a place with a floor of branches and a ceiling with strange illumination. But the branches had leaves on them, that's how I knew what they were. When I looked to the north, there was an impenetrable wall. It represented starvation, I think. To the west there was fire. Hell, maybe? To the east there were … monsters."

"Monsters?" asked Melissa.

"I don't know what they were. Monsters, demons, fallen angels. They were evil-looking and mad."

"Mad?" asked Seth.

"Yes, they were trapped behind glass, an invisible wall of some sort. There were thousands of them, and they all looked at me like they wanted to obliterate me."

Fox whimpered and slowly moved behind Melissa, hiding herself from any possible onlookers. Dauber, who had finally rejoined the others, looked equally frightened by Jimmy's story. He alighted on the top of Fox's head and the two remained as still as grasshoppers in front of a hungry frog.

"That leaves the south. What did you see in that direction?" asked

Melissa.

"Water."

Seth asked, "Like a wall of water? A flood? Or rain?"

Jimmy shrugged his shoulders, "Just water."

"It's obvious," said Melissa. "We go south. The vulture told us to find the living stream. Water."

"But which way is south?" asked Seth.

"What do you mean? Surely one of you knows which way south is."

Seth looked incredulously at his sister. "How are we supposed to be able to tell directions here? There's no landmark, no sun, nothing to indicate anything. You didn't happen to bring a compass, did you?"

"Why, yes. Yes, I did," said Melissa.

"Really?" asked Jimmy.

"Well, not a compass per se, but a compass nonetheless."

"What is that supposed to mean?" asked Seth.

"What's cleverer than a compass, just as good with directions, and pretty as pretty can be?" She smiled coyly.

"Oh no, I'm not trusting your sense of direction if my life depended on it."

"Not me, silly."

"Then who?"

"Why, Fox, of course!"

"Fox," repeated Seth.

Melissa smiled. "Of course, she's a girl and everyone knows boys won't stop to ask for directions."

"Very funny. I suppose we are blessed to have a fox with us," said Jimmy. "No animal has a better sense of direction."

"I would think birds and butterflies have a keener sense of direction than a fox," said Seth.

"Well, that's neither here nor there is it? Because I am a fox, not a butterfly," said Fox matter-of-factly, still hiding behind Melissa.

"Actually, Fox here uses the earth's magnetic field just like the best migratory birds," said Jimmy. "She is the perfect compass for a group of travelers finding themselves lost."

Fox stepped out from behind Melissa, beaming with pride.

"It is true, come to think of it, I have never ever, ever been lost," said Fox.

"But I'm not even sure we're on earth anymore," said Melissa.

"I'm betting that wherever we are, the laws of physics as we know them are still in operation. But either way, let's stop and pray," said Jimmy.

"Do you want to pray to get out of here and go home, like you did the last time you were here?" asked Seth.

"No. I want to pray for the strength to finish this journey and see it through this time. Everything in my life has led up to this point. I'm not going to let fear stop me again."

"Why is pleasing God so important to you?" asked Seth.

Jimmy walked back over to the hollow tree and sat down on the stump. "Just the other day when I was driving, I looked over at the car next to me and I saw this frail woman. I mean, she was a normal middle-aged woman, but she seemed very alone. She looked so unhappy. I guess we all look somewhat stoic when we're alone driving, but I saw something more in her. I saw a person who didn't know that she is loved. And I got sad. I thought, here is this lonely, frail woman, and she has no clue that she is loved by the biggest, most amazing being in the universe. I watched her as she drove ahead of me and disappeared and I just wanted to scream—YOU ARE LOVED. I can't help but think that she may never know."

"That's so beautiful," said Melissa.

Seth rolled his eyes.

Jimmy continued, "We are all loved. He loves every single one of us. And I know this with every fiber in my body. I made a vow that day, after the lonely lady disappeared. I'll never forget the look on her face, the worry in her eyes, her thin arms reaching out to the steering wheel. I made a vow to tell everyone that they are loved."

"And you think this place has the answers?" asked Seth. "You think something here is going to give you that voice?"

"I don't know. But I don't have to be right about this journey. I don't have to know why or how. We don't have to have all of the answers, because life is good and the one who gave that life is good. He is life. I am here to do His will. Just pray with me, Seth. Even if you don't know what you don't know, that doesn't mean you can't trust in something greater than yourself. You have to start somewhere."

Seth walked over to his sister and put his hand on her shoulder. "I don't have a problem with praying. Melissa and I prayed a lot the last time we were here, and maybe it helped. I don't know for sure. But at the end of the day, it's my feet—*our* feet—that have to do the walking, not God's. There's no sign posted, no explanation how to do this. We gotta figure this out on our own."

Melissa took her brother's hand in hers. She held out her other hand towards Jimmy, who took it. Fox whimpered a bit and pushed her head into Jimmy's free hand. Jimmy knelt down and wrapped his arm around the fox, who very much welcomed the embrace. Dauber buzzed around, wanting to connect with the others, but not sure how to do so. His interaction with humans had been nonexistent before this adventure. He then decided to land on Seth's free hand.

Seth froze, "I don't know if I'm ever going to get used to having a wasp around me, and on me."

Fox shook her head, "Not just a wasp, most certainly not just a wasp."

"Yes, sorry, dirt dauber," said Seth.

"Shall we?" asked Melissa. Everyone nodded, including Dauber—although no one could really tell because his tiny head barely moved. Melissa bowed and recited the only prayer she knew from memory. "Our Father who art in heaven hallowed be thy name. Thy kingdom come they will be done on earth as it is in heaven. Give us this day our daily bread and forgive us our trespasses as we forgive those who trespass against us. Lead us not into temptation, but deliver us from evil. For thine is the kingdom and the power and the glory forever. Amen."

"Well, again, I hope that prayer applies not only to earth but also to strange otherworldly places, like this one," said Seth.

"I'm sure it does, Seth," said Jimmy. "Fox, it looks like it's your turn. Use those electromagnetic prancing and pouncing skills to lead us to the river of life. Bumpy is counting on you!"

Fox already knew what direction was south, but she stood upright on her four legs and looked to the right and then to the left before proceeding straight ahead. She thought the whole looking to the right and left thing added a bit of flair to the moment. It worked. Everyone looked impressed, or so she thought.

She was careful not to move too fast. While it was not overly difficult, it was important to watch for any openings that could catch a foot. They all noticed that the branches had a little spring to them, which actually made it less jarring on their bodies.

Once again Dauber decided to hitch a ride and save his energy. He would never admit this to anyone, but he liked the way that Seth smelled—sort of musky. He had heard from a hornet acquaintance that humans often sprayed scents on themselves in order to mask their natural odors. The deception was intoxicating to the hornet, and while Dauber found it pleasant, he was absolutely sure that it was in no way intoxicating. Anyway, Seth had the backpack and there were more places to tuck into—at least that's what Dauber would tell Fox if she asked.

Other than Seth tripping and falling early on, the going had been easy. The journey atop the canopy was surprisingly uneventful. The only real drama was the debate between Jimmy and Seth concerning worldviews and religion. Jimmy argued that there was only one worldview that held up to reality, while Seth felt that there was no way to know for sure. By the time Melissa joined the conversation, it had moved on to humanism versus Christianity. It was hard for her to say much because she had only just begun learning about Christianity, and she had no idea what humanism even meant.

Seth said, "Hey, Dauber. Would you mind flying up into the fog, or whatever it is above us, to see if anything is up there?"

Melissa quickly interrupted. "You can't ask him to do that. It could be dangerous. We don't have any idea what might be up behind those clouds."

"What's the problem? We don't know what lies ahead of us, either. What happened to that no-fear thing you said was in the Bible?"

"I don't think that's what the Bible meant. It's not about putting someone else in harm's way."

"You think? Hey, Jimmy, why don't you pull out that Bible of yours? I know you brought one. Read what it says about being afraid of the unknown."

Jimmy reached down into his side pocket and retrieved a small Bible. He tossed it over to Seth. "Why don't you read it for yourself? Turn to the New Testament and look for the book of Romans."

"That's about three-fourths of the way in, in case you didn't know," said Melissa.

Seth looked at both Jimmy and his sister with indignation but reluctantly opened it. He turned a few pages, wrinkled his brow and turned a few pages more. He flipped through as if shuffling a deck of cards. "Is this a joke?"

"What do you mean?" asked Jimmy.

"There's nothing in here. All of the pages are blank. I didn't know Christians carried around joke Bibles."

Jimmy reached out and took his Bible. "Let me see that." He repeated the same actions as Seth. He shuffled through a few pages and wrinkles quickly formed on his forehead. He then examined the front and back cover to confirm it really was his Bible. "That's strange. It's my Bible alright, but it's completely blank. There's not a word in it."

"Let me see that," said Melissa as she reached over and took the small leatherbound book out of Jimmy's hand. She too flipped through the pages. "Are you sure this was your Bible? Maybe you brought your blank journal by mistake."

"I don't keep a journal. Never have. And I know that's my Bible. It's my pocket Bible, and I almost always have it with me."

Seth interrupted, "Maybe all the ink came off when we fell in the lake."

"Unless we fell into a washing machine with miracle bleach, I doubt it. There's no way water could cleanly erase every word on every page without leaving even a smudge," said Jimmy.

The travelers kept following Fox, who just realized her directional skills were far more advanced than the others. She refused to get caught up in any conversational distractions as she pranced ever so proudly in her new role as leader.

Dauber, unbeknownst to the others, had already taken Seth's suggestion and flown into the thick fog. It was difficult keeping up with such a small creature.

"Well, what does the Bible say about fear?" Melissa directed this to Jimmy who was still flipping through the pages of his Bible.

Jimmy looked up and paused, thinking, "Oh my gosh, there are so many. I couldn't possibly quote them all."

"Really? Well, I guess we are out of luck then, Sis. Both of our Biblical resources have gone blank."

Melissa ignored her brother and caught up to Jimmy. They walked side by side. "I know you must have a favorite verse or two memorized."

"Of course, I'm just weirded out, that's all." Jimmy turned around to look at Seth. "My favorite verse on fear is in Second Timothy. It says: For God gave us not a spirit of fear but of power and love and self-control."

"Did you hear that, Dauber? God gives you power. You can do it! Fly up there and see what secrets lie above," yelled Seth, not knowing exactly where Dauber was.

Everyone looked around for the flying insect to respond. They even listened for buzzing, but they neither heard nor saw him.

"Maybe he's back in your pack," said Melissa.

"Dauber is not here," said Fox, who never took her eyes off the course ahead of them. "He is there, up in the clouds. Dauber loves a challenge and he is the first to volunteer for the most dangerous of tasks if he thinks it will help his friends."

"Great, Bro, thanks to you, Dauber has risked his life to find out what, exactly? What's in the clouds? What difference could that possibly make?"

"Hey, you two are the ones that are supposed to have all this faith and trust. Everything is going to be alright, right?"

"I think I liked you better when you were all insecure and nervous," said Melissa, playfully punching her brother in the shoulder.

"Everything in prayer and supplication, I'd say," said Jimmy. "Bumpy needs our help. We have free choice to do as we like, but I do believe God is looking after us, guiding us."

"It's so confusing," said Seth. "Even if I wanted to, I don't know how I would ever understand what it means to be a Christian."

"It's a lifelong journey, but once you allow the love of Christ to dwell in you, He will give you exactly what you need to understand. I'm not saying it's easy, but it's the only way that makes sense to me—and it's the only way that made sense to those who actually walked with Christ. Eleven of the twelve disciples died professing the truth of Christ as God. They proclaimed Him the way the truth and the life. They could have denied Jesus and not been imprisoned, tortured, exiled, and martyred. But they all said they saw the resurrected Christ and they knew it was true. Someone may die for what they think is the truth, but no one would die for something they know to be a lie."

"Are you saying if the disciples had not actually seen Jesus come back to life, they would not have lied about it because it eventually got them killed?" asked Melissa.

"It's definitely something to spend a lot of time thinking about," said

Jimmy.

"I guess that explains it then," said Seth. "Dauber is willing to die for the truth. I'm sure he believes in God."

"I still don't think that gives us an allowance to be arrogant or careless about someone else's life," said Melissa.

Seth agreed, "Duly noted. What about the twelfth disciple? What happened to him?"

"I don't think historians know exactly. They know he was banished to the Isle of Patmos where he wrote the Book of Revelation. But I don't think we know how he died."

There were several minutes of silence as they all continued walking. Fox was as determined as ever to bring everyone safely to whatever lay ahead of them. She was in her element and as content as she ever remembered being. Melissa enjoyed watching her enthusiasm as the brave new leader of the pack. Melissa had grown madly fond of Fox, and the thought occurred to her that this time, should they make it back home safely, perhaps the two would remain friends there as well. She felt certain that she and Seth would remember everything this time around. In fact, she prayed silently to herself over and over that God would allow them to remember everything, especially the new friendships they had made.

Jimmy interrupted the silence. "Has anyone else noticed that the gaps in the branches seem to be getting larger?"

"Now that you mention it, yes. I've even had to jump over a few of them," said Seth.

Melissa was enthusiastic with her response. "Do you think that means we are nearing the end?"

"I don't know what else it could mean," said Jimmy.

Fox came to a sudden stop. She looked up at the fog and whimpered. The others took the abrupt halt seriously, as it was the first time Fox had done anything but march confidently ahead. No one said anything. They just focused on Fox, hoping to figure out the reason for her hesitation.

Fox circled around behind everyone, yapping all the while at the fog overhead. It was not long before everyone realized that Fox was tracking an object in the clouds. Melissa and Seth whispered as much to one another, and Jimmy nodded in agreement. Someone, or something, was hovering right above them.

"What is that noise? It sounds like a plane coming straight towards us," said Melissa. The sound intensified as it got closer. It quickly faded away only to return a few seconds later.

Everyone froze to concentrate on the noise. The sound seemed to come and go as if something were circling above them. Whatever was responsible for the noise could not seem to decide on a course of action.

The four of them instinctively huddled together for protection, scanning the sky above them. Their hearts raced as they whispered to one another in a desperate attempt to come up with a plan of escape.

Fox saw it first. Something horrible. It was so large and powerful that its wings caused the air to push Melissa backward into Seth. The fur on Fox's body undulated up and down. Jimmy and Seth did the best they could to shield the two girls.

"What is it?" shouted Seth over the noise.

Before anyone could propose an answer, large flapping wings descended upon them. Directly above them hovered a monster. Its grotesque figure exceeded anything they could have conjured up in the worst of nightmares. Melissa looked away and screamed. The usually brave Fox cowered. Seth, with his arms over Fox on one side and Melissa on the other, swallowed hard. Jimmy stepped in front of the others in a brave attempt to shield them. He froze, in terror. There was no escape. They were out in the open, defenseless.

The menacing creature ascended back up into the fog only to quickly return about fifty yards south of them. No one moved a muscle. They watched as it weaved in and out of the fog. Jimmy was shocked at how fast something so large could keep itself suspended in the air. The thing had to be the size of a three-bedroom mobile home with a hairy face and two gigantic, oval eyes.

Once he got his wits about him, Jimmy looked around for escape routes. There were none—just a wide-open space. Other options flashed through his mind like bullets from a machine gun, but nothing seemed sensible. Should he run towards the creature and offer himself as a sacrifice while the others ran? Should they all stand together and yell as loud as they could? He was not concerned for himself, but he felt an obligation to keep Melissa and Seth safe—and get them back home.

"No weapon formed against you shall prevail," whispered Jimmy. It was from the book of Isaiah.

Jimmy jumped up and began running away from the group. "Hey, over here! You big nasty, ugly, overgrown coward! Why don't you go pick on something your own size?"

The flying monster—with wings larger than a jet plane's—buzzed right over Jimmy's head. The force of the flapping wings knocked Jimmy to his knees. Why was this thing toying with them? He yelled to the others, "Run! I'm going to try and get it to follow me. Just keep running and don't look back!"

By the time Jimmy stood back up, the massive predator spoke, "What happened to everyone? You're so tiny."

Fox figured it out first. The big scary giant alien was none other than their trusted friend, Dauber. She jumped out from under Seth's arms and ran towards him. "Oh, my! We shrank, did we? I hadn't even noticed. My paws certainly look the same to me."

Jimmy stood up and took a deep breath. He was embarrassed for not being the first to figure out it was Dauber. But he knew something that Fox did not. "It's not us, Dauber. We didn't shrink at all. It's you, my friend. You have expanded … greatly."

"Expanded? Well, that's quite the understatement of the decade." Seth stared at Dauber. "Dude, you have grown to epic proportions! You are amazing. Just look at you. Even your voice is bigger. We can hear you now."

"Really? It's me that's changed? Isn't that something?" said Dauber.

"What happened up there, Dauber?" asked Melissa.

"I'm not sure exactly. It was very cloudy. The fog must have special powers."

"Does it end? Is there an end to the fog?" asked Jimmy.

"Not exactly. But it does thin out in places. And there is something up there," said Dauber as he landed a few feet away from the others. The canopy shook when his large feet took hold of the wooden branches. The others had to steady themselves from the abrupt jolt.

"What's up there?" asked Seth.

"I'm not sure exactly," answered Dauber. "Others. There are others up there."

"Others," repeated Fox. "I don't like the sound of that. I have my others right here with me. I don't want more others. These are the perfect others for me." Fox tiptoed around until she was directly behind Dauber. She sniffed his rear end, avoiding the giant stinger of course, and confirmed—yes, it was indeed their trusted friend.

"How do you know there were others if you couldn't see them?" asked Melissa.

"I heard them whispering. One of them even whispered into my ear, but I couldn't understand what it said."

"That's strange," said Jimmy.

"When has anything here *not* been strange?" asked Seth.

Jimmy walked over directly in front of Dauber. "Describe these whispering things."

"I would not know where to begin. I think they are very happy, joyful little creatures."

Melissa stood next to Jimmy and leaned her head back to look up at Dauber. "If you can't see them or understand them, what makes you think they are joyful?"

"I cannot explain these things. Come with me and meet them for yourselves."

"How are we going to do that?" asked Seth.

"I was very strong as a little guy. Imagine how strong I am now. Just jump aboard, all of you, and up we will go," suggested Dauber.

"Do you think we will come back as giants too? What if we expand? You won't be able to support us. We might crush you and fall to the ground."

Jimmy looked at Seth. "You worry too much. I want to go up there." He turned to Melissa. "Don't you?"

"Absolutely," she answered enthusiastically. "Are you up for it, Fox?"

"I must go where my friends go, this is my only desire," said Fox.

Jimmy motioned for Seth to help him. He then grabbed the slender part between Dauber's thorax and abdomen and pulled himself up. He sat far enough behind Dauber's wings as not to inhibit his flapping. It was not too different than sitting on a horse, minus the saddle of course. Seth helped Melissa, and Jimmy grabbed her hand to pull her the rest of the way.

Melissa sat behind Jimmy and held onto his sides. "Wow, you're a bit boney back here, Dauber, but actually not too uncomfortable." She looked down at Fox and yelled, "Come on, Fox." Without hesitation, Fox got a running start and rebounded up off of Seth's back, who had knelt down for her, and up into Melissa's arms. Fox nestled herself in-between Melissa and Jimmy. She felt as snug as a bug in a rug.

"You coming, Seth?" asked Jimmy.

"I guess so. But I just want to say I don't think you all have thought this out very well. It's on the two of you if anything bad happens," said Seth.

"And if something good should happen?" asked Melissa.

"Well, I did agree to it," replied Seth.

Melissa scowled as Jimmy chuckled.

Jimmy leaned over to grab Seth's arm but could not quite reach. Dauber lowered his body as far as he could—it was just enough. Jimmy heaved and Seth was able to grab hold of Dauber's waist and pull himself the rest of the way up. In no time at all they were all aboard.

"Hold on tight. Here we go," said Dauber.

Dauber flapped his wings and lifted up off the canopy with ease. There he was, a dirt dauber, with three humans and a fox riding on his back. He could not have been more proud. He had always felt strong and powerful, but this far surpassed his wildest dreams. If only Sticky could see him now. For a brief moment he missed his friend and the beautiful green woods of Garland County, and then Dauber giggled as he felt something he had never experienced before. Melissa tickled the side of his body. He had never felt a human hand. It was delightful. It was at that moment he knew that he was exactly where he was supposed to be. He was an important part of something bigger than even his big self.

Dauber knew that if what the vulture said was true—that evil was draining from this place into his world—then he had to do whatever he could to protect his new friends and those that he loved back home. There was no challenge that he could not face, and he had faith that together they would see it through to the end. It was an interesting perspective, he thought, just having flown up into a place where it was impossible to see any further than ten feet ahead. How exciting!

Chapter 17

The Whispering Foghorses

The air was thick and a bit cooler than below, but what everyone noticed the most was how quiet it was. The fog had a dampening effect. Even Dauber's rapidly flapping wings were barely audible. The quietness reminded Melissa of what it sounded like when she put her head under the water when taking a bath. Fox found the silence to be very off-putting as her acute hearing picked up nothing beyond the travelers themselves. The boys paid it little attention.

Such low visibility in the fog would not have been good for a pilot following visual flight rules. Fortunately for his passengers, Dauber did not need to see in order to fly—his antennae could sense anything in his path.

Despite not being able to see anything other than an endless white mattress of air, Dauber felt great joy soaring around with his friends holding onto him. He flapped vigorously, rising higher and higher, and then held his wings open wide as he glided down. Melissa's stomach did somersaults. It was the same feeling she got as a child when her father drove quickly up and down hills. She giggled with delight, both then and now.

"Dauber, where are the others you told us about?" asked Jimmy with a sense of urgency. Jimmy's stomach did not enjoy the ups and down nearly as much as Melissa's. He was doing everything in his power to keep from getting sick.

"They are everywhere, all around us, I do believe," answered Dauber. "Perhaps you can see them where the fog thins out."

Dauber darted to the left and then to the right, up and then down—looking for the ideal spot to see the creatures from his last trip into the fog. His passengers held on tight as they tried hard to detect figures in the fog. The task was doubly difficult because not only was it nearly impossible to see more than a few yards ahead of them, but also because they had no clue as to what exactly they were looking for. Fox had the hardest time, as Melissa was absentmindedly mashing her face into Jimmy's back in an effort to hold her securely. At times Fox found it problematic to even breathe. Yet she did not complain. Fox treasured the feeling of safety and warmth in her companion's embrace.

Dauber stopped abruptly and hovered. "Here, this is about as thin as the fog gets. Can you see them?"

"I don't see anything," said Seth with a sigh.

"Me either," added Melissa.

"Be patient, you two. We are strangers here. Maybe they are timid," said Jimmy, who was just happy not to be moving. "Just hold steady here for a while, Dauber."

"Sure thing, Captain."

Fox twisted her neck away from Melissa's belly and looked up at her, "What's a captain?"

"It's the leader of a boat, or an aircraft," said Melissa.

"Well, one thing is for sure," said Seth.

"What's that?" asked Jimmy.

"We haven't grown any bigger … or have we?"

"I don't think so. Everyone seems the same to me."

"Whew, that's a good thing."

"Should we try flying to another spot?" asked Melissa.

Jimmy shook his head. "No, I think whoever lives here is aware of our presence. If they wanted to greet us, it wouldn't matter where we went."

"Maybe that's not true. Maybe they don't want to be seen. Maybe we should go somewhere where the fog is thicker."

"You have a point, and it couldn't hurt to try," said Jimmy reluctantly. "You heard the woman, Dauber. Into the deep white fog we go."

"Aye, Captain!" Dauber lifted up and then flew straight ahead. When the fog seemed to be at its thickest, Dauber stopped and hovered as before. The layer of white was so substantial that no one could even see Dauber's head. In fact, it was hard to see one's hand at the end of their fully extended arm.

"I don't *see* how this is going to work, pardon the pun," said Seth. "If we want to see who, or what, is up here, isn't this the worst possible spot to do it?"

"I *see* your point, Seth," said Jimmy. Melissa laughed at the play on words and Fox giggled, not because she thought what Jimmy said was funny but because Melissa's belly vibrated against her head when she laughed. "Let's just give it a try and see what happens. I mean, well, let's just be patient."

Dauber continued to hover, but there was no indication of any whispering creatures. Everyone concentrated on listening, but it was difficult to hear anything other than Dauber's wings flapping and buzzing. There could have been something out there, but unless it was louder than Dauber how would they ever know.

They waited and waited but nothing happened. It was not long before boredom took hold. Melissa absentmindedly began to hum. It was a familiar tune, and Jimmy hummed along with her. Seth joined them. Fox did not recognize the tune, but she enjoyed listening to her human friends.

Perhaps it was because Fox was not humming—or perhaps it was due to her superior hearing—but she was the first to notice the harmony. It was beautiful. Although the voices were not loud, they were many. It was almost as though they did not want to be heard, yet they could not help themselves. Fox did not alert the others, as she was sure they would recognize the choir before long.

Dauber was the next to hear the faint voices surrounding them from all sides. Fox noticed that Dauber took it upon himself to slowly coast towards an area where the fog was less dense. He did it so slowly that the others, including the mysterious choir, seemed not to notice. They all just kept humming joyfully.

Jimmy put his finger to his lips and motioned subtly with his other hand for Seth and Melissa to stop and listen. Melissa caught on first, but it took a while before Seth noticed. He looked puzzled for a moment and then began to realize why the other two had stopped humming. He stared intensely, looking for where the voices might be coming from.

Dauber was now holding steady in the spot with the most visual acuity. He flapped his wings just enough to keep them in place, but no more. He enjoyed the sounds as much as the rest and did not want to frighten the choir away. One by one, Dauber and his passengers began to see things in the air floating or flying around them.

The objects in the air appeared to be small puffs of cloud, like cotton balls shaped into forms of seahorse-looking creatures. The Whispering Foghorses as they would eventually be called, were having so much fun humming that they either did not notice the visitors or did not care that their airspace was being invaded.

The fact was, the Foghorses were very much aware of the visitors, but could not help themselves. Their one weakness, if it could be viewed as such, was music and song. It brought them much happiness. It was in their nature to remain hidden from all outsiders, unless called upon to be seen, which was extremely rare.

The visitors from below watched as the puffs of clouds danced and floated all around them. Sometimes they would gather in small groups of three or four to form special ensembles. Melissa, having studied music, could hear the differences in pitch and melody among the different and ever-changing trios and quartets.

The Foghorses were now fully out in the open and much more boisterous than before. In fact, Jimmy was sure they were actually performing for their unexpected audience. This became obvious as they took turns positioning their little ensembles directly in front of his face only to quickly move on to Melissa and then to Seth. Even Fox received her own private serenades.

After a few minutes, Melissa felt it was safe to whisper without scaring off the remarkable performers. "What do y'all make of this?"

"I'm clueless," answered Seth.

"I'm speechless," said Jimmy.

"It's quite obvious if you ask me," said Fox.

"What's that?" asked Melissa.

"Well, they are singing," said Fox.

Everyone groaned and then Melissa responded. "Yes, we figured that much, Fox. But why, and who are they?"

"What do they want?" asked Seth.

"But singing is giving, not wanting," yapped Fox. "I most definitely can say they want nothing from us, but they are here to give something to us."

"I hope you're correct," said Seth.

"How do you know this, Fox?" asked Melissa.

"Do you know why very few animals sing? Because we know who our Creator is. We have no doubts. All that we do is in honor and thankfulness. We cannot do anything that our Lord has not given us instincts to do. Singing is instinctual to those with free will, and it was intended to praise the one who created everything."

"How would a fox know all of that?" said Seth. "I can sing with no intention to praise anything at all."

"Yes, yes indeed. But that's neither here nor there. Humans do many things that make no sense at all. But I know this: singing is powerful when it is used to give praise. Just listen for yourselves. Have you ever heard anything so delightful in your lives?"

"No, I haven't," said Jimmy. "I'm inclined to agree with Fox. I think they mean us no harm."

"Okay, that's cool. But what are they supposed to give us? We didn't risk our lives to end up empty-handed," said Seth.

"I don't know about you," said Melissa, "but I have been given one of the most awesome lovely displays of sheer happiness that I will never forget."

"Oh please!" Seth interrupted. "That's the sappiest thing I've ever heard. We need to figure out why we are here. What or who these things are?"

"Well, some of us already know why we're here, Seth," said Jimmy. "Besides, what do you want us to do? We can't exactly demand anything of these little guys."

"We tried," said Dauber, indicating it was time to head back down.

"Yes, we did," Jimmy said as he patted Dauber with his hand.

"I'm not leaving until we try harder," said Seth. "Hey, you white singy floaty things, who are you? Is this your home?" Seth waited for a moment but got no reply, at least none he could decipher. He yelled a little louder. "Okay, riddle me this, cloud choir of the skies: what happened to our friend Dauber? How did he get so big? Did you do this to him?"

There was no discernible response to Seth's questions, but their behavior did change. The Foghorses stopped giving choral serenades. They appeared to be just as happy singing individually as they were in groups. It was not until the travelers gave up and agreed to descend back to the canopy that the change was noticed. Whereas before the creatures seemed organized and unified, they now appeared to be randomly frolicking all around them.

Fox reveled in the beautiful vocalizations and dances of the Foghorses. The rest of the travelers had grown weary of the display and decided that they should return and continue on with their journey. They could not just hang out in the clouds on a giant dirt dauber forever. Dauber was bound to get tired sooner or later.

There were so many unanswered questions, and every moment should be spent in pursuit of finding answers. It was easy to get complacent, and Jimmy reminded them of the importance of staying focused. The idea that their world back home might be under siege by some malevolent force from this world gave their mission an added urgency. Perhaps such a grandiose notion was not to be, and they were simply on journeys of self-enlightenment—or maybe it was a mixture of both. One thing was for certain, the journey must continue and they must not become distracted by beautiful singing puffs of cotton.

With Dauber's new ability to carry them, the traveling would go much easier—or so they thought. When the decision was finally made to descend out of the fog and continue to the south, they observed an abrupt change in the Foghorses. The singing immediately ceased and all but four of the countless wonders blended back into the thickest part of the fog from which they came. The four that remained grouped together just in front of the visitors from below. Dauber and crew expected them to begin singing again. But that is not what happened.

In the blink of an eye, as fast as a bolt of lightning, the four remaining specimens quite literally disappeared into the ears of Melissa, Seth, Jimmy, and even Fox. It was Fox that put it all together. Her eyes were equipped to follow the quickest of movements, and while she could not see her own ear, she saw the ears of the others.

The whole experience was otherwise painless and uneventful. While odd and a bit disconcerting, there was nothing any of them could do—and according to Fox's account, the beings had nothing but harmonious intentions. It had also occurred to them that this was the reason they had ascended into the clouds in the first place. Perhaps this was the gift Seth was hoping for.

Fox explained to Dauber what had happened, as he could not see the action too well being just over the middle of his backside and under his wings. This gave the others time to gather their wits. There was a little discussion between Melissa and Seth as to what to do next. Everything seemed just as it was before, until Jimmy spoke. He uttered words none of them had ever heard before.

"Was that me?" asked Jimmy.

"Yes, it was. What were you trying to say?" asked Melissa.

"I don't have a clue what just came out of my mouth. I heard it but I didn't understand it."

"It was unintelligible gobbledygook, that's what it was," said Seth indignantly. The truth was that although the words were strange, Seth understood what they meant and they were directed at him. He would keep this fact to himself until he could fully make sense of it. He was not sure if what Jimmy spoke was a joke, a test, or a trap of some sort. He thought it best to keep it to himself, for the time being.

"Sorry. That's never happened to me before," said Jimmy. Although the strange utterances deserved more scrutiny, it made Jimmy feel awkward and he avoided further discussion. "Let's not waste any more time. Dauber, onward we go, to the south and to the river of life."

Dauber, excited in his new role as a passenger jet, energetically flapped his wings and darted quickly out of the fog. The passengers held on tight as the wind whipped their hair. Dauber leveled off and proceeded on course. The view was wondrous. Below them was a beautiful woven tapestry of tree limbs, but unlike what they had been walking on earlier, there were openings through the trees to the ground below. Somewhere, not too far ahead of them, was a river that would hopefully restore life back to their friend, Bumpy.

Chapter 18

THE RATCLIFFES

Bethany rarely took naps at home, but visits with her mother always took a little extra out of her. She had barely laid down and closed her eyes when the commotion began.

Her brother's bedroom, where she and Patrick slept, was located in the far corner of the house. It was almost impossible to hear any noises coming from the front yard where the commotion was happening. She briefly considered waiting it out, but her curiosity got the best of her. She ran her fingers through her hair and quickly put on her shoes.

By the time she made it to the front door, she had already figured out that her mother was arguing with the Ratcliffes. She could also hear Patrick's attempts to mediate.

"That tree has been here for over a hundred years, long before you and your selfish kids graced this world with your glorious personalities," shouted Azora.

"I'm not asking you to cut the tree down, I'm simply suggesting you might want to trim it back," said Ray Ratcliffe, Earl's son-in-law. Ray might have appeared to be pleasant and reasonable to the casual observer, but to those that knew him well, he was an overbearing, passive-aggressive troublemaker.

"I heard you the first time. I don't intend on hangin' around here to hear it again. We ain't trimmin' the tree. Why in the world would we want to trim a tree? Look around, we live in the cottin' pickin' woods!" exclaimed Azora.

"Like I told you before, that tree is dropping nuts all over our yard and it's a potential hazard," said Ray.

"How in tarnation is it droppin' nuts in your yard? The only nuts in your yard are you and that wife of yours. Complete nut-cakes, that's what you people are."

"Well, that's mighty Christian of you, Azora!" said Mrs. Bernita Ratcliffe.

"The wind blows em' all over the place and the squirrels toss em' here and there," said Ray. "The point is someone is gonna trip over em' and then it's gonna be a lawsuit."

"You can't sue someone cause a nut blew in your yard! What? You gonna take the squirrels to court? I wouldn't put it past you, Ratcliffe," said Azora.

Patrick looked at his mother-in-law in an attempt to calm things down. "Perhaps you should wait until Henry gets back from his trip and discuss this with him."

Ray tapped Patrick on the shoulder and in his most pleasant voice responded. "That would be fine, but he's rarely ever home."

"Oh please, you're too much of a coward to discuss things with Henry. You'd rather beat up on an old widow," said Azora.

Bethany stood behind the screen door. She had heard stories about the Ratcliffes, but she had never actually witnessed them in action. She knew her mother could be unreasonable, but family stuck together—and that included Bethany and her mother.

"Is that what it is I'm doin'? Beatin' up on you, Azora? I think I'd have an easier time with your son, quite frankly," said Ray with a smile.

"You probably would, but you hear me when I say nobody is touchin' that tree. Over my dead body!" shouted Azora.

"Let's just calm down—" said Patrick.

"Don't you tell me to calm down," Azora said. "You should be tellin' him to stop throwin' a hissy fit in my front yard. You should be advising him to get off this here property." She was only inches away from Ray Ratcliffe's face. If his belly did not stick so far out, she would have gotten even closer. As it was, she stood there, all five feet of her, clenching and shaking her fist up at him. Bethany had never seen her so angry.

"Don't you worry about that, Azora. I won't be stepping foot over here again. But if my father-in-law trips over one of your hickory nuts, you better believe there's gonna be hell to pay," said Ray, backing away from Azora.

"Who are you tryin' to kid? I'm surprised you ain't planted one right next to his stoop!"

Bethany could see Bernita scowling off to the right. No one really knew if she agreed with her husband or if he had brainwashed her. The consensus was brainwashed. No one could fathom a daughter treating her father as poorly as she did Earl. Case in point, the Ratcliffes had refused to repair Earl's air conditioner, and when one of the neighbors installed a ceiling fan for him, Ray had all the fan blades removed.

Bethany opened the screen door and momentarily distracted the crowd. She believed that kindness was a far better method of revenge than anything else. "Hi, Mr. Ratcliffe. It's nice to see you." She looked over in the direction of Bernita. "How was your Thanksgiving?"

"It was fine, thank you for asking," answered Ray. He then smiled unconvincingly, turned and began walking back towards his house. His wife followed behind without saying a word.

"What's his problem?" whispered Bethany.

"Well, he's got a valid point. That tree is huge and it does drop a lot of debris," said Patrick.

"You would agree with him," said Azora as she turned to go back into the house.

"I'm just sayin'—"

"There is nothing, and I mean nothing, to be agreed upon with that wretched man." Bethany followed her mother into the house.

Patrick walked over to a hickory nut lying in the yard and rolled his foot over it. He wondered if it would crack if he put all of his weight onto it, so he did a little hop into the air. When he landed down on the nut, it rolled out from beneath his foot and caused him to lose his balance. After the initial shock of finding himself on the ground, he looked up to see if anyone noticed. Actually, he did not care if just anyone noticed—he only cared if Azora noticed. As far as he could tell, he was in the clear.

Meanwhile, Azora sat on the edge of her bed, staring at the bucket of dirt with its fresh sapling in front of her window. She would have gently tapped on the glass and waved at her son-in-law, letting him know she had seen his unfortunate fall, but she was far too engaged with the new life before her. It occurred to her that she had never before passed up an opportunity to make her son-in-law feel like a nincompoop, but the thought was fleeting. Her attention would not soon depart from its new obsession.

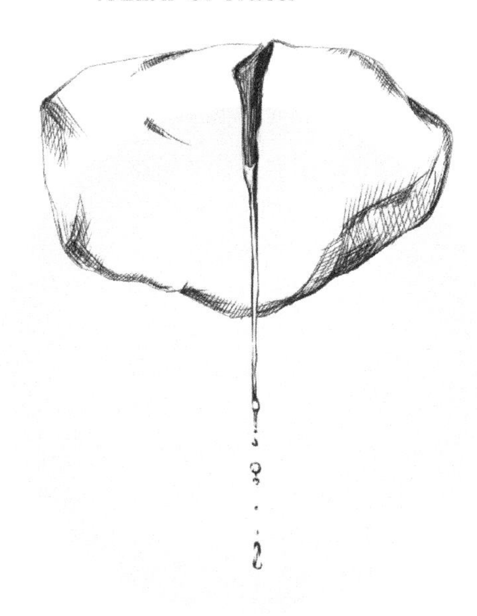

Chapter 19

The Interpretation

They had cleared the canopy miles ago. Dauber flew as low to the ground as he could so that everyone could get a better view of the terrain below them. While most of the passengers thought the view would have been better if they were higher up, Jimmy figured that the stream they were searching for might be too small to see from a higher altitude.

With everyone looking in different directions, they searched for anything that might possibly resemble a river or brook. Jimmy knew that if it was the only water source, it would not be far from its benefactors. But as they flew farther and farther away from the tightly interwoven canopy, the terrain began to resemble a deserted plain that had been cleared of most of the brush and trees. Try as they might, there was no flowing water anywhere to be found.

"We should have seen it by now," said Melissa.

"We must have missed it," said Jimmy.

"Should I circle back around towards the canopy?" asked Dauber.

Dauber leaned to the right and took a wide turn back towards the Dead Woods. He slowed down a bit and varied his altitude to give a variety of perspectives of the ground below. It was not long before Seth pointed at something a few miles ahead of them.

"It's over there."

"I don't see anything, where is it?" asked Melissa.

'It's over there. I'm sure of it."

"Dauber, head to your right at about a thirty-degree turn," said Jimmy.

Dauber turned and within seconds Seth confirmed that the Stream of Life was directly below them. He knew this because he was able to interpret the strange utterances that Jimmy had given in the clouds. Part of the interpretation was that the Stream of Life would begin by a large boulder in a dry creek bed. There was more revelation than just the location of the Living Waters, but Seth would refrain from telling anyone until he was sure what it all meant, or if it was even true.

Dauber found an appropriate spot to land and slowly descended, much like a helicopter. Fox, for one, was overjoyed to be back on the ground. She did not wait for someone to pick her up or help her down. She jumped so quickly and erratically that Melissa gasped and instinctively reached out to grab her, and in the failed attempt managed to push Fox just enough to throw her off balance. The usually graceful four-legged vixen landed awkwardly, causing her front right leg to collapse underneath her. She yelped in pain. The others were much more careful as they disembarked. After Jimmy eased himself off the side of Dauber, he reached up and offered a hand to Melissa. She gladly took it and carefully lowered herself to the ground.

"Are you alright, Fox?" asked Melissa.

"I think so," said Fox. But when she tried to walk, she could not help but let out a small whimper. Her leg was not broken, but it was badly sprained.

"I'm sorry, Fox. You startled me and I tried to keep you from falling."

"I'll be alright. I'm sure of it. It's not your fault."

"This is bad. We need Fox to scout ahead. How is she going to do that now?" asked Seth.

"Thoughtful, Seth, never mind that Fox is in pain," said Melissa.

"We'll make her a splint and we can all take turns carrying her, if necessary. Her nose can still lead the way. So where is it, Seth?" asked

Jimmy.

"Right over there," he pointed.

"What's wrong with you? Are you sulking?" Melissa asked Seth.

"No, I'm just ready to get on with this. Let's go."

Melissa and Jimmy looked at one another and shrugged. Seth's mood had changed since they left the fog.

Fox was not deterred by her injury as she happily, but gingerly, limped slightly ahead of her friends. The others followed closely behind.

"Take it easy, Fox. I think one of us should carry you,' said Melissa.

"I'm fine for now. I'm about to see real living waters. Have I ever seen living waters before? I'm not sure, but I can't wait! Won't it be the berries to see Bumpy fluttering around again. Besides, there's not far to go." Even with a limp, Fox was still quite nimble.

Dauber took the opportunity to rest and groom himself. He wanted to be ready in case he had to lift off at a moment's notice.

Fox stopped a few yards ahead of the others. She glanced back and forth between the approaching explorers and the gully at her feet.

"Well, it looks like there used to be a stream here," said Jimmy as he caught up with Fox.

"It's dry as a bone. This must be a mistake," said Melissa.

"Yes, a mistake I should say. We should scout in all directions and find where the water is," said Fox.

"There's no need for that. All we have to do is follow the dry bed up until we find the source," said Jimmy.

"There's no need for that," said Seth matter-of-factly.

"Okay, what do you suggest, brother dear?"

Seth reluctantly picked up a nearby stick and walked over to a large boulder that was next to the dry creek bed. He sighed and hit the rock with the stick. The other three—except for Dauber, who was too busy licking his limbs to notice—looked at one another quizzically. They all waited a few moments, expecting something to happen.

Melissa broke the silence. "Okay, well, that was weird."

"Yes, it was," responded Seth as he sat down on a nearby rock, staring at the boulder. He crossed his arms and lost himself in a memory he had not thought of in many years. He was seven years old, arms crossed as he wept and hit a mound of dirt with his red plastic shovel. The toy shovel was no match for the hard-compacted dirt. He broke the handle off and began to stab at the dirt. His mom sat down next to him and placed her hand over his.

"Sweetie," she had said, "I know it's hard, but Tuffy loved you very much. It was just his time to go. He would want you to remember all the fun you had together and not be sad."

"I asked God to bring him back, mommy. I prayed all night long … not all night, but until I fell asleep. I just knew he was gonna be there when I woke up, I just knew it. But he wasn't."

Bethany put her arms around her son and wiped the tears from his cheek. "Aw, honey, that's not the way it works. Tuffy is at peace now. Remember how he had a hard time walking up the steps and how it hurt him? Well, he doesn't hurt anymore."

"In church they said that God answers all prayers, all we have to do is believe." He looked up at his mom. "I believed, mommy. I really believed."

Seth felt Melissa's hand on his shoulder and the memory faded. He looked behind him to see that Fox, Melissa, and Jimmy had joined him next to the boulder.

"How did you know that was going to happen?" asked Jimmy.

"Are you talking to me?" asked Seth.

"Yes, I'm asking how you knew." Jimmy nodded his head, glancing in front of them.

Seth looked at the boulder he had only moments ago struck with the stick, and he saw a dark spot that was slowly getting larger and larger.

"I dunno, lucky guess maybe."

"I don't believe in luck," said Jimmy.

Fox began jumping up and down excitedly, but quickly stopped when her leg began to throb in pain. "I want to see something happen. Is it going to be fun?"

"Calm down, Fox. What's supposed to happen?" asked Melissa.

Seth and Jimmy answered simultaneously, "Just wait."

It began without even a trickle. The dark spot grew until water began to drip off the rock onto the dry ground below. One drip, then two, then eventually the drops connected to form the smallest of streams. Fox's eyes grew bigger and bigger in amazement. She trotted up next to Seth as if he was her new favorite person. Melissa smiled, and Seth even managed one, too.

By the time Dauber headed over to see what all the fuss was about, the water was practically gushing, as Melissa and Fox would later tell it. In actuality, it was nothing near a gush, but there was a solid stream of water and the dry creek bed was soaking it up.

Seth removed his backpack and slowly pulled out the jar where Bumpy was resting. As he unscrewed the lid, he looked up at everyone and said, "This doesn't make me Moses or Aaron or whoever it was in the Bible who hit the rock and water came out. This has nothing to do with that. Y'all got it?" Everyone nodded in agreement. Seth looked back down at the jar and gently took out the lifeless leaf. "Should I just hold him under the water?"

"Go for it," said Melissa.

Everyone held their breath as Seth placed Bumpy in the palm of his hand. With his thumb gently holding him secure, Seth put Bumpy under the stream. The droplets glistened as they quickly bounced off the leaf. Seth carefully rubbed the water into Bumpy in order to get it to absorb more quickly. He was sure the leaf was thoroughly saturated when it turned a darker shade of brown.

Everyone stared intensely at the palm of Seth's hand.

"Help me. Somebody help me!" The plea was heard clearly, but the leaf did not move.

"Was that Bumpy? Was it the leaf?" asked Melissa.

"It had to be, right?" asked Jimmy.

"I guess so. I mean, he's not moving, but who else would have said it," said Seth. Everyone became very still and looked at Bumpy on Seth's hand.

"Umph. Oomph! Phmph!

Seth lifted his hand closer to his ear.

"Ummmm, Mhph! Uugh."

"Yes, it's coming from the leaf!" Seth lowered his hand so everyone could see what was happening. Fox, nose first, squeezed in-between Melissa and Jimmy. She did not want to miss a thing.

"I can't move. What's wrong with me? Have I been drugged?" asked Bumpy.

"It's him for sure," said Jimmy.

"Why can't he move?" asked Melissa.

"Perhaps it is an imposter throwing his voice?" said Fox.

"What?" Seth asked, shaking his head and scrunching up his face.

"There are plenty of creatures that can make it seem they are somewhere they are not. It's quite a trick, I must say," said Fox.

"It's Bumpy. Give him a break. He's coming back from the brink of death. It might take a while to get his faculties together," said Seth.

Melissa said, "By faculties do you mean arms and legs? Well, being that we are talking about a leaf … I dunno."

"Help me! I can't move," yelled Bumpy.

Seth lifted the stem of the leaf with his thumb and index finger and slowly peeled him off the palm of his hand. He held it upside down dangling. Everyone tilted their heads a little sideways and lower to the position where Bumpy's eyes would have been.

"My body is so heavy," said Bumpy as a light breeze blew from behind.

"Oh, I get it. He's wet," said Jimmy. "Leaves don't usually absorb so much water. Blow, everyone!"

Jimmy began blowing on the leaf and it was not long before Seth and Fox joined him. Melissa chose to fan him with her hands. In no time at all they could see the little leaf begin to move his arms and legs. Everyone immediately stopped what they were doing when Bumpy let out a loud squeal.

"What is it? What's wrong?" asked Seth.

"My leg, what happened to my leg?"

"Oh, that. Well, we're not sure exactly. There was a fracas—"

Melissa interrupted Seth. "A fracas? Really, Seth? Bumpy, there was a scuffle and we lost you when a burst of air scooped you up. There was all this dust and everyone was trying to catch the buzzards and we lost you in all the commotion."

Jimmy said, "When we finally did find you, thanks to Fox, you were covered with that nasty moss and missing a piece of your leaf, I mean your body, or your leg or whatever—"

"Well, where is it?" asked Bumpy.

"Where is what?" asked Melissa.

"My missing piece! How would you like to be missing a piece of yourself?"

"Most unhappy I would be to miss a paw or something that once was attached, no matter how small," yapped Fox.

"We don't know where the rest of you is," said Seth. "I'm sorry. I guess I'm not doing my job very well, am I?"

"Hogwash, young feller," said Bumpy. "It's a miracle is what it is. A straight up, flat out miracle. I mean, I knew it was going to happen. But how and when, I had no clue."

"It is a miracle, you coming back to life, that much is obvious," said Jimmy.

"No, no. God has much bigger things in store than that. So I see you found the Living Waters."

"Wait a minute, not so fast. Then what miracle are you talking about?" asked Melissa.

Bumpy stretched out his right arm and then his left. "There's plenty of time to see the evidence of the miracle that's unfolding but no time to tell the tale now. Nor would it matter or change the course we are to take—"

"Which is?" asked Seth.

"Now that I do not know."

"How could you not know that?"

"What I do know, is the good news we have here. The Living Waters are flowing again. Thanks to all of you," said Bumpy.

"All of *us,*" added Melissa.

"Yes, all of us. There is only one thing to do with good news."

"And that is?" asked Seth.

Fox jumped up from her comfortable spot—and after flinching a bit because her leg still ached when pressed upon—cheerily answered Seth. "Good tidings must be shared with anyone who will hear."

"That's true there, four-legger. There's only one thing to do with good news and that's tell it," said Bumpy.

"No one will believe us back home. What's the point?" asked Melissa.

"Two points. Don't judge who may or may not believe and don't assume you know the audience that needs to hear. Just tell it. Here, there, and everywhere," said Bumpy.

"The Word will not return void," added Jimmy.

"And as for you there, my four-legged friend, why have you not partaken of the healing waters? The water is for everyone," said Bumpy.

Fox tilted her head quizzically and limped over to the small pool that had collected in front of the large boulder.

"Of course, why hadn't I thought of that before," said Melissa.

"Go for it, Fox," shouted Jimmy.

Fox took her lame leg and gently dipped her paw in the small puddle. After a second or two passed, she took both paws and thrust them into the mud. What little water was there splashed out but was quickly replenished with more from the stream coming out of the boulder. Fox seemed to enjoy splashing the water and kept thrusting both paws in and out until she had all of the onlookers laughing. She had completely forgotten why she was at the puddle in the first place.

"What's so funny?" asked Fox.

"Nothing, nothing at all, little red. How's your leg, by the way?" asked Jimmy.

"My leg? Oh, my leg you say. Well, let's see." Fox quickly darted up and out of the riverbed. She circled all the way around Dauber and the entire group, yapping the whole time. During her second lap around she yapped, "My leg is …" And the third time she said, "quite fine …" On her fourth lap Melissa jumped out in front of the fox, but Fox jumped over Melissa and happily proclaimed, "As good as good can beeee." Fox landed on the ground, steady and sure. She ran back over to Melissa and nuzzled her.

Melissa patted Fox on the head. "I'm so glad you're feeling better." She looked at the rest of the group and asked, "So where to now?"

"Apparently there are some folks that need to hear a little good news," said Jimmy, "so I say we follow the riverbed downstream and see if we can find anyone. It won't be long until this creek, or river as it were, is flowing again."

"Sounds like a plan to me," said Seth.

"Why don't we just fly on Dauber? It would save a lot of time," said Melissa.

"Oh, you youngins will take any opportunity to make the way easier, won't ya? No, we won't be flying on this journey. Ears are on the ground, not in the air," said Bumpy.

"Tell that to Dauber," said Melissa. Dauber was already up in the air and flew directly over as Melissa pointed up.

"I do declare, what in tarnation might that be?" asked Bumpy.

"That there is Dauber, he flew us down from the top of the forest," said Fox.

"Miracles never cease, and quite a story that must be, but on the ground we shall continue now," said Bumpy.

Jimmy, who had already begun walking downstream, looked back at the group and shouted, "Listen to the leaf." He motioned with his hand for everyone to follow. "This way." And follow they did. Seth placed Bumpy into his shirt pocket. Fox trotted alongside Melissa, weaving in-between her legs when she got the notion. Dauber, of course, flew above, sometimes remaining in sight and sometimes not.

All of the travelers were excited to see what might lie beyond the river bend.

Seth caught up with Jimmy and the two had quite a conversation. Bumpy sat contentedly in Seth's shirt pocket, using the time to rest and dry out. Melissa and Fox routinely trailed a few yards behind, as it was nearly impossible to keep Fox from following her nose to every new scent.

Dauber could not resist utilizing his newfound strength and vigor. He flew up high and down low, in front of and behind, anywhere and everywhere his whims suggested. Before he got too far, however, he went back to the boulder with the healing water and took a long drink. He knew the journey might be a difficult one, and it was important to stay hydrated.

Chapter 20

The Terra Two

There were three bright, white, puffy clouds floating in the otherwise crystal blue sky. They were three of the laziest clouds to ever meander about on such a crisp fall day. One resembled a puppy dog holding a bone. The middle cloud looked like a man in an astronaut's suit when viewed from directly underneath, but to the eagle flying to the east, it looked more like a fish jumping out of the water. The third cloud, trailing quite far behind the other two, resembled no discernible shape at all—at least not to the few onlookers taking the time to imagine.

The eagle, having just caught a real fish of his own, landed on the tall pine in the middle of the state-owned acreage just north of Crystal Cove on Lake Ouachita. He would dine with one of the best views around. All the way down at the bottom of the tree, beneath the roots, sat two prominent members of the woods also having dinner.

The Terra Two would normally be hibernating this time of the year, or at the very least preparing their beds for the long winter ahead. Instead, they were having a nice meal of freshly dug grubs and vegetables while chatting about the day's new revelations.

The Terra Two were no ordinary box turtles. They were older than the lake itself and keener than the eyes of an eagle. They were the ones that wise critters came to for advice and adjudication. When there was a dispute to be settled, the Terra Two were the ones to do it. As odd as it may have seemed to have a judge and jury of two (as most juries consisted of an odd number), the Terra Two almost always came to a verdict. The few cases, never mentioned and barely remembered, where there was a dispute, were sent to the Council of Three.

Their given names, quite impossible to pronounce, had been supplanted with human monikers given to them by a young boy who found them years and years ago. That's how the Terra Two came to meet, in a little boy's wooden milk crate. He named them Kenneth and Geneva. Neither one of them looked like a Kenneth nor a Geneva, but the names stuck.

Geneva was an expert at finding the plumpest and tastiest worms, grubs, and vegetables. That was the main reason, so it is told, that Kenneth remained forever in the good graces of his beloved Geneva. It was also rumored this was why there was almost always unanimous agreement between the two.

"Where on earth did you find these English peas?" asked Kenneth. "They are as fresh as spring."

"There's more where those came from. In fact, there are all kinds of veggies still hangin' on the vines in pert' near every garden from here to town. Such a bumper crop that folks just left the extras for us, I reckon," said Geneva.

"Just be careful at that old woman's house on the corner with the giant red blooming camellia. She's thrown many of us in the garbage bin. I think that's why Uncle Vern turned up missin' a few years back. Ended up at the city dump and never found his way back. Probably buried so deep he couldn't dig himself out. Wretched woman."

"Horrible way to go. Gives me the heebie-jeebies thinkin' about being stuck so deep underground that you couldn't dig your way out."

"It could be worse than that for the rest of us if the Council of Three refuses to deal with all the revelations manifestin' around here lately," said Kenneth. He was becoming increasingly frustrated at not being able to get the last little pea out of its pod. Most years he would have eaten the whole thing, but now that food was so plentiful, he had become rather picky.

"What good would it do for them to say anything? What will be will be. We can't do nothin' about the prophecies—the true ones anyway."

"Do we just hibernate as usual?"

"Of course not. We do what every cold-blooded reptile should've always been a doin'. We remain thankful for the food we got. We spread joy and praises wherever we can, and we share the good news with anyone that'll listen."

"Ain't no one payin' attention. Most of em' can't even see us. The ones that can, can't hear us, and the one's that can hear us don't listen." The pea he had been working on finally burst through the membrane and flew all the way across the small burrow. Frustrated but determined, Kenneth slowly made his way to the tasty morsel.

"Nothin' worthwhile is ever easy," said Geneva. Always the practical one, having barely escaped the Great Depression alive, she ate the pods that Kenneth left behind. Frugality was her strong suit. "It is not for us to predict who is going to listen or act. We are simply to do."

"Do? As God is my witness that's all I've been doin' for the last seventy-plus years. I've been settling petty arguments between ungrateful souls from here to Mountain Pine."

"I know you have. I know it. Yes, sir, you certainly have worked hard all these years."

"And you right along with me."

"Yes, sir, I have. Right here next to you. And all I'm a sayin' is that we are not to judge the hearts of men. What's more, we may never know how much good our work has done to help humanity."

"True that, Mama. True that. But I still wish the Council would just shed a little light on the current happenings."

"And what light would that be?"

"For one, if the evil is upon us, we need to act. If those two youngins brought something wicked back with them into this world, we need to squash it," said Kenneth as he finally secured the pea under his right foot. He took a bite and snorted with delight.

"Don't you trust God enough to know that He has everything under control?"

"What if *we* are His control? What if we are supposed to do something?" Kenneth stopped with a look of wonder in his eyes. He licked his beak and said, "Mmm, wow, that was really good. The best pea I have ever had. Thank you, Mama."

"Don't thank me. One of the robins dropped it off this morning. On purpose, I do believe."

"You don't say? Probably tryin' to butter us up for somethin'"

"Or just bein' nice."

"We shall see. I for one, think it imperative that we share what we know with any and all who will heed. We have knowledge that the others do not and it's time we share what we know. Perhaps the robins or even the eagles will help us get the word out."

"You just sat there in your beautiful shell and said that no one listens to us anyway."

"And you sat there in your smooth, curvaceous, crustaceous shell and said we should proclaim the Good News to everyone."

"What exactly are we to say?" asked Geneva.

Kenneth moved back over to the remaining pile of food. "What we know. The truth." He dug through the delicacies that Geneva had collected, scrounging, digging, and pushing the less desirable fare to the side with his nose until he finally landed on a half-eaten carrot.

Before Kenneth could fully pull the carrot out of the pile, there was a loud thud outside the burrow. The ground shook and the tree above them creaked as it swayed from side to side. Clumps of dirt fell to the ground all around them as a few more roots sprung from the ceiling of their modest home.

When a minute passed with no more falling debris or pops and cracks, Geneva and Kenneth slowly stuck their feet and legs out of the safety of their hard shells. Their bodies remained motionless as their heads stuck out as far out as they would go.

Geneva fully extended her neck to the right and then up towards the ceiling, taking an assessment of the damage. Kenneth looked to the left and down, wondering if his food survived. Never before had they experienced such a quake.

Other than a little dirt and a few new low-hanging roots, there appeared to be no real harm done. They no sooner had begun to relax when it happened again. Both terrapenes retreated quickly back into their protective shields. More dirt fell and what little light had been entering their home under the tree was completely snuffed out.

Kenneth was the first one to speak. "You think this is a coincidence?"

"Not at all. Not one bit, my dear."

"Is that so? Then what say ye?"

In the quietest of whispers Geneva scratched out her message in the dirt. There was not enough light for Kenneth to see the markings, but his hearing was acute. By the sounds of the scratching, he knew that once again they were in agreement. It was time to get to work. They had a new mission. It did not matter to them if the Council was too scared or simply unwilling to get involved—they were going to sound the alarm. It was time everyone in Garland County had a chance to prepare for what was coming. And those who would listen would be ready.

In the now-quiet burrow, there was a loud crunch. Geneva gasped and retreated once again into her shell. She listened carefully and then another crunch, followed by yet another. Once she realized what the sound was, she sighed, "How can you eat at a time like this, K.P.?"

"Waste not want not, isn't that what you always say, Mama?"

"Go ahead and finish. You're gonna need all your strength to dig us out of here. Whatever caused that quake also collapsed our tunnels."

"Don't you worry none. If there's one thing I'm good at, it's clawing through dirt. I'll get us outta here."

"Our first order of business is to test our allies. We need to know who we can trust to spread the news. It's got to be someone that everyone knows and we need to do it before the weather turns. We haven't got much time. That seed the girl brought into this world must be destroyed before it sprouts, if it hasn't already. Once it begins growing, the evil will be much harder to stop."

Kenneth took his last bite of carrot and crawled over to his beloved. He extended his neck and rubbed her nose. "I got this, Mama. As soon as I get us out of here, we will find help. I have a feeling many of the other animals in the woods are already aligned with us. It won't be hard to find the chosen, because they will find us. The remnants of God's chosen will unite."

"That may be, but the evil one must know our inclinations, and this quake was an attempt to keep us quiet," said Geneva.

"Perhaps evil knows the times, but the wicked never take the time to know the hearts of the faithful. And that's why they shall fail."

Chapter 21
The Wall

"My feet are killing me. I knew we should have flown on Dauber. Who in their right mind would pass up flying on a supersized insect? A *friendly* supersized insect, at that," exclaimed Melissa.

"I haven't walked this far in, well, as long as I can remember," said Jimmy.

"Speaking of flying, I haven't seen Dauber in at least a few hours. You don't suppose he left us?" asked Seth.

"Maybe he got lost," added Melissa.

"If he did, he's clever and I'm sure he will find his way back to us," said Jimmy.

"I hope so. And soon."

"Dauber is loyal too, just like me and you," said Fox as she rubbed against Melissa's leg.

After hours of walking and talking, the group had become tired of both. The only sound that could be heard was the dirt beneath their feet. Fox had even stopped exploring the riverbed, choosing instead to trot steadily and quietly next to the others. She ignored the temptation to paw at the small rocks or dig in the soft sand. Their thoughts were absorbed with the task before them. The only problem was, most of them were not quite sure exactly what that task was.

They had left the boulder and its emerging spring miles ago. The riverbed, once hardly distinguishable from the surrounding landscape, had become deeper and wider. The change was so gradual that no one paid attention to the fact that the walls of the riverbank were now at least a full body-length deeper than Jimmy, the tallest one in the group. There was no mistaking that this was once the course of a mighty tributary.

Much like the Dead Woods, there was no other visible life to be found. No signs that anything living had ever been there. No shells, bones, driftwood—nothing but an empty riverway. Earlier in the day, Seth and Jimmy had discussed how animals might return and plants might spring up once the water began flowing again. No one was sure how long that would take. If the trickle out of the boulder remained constant, it could take months, if not years. If the trickle increased to a steady flow, it might take as little as a few weeks or days. No one could be sure.

Bumpy informed everyone how the living waters were essential to life and that anything was possible once the water spread. But not even Bumpy was privy to the future. He only knew the task that had been assigned to him, which had nothing to do with anything they had yet encountered. He was not told he would lose part of his leg in the Dead Woods or that he would need the living waters to restore his vigor. Yes, much of this journey was a mystery even to him.

Melissa, more than anyone else it seemed, had a calm sense of purpose. She had been through this world before and she had come out on the other side safe. She knew she was there for a reason even if that reason had not yet been fully defined. Her faith was strong and the others sensed it. Even Jimmy, who perhaps knew more about God, eternity, and the mysteries of the Bible than any of them, was almost envious of her trust and confidence. He was also thankful. It was going to take a lot of what Melissa exuded to finish the tasks before them, whatever those tasks might be.

As everyone wondered exactly what their role in this world was, Seth knew, at least in part, what he was there to do—and it was Jimmy that told him. While everyone else just heard Jimmy speaking gibberish in the fog, Seth had heard actual words. He never told anyone what Jimmy had spoken because he was not even sure what he heard was real. He also considered the possibility that the others were playing a joke on him. But once he found the boulder and the water sprang fourth, he knew the words were true. He also knew there was yet one more thing he was supposed to do. He did not know how or when, but he knew what. He, was going help bring back the Word, the Good News, as Jimmy uttered, to everyone in this world. He did not feel worthy of such a mission, he was not even sure the Word of God was true. Why would God choose him?

"What's that?" asked Melissa as she pointed ahead.

"It looks like the river ends or maybe it just makes a turn or something," said Jimmy.

"Hey, Fox, run and take a look up ahead, would you?" asked Seth.

Without saying a word or yapping a yap, Fox obliged. She darted off to inspect what lay ahead of them.

"I don't think we are going to be expected to walk much more. I, for one, am just about at my walking capacity," said Melissa.

Bumpy pushed his way out of Seth's pocket and used the breeze to lift up higher to get a better view of the surroundings. He fluttered higher than the riverbank and almost out of sight before gliding back down. He was quite adept at using the wind to control his movements. At moments he looked like a hummingbird hovering in place, and at other times, he resembled a small piece of paper surfing on the wind.

"There's something blocking the way and the dead trees are back, not too far from the riverbank," reported Bumpy. "I think we are back near the Dead Woods again."

"What's taking Fox so long?" asked Melissa.

Actually, Fox had not been gone that long, but she failed to return in her usual eager fashion. No alarms were sounded, however, because it was only a matter of minutes before they reached the end of the riverbed. Each of the travelers had become distracted with figuring out what exactly was blocking the way. Their imaginings of the challenge ahead were only hindered by what their limited farsightedness could see.

Even though Melissa was weary and her feet worn, the walk up to the barrier before them seemed effortless. There they were, at the bottom of a huge pile of limbs and sticks. It was gigantic—so tall that from the base one could not see the top.

Melissa said, "Funny, I thought for sure it was going to be a magical wall made up of some strange, never-before-seen substance. But it's just a bunch of sticks."

"It's a dam," said Jimmy.

"But who built it?" asked Seth.

"Beavers, of course."

Seth shook his head. "Beavers? It would take a gazillion beavers to construct this monstrosity."

"Or maybe a few hundred over many, many years," offered Melissa.

Jimmy rubbed the wood with his hand. The smooth, twisted limbs were pleasant to the touch. He pulled on one of the branches and nothing budged. Melissa and Seth tugged on a branch or two of their own to the same effect. The structure was firm and woven tightly together.

"I'm not about to climb over this thing," said Melissa.

"Me either. I say we wait for Dauber and fly over," said Seth.

"Otherwise, we're going to have to try climbing up the riverbank," said Jimmy, "which probably isn't going to happen because there is nothing to grab on to. If Dauber doesn't come back soon, we may be forced to head back to where the riverbank is more manageable."

"But that was miles ago," Melissa protested as she kicked the dam out of frustration. Within a matter of seconds, a huge creature stuck its head out of a hole directly above their heads.

"Hey, hey, hey, now that's no way to treat a work of art," said the creature.

The big beast, at least seven-foot-tall when standing upright, crawled out of its hole and scurried down the dam to greet the visitors. Its head was oddly small for such a large, plump body. Its brownish-purple ears were so large that they almost drug on the ground. Most of it was covered in orange fur, except for its ears and odd rear appendage that seemed so out of place it appeared to be surgically attached.

No one on the ground knew what type of greeting the thing had in mind, so they each took a few steps backward. There was no sense in running because, even with the strange, flat, rubbery thing attached to its rear-end, it was doubtful they could outrun it. Better to stand their ground and attempt to display a confident manner than a weak retreat.

Bumpy, who had been drifting, slowly made his way down in front of the creature. "Hi there, my name is Bumpy. My friends and I are on a journey of discovery and inspiration. We need to get to the Land of

Indulgences, or so we think, and the most economical way, it seems, would be to continue down this riverbed."

"I see," said the creature, who at first did not seem at all alarmed by a talking, floating leaf. Then came the scream. The shriekiest, loudest squeal of a scream anyone there had ever heard. It was emanating from another creature poking its head out of the same hole. "Well, so much for decorum," said the calmer of the two furry creatures.

After the second one climbed out of the wooden barrier, it stood on its hind feet in order to get a better look at the floating leaf. It sniffed, squinted, and even tried to touch Bumpy with one of its claws. Bumpy did not welcome the unwanted advances and so he lifted higher, out of reach.

"Extraordinary. Exquisite, I'd say. Wouldn't you, McClanahan?" the second creature demanded, more than asked.

"Yes, yes. Absolutely beautiful, but a bit blemished. Not perfect."

"Perfection is overrated, dear. It is the imperfection that adds character to this otherwise titillating find. Just look at the color. The curves. Ohhhh, the lines. The divine inspiration that was behind this deserves nothing short of applause," she said. The creature then sat on her rear and applauded Bumpy.

"Yes, applause is most deserved, Mackenzie." And he too sat and clapped his two paws together. They were not loud claps, because the webbing in-between their digits muffled the sound.

Bumpy, feeling a bit more secure, glided down and asked, "And what may I ask are the two of you?"

"It speaks! Dear Lord, it speaks," said Mackenzie. She rolled on her back and fanned herself with both of her rear webbed feet.

"Isn't it obvious what we are?" McClanahan turned towards the others for the first time. "We are beavers."

"Beavers? That makes all kinds of sense, but you're the oddest and the biggest beavers I've ever seen," said Jimmy.

"Well, I have never!" shouted Mackenzie.

"You might not want to insult the little woman. She's actually at the ideal weight for our kind," said McClanahan.

"Oh, no. I didn't mean fat, I just meant large. As in gigantic. Enormous. Larger than life."

Melissa waved at Jimmy to stop talking. "What he means to say is that beavers are little creatures where we come from. They have large flat tails, tiny ears, two buck teeth, and cute whiskers on their cheeks. They are not much bigger than a milk jug."

"What is a milk jug?" asked Mackenzie.

"It's a container that holds cow's milk."

"And a cow?" asked McClanahan.

"Never mind, it's really not important," said Seth. "Suffice to say we are very impressed by your size and color and ears. Now it makes sense how beavers of your sort could have built such an impressive structure!"

"Impressive. Did you hear what he said, McClanahan? He said impressive."

"Yes, Mackenzie, I'm less than five feet away from the boy, I heard what he said."

"Impressive, that is a good word. What else would you say about it?" asked Mackenzie.

"About the dam? I don't know. What else is there to say? It's big, sturdy, and really, really impressive."

"I see." Mackenzie was obviously not pleased with Seth's additional comments, but Melissa came to the rescue.

"It's beautiful. The interweaving of the wood pieces is like nothing I have ever seen. It's a work of art, actually."

"Did you hear that, McClanahan? She said it is a work of art. Go on dear, you're obviously the creative one in the group."

"Just look at how you managed to create a circular pattern in the weaving."

Mackenzie squealed with delight, "She noticed the circular pattern, McClanahan. Did you hear that?" She rose onto all four of her legs and ran to McClanahan. Standing nose-to-nose, she joyfully repeated, "She noticed!" She then turned back to Melissa. "That was my idea. I thought why not make it more than just a horizontal sculpture."

"Sculpture?" repeated both Seth and Jimmy somewhat incredulously. McClanahan quickly quieted them by shaking his head and waving his paws in a motion indicating to proceed with caution.

"What else do you notice? What is your name?" asked Mackenzie.

"I'm Melissa. That's my brother Seth over there, and this is our friend Jimmy. You already met Bumpy, he's the leaf. And somewhere around here are our friends. There's Fox, she's a fox, and then there's Dauber, flying around, I guess."

"And?" asked Mackenzie.

"And what?" responded Melissa.

"Sit down, boys," said McClanahan to the others. "This could take a while. It's been a long time since we've had visitors to the gallery." Seth and Jimmy sat on the base of the dam as Bumpy continued to drift around.

"Well, go on dear girl," said Mackenzie. Mackenzie was hoping that Melissa would see the symbol discretely interwoven with the sticks in the dam. In fact, the pattern, which was in the shape of a large cross, was so subtle that no one had ever noticed it.

Melissa glanced at the others and shrugged her shoulders. She then backed up from the dam in order to get a better view. After a moment, she backed up even further. Her eyes widened and she began shaking her head in disbelief. "That's simply ingenious, it's a cross."

"She spotted it, McClanahan. She has the eye. She has an amazing eye. She's a real artist, this one."

Seth and Jimmy stood up and walked over to where Melissa was standing. They looked in the same direction as her, but did not see anything remotely out of the ordinary.

"Okay, I give up. What's the big deal?" asked Seth.

"Don't you guys see it? It's right there," Melissa pointed.

"Sorry, I don't see it, either," said Jimmy.

Mackenzie quickly scuttled over to Melissa and whispered in her ear. "Don't bother to tell them, dear. You can lead a patron to the museum, but you can't make them see the art." Everyone heard her, mostly because she wanted them to, but also because a beaver her size was incapable of whispering.

"Now, dear, don't be rude to our guests," said McClanahan. "They may not want to see the rest of your work."

"There's more?" asked Jimmy.

"Of course, there is more! Once the dam was completed many, many years ago, there was little else for us to do. I must admit, she's quite good," said McClanahan.

"How very kind of you to say so, McClanahan. He's not so bad, either. Where I excel in sculpting and weaving—the finer arts, you might say—he outclasses the best whittlers you have ever seen. Whittling may not be a fine art per se, but it does impress the local folk."

"The local folk? There are more of you?" asked Seth.

"There are more, yes. Not like us, but there are plenty of others in the town on the other side of the dam. I dare say you would not want to venture into their territory, however. You will not find them to be as enlightened as Mack and I."

"Who are these other folks?" asked Melissa.

"We call them the Mara People," said Mackenzie.

"Not immediately on the other side, but not too far down the canyon," added McClanahan.

"Yes, they live in the actual banks of the old river."

Bumpy drifted in front of McClanahan and said, "It's very smart of them to have had this dam constructed, because sooner or later the water is going to arrive here."

The two beavers laughed heartily and McClanahan said, "Water? There hasn't been any water in these parts for longer than we have been alive, and no rain to speak of, either. Not a cloud in the sky. Ever."

"The leaf is right, the water is going to come and it's not going to come from the sky," said Seth. Both beavers rushed over to him, who now had their undivided attention. "It's coming out of the ground—or a boulder, as it were. It was just a trickle when we left, but I'm pretty sure it's going to pick up the pace in the coming days."

"A boulder. You don't say," said McClanahan.

"That's exactly what he said," said Mackenzie.

"We must warn the Mara People."

"Good luck with trying to tell that group of commoners anything," said Mackenzie. "They won't listen."

"Like I said, it's a good thing you built this dam to protect the city," said Bumpy.

The two beavers looked at each other and sighed. "We did not build it to protect the city. We were simply bored. We've never even seen more water than one could drink with dinner. How in the world could we be expected to build something to withstand a wall of water?" asked McClanahan.

"No, it's a work of art," said Mackenzie, "and art needs no function other than to be beautiful. I'm quite sure the water will penetrate this thing quicker than an arrow penetrates the air."

Melissa said, "We have to warn everyone. They will have to abandon their homes and find some other place to live."

"What's the quickest way to this city?" asked Jimmy.

"Through the wall of art, of course," said McClanahan.

"Delightful. Might you all have time to see my, I mean *our*, beautiful work? We have the most influential gallery in the entire region," said Mackenzie.

"Don't you think there are more pressing matters at hand?" asked Seth.

Melissa elbowed her brother and said, "Of course we have time. It's on the way, right?"

"Not only does she have an eye, but she has superior intelligence as well," said Mackenzie.

Seth looked at his sister and rolled his eyes.

"This way, careful not to slip," said Mackenzie as she began to scale the wall back to the hole from which she originally emerged. Seth went first after Mackenzie, followed by Melissa and then Jimmy. Bumpy alternated in-between. The last to climb up was McClanahan.

McClanahan, as he took a look back, realized something that Mackenzie did not. If the water did come and the riverbed did fill, their masterpiece—and their home, no less—would be submerged. It is true that they were beavers, but they had never even swum in water before. What if they were not able to swim? What if the water washed everything downstream? He was not one to let worry get the best of him, but he could not say the same for Mackenzie—and that is what worried him most.

Chapter 22

INSIDE THE ART

Inside the hallowed halls of the beaver dam were many rooms. Each one contained meticulously carved sculptures, handcrafted baskets, or transformed treasures collected from the riverbed.

Melissa, never one to voluntarily tour a museum or art gallery, found herself mesmerized by all the works of art. How could a beaver with webbed hands and feet ever accomplish such a thing? When she came across a giant form hanging over her head, she reached up to feel a long translucent tentacle protruding downward. Seth scolded her for trying to touch the flying jellyfish—or at least that's what he thought it was—but the beavers were so delighted by her enthusiasm that they encouraged her to touch anything and everything.

"I guess you are wondering what those translucent waves trailing behind the main form are made of," said McClanahan. "Many years ago, some of the wood pieces still had resin in them. I extracted what I could and Mackenzie did the rest."

Melissa said, "It's beyond words. I've never seen anything like it. But why do you do this? Who sees your work?"

"Only a few have ventured to these parts, and even fewer to our home here. Unfortunately, not many have gotten to see the collection," said McClanahan.

"Then why do it? What's the reward? Every artist needs an audience," said Seth.

"That may be," said Mackenzie. "But we are simply thankful for not only the opportunity to create, but also the ability and the desire to do so. I, for one, am thrilled to see your reactions, but I also know that busy beavers are happy beavers. Isn't that right, dear?" Her husband acknowledged by simply nodding in agreement.

"What a great perspective," said Melissa.

"I don't know, I think I would need a more immediate response myself," said Seth. "All of this work and no one to appreciate it. No thanks."

The beavers looked at one another and made a noise that was either the equivalent of a chuckle or a grunt. No one was quite sure and no one wanted to clarify.

Jimmy, although very impressed with all of the pieces on display, was most awed by the hardwood floors that connected one room to another. The planks were smooth and seamlessly connected. It was like a carpenter had cut them to precisely match. They had been polished and were a beautiful dark burgundy color.

Bumpy, who had made his way back into Seth's front pocket, noticed the light more than anything else. Somehow the beavers had managed to create skylights that illuminated the pathways. Each work of art was also illuminated by a spotlight. The best he could surmise is that they were able to bounce the light off of reflective surfaces until it reached the desired area. It reminded him of his days hanging on the oak tree and how light seemed to filter down and bounce from leaf to leaf as if it had a life of its own. He could not help but wonder how the beavers managed to see at night. Surely, they would never burn a torch in a place like this.

"Here we are," said Mackenzie. "The grand finale before heading out to the other side of the riverbed. One of my personal favorites."

"Wow!" exclaimed Seth.

"What was that, dear?" asked Mackenzie, looking Seth square in the eyes.

"The staircase, it's amazing. It's like right out of the neoclassical period," said Seth. Melissa and Jimmy gave each other a quizzical look. Mackenzie stopped in her tracks, lifted her head, and put her right foot up to her throat, as if to stop herself from gasping.

"You have done it, young man. This is the first time in eons I have seen someone render her speechless," said McClanahan.

"I'm sorry. I didn't mean to say anything offensive. I just think it's beautiful. The workmanship that must have gone into this is nothing short of mind-boggling. You did this all on your own?"

Since Mackenzie was still unable to speak, McClanahan spoke up on her behalf. "Yes, she did indeed. I mean, I selected some of the wood, but she did all the real artistry."

Mackenzie was finally able to speak. "That is what I was going for—the neoclassical period. The neoclassical period seemed so overshadowed by the romantic period. Undeservedly so, I do believe."

"Yes, perhaps in painting and literature, but not in architecture and sculpture. Perhaps that's why you are so drawn to it," said Seth.

"Drawn to it, pardon the pun," laughed Melissa. When no one else laughed, she looked at Seth and grimaced. "Since when did you become an expert on art?"

"It's a required course in college. I'm not an expert, but I know what I like. And this is extraordinary."

"I am most flattered by your gracious praise, Seth," said Mackenzie. "Perhaps you would like to be the first to take the stairs out to the other side of the dam?"

"She means the first one *ever*," said McClanahan. "No one has ever walked the entire thing before. We ourselves have never even been to the other side since this was originally constructed."

"A prophet told us to prepare a way, that a time would come when strangers from a far land would need to travel this way. And well, here you are it seems," said Mackenzie.

"But why didn't you say anything earlier?" Jimmy asked. "You never mentioned any prophecy."

Mackenzie said, "We had to be sure, did we not? We were told that two young ones would see the way. Melissa saw the pattern on the front and Seth has identified the staircase. I myself have not a clue what

Neoclassical' means. It has been so long since I heard the term that in my own head, I had been pronouncing it the Knowclass Period. As that sounded more astute, wouldn't you agree?"

"No class? That sounds like the opposite of astute," said Jimmy.

"No dear, Knowclass. As in you must know things and have class in order to see it," said Mackenzie.

"I see," said Jimmy.

"But do you?"

"Well, I do now."

"How very exciting!" exclaimed Mackenzie. Looking at Seth, she continued, "You should be the first to climb the stairs to the other side."

"I would be honored, but I think we should wait on our friends."

"Don't you worry about them," said McClanahan. "We will send them along after you, should they come this way. There is little time to waste if the water decides to start pouring forth."

"Would you mind too terribly if I waited here for Fox? And then we could continue on?" asked Melissa.

Dauber and Fox had gone over and around the dam hours earlier. Melissa was right to worry about them, as they would soon find out. The Mara People did not have many visitors and there was good reason.

"Your lost friends will find you, of this I have no doubt. There is but one trail: the riverbed itself. And getting lost would take more skill than any of you have, I should think," Mackenzie assured them.

Bumpy peeked out of Seth's pocket and said, "They are correct. We should continue on. We must warn the people. Fox and Dauber will understand. Besides, maybe they've already found a way to the other side and are waiting on us."

"I agree," said Seth. "There is something I'm supposed to find, and I have no idea where it might be. We need to get going and I need everyone's help."

"This is the first we have heard of this, Seth. What are we supposed to be looking for?" asked Jimmy.

"Why are you keeping secrets from us?" asked Melissa.

"It wasn't a secret. I just wasn't sure of the details, that's all. Now I know. It all makes sense."

"Well, would you mind filling us in?"

"Yes, of course. On the way. Let's go." Seth proceeded to walk up the stairs. Melissa and Jimmy followed.

Seth stopped and looked back, "Aren't you coming with us?"

"I'm afraid not," said McClanahan. "We have much work to do here. Apparently, we have a flood to prepare for."

"Will we see you again?" asked Seth.

"We certainly hope so. We never like to leave a story in the middle," said McClanahan.

Mackenzie made her way over to Seth and handed him a small wooden stake. "We were told to give this to the one who deciphered the signs. You and the girl have both had a part in doing so. Mack made it himself to exact specifications. We are not sure what it is for, but only that you will know when the time is right to use it. Guard it with your life. Take it with you to where you come from as it has no usefulness here. That's all we know."

Melissa moved in to get a closer look, "What is it?"

"It is the hardest wood in the five realms," answered McClanahan. "Nothing that can grow is stronger."

"We will take good care of it," said Seth. He placed the smooth, tapered stake into his backpack.

Melissa smiled warmly and said, "Thank you for inviting us into your home and for providing us such a grand exit."

"You are quite welcome. Be careful on the other side. We rarely encounter those who live there but when we have, it's been rather frustrating," said McClanahan.

"What do you mean, frustrating?" asked Jimmy.

"Let's just say that it's rather hard to pin them down on anything. Pay very little attention to what anyone says and more attention to what they do. And even then, you must rely heavily on what you already know."

"Are they totally untrustworthy?" asked Melissa.

"You may find a few honest souls, but just don't depend on it," said McClanahan.

"You all will be fine. Trust in each other and what you know to be true," said Mackenzie.

With that final word of advice, the four travelers ascended the elegantly crafted stairs, the first to ever do so. They felt a little like nobility, especially Seth. But the feeling would not last long. They had come so far in this world already, yet it felt like their journey was only just beginning.

"Since no one else asked, I'm just going to throw this out there. Why have we been climbing *up* the stairs for the last ten minutes?" asked Melissa.

"How do you know it's been ten minutes?" asked Jimmy. "You don't have a watch on."

Seth said, "She has a pretty good sense of time. Always has."

"That's not the point. We have been going up. Shouldn't we be going down?" Melissa asked.

"I just assumed we had to go up in order to go down," said Jimmy.

Melissa disagreed, "That makes no sense."

"It could make sense in the right situation," said Seth. "Maybe we need to go up and over something and then back down to the ground level."

Melissa accepted the answer but was still agitated about something.

"What's bugging you, Sis?"

"I just find it odd that they didn't come with us. It's not like they had to go all the way. They could have come to the end of the stairs with us and then said their goodbyes."

Bumpy decided to chime in, "Are you suggesting they have ulterior motives? Or that something is awry, lassie?"

Melissa looked at the leaf, bewildered. "Lassie?"

"It means young girl, I think it's an Irish word," said Jimmy.

"All I'm suggesting is that it should cause one to pause, that's all," said Melissa. "We should be careful, just in case. The last time I was in this world, I learned to be as gentle as a dove and as wise as a serpent."

"That's not a bad idea. We'll be careful," said Jimmy.

"Bumpy, why don't you flutter above and make sure everything looks okay?" said Seth.

"I use the wind to move around and there isn't the slightest breeze in this place. Wish I could be of more help."

"It'll be fine everyone," said Jimmy. "Let's just take it one step at a time and keep an eye on one another."

If the ascension had been slow going before, it now felt as slow as a snail's pace, or so it felt to Seth. He tried to find a good time to bring up what the Foghorses had revealed to him while they were up in the clouds over the Dead Woods, but he would rather be looking at everyone face-to-face and not in a line going up some stairs. He planned to tell them once they were out on the riverbed.

Though his sister may not have realized it yet, Seth had a moment of recognition last month. He believed that the God of the Bible might indeed be the creator of the universe. He might even be able to grasp that Jesus was the Son of God. But he was not quite ready to proclaim it from the rooftops. He needed to know more. He still had too many doubts and too little faith. He wanted the knowledge that Jimmy had, but he also knew that it would take time. Jimmy had spent many years studying and reading the Bible. Seth also wished he could be as confident as his sister. She didn't seem to need anything more than her faith. Seth admired them both, but he also could not help who he was. He knew that this was his journey and that the answers he needed were not too far away.

"Hey. Hey, Seth! Are you with us?" Melissa was practically yelling. When he finally heard her, he stopped walking.

"What?" asked Seth.

"Jimmy needs your help up ahead."

Seth passed Melissa and climbed a couple of more steps until he reached Jimmy, who was crouching down.

"What's up?" asked Seth.

"Have a look," Jimmy pointed in front of him. The stairs that they had been climbing came to an abrupt end. No more steps. There they were, in the middle of the dam with a gap of air below them. There was no way to continue ahead without falling to certain death below.

The three of them rested on the final few steps and stared ahead. Melissa shook her head as if she knew something like this was going to happen. Seth put his hand on his chin and thought hard. Jimmy sat and did the same.

After a minute passed, Melissa took it upon herself to start walking back down the stairs. "Well, this was a big waste of time. I knew those beavers were up to something!"

"What is happening?" asked Bumpy who's view was not quite as good as the rest.

"They're gone. The stairs. They just disappeared. There are no stairs, so we've got to go back the way we came," said Melissa.

"But how can this be? Perhaps it is too dark for human eyes to see. Lift me up, youngin'" said Bumpy.

Seth obliged the leaf. He did not figure the leaf could remedy the current predicament, but it would not hurt to let him see the situation more clearly. Bumpy, after seeing the missing steps, was just as perplexed as everyone else. And true to Seth's prediction, the leaf could not offer any solutions.

"What happens if the steps we are on now just vanish into thin air?" asked Melissa nervously. "What happens to us?"

"I refuse to believe that those beavers meant us any harm," said Seth. "I don't think they sent us here on a suicide mission."

"Simmer down everyone," said Bumpy. "There must be an easy peasy lemon squeezy solution to be found."

"Easy for you to say," said Melissa. "Wind or not, you just float to the ground. Us on the other hand—easy peasy lemon *squashy*!"

Jimmy said, "So far, we're fine. Let's just take some time and try to figure this out. I tend to agree with Seth. I don't think the beavers meant us any harm. I think it's another test. They seemed to be really into tests. You two saw the signs. Maybe there's another sign of some sort."

Everyone sat, huddled as close together as possible, and looked around. It was fairly dark except for a dim light illuminating the stairs directly behind them. Not much else could be seen.

"I am surprised it's so dark here. The beavers had everything lit so well below," said Bumpy.

"True. It's not like Mackenzie not to have every inch of these stairs fully spotlighted," said Seth.

"It is her masterpiece, after all," said Melissa.

"You're right," said Jimmy. "The stairs were very well lit up until this point. And the way they utilized the light is nothing less than miraculous. How in the world did they get all that light to shine through this huge structure, hitting just the right points? Maybe we need that wood stake thing they gave you."

Seth shook his head, "No. She said it was to be used back home. If we trust them, we have to believe what they said was true."

Jimmy stood and walked back up to where the stairs had ended. He then turned back and asked Melissa a question: "So just how good is your sense of time?"

"I'm usually right within three minutes. It's a gift."

"It's true. I've lost many a bet with her," said Seth.

Jimmy asked, "What time do you think it was when we started? Now that I think of it, they were kind of stalling, and then all of a sudden, they were ready for us to go. There were many more rooms full of art they could have showed us, so why stop when they did?"

"I would guess it was about twenty minutes to noon, in our world. Not sure what time it would be here," said Melissa.

"That would make it noon now, right?"

"Yes, I think so."

"Noon. That's a specific time of day," said Jimmy. "Give me your backpack, Seth."

"Why?"

"Just give it to me."

"You better not lose it." Seth slipped his arms through his backpack and handed it reluctantly to Jimmy.

Jimmy took the backpack and walked to the very last step. He looked up and down, paused for a moment, and then rubbed his eyes with his free hand.

"What is it, Jimmy?" asked Seth.

"Forgive me, but I have a gut feeling—"

"Nooooooo," yelled Seth. But it was too late. Jimmy had tossed the backpack down the dark chasm below. Everyone quickly joined Jimmy on the last step and looked down. But there was nothing. No backpack.

"Why did you do that? I had important things in there. That wasn't cool!" exclaimed Seth angrily.

"Relax, Bro, it's not like it matters right now," said Melissa. "If we don't find a way out of here, what difference does it make if you still have your backpack?"

"We will find a way out of here, but I was hoping not at the expense of all my stuff!"

"You're correct. We will indeed find a way out of here. And all thanks to your backpack," said Jimmy.

"What do you mean?" asked Seth.

"Your backpack is right there," said Jimmy, pointing below them.

"What are you talking about? There's nothing there."

"I do believe Jimmy is correct," said Bumpy.

"How did you know that?" Jimmy asked Bumpy.

"If I can hear a leaf hit the ground from thirty feet high, I can most certainly hear a big bag hit a wooden step only a few feet below."

"You're telling me that my backpack is sitting right below us on a step?" asked Seth.

"Yes, siree. I don't know exactly how it works, but I think it's like a lot of tricks that magicians employ. They call it smoke and mirrors but, in this case, I'd say its light and mirrors."

"So how do we get down there?" asked Melissa.

"We jump," answered Jimmy.

"After you."

"Sure, no problem." Jimmy, very sure of himself, sat on the edge of the last step with his legs dangling. He then scooted as far as he could while holding on to the edge with his hands.

"Are you sure about this?" asked Seth.

"I'm taking it slow. I'm not really going to just jump. Watch me and do exactly as I do. Melissa should go after me, and then you, Seth."

Both Melissa and Seth nodded in agreement. Jimmy, still seated, held onto the edge of the stairs with his feet hanging over. He then crossed his left arm over to his right side and slid his body over the edge. He now faced the others as he held his upper body above the step by stiffening his arms and locking his elbows. He gave the siblings a wink right before he lowered the rest of his body over the edge until only his hands were left holding him up. He made one last comment before completely dropping out of sight. "See, nothing to it."

"I'm sure you all heard that loud thud," said Bumpy.

"Yes, we did. Thank you, Bumpy. Is everything alright down there?" asked Seth.

As Seth was looking over the edge of the stairs, he saw something quickly coming at him. He fell backward, catching his backpack. "You could have warned me first."

"I just wanted to send up some proof. Okay, Melissa, your turn. Just ease over the edge like I did and I'll be here to catch you. It's not that far."

Melissa looked at Seth and said, "Here goes." She repeated the same motions as Jimmy and quickly disappeared out of sight. Seth, with Bumpy and backpack in tow, followed right after his sister. After everyone got their footing and a good look at their surroundings, they were ready continue. They were no longer going up the stairs. They were now descending.

The staircase was far less ornate on the way down, but was still encased by a very wide, smooth handrail. It was several minutes into their descent when Jimmy got the idea to slide the rest of the way down on the railing. It would not be long before they reached the door that would open to the outside of the dam. The angle was not too steep and everyone was ready for a little fun. Jimmy went first and they could hear him laughing long after he disappeared into the darkness. Melissa went second, followed by Seth who promised not to crush Bumpy. Bumpy, being the wise leaf he was, insisted on taking the ride down the banister while safely tucked away in Seth's backpack.

Chapter 23

THUMP IN THE NIGHT

After sliding down the beautifully carved banister, they were greeted by a small opening that had been covered by tumbleweeds and dead vines. It led outside to a deep, long, wide ravine under a clear, blue sky. Exiting the dam—or museum, or whatever it was the beavers had built—left everyone feeling pensive. Everything was so much larger than they had expected or were accustomed to. The continued journey suddenly began to feel overwhelming.

Melissa was the first to comment that this part of the riverbed reminded her of the Grand Canyon. The sides of the towering walls were flat and sheer in some places, and in other areas they were craggy and terraced. Everyone, including Bumpy, who was happy to be free-floating in the breeze once again, took in the landscape. On one side the walls were a deep orange with highlights of amber and gold. On the flat landings, where terraces jutted out, the dirt was dark purple. The edges glimmered as if lined with copper.

There were many tall pillars on some of the terraces that had been carved out by wind and water. They looked so thin that a simple touch could topple them over. The other side of the canyon, now in the shadows, was far less colorful, dressed in grays and browns. There seemed to be little or no life, much the same as the more colorful side. No trees or plants that they could see. No birds in the air or lizards scurrying about the ground below. It was eerily quiet.

"The canyon valley will soon be in the shadows," said Jimmy. "We probably need to find a safe place to hunker down till morning."

Melissa said, "Oh, no, if it's getting dark here, it must be getting late at home, too. Please tell me that this is not going to be a repeat of our last visit to Grandma's house."

"What can we do?" asked Seth. "We can't go home until we get home. I don't even know how we got home last time, but however it was, I don't think we had much to do with it."

"They're going to be so worried about us."

"And they're never going to trust us to come out here on our own again."

"We can't worry about that right now," said Jimmy. "Unfortunately, there is nothing we can do about it. I'll take the heat if it comes to that. Now let's get going. We need to find shelter before it gets pitch black down here." Jimmy led the way as the rest followed behind.

Bumpy floated down in the midst of the travelers as they walked. "Don't worry, I'm the one who was told to make sure you all made it here, and I was also told that it was not time for those in our world to know this world."

"What does that mean?" asked Melissa.

"I don't know exactly, youngin', but I speculate that whatever is goin' on with us here isn't supposed to be too obvious as to start people questioning yet."

"Yet?" asked Jimmy.

"There will be a time when no one can deny a battle is brewin'. What? You thought this here journey was just about your personal enlightenment?" Bumpy laughed heartily. "Isn't that just like young folk to think the world revolves around them? *Two* worlds, in this case."

"I did think it was about me discovering the truth of the universe and existence and the meaning of life—" said Seth.

"Yeah, yeah, yeah, there's that," said Bumpy. "You would have to be a blind fool not to have figured out a lot of that by now. Not everyone gets to ride a big fish and live to tell the tale, or talk to angels, or, in your case, travel to this place. Don't ask me why the Creator does things the way He does. I pretty much reckon He is willing to do just about anything to get the attention of those He loves. And from what I've heard, He's been doin' just that for thousands of years. He won't stop here."

Jimmy responded, "If Jesus didn't get their attention, I'm not sure anything will." He continued as he walked. "There's no precedent for any of this in the Bible. Jonah was swallowed by a big fish, sure, but that was in real time in the real world."

"There were those three dudes that went into that really hot furnace and walked out the other side alive," said Seth.

"Still, that was in the real world, real time," said Jimmy.

Melissa said, "Okay, but who is to say that other people haven't had otherworldly experiences like this. The Bible didn't record every single thing that has happened in the history of mankind or the world. Maybe this has happened before, but it's just not in the Bible."

"I don't know," said Jimmy shaking his head.

"I don't either," added Bumpy.

"But what I do know is this. Jimmy wasn't speaking gibberish in the fog when we were riding on Dauber," said Seth.

"What do you mean?" asked Melissa.

"He said two things that were very distinct and clear," said Seth.

"Why didn't you tell us this before?"

"At first, I thought y'all were playing a joke on me. When I found out that it wasn't a joke, I wanted to make sure that what I heard was really what I heard."

"What do you mean?" asked Jimmy.

"The first thing you said was to find the boulder in the creek and to hit it with a stick. So, I reluctantly hit the boulder with a stick. I didn't really believe, but I guess I did believe a bit, because anything in this world is possible. Anyway, when the water came out, that's when I knew for sure that what you said in the fog was for real."

Bumpy floated down in front of Seth, "And what was the other thing he said?"

"The other thing he said was to find the twelve."

"And?" asked Melissa.

"There was also something about bringing back the Word to this world with the twelve. Find the twelve and bring the Word."

Melissa looked at Bumpy, "Do you know what that means?"

"Heck if I know, kiddo."

Bumpy, feeling somewhat inept, lifted above the walkers to help in another way. Without Fox, it was up to him to scout out the path ahead. But not even a leaf can see in the dark. He, like Jimmy, was beginning to get worried—not for himself, but for the others. Bumpy was used to the elements. Having spent his whole life hanging on a tree, he was subject to fierce wind, heavy rains, and one time even hard sleet pelted him. If the canyon got cold, his fellow travelers would be in danger, because unlike him, they needed shelter.

"I don't know what or who the twelve are, obviously. I figure we will know when we get there," said Seth.

"Get where?" asked Melissa.

Jimmy saw Seth getting frustrated with his sister and decided to step in. "I think what Seth is saying is that we have a clue and the rest will be filled in as we go. I agree, I think it will be clear when the time comes. Let's just keep our eyes and ears open." Melissa must have been satisfied with Jimmy's answer because she did not pursue her line of questioning any further.

The three of them continued walking deeper into the canyon. The riverbed, which had been wide and shallow before the dam, had now become very deep. It wound and turned so many times it was nearly impossible to know whether they were headed north, south, east, or west. Since the sun was setting, the path became dark and full of shadows. It was very clear that soon they would all be walking blind.

"I don't suppose you brought a flashlight in that backpack of yours?" Jimmy asked Seth.

"I wish."

"What are we going to do when the sun goes down completely?" asked Melissa.

Jimmy looked up to find Bumpy and asked, "How's it looking up there?"

Bumpy floated back down and answered, "As far as I can tell, it's pert near the same as far as the eye can see. I don't see any life at all."

"What about something that we could use to make camp for the night?" asked Jimmy.

"Just more of what you see now," said Bumpy.

"If you're tired of floating around, my pocket's here waiting for you," said Seth.

"I reckon I'll take you up on that offer. This breeze is very drying on my membranes. Not much moisture in the air." Seth held his shirt pocket open as Bumpy made a perfect landing.

They continued walking until the path was completely dark on both sides. There would be no choice but to stop and wait until morning. It would be too dangerous to walk in the dark. Melissa, exhausted, found a rock and sat. Seth took his backpack off and used it as a headrest on the ground. Jimmy leaned against the canyon wall as he contemplated what to do next. Even though they were all in this together, and Seth was technically a legal adult, Jimmy felt responsible for their well-being and safety. The pressure was all on him, whether or not the teens saw it that way.

"I miss Fox," said Melissa.

"Me too," said Seth.

Jimmy agreed, "Yeah, she's quite the little personality, isn't she?"

"If you only knew," said Melissa. "When I first met her, she was the most innocent, unassuming creature I had ever encountered. Don't get me wrong, she drove me crazy for the first few hours. I just couldn't get used to all the optimism. But she grew on me."

"How did you meet?" asked Jimmy.

"In the Dead Woods. I think she saved my life no less than three times. There was the time when the vampire moss tried to cover me. She had warned me about it, but I didn't listen."

"You? Not listening? Never," teased Seth.

"And then there was the Land of Indulgences. Wow. That was scary. I basically went into some sort of trance after eating this infected fruit. They say no one ever leaves the Land of Indulgences, but I guess whoever said that never met Fox. Where is she?" Melissa looked very concerned.

Jimmy came over and sat next to her.

"She will be alright. You know the saying, 'as clever as a fox.' There's a reason why people say that."

"I hope you're right."

"I know we might have bigger things to worry about, but is anyone else getting hungry?" asked Seth.

"Weird, now that you mention it, I'm not hungry at all," said Melissa.

"That is strange. We've been gone a while," said Jimmy.

"Last time we were in this world, we never really got hungry. Maybe it was all the fruit I felt compelled to eat in the Land of Indulgences."

"I remember getting very thirsty in the Salt Lands—I almost died of dehydration," said Seth.

Jimmy said. "Yes, things are a little different here, off-kilter a bit. Now that we are talking about it, I haven't had anything to drink since the boulder and I wasn't really even thirsty then. Not thirsty now, either."

"Me either," said Melissa. "I'm starting to feel a chill in the air. I'm not dressed for this."

"What's in that backpack of yours, Seth? Anything else we can use?" asked Jimmy.

Seth tried to answer as nonchalantly as possible. "I wish there was. I didn't know we were going to be camping in the middle of the Grand Canyon."

"Then what's in there? Why would you bring a backpack if you didn't bring anything useful?" asked Melissa.

"That's a good question, Sis. If you will recall, I had to bring Bumpy in something, and I brought the candy bar that we used for the vultures. Other than that, I just have a couple of books and—"

"Books! Why would you bring books?" asked Melissa.

"To read, of course. You know I love to read, and I thought I could kick back in the canoe and read in the sun."

The truth was, Seth did bring a book. But that book was tossed out in order to make room for all the treasure he loaded into his pack at the table of illusions. He knew deep down in his heart that he should not have taken anything off that table, but he could not resist. Nothing on the table belonged to him, and in fact, it was nothing less than stealing. He rationalized that he would use his newfound wealth to help those less fortunate, but what started out in his mind as a donation to the needy had turned into his college fund, a new car, and perhaps a little something for his parents and sister. There would of course be some left over for the poor, but even that was dwindling with each passing hour.

"Books! No wonder it was so heavy," said Jimmy.

"I'm the one that has to carry it," said Seth. "Don't worry about what I have. Just worry about yourselves!"

"Gee. Touchy, touchy," said Melissa. "Scoot over, I'm getting cold." Melissa sat down next to her brother in order to shield herself from the decreasing temperatures. He quickly shoved his pack further to the side, away from his sister. He didn't want her to feel the odd shapes in his pack and start asking more questions.

Jimmy found a rock to sit on, not far away from the other two. No one could see the worry on his face because the sun had finally set. It was dark and would only get darker as the night went on. Everyone sat in silence, each contemplating what to do next.

Seth once again rationalized taking the treasure because he knew that if anyone showed up, he could pay them to take their little party to safety. It was good to have money, he thought. The treasure he held would eventually save them, he just knew it.

Melissa considered calling out to Fox. Maybe she would hear her and come running to their rescue. But she knew that if Fox was anywhere close by, she would have come already. No one was more heroic or caring than Fox. No, Fox was nowhere near, and Melissa knew this. It made her terribly sad and lonely. If only she had waited until Fox returned. She felt guilty for leaving without her.

Jimmy prayed silently to himself. He then tried to think of a scripture that would build them up at a time like this. He thought of Psalm 23 and laughed aloud at the obviousness of it.

"What's so funny?" asked Seth.

"Even though I walk through the valley of the shadow of death, I will fear no evil, for you are with me; your rod and your staff, they comfort me."

"That's funny? Walking through the valley of the shadow of death, is that what this is?" "Maybe it's more ironic than funny. That's a proverb, right?" asked Melissa.

"It's in Psalm 23. That should be your next thing to memorize. It comes in handy at times like this," said Jimmy.

Bumpy suddenly pushed himself out of Seth's pocket and exclaimed, "Hey, does anyone else feel that?"

"Feel what?" asked Melissa.

"That thumping."

"Thumping?" asked Jimmy.

"Yes, thumping," repeated Bumpy.

"Not me," said Melissa.

"Me either," said Seth.

"Are you sure it's not Seth's heart pounding out of fear?"

"My heart is not pounding, Melissa!"

"No, I know the difference between the rhythm of the heart and what I'm feeling now," said Bumpy.

"Where is it coming from?" asked Jimmy.

"The ground."

"Is it coming from the way we came or the way we are going?"

"I'm not sure. Is it possible to walk a little further down?"

"I guess if we all stick together and keep to the right along the wall. And go slowly," said Jimmy.

"Well, what are we waiting for?" said Bumpy.

"No way!" said Seth. "I'm not walking in a canyon in the pitch black. One wrong step and we could fall hundreds of feet to our death!"

"We are at the bottom already. I doubt it goes any lower," said Jimmy.

"You don't know that. It's not worth risking."

"So do you want to spend the night here without shelter or protection?" asked Melissa. "I'm willing to take the chance on walking in the dark. Let's go."

Melissa enthusiastically, if not irrationally, jumped up and immediately began walking. She kept her hand on the side of the canyon wall and proceeded forward to what she hoped was a warm cup of tea and a fireplace in some welcoming stranger's home.

Jimmy said, "Melissa, slow down. Don't go without us. We need to hold hands and walk slowly together. We have to all agree or we wait till morning."

"Too late. Come on Seth—get up and move it," said Melissa.

As Seth reluctantly rose to his feet and brushed the dirt from his pants, Melissa let out a loud scream.

'What happened? Melissa, are you okay?" yelled Seth. It had become so dark that he was not able to see anything more than an arm's length away. He knew this was a bad idea.

"Melissa, where are you, what's happening?" asked Jimmy.

"I'm not sure. There's something very big and hairy right here in front of me," said Melissa.

"Be still and don't move," said Jimmy.

"I couldn't move if I tried, it has me pinned against the wall. Please help me."

Melissa was obviously in fear, but she tried her hardest to hide it from the others by remaining calm. She was right. Something very big and hairy stood next to her and had her pressed against the wall. She was immobile, but still able to breathe. She tried with both hands to push the creature away. It didn't budge. And then the unthinkable happened. Something wet slithered across her face. It was a foul-smelling tongue that felt like fine sandpaper. She felt the hot air of an animal exhaling its breath on her.

Melissa froze. Unable to move. Unable to speak.

"I'm almost there, Melissa. Hold tight," said Jimmy.

"I'm right behind you, Jimmy," said Seth.

He felt his way along the wall as fast as he could. Jimmy was there in a matter of seconds, but it seemed like forever to Melissa. He halted when he heard the beast breathing. His mind raced to think of a way to make it all the way to Melissa's side without getting mauled to death. He instinctively closed his eyes as he reached out to touch the unknown. He was terrified, but he would never let it show—not that anyone could see his face in the pitch black. And then it happened. He made contact. It was hot and its hair was coarse. The hot, hairy beast was solid muscle. Jimmy knew that at any moment his hand could be torn off. There was no choice—he had to save Melissa even if it cost him his own life.

He repeated the psalm aloud, "I will fear no evil, for you are with me; your rod and your staff, they comfort me."

Chapter 24

The Mara People

As it turned out, the hairy animal was nothing more than a beast of burden heading home. He meant them no harm. He knew the area very well and was able to lead the way down the canyon trail in the dark. With the help of the beast, they had safely arrived on the outskirts of the town.

After rounding the umpteenth corner, they could hear the music in all its fullness. There were hundreds if not thousands of lights. All sorts of people milled around in elaborate costumes. It was stunning and quite beautiful. Everywhere they looked people were dancing, eating, and drinking; it was a festival unlike any they had seen before.

Their newfound hairy friend directed them towards the center of town before he turned to make his way home. The lonely creature reminded Melissa of Eeyore, a character from one of her favorite childhood stories. He had very little to say and seemed rather gloomy, but he was helpful and well-intentioned, as best she could tell.

There were many terraces protruding from the canyon walls, and each one had a large pole, some of which appeared to be at least a hundred feet high. On top of the poles were burning torches that lit up the canyon in the most spectacular way. Paper lanterns of all colors floated in the air. Now that there was light, they could make out the dwellings carved into the sides of the canyon. This was a thriving community and the inhabitants were having a major celebration. Finally, things were panning out for the weary travelers. Just an hour ago they were in danger of succumbing to the elements, and now they had found civilization. Things were looking up indeed.

Melissa pointed directly above her head. "Look, I think someone lives here. There's a door and steps leading up to it. There's even a window."

"Should we go up and knock?" asked Seth.

"No, I don't think anyone is home. It looks as though the whole town or city, or whatever this is, is down there," said Jimmy.

"Well, let's go join the celebration," said Bumpy from the top of Seth's front pocket.

"Sounds like a great idea to me," answered Seth.

They continued down a gentle sloping trail. Along the way they encountered more homes carved into the canyon wall. But Jimmy was correct, no one was home. The entire town, it seemed, had joined the party. And a fun party it appeared to be. As they got closer, they heard laughter and singing and music featuring instruments they had never seen before.

When they finally met their first canyon dweller, they were surprised at how tall he was. Melissa assumed he was on stilts, but it turned out she was wrong. Most of the people who lived there were at least ten feet tall—giants. Their new friend was on the shorter side, at just over nine feet. He made a point of insisting his small stature did not reflect on his prominence in the community.

His name was Tontic. It was short for something that none of them could pronounce. He was very nice as he led them the rest of the way down to the heart of the town where the celebration was happening. Jimmy asked if he was one of the Mara people, and Tontic said he was. The beavers had told them that the Mara people had been in the canyon since the waters dried up over three thousand years before. McClanahan had also warned them to be wary of these people.

"Where do you get your water from?" asked Jimmy.

"Don't you see him? He's all around. Our sovereign," answered

Tontic.

"Who? Where?" asked Melissa.

"There, right there," said Tontic, pointing to someone dressed in what looked to be a merman costume with a coiling fish tail and a head crowned with a horn.

"That's your king?" asked Seth.

Tontic laughed heartily, "Of course not, that is a Mara dressed as Achelous. There are many here who honor our water god with costume."

As they looked around there were many more Achelous costumes of varying quality and complexity. There were kites resembling mermen. There was even one that appeared to be swimming in a large clear fish bowl filled with clear balls, to simulate water. Melissa thought if there was actually a god named Achelous, he would be embarrassed at the various representations.

"Tonight, we celebrate the arrival of an honored dignitary. She shall be making her grand entrance very soon," said Tontic. "In the meantime, enjoy the celebration. Eat, drink, and be merry!"

Tontic disappeared, singing and dancing, into the crowd. Jimmy, Seth, and Melissa looked bewildered. They had no currency or anything of value to trade. The only person that could have helped them had just left. And even though they had found civilization, they still were in need of a place to rest for the night. The day's travels had taken their toll. Everyone was mentally and physically exhausted.

Just as Jimmy was about to suggest a course of action, a giant reached down and handed Melissa a toy of some sort. Another giant gently ushered the three of them in front of a food cart and proceeded to hand each of them a delightful smelling treat. These people did not use money, or perhaps everything was free during celebrations. Melissa was handed what looked like a gyro. Seth received something resembling a corndog. Jimmy was the proud recipient of what could only be described as a caramel apple. Seth looked at Jimmy and shrugged his shoulders. He was not about to take the first bite, so Jimmy obliged and ate. After chewing for a short bit, he smiled and gave an enthusiastic thumbs up.

They wandered around the town. Everyone, including Bumpy, was full of curiosity. All of the Mara people seemed very friendly and welcoming. Even though there were other short people that lived there (although slightly taller than Seth and Jimmy), they still felt like fish out of water amongst all the giants.

The depictions of Achelous walked, floated, and hung all around them. There were other deities as well. There were even animal costumes. Giant winged creatures, horses, and, to Melissa's delight, little stuffed animals and toys hanging in shop entrances and over windows. The one she was given reminded her of Fox. She hoped she would be able to take it back home with her.

Bumpy chose to stay within the safe confines of Seth's pocket. The crowds were large and the possibility of personal injury to someone of Bumpy's delicate nature was great. Jimmy thought it best for Bumpy not to be out in the open for other reasons as well. The beaver's reaction towards Bumpy, although positive, was worrisome. These people seemed to put a lot of attention toward mythical beings. What if they met someone with bad intentions? A talking leaf was bound to stir the pot. It was best, they agreed, to keep Bumpy under wraps for the time being.

The music and the crowds were louder on the valley floor. It was hard to hear one another and so they kept quiet as they mingled amongst the revealers. By the look of things, the party was going to go on all night. The travelers were tired, however, so Jimmy kept an eye out for lodgings as the others partook of more festive sights. Of course, Jimmy did not even know if such a place had accommodations for visitors. Hopefully one of the nice townspeople would help answer some questions when the celebration ended. Soon, Jimmy hoped.

Melissa sat on a bench between two shops and motioned for the others to join her. Seth was happy that it was Melissa, and not himself, who had stopped first. His feet were swollen and sore, but his pride still had life left to give.

"Shouldn't we be looking for the twelve?" asked Seth, sitting down.

"What?" Melissa asked.

Seth yelled louder to be heard over the noise. "Shouldn't we be looking for the twelve?'

"I think we need to find a place to hole up for the night. We can look for the twelve in the morning," said Jimmy.

"Oh, look, it's a parade!" exclaimed Melissa.

"What? A parade? I want to see. Lift me up there, youngin'," said Bumpy.

Seth looked down and spoke into his pocket, "It's just more of the same, Bumpy. Giants in outlandish mermaid costumes. Well, merman costumes, I guess. Lots of big animals made out of I dunno what. You're not missing anything."

Melissa rolled her eyes because she knew Seth was not being honest with Bumpy. The parade was amazing. The costumes and the giants were larger than life. The colors were more vivid than anything she had ever seen in parades back home. There were even little skits being performed—enacting some type of ritual, or so it seemed.

"Did anyone stop to think that these people are going to have to leave their homes? This whole place is going to be underwater soon," said Seth.

"We'll warn them, but there's time," said Jimmy. "We can't just spring it on them all at once."

"Pardon the pun there, young fella," said Bumpy.

"Pun?" asked Melissa.

"*Spring* it on them," repeated Bumpy.

"Oh, ha ha."

"That's pretty funny, Bumpy!" said Seth.

"It's not going to be very funny to them," said Jimmy.

"I say we find the twelve and let them announce the coming catastrophe. These mermen better live up to the hype, because they're going to need to be good swimmers, that's for sure."

"Seth, quit yelling everything so loud," said Melissa. "Someone might hear you. Besides, you sound so heartless. This is a whole town. People live here. It's their home."

"Okay, okay. Geesh."

Unbeknownst to Melissa, there was in fact someone listening in on their conversation. She had been following them since they arrived on the canyon floor.

Jimmy continued to scan the area but had not found anything resembling guest lodgings. The valley of the Mara people rarely had visitors, and therefore there was no reason to offer rooms for rent. Visitors, such as they were, did not go unnoticed. The only reason they had not been spotted by more inhabitants was because of the celebration. Most everyone was unrecognizable in their costumes.

A stranger startled Melissa by whispering into her ear, "Did I hear you say you are looking for the twelve?" She slowly dropped down next to Melissa. She was actually hanging upside down, and she was uncomfortably close. None of the others noticed the stranger. They were too busy chatting about their swimming skills.

"What?" asked Melissa. She was taken aback by the invasion of her personal space. It took her a second to realize how the eavesdropper was situated. When she saw what it was, she instinctively leaned in the opposite direction. She was speechless and did not know what to say.

The eavesdropper gently moved towards Melissa and whispered, "I'm sorry dear. I overheard your group talking about the ..." she mouthed the word twelve. "No one mentions that number here. It's a number that sticks out, you might say. I suggest you never repeat it again."

"Eww! Are you a bat?" Melissa was disappointed with her greeting, but she had never seen anything like it before. She was so transfixed that she failed to alert the others. The creature hung from a light pole protruding from a wall only inches away from Melissa. Its feet, a cross between bird claws and human hands, were wrapped securely around the post. It had a furry face that could only be described as a very human looking French Bulldog.

"Please try not to look at me while speaking. Don't be too obvious. It may not seem like it, but there are always people watching and listening." Both Melissa and the bat looked away from one another. "Is that what you call my kind where you're from? It's not a very flattering name—bat, is it?"

"Well, it's the hanging upside down thing," Melissa said looking back at the bat. Realizing her mistake, Melissa quickly turned her head and stared directly at the ground. She spoke in softer tones. "You look more like a cute little dog with an overcoat than a bat. But then I've never really seen a bat this close up, or this large."

"Dog? That's not any better," said the lady.

"A very cute dog with a very pretty, black shiny overcoat. I've always thought bats were cute, actually. Honest."

The bat lady seemed pleased. "Thank you. I'll take cute any day."

"Is it a bad thing? Are the twe ... that number ... those people ...bad people?"

The bat lady pulled a masquerade mask from underneath her wings and handed it to Melissa. "Hold this up to your face. The only reason you and your friends have not been detected thus far is because you look like you are already in costume. But costumes no one would really be wearing to this celebration. We need to get you away from here, to somewhere safer, quieter."

The lady, still hanging upside down, pulled two more masquerade masks from under her wings and gave them to Melissa. "There is an alleyway two left turns from here. At the end of the alley is a small door, too small for a giant. It will be safe to talk once inside."

Melissa turned to her companions and said, "Hey guys, don't ask any questions. Cover your faces with these. Don't look now, but there's a bat-slash-dog-like lady hanging right next to me and she says we need to get out of here as quickly as possible."

Seth and Jimmy looked at each other before examining the masks. It was obvious they were confused.

"Here, right here to my left." Melissa whispered as she nodded her head in the direction of the bat. When the guys still seemed confused, she looked back herself and saw that the bat was gone. "I swear it was there! A cute, huge bat with black shiny wings was hanging right here."

Both Seth and Jimmy shrugged and held the masks up to cover their faces. "We believe you," they said in unison.

"Where did she go?" asked Melissa. "Or why did she go, is a better question. What should we do?"

"How should we know?" said Seth.

"What did she say?" asked Jimmy.

"She told me that we should disguise ourselves and follow her up the road, take the second left to the end, and then there would be a small door—a door too small for a giant. She also said never to say the word," she mouthed the word twelve, "out loud. She said it was very dangerous."

"Twelve?" asked Seth.

"Shhhh. I just told you not to say that number out loud!"

"I wasn't sure that's what you were trying to say."

"To be fair to Seth, I wasn't quite sure either," said Jimmy.

"Whatever. Just don't say it again," said Melissa.

Jimmy mouthed twelve and shrugged his shoulders inquisitively.

"Yes," said Melissa, mouthing twelve again.

"We shouldn't say the number in between eleven and thirteen, right?" yelled Seth, sarcastically.

Melissa rolled her eyes. "That's right, Seth. And I'm sure no one within shouting distance can put that one together."

The four of them—Bumpy had lifted himself up just enough to see over Seth's pocket—peered up and down the street before they went the way the upside-down bat lady had instructed.

"Come on, it's our only lead," said Jimmy. "If the bat lady meant us harm, it probably wouldn't matter if we stayed here or went in the opposite direction. She knows the lay of the land. Let's go find that door."

Jimmy led the way and the others followed.

"I think we need to prioritize finding Fox and Dauber," said Melissa. "They've been gone far too long. Something is not right. I just know it."

"Speaking of Fox, did anyone else notice how much these masks look like her?" asked Seth.

"Now that you mention it, they do look like a fox," said Melissa.

Jimmy said, "The festivities will surely be over tomorrow. It'll be easier to make sense of things then. Besides, maybe this lady knows something about Fox and Dauber and she can help us find them."

"I hope you're right, but I'm still worried," said Melissa.

"Don't worry about tomorrow, for tomorrow will worry about itself. Each day has enough trouble of its own," said Jimmy.

"You got that right," said Seth.

"You really need to start reading the Bible, Seth," said Melissa.

"I knew that was from the Bible, Melissa. Just because I don't read it doesn't mean I've never heard of some of the stuff in it."

"She's right, you need to start reading it for yourself," said Bumpy.

Seth removed his mask and looked down at Bumpy, "What do you know? You're just a leaf."

"You should be so lucky, whippersnapper," said Bumpy as he retreated out of sight to the bottom of the pocket.

"That wasn't very nice, Seth," said Melissa.

"What's so lucky about being a leaf? Let's go find the door," said Seth.

Chapter 25

TUNNELS OF LIGHT

"Are you sure we didn't miss it?" asked Seth.

Jimmy stopped walking and turned to look at Melissa. "Are you sure this was the right direction?"

Melissa put a hand on her hip and used the other one to point at Seth and Jimmy. "Don't everyone start blaming me. This isn't my fault. The old bat pointed this way and said to take the second alleyway on the left."

Bumpy began giggling in Seth's pocket.

"What's so funny, Bumpy?" asked Melissa.

Bumpy peeked out of Seth's pocket and in between laughs he said, "The cute bat suddenly turned into an old bat. I've seen a lot of both in my days."

"Yes, well, I don't appreciate being lied to," said Melissa.

Jimmy handed Seth and Melissa two lit poles that he had just taken off a nearby canyon wall. The lights reminded Jimmy of torches, but he wasn't quite sure what their source of energy was—they were not made of fire, nor were they hot to the touch. "We don't know that anyone lied, we just haven't reached the second left yet, and it's hard to see very far ahead in the dark. Onward we go."

Walking down the road amongst the crowd was getting more difficult. The number of revelers increased the farther they went. They were also going against the flow of the crowd, making matters even worse. They stuck as close to one another as possible.

"Let's just wait here until everyone passes," said Seth.

Jimmy agreed, "We must be walking directly on the main parade route. Once the parade passes, the crowd should thin out."

"At least we have a front-row seat to watch all the crazy costumes and characters," said Melissa.

"There are two problems with that statement," said Seth. "First, there is nowhere to sit, and second, I can't see over these giants."

Jimmy pointed to a spot free of pedestrians. Seth and Melissa followed him, quickly finding a wall to lean against. They stretched their necks and stood on their toes in an attempt to see as many costumed giants, musicians, and spectators as possible.

Seth turned to Jimmy and whispered, "You think we should ask one of these people where the alleyway is?"

"I don't think that would be a good idea. Whoever gave Melissa the information was obviously worried about secrecy. We'll start walking again when the crowd lets up. It can't be too much farther."

But instead of getting lighter, as they had expected, the crowd grew larger by the second. The passersby were so thick that those standing along the side were getting pressed against the wall. Jimmy's idea to stop and wait for the parade to pass was a bust.

Jimmy offered to lift Melissa onto his shoulders above the rambunctious crowd. She gratefully accepted and Seth locked his hands together so she could step up. At first, she sat on his shoulders but then, in order to get a better view, she stood on them. Her weight was partially supported by the wall they were leaning up against. On the ground, she could hardly see anything, but now that she was taller, she had a giant's view.

The crowd was thickest directly in front of them, and she could see that it started to thin out not too far ahead. Just as she was about to get down to share the good news, she thought she saw Fox. She squeezed her eyes shut and rubbed the palms of her hands over them. When she opened them again, it was true. Her eyes did not deceive.

She watched as Fox, in a large ornate cage, was being carried over the heads of four giants. There were two poles extending through the bottom of the cage. Four giants, one on each end of the two poles, rested the cage on their shoulders. Their gait was so smooth that the cage appeared to be floating in midair.

Fox did not seem to be alarmed or distressed. In fact, she never looked better. She sat perfectly perched on a beautiful red pillow trimmed in gold. The cage itself was trimmed in gold tassels hanging from the top. The tassels sparkled so much that Melissa thought they must have actually been made of real gold. She wanted to quickly get down off of her perch to tell the others what she was seeing, but she could not stop staring. She was mesmerized and did not want to miss a thing.

The longer she stared, the more details she noticed. A giant holding a large fan trailed behind the cage. His only job, it appeared, was to fan Fox. There were also creatures—it was hard to tell if they were animals or otherwise—on each side of the cage. They seemed to be bowing at the waist with their arms and hands in front of them. If she did not know better, Melissa would have thought they were worshipping Fox. Still other creatures carried torches. There must have been a hundred torches lighting the parade.

She had seen enough. Besides, Jimmy's shoulders must have been getting sore. Melissa, with the help of Seth, landed on the ground. She immediately motioned for Seth and Jimmy to come closer. She rushed through an explanation of what she had just seen. The three of them instinctively began pushing their way through the crowd in the direction of the fox. The parade participants and onlookers were not being cooperative. Everyone was so tightly packed that it was impossible for anyone, especially regular-sized people, to get through.

Melissa yelled to Fox as loud as she could, but Fox could not hear her over the noise and music. Jimmy and Seth also tried calling out her name. They even tried counting to three and yelling in unison, but Fox could not hear them. They were losing ground and could not even see the cage anymore.

Jimmy pulled the two siblings to the edge of the crowd and said, "This isn't working. At least we know Fox is okay. We will catch up with her later. I think we need to go find this bat creature and figure things out from there. She might be able to take us to Fox."

Melissa and Seth nodded in agreement. The crowd had thinned out, and they were able to backtrack more easily towards the direction the bat had given.

It was not long until they found the second alleyway on the left. The path was obviously not a major thoroughfare for the locals, as there were no shops, windows, or points of interest. It was just a bleak cobblestone passageway that was much darker than the main street. They turned and followed it all the way to the end where, true to the bat's words, there was a door too small for a giant to go through.

It was almost too small for regular folks to go through, but they managed. Seth knew they had been in this world too long by how they didn't think twice to just open a strange door and enter. It was certainly not something that was a common occurrence in their world. One would knock first and wait for a reply, or at the very least ask if anyone was home.

As it turned out, the door did not lead to a home, but to an outdoor vestibule of sorts. There were walls and more passageways, albeit smaller than from where they had just come, but there was no roof or ceiling. The outside elements were free to enter in as they wished. That was the strangest thing of all. In this place, on the other side of the door, the sun was shining bright—in the middle of the night.

Bumpy finally felt safe to flutter about, much to the chagrin of Jimmy. Jimmy was still not convinced it was safe for the Mara people to know about their special leaf. "Look, when you hear or see someone—*anyone*—find the first good hiding spot and keep quiet. We don't need you disappearing too." Jimmy looked around. "Well, where is this bat lady?"

Melissa and Seth could sense Jimmy's tension. When they met him last spring, he seemed so much older and wiser. He was the guy who knew a lot of stuff about science, astrophysics, and the Bible. He was the person they went to for answers to their questions. But the truth was that he was only a few years older than Seth. His life experience might have been a little greater, but he was still just a young man trying to make his way in the world—their world, not this world. But because he was older, even if only by a few years, he would always be held more accountable.

Melissa put her hand on Jimmy's shoulder to reassure him, "Hey, Jimmy. It's going to be alright."

"Thanks. I hope so. It just seems like every new road or door leads to exponentially more choices. Every time I think we get a step closer to an answer, we get presented with more questions."

Seth stepped in front of Jimmy and Melissa. "Yeah, look at this place. I mean, what the heck! What is this?"

A voice from the shadows answered, "It's a place we can talk without the giants hearing us. It's a place for small people, like you."

"Who said that? Where are you?" demanded Seth.

"I'm the one who told the girl how to get here," said the lady.

"Why don't you show yourself?" asked Jimmy.

"I would be delighted to, but I must remain where it's darkest. Step a little further down, where the sun does not stream, and we can chat face to face."

Seth walked down the corridor as it curved towards the left. Jimmy and Melissa followed. Bumpy discreetly hung in the rear just before the bend, remaining in the sunlight. Whoever was speaking would not be able to see the miraculous leaf, not as long as they stayed on the dark side.

"Hello?" Seth looked all around, including up high, but he could not see anyone. He decided to introduce himself anyway. "My name is Seth. This is my sister, Melissa. She's the one you spoke to earlier. The other guy here is Jimmy."

"Hi," said Jimmy, also looking around but seeing no one.

"I'm assuming it's safe to talk here, like you told me," said Melissa. "We have a lot of questions."

"Questions. Everyone has questions. I'm good at answering them, and yes, it is safe here," said the bat lady. She then quickly dropped from somewhere above and clung to the wall directly next to Seth.

"Okay. Well, that's not creepy at all." Seth, not wanting to appear as frightened as he actually was, slowly inched away from the bat. "I'm sure you would like to speak to my sister. And here she is …"

"Thanks, Seth," said Melissa. "You know our names, how about telling us yours."

The bat lady chuckled and said, "He's adorable, your brother. So fragile." She reached out her wing and touched the tip of Seth's nose. Seth yelped a little and moved quickly out of the bat's reach. "My name is Athaliah."

Jimmy moved around in front of Seth. "Nice to meet you, Athaliah."

He reached out his hand, not realizing the custom was probably not familiar to a creature with wings. But to his surprise, Athaliah reached out and embraced his hand with hers. Her other arm—or wing, as it were—remained attached to the wall.

"Nice to meet all of you. It's quite refreshing to have new blood in town."

"New blood ..." repeated Seth incredulously.

She laughed. "So adorable! Oh, dear, don't you worry. My kind only eat fruit."

Jimmy spoke up again. "May I be frank?"

"Absolutely," said Athaliah.

"What do you want from us? We don't have anything to offer in exchange for information."

"Ahh, the pragmatist of the group, are you? Well, of course, you are right. I *do* want something. Nothing, it is said throughout the kingdoms, is free."

"Are you alone?" asked Melissa.

"At the moment, yes. But my kind are everywhere. In the cracks and crevices. I can't promise we will be alone for long. This is why I have chosen to meet you in the tunnels of light. No one would expect me here, especially at night. But there are other creatures that use these passageways for their own agendas. It just so happens the parade has distracted nearly everyone—for the moment."

"We should get to the point quickly, I take it," said Jimmy.

"It couldn't hurt," said Athaliah.

"You first," said Jimmy.

"We know you are from the other world. The first to make it this far in. We want to help you with your mission. Your mission is our mission."

Jimmy said, "Great. You're going to be more help than we thought because we have no idea what our mission is."

Athaliah seemed to be taken aback by Jimmy's last statement. How could a group make it this far into her world without knowing why they were even there? But she quickly covered her surprised expression by mentioning something they obviously knew something about: the twelve.

"I can tell you where to find the twelve, but first you all must swear an oath. Before you swear the oath, I must know who it is you call Lord? Who is it you worship?"

"Why does that matter?" asked Melissa.

"Your oath is only as strong as your belief in the one you worship. Tell me, what is its name?"

"Our God is not an it," said Jimmy. "He is the creator of the beginning, the middle, and the end. He created all that is and ever was. He is the One who died and rose again so that I may live. To some He is the unknown God, to others He is ignored, and still others He is an enemy."

"Interesting. And which of those 'others' would you say am I?' she asked.

"I have no idea. Only God knows the heart. I cannot judge your belief or disbelief. But if you claim to know *my* God, it will show in what you do, how you live."

"And you?" she asked Melissa.

"What he said," she answered. "I believe in the God of the holy Bible. The one that even the stars declare."

"And you?" She looked at Seth.

"I, I guess I'm a believer, too. I'm still learning, but yeah," stammered Seth.

"You, the adorable one, go wait by the door from where you entered. That is where you will be leaving again. I must speak to these two alone."

"What? Are you serious? We're a team, you can't just divide us. Besides, it's not like they won't tell me everything, anyway."

"If you want to know where to find the twelve, you will do as I say and adhere to my requests," said Athaliah. "There is no other option."

Jimmy said, "He's right. We are a team, and we are all in this together."

"Very well, I wish you a safe journey," said Athaliah as she quickly began ascending the wall.

"Wait!" yelled Seth. "We don't have time for this. I'll leave." He looked at the others, "You know where I'll be. Make it quick."

"Seth, you don't have to leave. If it's meant to be, we will find the twelve with or without her help," said Melissa.

"Thanks, Sis. But it's not a problem. Really, I don't mind. It's for the greater good. I'll see y'all in a bit." Seth turned and followed the path back the way they came. He was happy to get far away from the odd creature.

Once her brother was out of sight, Melissa spoke. "You do realize there is nothing you could tell us that he won't soon find out for himself?"

The bat crept back down the wall and over to Melissa. "Rarely do we see the weakness within ourselves in the way others can. We must strive to see a reflection and not an interpretation if we are to change. Your brother is conflicted, but this you already knew. What you don't know is that he can't be trusted. He will turn against the one you claim to follow."

Jimmy turned to Melissa and said, "We don't know that's true. No one knows that except God Himself." He then turned to Athaliah, "Don't think for a minute that we are just going to trust you blindly."

"I would never dream of asking a stranger to trust me. Not until I've proven myself worthy."

"I have no reason not to trust you," said Melissa. "I suppose if you meant us any harm you could have already taken advantage of us. I obviously trusted you enough to follow your directions here."

"The faith in this one is strong, is it not?" Athaliah said to Jimmy. "But have no doubt, it is not me she trusts. It is the God you spoke of in which she places her faith."

"I think you're right. Our faith has gotten us this far, and it will see us the rest of the way," said Jimmy.

"Is not your god a practical god, like most gods? If so, heed my warning about the adorable one," said Athaliah.

"Our God is not like any other god," said Jimmy. "What's in this for you? Why are you helping us, if indeed that's what you are doing?"

"Simple. I want the twelve on my side. I want them to know that it was I that helped you to find them."

"Why? What can they do for you?" asked Melissa.

'That's none of your concern," said Athaliah. "But let's just say I want to be on the winning side when it's all over."

"When what's all over—why so cryptic?" asked Jimmy.

"You really don't know what's going on, do you? There is a war. A war that's been brewing since the dawn of time. The signs of the end are near. I'm sure that you are part of the unfolding. You came with the Crimson one, did you not?"

"The crimson one?" repeated Jimmy.

"You mean Fox? What about her?" asked Melissa.

"To prove my loyalty to the twelve and to you, I am going to tell you how to free the Crimson Goddess of Fire."

"What are you talking about?" asked Melissa.

"I know the fox is not a Goddess, but the Mara people worship everything. It did not help that they heard a skewed version of the prophecy that speaks of the Crimson one arriving on the night with three stars. The part with the three stars they got correct, but the rest of the prophecy was entirely misunderstood."

Once Athaliah mentioned Fox, she had Melissa's complete attention. Jimmy understood Melissa's affection for Fox and would do anything to bring them back together. Both Melissa and Jimmy moved close to the upside-down bat lady. They wanted to hear every word she had to say.

Athaliah first spoke about the twelve and where to find them. She gave specific directions complete with clear and unmistakable landmarks. Jimmy felt confident in his ability to locate them. What seemed more troubling was how to get to Fox. Apparently, according to Athaliah, the Mara people were taking Fox back to her eternal home. In fact, Fox was the reason for the celebration and the parade. It was all about Fox.

When Melissa nearly fainted, Jimmy was there to catch her. It seems that the eternal home of The Crimson Goddess of Fire was in a real fire. They were going to burn her alive!

Jimmy assured Melissa that they were not going to let any harm come to Fox. Athaliah would not be able to aid in any rescue attempt, her kind preferred to remain neutral, and if she were discovered helping the strangers, she would certainly be executed. She was, however, willing and able to give valuable information on where they were taking Fox. She warned them that the Mara people were foolish and superstitious. She could not predict what would happen if the Mara people caught them trying to free Fox. In fact, she urged them to not even try. Jimmy had never heard Melissa angrier, nor would he ever again. She laid into the bat lady like a mother bear rescuing her cub. That's when Jimmy knew that whatever was in store for him, God had chosen the right comrade to join him in battle.

Chapter 26

The High Place

The parade was over. It was still dark and mostly quiet. The only light was from the torches surrounding Fox. Most of the revelers had either headed to their homes or fallen asleep under the stars. Others chose to camp around the small hill, known as the High Place, where Fox slept in her cage. It was hard to see exactly how many of the Mara people had remained, but by the sound of the snoring it was quite a large number.

Jimmy and the others had found an out-of-the-way spot about five-hundred yards to the west of Fox. They were secluded in between several large boulders on a small knoll. Seth sprawled out on the ground, resting his head on his backpack. Melissa followed suit, using her brother's leg as a headrest. Exhaustion was getting the better of them.

They had a good view of their surroundings, and they whispered to each other without fear of waking the giants. The bat lady gave good directions to where the Mara were taking Fox. Jimmy felt assured that once they rescued Fox, they would be able to follow the bat lady's directions to find the twelve, but first things first.

"Plan A or plan B?" asked Jimmy, who did not appear to be quite as tired as his traveling companions.

On their way to the High Place, the group had come up with two plans. Plan A was the most basic: wait until everyone was asleep and send Bumpy over to warn Fox and do reconnaissance. Plan B required more diplomatic skills. They had information that the Mara people needed. Sooner or later the town and perhaps the entire canyon was going to flood, and they would freely exchange this information for the release of their friend. Unfortunately for them, it was midnight, and it was impossible to tell who was in charge. Besides, who was to say that the Mara people would even honor such an agreement?

"It's obvious, isn't it? Plan A. These Mara people are nuts. We can't risk trying to talk to them. They burn people alive!" exclaimed Seth.

"He's right, we can't trust people with no higher moral authority," said Jimmy. "What basis is there for agreement?"

Bumpy, already hovering above the group, lowered himself to their level. "Fortunately, we are blessed with a nice, strong breeze. It will be easy to drift over to Fox and make an assessment. In fact, I daresay that Fox and I can manage an escape all on our own."

Melissa yawned and said, "If Bumpy is willing to do it, I'm all in."

"Plan A it is. Let's say a prayer, y'all," said Jimmy.

After leading the prayer for Bumpy and Fox's safety, Jimmy carefully took Bumpy in his hand and climbed on top of a mound of rocks where they were hiding out. He wanted Bumpy to have the best lift possible just in case the wind died out on his way. If he started high enough, he could coast down the rest of the way to Fox.

The canyon floor was no more than several hundred yards wide. It narrowed even more further down. There was nowhere to run and very few places to hide. If Bumpy failed in his mission, and they were discovered, they would have to rely on plan B.

"Alright, Bumpy, it's all yours," said Jimmy. "I guess I don't need to tell you to be wary of the campfires. If you find yourself in trouble, just find a good hiding spot and hang low until it's safe. As long as the Mara people don't see you talking, you're just another leaf to them."

"Just another leaf? I don't reckon you've noticed but I'm the only leaf in this entire world. I'm bound to stand out no matter what I do."

"All the more reason to keep your options open. If anything goes wrong, find someplace to hide and stay low."

"Don't worry about me. Everything will be fine. Just be ready to skedaddle when Fox and I make it back over here."

"We'll be ready. God be with you," said Jimmy as he carefully released Bumpy into the wind.

Jimmy watched until Bumpy was out of sight, which because of the darkness was only a matter of seconds. And although he was careful in handling Bumpy, who had become noticeably more brittle during their travels, a small piece of the leaf broke off and disappeared into the wind. Jimmy thought nothing more of it as he made his way back to Seth and Melissa who had already fallen asleep. Jimmy was tempted to join them, but someone needed to remain on the lookout and in prayer.

Bumpy felt a part of himself crumble as Jimmy released him into the breeze, but he was not concerned. It was just a small part of his lower left extremity. He still felt strong and able. He put it out of his mind and concentrated on the mission before him. As he floated above the camp of giants, he wondered if Fox was aware of the plans these pagans had for her. He also wondered if he would be capable of undoing any locks or restraints that might be holding her. His dexterity was obviously limited—he was, after all, just a leaf.

The wind currents were in his favor. They were going in the right direction, but he was not quite as high up as he had hoped to be. He was no higher than a giant's arm length most of the time. Since all of the Mara people were sleeping, however, he was not worried about them reaching up to grab him. What he did fear were the campfires. And it just so happened that there were several on the way to Fox. Warm air currents can cause unpredictable turbulence, and Bumpy knew it would be hard to navigate. His first test was less than thirty feet away.

The leaf leaned to the right until he was totally perpendicular to the ground. The breeze pushed him to the left away from the fire below. It also raised him another giant's body length in the air, making him untouchable to any light sleepers below. Bumpy gave a sigh of relief as he continued to make his way towards Fox.

He was surprised at how so many people could be outside resting peacefully together. From his view above, he estimated at least a thousand giants and many other life forms. There were donkey-type animals, monkey-like creatures, and even a few normal-sized people like his friends. Since it rarely, if ever, rained, there were no tents or coverings of any kind.

He wondered what they were burning, since there were no trees or wood to speak of in these parts. Upon their arrival here, they had noticed most of the lights and torches were made of some type of illuminating gel, but the campfires looked just like the ones back home. The ones made from his kinfolk.

Fox was no more than one hundred yards away, but the wind currents had died down. Not only was Bumpy barely moving, he was also sinking closer to the ground. Unfortunately, the lack of wind could not have happened at a more inconvenient time. He was approaching another fire, and Bumpy was heading straight for the incinerator with no ability to alter course. Nothing he did made a difference. He leaned to the right and then to the left, but all he did was sink toward the ground.

Bumpy quickly lamented his lack of caution. He had gotten cocky and taken the shortest route rather than the safest. He felt the heat. He was that close. He could feel his membranes shrink; what little moisture he had left was being sucked right out of him. For the first time in his life, Bumpy was scared. Was this the end? Was this the Creator's plan?

He was about to give up all hope—something very unusual for a leaf, as leaves have never been known to lose faith. He closed his eyes and prayed it would not hurt. He knew of many leaves that had been burned in fires, but none had survived to share the details. He had no control over his fate. It was over. He was spinning out of control. The hot air currents were pushing him up only to be pushed back down by the cooler currents. The mix of temperatures created what felt like a rollercoaster in the middle of a tornado.

Bumpy was heartbroken that he would no longer be able to help his new friends. He had grown to really love them all. Seth, unnoticed by the others, had always taken the utmost care to protect Bumpy from harm. Placing him in a mason jar and using tissue paper was the kindest and sweetest thing for a human to do. Bumpy also adored Melissa. Her affection for the Creator's creations was obvious. Bumpy was sure there was no human more trustworthy than Jimmy, the strong and noble one.

The leaf looked below him and knew it was over before he even hit the fire. There was an ember rising quickly towards him. It would reach him in a matter of seconds. He would more than likely go up in flames before he ever hit the ground. As Bumpy thought of the others and the brevity of his new friendships, he felt something strange. Something deep inside of him welled up. It was like nothing he had ever felt before. It was an intense sadness—an overwhelming sense of loss. Then the strangest thing of all, a single drop of water fell from Bumpy. The drop of water came from nowhere, but from somewhere deep within him. He had never felt anything so intense. He watched as that single drop of water fell directly onto the ember, extinguishing the burning fire that would have surely destroyed him.

Bumpy was so shocked at what had just happened that he forgot all about the fire waiting below. As it turned out, he need not worry. A current swept in from the west, pushing him out of harm's way. He was safe again, and only a few yards away from Fox. Never had a leaf smiled as big as Bumpy did in that moment. His joy erupted into a dance. And that's what Fox saw, a leaf dancing on the wind.

"Bumpy, is that you?" asked Fox.

"Shh. Not so loud there, little critter. We mustn't rouse the evil spirits, don't ya know?"

"Evil spirits? Where? Where?" Fox turned circles in her cage, looking in every direction as fast as she could.

"All around us, they're sleeping. Let's make sure they stay that way."

"What? The Mara people? Oh, no, Bumpy. These are the sweetest people. They have been so nice to me."

"Nice? Then why do they have you locked in a cage?"

"Cage? This is not a cage. And it's not locked."

"Then why are you here?"

"I was just waiting for my friends, and here you are. I thought this place was as good as any. The pillows in here are so soft and can you smell that? They call it intense. Is it not the sweetest intense you have ever smelled?"

"I think you mean incense, Fox. But this is not at all what it seems."

"What do you mean?"

"I don't want to alarm you, little lassie, but we need to get out of here. Quickly and quietly."

"I think you are being so very silly. Where are the others?"

"They are waiting about five-hundred yards away."

"I am very happy to see everyone again. As nice as the Mara people have been, I have missed Melissa and all of you very much." Fox nudged the cage door open with her muzzle and eased out.

"How will you be getting back," Fox asked Bumpy.

"I hadn't thought that far ahead. The wind is indeed blowing in the wrong direction. You don't have pockets, do you?"

"Don't you worry, I'm a fox." Fox took a small pillow from her padded palace and ripped a hole in it. She rooted most of the stuffing out and slipped her head through the hanging fringe. "A pouch fit for a king."

"Indeed, it is. Quite crafty, Fox. Just remember to be stealthy and quick. We mustn't wake the giants."

"If stealthy means sneaky, we got it made," said Fox proudly.

Bumpy slid into the newly made pillow-pouch hanging around Fox's neck. It was very comfortable. The lining inside was the softest material Bumpy had ever felt, much softer than Seth's pocket. And there was just enough stuffing to keep it nice and airy, which kept Bumpy from getting squashed.

Bumpy peeked out to see that Fox was darting around and over the sleeping giants. She was in stealth mode, that was for sure. What should have been a rough ride, even in a soft pillowcase, was very comfortable. Fox was as smooth as the wind.

Bumpy looked down just as Fox leaped into the air. Directly beneath them was a giant. This was the first time he saw a giant's face up close. Not the most attractive creatures. A tiny nose and almost indistinguishable ears attached to a big round face with a long pointy chin and the biggest forehead imaginable. The eyes were cute, though: big and round like a cow's.

No sooner had Bumpy starting to enjoy the trip than Fox had found their friends. "How in the world did you find them so fast?" asked Bumpy. "I didn't even tell you exactly where they were."

"I could smell them, of course," said Fox.

"Hmm, is that so? You might reckon you would have smelled us before I risked flying over giants and bonfires to rescue you."

"I'm sorry, Bumpy. I guess you have a point, but I was having oh so much fun with the Mara people that I didn't even think about it."

"Are they sleeping?" asked Bumpy.

"Yes, every last one of them."

Even Jimmy had succumbed to the warm night air and fallen asleep.

"Aren't they all so wonderful? I have missed them. Maybe we should let everyone rest and we will leave before first light," said Fox.

"Do you think it wise, Fox?"

"I'm awful tired too. It's been a long day. You could wake us in a few hours. Leaves don't sleep, do they?"

"This is against my better judgment, Lassie. But warm-blooded creatures do need their sleep, so I hear. Alright, get some rest and I'll stay on the lookout."

"You're the best leaf ever, Bumpy."

"Yeah, yeah, yeah … Well, you never met my cousins on the branches above mine. You talk about some good-hearted leaves. They would always take the brunt of the hard rains and hail. By the time anything reached us, it was as harmless as could be. They took some hard beatings. I could only hope to be as brave and strong as them someday, but thanks for the kind words, Fox." By the time Bumpy had finished speaking, Fox had already crawled in-between Seth and Melissa. Her chin rested on Melissa's arm. She was fast asleep with the rest of them. Everyone looked so peaceful.

But the peace would not last long. The giants, although their noses and ears were tiny, could smell as well as a bear and hear just as keenly as an owl. The noise and the smell of the strangers had aroused the giants from their slumber. And while the Mara people were usually nice and hospitable to outsiders, nothing ever got in the way of their ritual sacrifices.

The Abaddons, the dwarf giants of the Mara people, had spent the entire night stoking the fire to get it ready for their evil purpose. The flames were finally ready to receive their prize, the Crimson Goddess of Fire.

As the travelers from the other world slept, the Abaddons, along with several of the Giants were forming an impenetrable circle around them. Escape was most unlikely.

Chapter 27

CHOICES

It is true that everyone appeared to be resting peacefully. But for Seth, sleep was full of unwelcome dreams. He found himself back in the Tunnels of Light. After having just left the others at Athaliah's request, Seth sulked on the way back to the entrance. But it was hard to tell which way they had come. Seth was confused and disoriented. He was lost.

The tunnel walls began to move and morph in new directions. Seth quickly walked towards what he thought was the entrance, but the pathway suddenly expanded from one path into two and then three. Seth was sure there were not as many options when they first entered. It was a simple and straight path. Something or someone was playing tricks on him.

Every way he went seemed to be wrong. His instincts told him to try another way and then another way and another way. He went back and forth. He tried to trace his steps. His anxiety was growing and he started to breathe heavily. It became arduous to lift his feet or to even think about his next move.

Seth stopped and leaned against the wall. He remembered what his dad had taught him: If you get lost, don't make matters worse by going further, stop and wait for someone to find you. He felt sure that Melissa and Jimmy would find him soon.

But it was not his friends that found him, it was Athaliah. But instead of a bat creature, she looked like a normal girl. She resembled a classmate from college. Seth sighed a little—some part of him knew that this must have been a dream. Now all he had to do was wake up.

"Are you lost?" she asked.

"I don't know how. It seemed easy enough when we came in, but yes. I seem to have lost my way."

"The way is easy. I can show you. You're not far at all."

"But I don't understand, I thought you wanted to talk with my sister and Jimmy. Why are you here? How did you get here so fast?"

"Time and space are different in the Tunnels. I am most glad I happened to run into you."

"I am too, I guess."

"There is something I wanted to mention to you without the others hearing."

"I thought it was *me* that you wanted to keep secrets from."

"Quite the contrary. It is you for which I have a special revelation."

"What makes you think I won't tell the others?"

"Because I know what you're hiding in your pack. You stole from the table of illusions. And like all men, you want to take the riches back to your world. Don't you?"

"How do you know what's in my pack?'

"You're just like me, that's how I know. You and I want the same thing. And if we help one another, we can both get what we want."

"Assuming you are right, and I'm not saying that you are, why would I need your help?"

Athaliah laughed. "You can't take an illusion to a world where miracles are not appreciated and faith is as scarce as the riches you seek."

"I don't understand."

"I know you don't." Athaliah ran her fingers through Seth's hair and whispered in his ear, "Your sister took something from this world when she was last here, and I want it back. She somehow escaped the Land of Indulgencies with a seed of the Glouscenshire. The seed will not be useful in your world, but it will be in mine. The tree of the Glouscenshire is no more, so the seed is the last of its kind. You must bring it to me."

"If I do this thing, what do I get out if it?" asked Seth.

"I can make your illusion a reality, I can make it so you can take the treasure from our world to yours." she answered. Athaliah began to walk away.

"Where are you going? I thought you were going to show me the way out of here?"

She turned one last time before disappearing into one of the passageways, "The choice is yours. You have nothing to lose and everything to gain. You keep your end of the bargain and I'll keep mine."

"But I didn't agree to anything." he said. But it was too late. She was gone. As Seth stared in her direction, he noticed that all of the tunnels began to shrink. Even the space where he was standing began to close in on him. He reached out to hold the walls back from crushing him. If it was just a dream, he would have woken up by now.

"Seth! Seth, wake up," said Melissa as she stared down at him and shook him by the shoulders.

"Oh wow, you have great timing, Sis. I owe you one," said Seth as he rubbed his eyes. "I was having a dream about something that happened earlier and then the walls started to close in on me." Seth stopped talking when he noticed all the many giants staring at him. It seemed that he was the last to realize that the Mara had discovered them. It was still night, but there were enough torches to make it seem like the middle of the day. There must have been a hundred giants surrounding them.

"I fell asleep too," said Jimmy.

Seth saw Fox and exclaimed, "Fox, you're okay!"

"Yes sireee, I'm so happy we're together again," said Fox.

"Where's Bumpy?" asked Seth.

Jimmy nodded towards the giants and gave Seth a stern look. Jimmy was not sure where Bumpy was, but he was sure the giants should not know either. "Everyone is accounted for."

Seth understood and he hoped the giants were not too inquisitive. There was no telling what the giants would try to do with a talking leaf.

"These things want us to follow them," said Melissa.

"Well, *want* is a generous term," said Jimmy. "We have no choice, it seems."

"There's always a choice," said Seth. He stood up and yelled, "I'm not going anywhere with these barbarians."

The last thing Seth would remember before waking up the next time was a rather hard thump. One of the dwarf giants whacked him on the back of the head with a torch pole. Melissa and Jimmy kept him from hitting the ground, and they were assigned the task of carrying him to their new accommodations.

It seems that Fox's pillow-laden palace could also act as a prison cell. This time there was a lock, and it was a lot more cramped with its additional occupants.

Jimmy was able to convince the dwarf giants to summon the leader of the Mara people. He warned them that he had information that they would want to hear. When the leader of the Mara people finally came, he introduced himself as Porpion. He was half as tall again as most of the other giants. He towered over everyone and everything. Yet he seemed to have an easy-going disposition. His features were a little more balanced than his fellow giants. His ears and nose fit his face quite well, his chin was not nearly as long or pointed as his shorter comrades, and his forehead was almost proportional to the rest of his head.

Melissa was in fact charmed by Porpion. He reminded her of the TV evangelists back home—the ones her dad called smiley and smarmy. On the downside, it did feel like he might expect a donation or a tithe. He had the persona of an incumbent running for re-election—secure, but always on the lookout for his next opportunity.

Jimmy was immediately impressed with Porpion as well. After meeting him, behind the cage bars, Jimmy felt as though the giant would hear him out and possibly accept his proposition. He felt even better when Porpion ordered the dwarf giants to let them out of the cage. It only made sense. It was not likely anyone, let alone these small humans, could escape all of the guards.

Jimmy informed Porpion that he had information that could save all of their lives. All he wanted in exchange for this information was their freedom. The giant of giants seemed intrigued. What could these fools possibly know? His attitude suddenly changed from a polite host to a smug know-it-all. And to everyone's surprise, he considered Jimmy's proposal. He would release them all if the information Jimmy gave could meet two criteria. The first was that it had to be new information and the second was that it had to have implications large enough to warrant their freedom.

Jimmy explained that the river would soon fill up and the whole canyon valley would be flooded with water. He also explained that the beaver dam was really not a dam at all, and would only further exacerbate their problem. When the structure broke, a wall of water would engulf the canyon so quickly that no one would have time to escape.

The news seemed to have had its desired impact. What was once a loud and bustling group of religious zealots had become a quiet sanctuary of contemplators. The giants were perfectly still, almost frozen. A dwarf giant next to Melissa scratched his head. Another giant looked up into the sky as if to look for rain. He even stuck out his tongue in hopes to wet his whistle. Still others just looked at each other to see how they should react. This went on until Porpion erupted into a burst of laughter. He leaned his head and shoulders backward and the ground rumbled when his stomach began to heave up and down as he let out short rhythmic bursts of sound.

"You must know that giants don't swim," said Porpion, finally regaining his composure. He paused expecting an answer, but no one dared offer a reply. "It is true. We don't swim because there has never been, nor will there ever be, water in these canyons. And if there were, we would simply walk to the other side. Water is controlled by the Goddess Amphitrite, and even if it were not, mere water would never match the power and might of a giant." He erupted into laughter again, but this time all of the other worshipers joined him. The ground quaked as giants rolled on the ground in hilarity. They slapped the ground with their hands and laughed harder and harder. The vibration was enough to crack the very ground beneath their feet.

As the giants continued with their display of raucous contempt, one of the dwarf guards ushered Jimmy, Fox, Melissa, and Seth back into the cage. He giggled to himself and shook his head in disbelief as he locked them back into their prison cell. What none of them knew at the moment, however, was that the laughter of a thousand giants was enough to crack a dam, only a few miles away.

The sun had not yet risen but the dawn was upon them. All of the torches had been extinguished now that enough light crept onto the valley floor. Seth made sure that Bumpy was safely tucked away into his new carrying case. Melissa held onto Fox. Jimmy held onto the locked door, wondering how they were going to get out of this one.

Jimmy could see the smoke rise from the fire less than a few hundred yards away. He assumed it was coming from where they make their ritual sacrifices. He also surmised that it was no longer just Fox that these blasphemous creatures planned to burn alive. He saw the look in the eyes of the dwarf giant as he secured the lock. It was a haughty look—with just a hint of pity. They were all going to be sacrificed in the fire, unless Jimmy could think of something quickly. His plan B had failed to work, and unless he could come up with another plan quickly, they were all doomed.

"Don't worry so much, Jimmy," said Melissa. "If those three guys with the funny names could come out of a furnace with not even their clothes singed, God will provide a way for us."

"That's great, Melissa, but I'm sure God appreciates a little effort on our part as well," said Seth.

Jimmy shook his head and responded, "No, the Book of Daniel states they did nothing but hold firm in their faith. Shadrach, Meshach and Abednego sang God's praises and God delivered them from the fiery furnace. You're right, Melissa. We have nothing to fear."

The giants used the two long poles and lifted up the cage with relative ease. Even though there were now three additional people along with Fox, it still only took four giants to lift them. Seth sat up on his knees, as that was as far as he could go without his head hitting the top of the cage. He used all of his strength to shake the cage. He yelled defiantly at the giants. "Let us out of here. You'll pay for this, I promise you that!"

Seth only stopped his ranting when one of the more overweight followers of the caravan spit a wad of something green onto him. It smelled putrid and was so slimy that it left a sticky residue all the way down Seth's check to his pants. Seth sat back down and said, "The least you think they would do is serve us breakfast before the main event."

Melissa, seemingly unaffected by all that was going on around her, had already eaten and filled her pockets with the food that was left for Fox—the Crimson Goddess of Fire. She gave some to Jimmy, who accepted the food but was too preoccupied to eat it. When she tried to get Seth to fill up his backpack, he just shrugged his shoulders and shook his head as if to say what good is food when they were about to die. Melissa knew better, however. She knew this was not the end of their journey.

There was more music, like the night before, but this time it was simply drums with a repetitive beat. The onlookers were more focused today and less festive than the night before. They were on a holy mission to appease their god. The party was over and the finale was just moments away. Still, Melissa peeled something resembling a banana, Jimmy thought hard on another strategy to free them, and Seth looked for something to wipe the slime off of his face.

Fox, like Melissa, was not concerned. Nothing could phase her optimistic outlook on life. She was never really convinced that the Mara people really intended any harm. Her mind was just not conditioned to think in that manner. Even though she had seen her fair share of hardships and struggles in the woods back home, she had never witnessed pure evil before. And if these people planned on throwing her and her friends into a fire to burn them alive, they were indeed pure evil.

The fire was now in full view. The smoke was gone and replaced by flames that shot into the sky. This was the largest fire any of them had ever seen. Jimmy could feel the heat from where they were.

The giants carrying the travelers stopped abruptly. Fox jumped to her feet and yapped, "See, I told you it wasn't so!"

As quickly as the giants stopped, they lowered them to knee level, and several Abaddons ran up and doused the prisoners with water. And then another group right behind those tossed more buckets of water on them, and yet a third group of dwarf giants followed with even more buckets of water. It was both shocking and refreshing. Seth took the opportunity to clean the rest of the giant spittle from his face. Fox immediately shook the water off her fur, not ever having liked baths. She wondered why they would be wasting such a precious resource like this.

"The water ritual is ancient with our people," said Porpion. He was obviously addressing his flock and not the captives. He continued, mostly reading from a scroll of some sort, "The ancient text reads: 'May the Goddess Amphitrite have mercy on all who call her name.' We offer this precious gift, the drenching of the sacrifice. For it has been told that if the Goddess Amphitrite deems a sacrifice worthy, her clothing shall protect and save them from Hephaestus, and Achelous shall then have his will." The scroll was blank and had no writing on it at all, but Porpion was quite proficient at disguising this fact from his followers.

"Who is Hephaestus?" Seth asked.

"I'm sure he's the dude that likes the fire," said Jimmy.

"Quiet!" exclaimed Porpion. He had excellent hearing, surprising Seth and Jimmy who were whispering. He continued reading form the blank scroll, "The ancient text reads: 'When the three stars align in the night sky on the same night that the Crimson Goddess of Fire appears, the battle will begin. The town shall be wiped clean and all will perish.'" There were many rumblings among the crowd. This did not appear to be a well-liked part of the text.

Porpion lifted his huge arms into the air and spread them wide as he commanded his people to be still. "The text reads: 'There is no greater love than to lay down one's life for his friends.' And we are so very grateful that these friends have offered to lay down their lives to appease the gods to save our great metropolis."

"Uh, just a second there, buddy. I don't think any of us offered to lay down our lives. I think you're taking that text completely out of context—" Jimmy was quickly interrupted.

"Quiet!" Porpion looked condescendingly at Jimmy. He then looked back to the crowd. "If our friends are deemed worthy, our beloved Goddess Amphitrite will save them. Listen, my people. These friends come with great knowledge. They say that Our Goddess is sending water to us any day now. But they say it will destroy us. They have contrary spirits, do they not?" The crowd roared and cheered in agreement. "Our Goddess has always provided us with what we need. But the wells are drying and the prophecy is at hand. Shall we let the gods decide? Shall we live in abundance or shall we live in need?" The crowd roared and applauded. Some of the crowd began to chant "abundance" and others simply cheered.

"It is written and practiced that a man willing to lay down his life for his friend shall be offered a time to speak his peace. The time has come. Which of you shall speak?" For the first time since they met Porpion, he addressed them as intelligent, worthy beings.

There was obviously not much time to decide on a representative, so they quickly elected Jimmy to speak for them all. The Mara culture did not seem to esteem women very highly, so that left Melissa out. Seth was much too angry to help matters, and Fox was much too kind. If anyone could speak their way out of this mess, it was Jimmy.

Dwarf giants stood on each side of the cage door and escorted Jimmy out. The shorter of the two held out his hand for Jimmy, who, for no other reason than to experience what a giant felt like, grabbed his large, thick thumb. It was awkward for both the giant and Jimmy. Jimmy's feet actually lifted off the ground when the giant helped him over the threshold. It was embarrassing, and Jimmy hoped no one noticed.

He was placed right next to Porpion, who was at the highest point on the valley floor, giving everyone a good view of their leader. The usually confident Jimmy felt small and vulnerable. He was sure the crowd was quietly ridiculing his diminutive stature. When he released his grip of the guard's large thumb, he stumbled a bit. If the crowd was not amused before, they surely were now. Melissa felt bad for Jimmy, but there was nothing she could do but watch along with everyone else.

Jimmy quickly regained his composure and assessed his new vantage point. Porpion stood to his right. His large hand dangled right above Jimmy's head. Porpion's thumb was not quite as thick as the dwarf's. The crowd standing before him numbered in the thousands. There was a larger assortment of people than he originally thought. The giants and dwarfs were numerous, but there were also many smaller creatures not much larger than himself.

He cleared his throat and began speaking. "Hello. Thank you for giving us a chance to speak," The crowd erupted in laughter and chatter. Jimmy immediately began to feel insecure again. He looked over to Seth and Melissa who smiled and gave him a thumbs up. He said a quick prayer to himself, remembering 2 Timothy 1:7: For God has not given us a spirit of fear, but of power, love, and of a sound mind.

It occurred to Jimmy that God loved all of these creatures, whether or not they returned his love. He suddenly had an overwhelming sense of compassion for them. Here he was, about to beg for his life, but yet it was these people who faced certain death. Jimmy knew that no matter what happened to him, he would live eternally in paradise with his Creator. But he could not say the same for the crowd before him. His compassion strengthened his resolve, and he would never again feel insecure because he was small or seemingly insignificant.

"Part of the passage you quoted from your great scroll is also contained in a book I study. It's called the Bible." The crowd booed and roared; it was blasphemous for someone to claim scripture as their own.

Porpion quieted the crowd by simply raising his arms.

Jimmy continued, "There is no greater love than to lay down one's life for his friends. It was written by the Apostle John in Chapter 15, verse 13 in the Book of John. You see, there was someone who died for all of us. If we believe in Him, we should not perish, but have everlasting life." For the first time the crowd completely hushed, and there was genuine interest in what Jimmy was saying.

"This man was Jesus and He is also the one and only God," he said. The crowd mumbled a bit, but it was obvious they wanted to hear more. Melissa noticed that Porpion appeared somewhat uncomfortable as he looked out over his subjects, but he said nothing as he nodded at Jimmy to continue.

"Unless a friend lays down their life willingly, the gesture is meaningless. Forcing us to die in that fire of your god or goddess is not what the scripture your leader read intended. What you are proposing is murder."

The crowd went wild. But the consensus was not unanimous. Some were outraged that they would be accused of murder or that their god would be blasphemed. Others seemed to be in agreement as if they had questioned these sacrificial acts in the past. Porpion became increasingly uncomfortable, yet there was little he could do. The ancient ritual demanded that the sacrifice should speak and if he were to stop Jimmy now, there would surely be repercussions.

"Jesus was completely innocent, yet he allowed his captors to crucify Him because He loved us—you and me. He alone became the sacrifice for our guilt. No matter how many people you sacrifice to your gods in your fires, you will never attain what you are seeking: peace, the surety of salvation, and most of all eternal love."

Jimmy's voice got louder, his conviction grew stronger, and everyone could sense his unabashed passion. "Whether or not you believe that the river is filling and that the dam will break, you will all face death one day. Even if this valley doesn't flood today, or tomorrow, someday each one of you will die. I tell you to not face death alone. Only our God lived and conquered death. Believe in the way, the truth, and the life …"

Some in the crowd began to chant "Burn them!" and others wanted to hear what else he had to say. Jimmy sensed the crowd becoming increasingly agitated and they would not hear too much more. Jimmy raised his voice as loud as possible, "Because I know how much my God loves me and even you, and because I know I will be with him for eternity, I will offer my life as my testimony to the truth. But I ask you to spare my friends. Take me as your sacrifice and let them go."

Melissa screamed, "No!" But there was no hearing her over the crowd, which was now completely out of control and divided. It seemed that a third of the crowd wanted to set them all free, while others were willing to accept Jimmy's offer. But the majority still wanted them all to burn. They were not persuaded. The dwarves pushed Jimmy back into the cage and looked to Porpion for guidance.

Porpion quieted the crowd and spoke. "The small one spoke elegantly, did he not? If his words are true, will not our goddess of water protect him?" The crowd cheered in affirmation, even the ones that seemed to agree with Jimmy only moments before.

"No innocent shall die here today. Our gods are not cruel. Have they not provided for us? In a land of no rain, lakes, or oceans, have we not found drink in the very earth itself?" The crowd cheered again. They were ready for the climactic end to the ritual. They wanted the familiar, the tradition. They wanted a sacrifice.

Melissa rubbed Jimmy's arm and whispered in his ear, "Thank you for trying. That's the most heroic thing I've ever witnessed."

Porpion shouted, "Achelous will have his will. Amphitrite has spoken and Hephaestus awaits! To the fire!"

The giants lifted the cage and marched towards the fire. Melissa and Seth were suddenly frightened for the first time. The immediacy of their fate was undeniable. The last opportunity for freedom slipped away like sand in an hourglass. They were close enough to the fire to feel the heat. Drops of perspiration formed on their foreheads. Fox panted and whimpered, and Jimmy prayed.

After a short break of silence, the drums continued. They were loud and steady. Boom … boom … boom … boom. The onlookers were mostly quiet, as if in church. They looked hungry, ready for a meal. It had been a long time since their last sacrifice, and the stakes were higher than ever. The prophecy, the dam, the water, and the mysterious strangers had driven the Mara people to near hysteria. Seth would have sworn he actually saw a giant licking his big fat lips, as if the smell of burning bodies would satisfy his hunger for redemption.

The beat of the drums quickened. Boom, boom, boom, boom. The giants held the captives, cage and all, over their heads. They intended to throw them into the fire all at once. Melissa could not believe it. She refused to believe that this was it. Even though death was imminent, and the reality of their predicament unavoidable, she somehow had a peace that surpassed all understanding.

The drummers were beating violently. The atmosphere was chaotic. The crowd was now chanting something indistinguishable to the travelers. It sounded like "humoshgodlio" or "emumushollow." But it did not matter what the crowd was chanting or how fast the drummers were drumming. No matter the pomp and circumstance, they were wrong, and everyone in the cage knew it. What they were doing was evil, and there would be consequences.

All of a sudden, everyone and everything stopped. It was as if it were a choreographed dance. The dwarf giants, as if on cue, bent their knees. As the last movement of their performance, they used all the strength in their mighty legs to hurl Jimmy, Melissa, Seth, Fox—and, unknown to them, the only talking leaf in the universe—into the fire. All that could be heard was the grunting of the dwarfs as they gave it their all. It was their moment to shine. All eyes were on them. The cage lifted up into the air and turned over, tossing its occupants to and fro.

But the show was not over. Out of the sky came something larger than the giants. With lightning speed, it swooped down and took hold of the cage with its powerful legs. It immediately reversed course after seizing the cage and flew upwards, away from the flames and the heat. It was Dauber. And he had come just in time. It took a few seconds for the prisoners to realize what was happening. Once they recognized it was Dauber, everyone in the cage cheered loudly.

The moment did not last long, however. Suddenly Dauber and his caged companions began sinking back down into the flames. Dauber was strong, but for some reason the weight had almost doubled. Jimmy looked below and saw that one of the guards was hanging onto the cage. And right before his eyes he saw another giant jump up to grab the guard's ankle. They descended even faster. The weight was too much for Dauber as he struggled to maintain altitude. Melissa and Seth immediately began hitting the giant's fingers to loosen his grip, but he was much too strong.

The giant looked up at Jimmy and spoke, "Take this key, you will need it to unlock the cage." The giant released his grip on the cage and as he fell into the fire below, he spoke his final words, "I believe." Everyone stared as the two giants quickly fell into the inferno below them.

Chapter 28

BEHIND THE SHADOW

"This is amazing," Seth shouted into the wind. He was looking through the bars of the cage down at the hills and canyons below. A cool breeze blew through his hair, a welcomed respite from the furnace they faced only a short time before.

Fox sat in the middle of the cage on her pillow with Bumpy safely tucked in the pouch around her neck. Melissa and Jimmy were kneeling down at the rear of the cage, looking back from where they came. The giants were long gone and the canyon was once again devoid of life. Everyone felt a sense of exhilaration. They were not only safe, but they were flying first class. The air was fresh, the view stretched for miles, and they were not walking. What more could anyone ask for?

Melissa turned to Jimmy and said, "I don't understand why he gave up his life to get us the key. We could have gotten out of this thing on our own."

"Perhaps he was moved by what he heard, and he just wanted to make sure we knew it," said Jimmy.

Melissa said nothing in response. She contemplated Jimmy's answer and wondered. She wondered if it was worth it; for someone to give up their life like that. The giant knew they did not need the key. Sure, it would help speed things up, but they would have eventually gotten out of the cage one way or another. Could that giant have been so moved at Jimmy's words and actions that he was willing to die so selflessly? If so, if that was really the motivation, it was beautiful. Something she had never witnessed before. It also made everything they were doing here so much more important. More than ever she wanted to find the twelve and accomplish their mission.

No one spoke for a while as they rested and took in the view. Jimmy had given Dauber directions on where to go, the place that the bat lady had told them about. It would not be long until they were at the last known whereabouts of the infamous twelve.

Melissa was not sure if the land below was actually becoming more beautiful or if she was just getting used to it. But there was a sense of grandness to the blandness. The canyon was inspiring, the rolling hills above it were peaceful, and the sky was not too unlike the one back home. Except that it was bluer, probably due to the lack of pollution from industrialization.

"What are we supposed to do when we find the twelve?' asked Melissa to anyone who would answer.

"I assumed they would tell us," answered Seth.

"What if we are supposed to tell them?" said Melissa.

Bumpy lifted himself part way out of his pouch and said, "I would suspect your purpose here is not at all unique from the purpose you have in your world."

"I'm not sure that's much help, Bumpy," said Melissa.

"To love God with all of my heart, soul, strength, and mind. And to love my neighbor as myself," said Jimmy.

"Good luck with that," said Seth, who was now sitting next to Fox and scratching her chin.

"Look," said Jimmy, pointing to a large monolith. "The bottom half is orange and the top half is a reddish-brown. That's got to be the landmark that Athaliah told us about."

Dauber found a flat place to set the cage down a few yards away from the tall monument. The giant's key was too large and cumbersome for just one of them to manage on their own, so both Jimmy and Seth held it as they unlocked the cage door. Seth stepped out and stretched, and Jimmy and Melissa followed Fox and Bumpy out onto the hard sandstone.

"Maybe we should use this for the rest of our travels," suggested Jimmy as he tapped the cage. But when he noticed how tired Dauber looked, he retracted the statement. "Or maybe it would be more productive to walk."

Dauber, in between breaths, reassured him, "It's not a problem. I've carried heavier cargo many times."

"I'm not sure cargo is the appropriate word for your unfortunate victims," said Seth.

"That's not fair," said Melissa. "Everyone has to eat."

"Hey, as long as he doesn't start flying into a big mud house with me in his talons, I'm good," said Seth.

"Come on, y'all, let's be quick about this," said Jimmy. "We don't know if there are folks following us. We need to get away from this canyon and the Mara people as soon as possible." He did not wait for them to fall in line after him. He immediately headed towards the tall monolith.

The plateau was about halfway between the bottom of the valley floor and the top of the canyon ridge. It was a relatively large crest, perhaps one hundred yards in total. Jimmy scanned the side of the canyon wall and could not imagine how anyone could have scaled down from the top without ropes and gear. There was an overhang at least fifty feet up, a sizable drop even for a giant. He wondered if perhaps the twelve climbed up from the bottom.

As the other travelers—aside from Dauber, who decided to rest his wings—were slowly making their way towards the monument, Jimmy had already circled around it twice. He was not quite sure what he should be looking for. There was no door on the monolith or in the surrounding rock.

"Well, where are they?" asked Seth.

"Why don't you help me look?" said Jimmy as he continued to inspect the area for clues.

"There are not that many places to look. I think you've just about covered it. Maybe this isn't the right place."

"The least we can do is look, Seth," said Melissa.

"Fine, I'm looking. I'm looking." Seth's eyes quickly darted about as he stood in one spot and turned a complete three-hundred and sixty degrees.

Melissa walked over to the edge and looked down.

"Careful there, Melissa," shouted Jimmy.

Fox, in the meantime, seemed to be preoccupied with a flying insect of some kind. Bumpy crawled out of the pouch hanging from Fox's neck and fluttered around as best he could. There was not much of a breeze and what little there was kept pulling Bumpy towards the ridge of the crest. He did not want to find himself floating helplessly down to the canyon floor below, so he maintained a relatively narrow search field. Neither he nor Fox were much help.

The other three came together and stared up at the tall monument. Seth thought it resembled petrified cake icing in the shape of a super skinny Snoopy dog. Melissa thought it looked more like a huge wax candle that had dripped wax on one side. Jimmy, having visited Utah as a child, which had many similar structures, simply regarded it as a sandstone pinnacle carved by the wind.

Their attention was diverted when they became distracted by Fox's yapping. She sat up on her hind legs and pawed at the air.

"What is she doing?" asked Seth.

"I think she sees something," said Melissa.

They walked over to Fox, who was about halfway between the monolith and the canyon wall. They immediately noticed that it was not an insect she was chasing, but a leaf floating up and down in the air.

"Oh, it's just Bumpy. I think we have more important things to do than play," said Seth.

"Why shouldn't they have some playtime?" said Melissa.

Jimmy was the first to notice something peculiar. Bumpy was indeed floating up and down, but it almost appeared that he was disappearing and reappearing at different points. "Melissa, go walk across that line," suggested Jimmy.

"What line?" she asked.

"The shadow right there." He pointed. "The monolith is creating a shadow from here to there, see?"

"Okay. I don't know why you don't just do it yourself, but no problem, here goes ..." Melissa walked across the shadow and nothing happened. "Is that what you were expecting?"

"I'm not sure what I was expecting. But doesn't anyone else other than Fox notice that Bumpy is disappearing and reappearing?"

"Am I really?" asked Bumpy.

"Oh yeah, I see it now," said Seth.

"Me too," added Melissa.

"Hey, Bumpy, drift away from us as far as you can and give it a count of five and then come back towards us," said Jimmy.

"Can do ..." Bumpy's voice was cut off at the same time he disappeared out of sight. After about five seconds he reappeared. "Did I do it?"

Melissa and Seth both walked across the shadow again, as Bumpy had just done, but neither of them disappeared.

"Maybe it's because he's a magical leaf," offered Seth.

"No. The same set of laws has applied to him as us the whole time. Why would they differ now?" said Jimmy. "It's got to be something else.

"Fox you try it," said Melissa. Fox gingerly stepped over the shadow and back again. But nothing happened.

"What's on the other side?" Seth asked Bumpy.

"It looks the same as here, from what I can tell," answered Bumpy.

"I think I've got it. We jump into the air as we cross over the shadow. If we are touching the earth as we cross, it won't work. I'll see you on the other side," said Jimmy. He then looked towards Dauber, who was several yards away and yelled, "If I'm right, we won't be gone long, Dauber. Hold tight and rest up." Jimmy then walked to the shadow and jumped up and over, disappearing in the process.

When the others joined Jimmy on the other side, in yet another dimension, they found him reading something written on a stone near the base of the monolith. Other than the stone the message was written on, everything looked exactly the same as before they jumped over the shadow.

"Have no fear. You are here. But should you choose another step, my dear, make sure you know true scripture or you shall never reappear. If in doubt, do not pout, simply turn and step back out. Through the next shadow you shall see a word that is truly divine. If you know the answer, the answer there you'll find." Everyone read the message to themselves except for Melissa, who read it aloud for Fox and Bumpy.

"I nominate Jimmy," said Seth.

"I'm pretty sure we are all supposed to go," said Jimmy.

"What if we don't know the answer?"

"If it's about scripture, Jimmy will know the answer," said Melissa. She examined the shadow, and bit her lower lip and then snapped her fingers. "If we jumped in this way, I would suppose the way back out is the opposite." She walked around to the other side in order to jump forward. She disappeared.

"I think a group vote would be in order. But I suppose it's a little too late for that," said Seth, shaking his head. "Maybe I should just wait here, in between."

"No, y'all go back and wait. I'll go forward with Melissa. Fox and Bumpy, stay with Seth. Melissa and I will be back as soon as possible." Jimmy wasted no time following Melissa over the shadow.

Once on the other side, he found Melissa reading another message on another stone. He looked around and noticed that this place was exactly the same as before, with one horrifying difference. There were skeletons all about. He wondered if Melissa even noticed. He hoped that she was too preoccupied with the message.

"What does it say," he asked.

"One thing in common these things have, say it aloud and you will pass. Heed this warning before you speak, or a worse fate you will meet. Once your hand is on the stone, just one chance or rest forever with the bones. This was in the beginning, This became flesh, and This was God."

"Praise God. I know the answer," said Jimmy excitedly.

"Is it just one word?" asked Melissa.

Jimmy laughed. "Yes, indeed it is."

"What's so funny? You better be sure you know the word or we're done for. All of these people probably thought they knew the right word too," she said as she looked around at all the bones around them.

Jimmy was surprised that she had noticed the corpses and was still able to concentrate on the clue. She seemed to be handling the stress well. "These people obviously did not know the one true God. You've read enough of the Bible to know the answer yourself."

"There's no way I would take a chance on guessing. I wouldn't dare risk it."

Jimmy placed his hand on the stone monolith and winked at Melissa, and just as he started to speak the word, she shouted, "Wait! You have to be sure. How are you so sure you know the right answer?" Jimmy removed his hand

"I've read the Bible several times through. I studied it for the last ten years and prayed about it even more. I'm confident in two things: God's word is true and God is faithful. We got this because, if nothing else, He's got us first."

"You mean because He loved us first? I admire your faith. I hope my own faith will be as strong as yours someday."

"I also have a lot of faith in you. You are going to do great things. I know it. But for that to happen, we need to take the next step. Ready?"

Melissa took a deep breath and said, "Ready."

Jimmy placed his hand back on the rock and almost whispered as he said, "Word."

Melissa, more or less to herself, repeated the clue with the answer: "The Word was in the beginning, the Word became flesh, and the Word was God. The Word …"

They both remained silent. Jimmy looked to the right and then to the left, but he did not move his head. Melissa, taking a cue from Jimmy, also remained still, but more out of fear of being struck dead than missing anything.

Jimmy finally broke the silence. "I know without a doubt that was the right answer, but why isn't anything happening?"

Melissa pointed to the ground and said, "That shadow wasn't here before. I know because while you were reading the clue, I was looking for a way out, just in case. There was no shadow line to cross."

"Well, shall we?" Jimmy stuck his elbow out towards Melissa and she in turn put her arm through his and they both jumped over the shadow together.

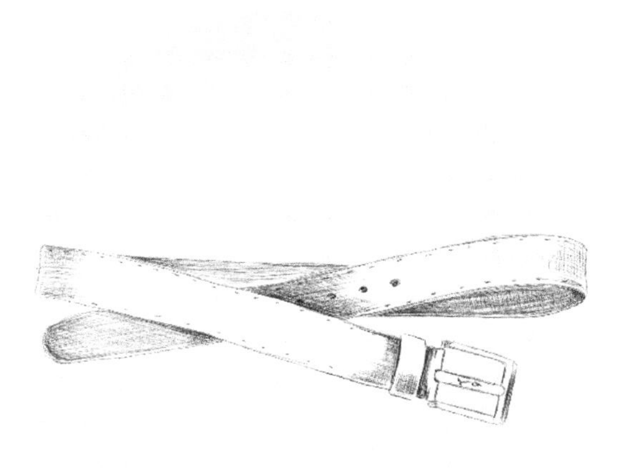

Chapter 29
The Twelve

They had no idea what to expect on the last shadow jump. There was no time to imagine the possibilities. Would it be more of the same? Another flat plateau just like the previous three, or would they be transported to some exotic paradise with strange beautiful plants and creatures? Would the twelve be there to greet them with an amazing mystical assignment? Or would there be yet more clues and hurdles to traverse?

Melissa was hoping for lots of fanfare, which would mean that everything was as it should be. Jimmy was simply hoping that they did not have to pass any more tests. As confident as he was in his ability to answer Bible trivia, he was not a fool. The sooner they found the twelve, the sooner they could get back home. He was not worried about himself, but he felt responsible for their group and he had no idea how he was going to explain their absence.

Neither said a word as they took in the latest terrain. It was, to Melissa's chagrin, much the same as where they had originally come from. There were a few benign variations, however. To the right of the monolith, against the canyon wall, there were doors that most likely led to dwellings of some kind. There was an outside sitting area with chairs and a table. There were even planters with walkways in between. The place had been landscaped and cared for, that much was obvious.

Jimmy noticed a ladder made of jute and wood rungs resting on the side of the canyon, hanging down from above. He could not see how far it went up or where it originated from. Although it looked sturdy, he was not interested in climbing to find out where it went. The terrace looked both lived in and recently forgotten. While the planters had plants in them, many of them had dried up and died. The wooden chairs were dusty and randomly placed, with one of them turned on its side.

Needless to say, it was not the welcome Melissa had hoped for. There were no singing disciples or dancing elves. To her, the place looked a bit forlorn. She could see that someone had put a lot of work and care into making everything homey, and it made her sad to see the neglect. It was like a home that someone had to leave in a hurry, without getting to say goodbye.

"What now?" she asked.

Jimmy cupped his hands around his mouth and shouted, "Hello, anybody home?"

Melissa gave it a try as well. "Hello? We're looking for the twelve. Is anyone here?"

There was no response.

Melissa moved over to one of the wooden chairs and sat. Jimmy picked up the chair next to hers, placing it upright, and joined her. They contemplated their next move.

"This is not fair," she said.

"What do you mean?"

"We answered the question. We followed all the rules. We risked our lives to get here. And nothing. No one. It's not fair."

"Well, that's an interesting response. I'm not sure 'fair' is part of the equation."

"Maybe not, but for once I just wish things would go as planned."

"Maybe this is the plan. We don't know everything. I think we should explore a little more. Maybe go inside one of the doors and see if there are any clues as to what happened here."

Before they could get up to investigate, they heard a voice come from behind. They turned to see an ordinary man who did not look much older than Jimmy. He was thin, average height, and had a kind face. His eyes were deep-set and somewhat sad, or so Melissa thought. "There was a plan, or so we thought, but you are several months late arriving," he said.

Jimmy asked, "Who are you? Are you one of the twelve?"

"Ah, the twelve. Is that what they are calling us now? There were twelve of us, so that seems as good of a title as any," he said. "My name is Propo, and I'm from the Fifth Kingdom. It's nice to finally meet you."

"What happened to the others?" asked Jimmy.

"We were discovered, even with all the precautions. We received word months ago that you were on your way, but alas, it did not happen as we had thought."

Melissa noticed that the man's eye twitched nervously when he spoke. "Who discovered you?" she asked.

"It was only a matter of time," he said as his left eye twitched again. "I'm very much aware of the world from which you come. We—this world, if you will—is not unlike yours. There is a battle being waged here and there. Jimmy undoubtedly knows the scripture, 'For we wrestle not against flesh and blood, but against principalities, against powers, against the rulers of the darkness of this world, against spiritual wickedness in high places.' There is one God of the universe. One Savior for all. One Word."

"You're saying that our Savior is the same?" asked Jimmy.

Melissa was not sure if the man's nervousness came from insecurity or just lack of sleep, but either way she found him oddly charismatic. "But how can that be? Most of the creatures here are not even human. And the animals don't talk in our world like they do here. Everything is so different," said Melissa.

"There is only one God. Of this, you can be sure. There is only one creator of everything," Propo said.

"I don't understand," she said.

"You will. Your name is Melissa, correct?"

"Yes," she answered.

"The reality is that both our cultures have fallen, and all who were created in His image have chosen their own will over His. We all have allowed evil to persuade us. The penalty, of course, is obvious and deserved," said Propo.

"Penalty?" asked Melissa.

"Dying, death, disease, violence, hate, war … the list goes on. Justice has to be met for all the evil we choose to do."

"And like us, you need a savior too," said Jimmy. "Someone who paid the penalty."

Melissa said, "Wait a second. I'm not at all clear on why we all need someone to pay a penalty. I understand Jesus died for us to offer a way to heaven, to be with God, but I don't understand why the savior needed to pay anything. Isn't He God? Why would He need to do that?"

Propo looked at Jimmy and said, "I'm surprised the One chose someone so young in the faith to lead the way here. It is not at all what I expected."

Melissa was not outwardly bothered by Propo's opinion of her. "Don't worry, Jimmy here can make up for my lack of understanding, and if you think I'm clueless, you should meet my brother, Seth."

"She's learning and she has more faith than you and me combined," Jimmy said. "That I can guarantee. She also has an amazing heart. She has a gift when it comes to communicating with the people in your world. She will learn the rest in due time."

Melissa smiled. "Aww, thank you Jimmy. That's so sweet of you. I didn't know you thought so highly of me. A few months ago, I was just a silly teenage girl to you."

"I never said that."

"You didn't have to."

Jimmy returned her smile, then looked back to Propo. "Why are we here?"

"The Word. It has vanished from our world. The originals, as we call them, those who knew about God and passed the stories down orally, have long since passed away. They were experts in memorizing and transferring truth to the next generation until it would be written and preserved for all time. But the evil one vanquished all books. All writings of any importance and truth were erased."

"How can one person do all that?" asked Melissa.

"They call it magic, wizardry, but call it what you will—it is evil and it is a lie," said Propo.

"That explains why your Bible was blank, Jimmy. When we opened it, there were no words whatsoever."

"What can we possibly do?" asked Jimmy. "We are just regular folks from a very simple place. We have no magic. We can't compete with those in this world."

"I'm not the one that chose you. Only the one that did knows why and how. I'm a blind believer. I have faith but I have never seen, not even the Word. You two have vastly more knowledge of the Creator than I do. I suppose that's why you are here."

"In a nutshell, you don't know what it is we are supposed to do?" asked Melissa.

"I know a part of it. But not all," he said.

Jimmy walked over to the edge of the landing and was looking down when he said, "Where are the other eleven?"

"There were indeed twelve of us in the beginning. But that was years ago. The number of us was never the important thing. It was what we represented."

Jimmy walked back over to Melissa and Propo and said, "And that is … was?"

"The Five Realms of Here."

"The Five Realms of Here?" Melissa repeated.

"Yes, I am from the land of Pixinese."

"And where are the other … representatives?" asked Jimmy.

"After you failed to show up, we waited for months. Most of the others lost hope, some lost faith, and others simply thought we misunderstood the fragments."

"Fragments?" asked Melissa.

"Fragments are writings that survived from the accounts of the originals, but there are very few and it's difficult to verify if they are authentic or not. I can't really blame the doubt of my comrades. We have so little to go on."

"I still don't know why we are here," said Jimmy.

"It's my understanding that you were to bring the Word, but I am not sure. We were assembled, the twelve, to help disseminate the Word to the five realms. But the others starting hearing of changes. The dark woods have been rumored to be sprouting life again. The Lake of Entitlement has apparently been filled with water. And the latest news is that the river of life has begun to flow once more. If that is true, our world is changing in ways unimaginable to my people."

"Wow. It's true. I witnessed the Lake of Entitlement fill with water myself. I was there," said Melissa.

"You were?" asked Jimmy.

"Long story, but yes, Fox and I were both there."

Jimmy became excited as he confirmed Propo's suspicions. "If this canyon is the river of life, then you are correct, that too has begun flowing again."

Propo looked pensive and his eye twitched as he considered the words of his guests. "Everything is happening out of order and much too quickly. I don't understand. You two must get to the vanquished Library of Truth. It is in the realm of Matana. I will try to find as many of the twelve as possible, but time has gotten the better of us, it seems. I'm afraid your charity would be welcomed. If you can find the ancient writings that verify the truth of the Originals, we can get it to the five kingdoms."

"I see. We are to help spread the Good News of the Creator and Savior to your people, but why do you need us to do this?" asked Jimmy.

"I understand your frustration. Let's go inside, shall we? There is food and drink. It will take a while to explain everything that I know. And unfortunately, what I know is not nearly enough."

"Our friends are waiting in between here and there," Melissa explained, "and I don't think we should stay too long. My brother is not the most patient person in the world."

"I see. There is a reason there were twelve representing only five kingdoms. The evil one knows us and can follow us. The plan was to send one to each kingdom, but her deception is deep. The thought was that if we had twice as many plus two, we would be able to overcome any loss and perhaps confuse her. But alas, we are down to only one, me, and we haven't even begun. I'm sure the other eleven, those still alive anyway, will rally to the cause once they hear of your arrival. You, on the other hand, can travel through our kingdoms undetected. She can only track you in real time—she has no otherworldly power over those of another world. But don't get me wrong, the evil one will seek you out, and should she find you, the consequences will be severe."

"If you were to come with us?" asked Melissa.

"I would act like a tracking device. We, the twelve, have to be very clever to evade her detection, and that would be nearly impossible traveling with all of you. The evil one can take any shape or form, but will most likely emulate something recognizable to you, probably human, like yourselves. Be leery and always vigilant."

"So how do we find this library in Matana? How do we get there?" asked Jimmy.

"I have no idea. This is as far as I have ever traveled in my world. But I do know who does know. This canyon leads to the Lake of Entitlement. There is someone there who is as old as the ages. She knows everything. You can trust her and she knows you are coming."

"Willow?" said Melissa.

"Yes, the rumor is true then? You have met her?" said Propo.

"I should say so. She saved my life. She's amazing."

"If she is so knowledgeable, why can't she come to us?" asked Jimmy.

"Well, she's deeply rooted to where she is," said Melissa.

"If you have met Willow," Propo said, "then you know to avoid the Land of Indulgences. Stick to the canyon valley where the river once flowed and you will see Willow on the banks of The Land of Indulgences. Go no farther than where her roots grow and you will be safe. I wish I could go with you. I wish I could tell you more, but there is little time. All I can do is thank you from the bottom of my heart for all that you have done and all that you will do to help save the lost in our world."

"I suppose the way back to our friends is up and over the shadows," said Jimmy.

"Yes," he answered. "I have been told that you will need a way to float on water. Which makes no sense to me at all, but you must take that table back over the shadows with you." He pointed to the table in front of the chairs where they had been sitting.

"How is a table going to help us float on water?" asked Melissa.

Jimmy, who had already examined the table up close, said, "Because it's not really a table at all. It's a small, flat-bottomed boat." He flipped the boat over and continued, "Nice craftsmanship, considering no one around here has probably ever needed one."

Melissa looked at Propo and asked, "Will we see you again?"

"We shall see. I will do everything in my power to help you when the time is right. There will be more with me, I'm sure. At least a remnant of the twelve must exist. Please guard the Word with your lives, a whole world depends upon it."

"You have my word," said Jimmy.

"Pardon the pun," said Melissa with a chuckle. Propo missed the joke but smiled anyway.

"One more thing." Propo pulled the belt from around his cloak and gave it to Jimmy. "Take this and keep it always on your person. If you ever meet anyone from my Kingdom, they will recognize it and they will give you safe passage."

Jimmy took the belt and slid it between his fingers. The brown leather had been worn smooth from years of use. Not wearing one of his own, he quickly slid it through his belt loops. It was a perfect fit. The buckle was a small copper rectangle, nothing out of the ordinary. Jimmy thanked him.

Melissa hugged Propo goodbye and assured him that they would meet again. She, to Jimmy's surprise, initiated a prayer. Propo seemed taken aback and not quite sure what to do. Jimmy briefly explained the tradition and its purpose. This seemed to give Propo much pleasure. Melissa had never seen anyone so excited to pray. She would never again take the act for granted.

After they finished saying their goodbyes, Melissa and Jimmy picked up the small boat. They were surprised at how light it was, and they jumped over the shadows to rejoin the others back on the original plateau. It was none too soon, as Seth was quite irritated and had the other three in a tizzy by trying to persuade Dauber to take him to the top of the canyon so he could scout their surroundings.

Fox was so excited to see Melissa and Jimmy return that she wet herself. No one noticed except Melissa, and she said nothing. Fox circled around them and stood on her hind feet and yapped as fast and as loud as she could manage.

Bumpy was less focused on the return of his friends than the canyon below. He did not want to mention it to the others, so as to not scare them, but he had been monitoring the Mara people gathering below. They had been discovered, and the giants were climbing the canyon walls towards the plateau. If it were not for Dauber, they would be trapped with no place to go.

"I suggest we fly away from here as soon as possible. Look below," said Bumpy.

Everyone, including Dauber, walked to the edge and looked down. The giants were adept at climbing and had already managed to scale halfway up the canyon wall. There must have been hundreds of them. They were so eager and careless that some of the giants were being knocked back down to the ground below by their fellow giants. This was evident by a brief descending scream followed by a puff of dust.

Jimmy looked over at Dauber and shouted, "Are you up for another flight?"

Dauber flapped his wings, his equivalent of a preflight warm-up. He then made several attempts to lift off the ground but only managed a short hop in the air. "There's something wrong with my wings, I can't get any lift. This has never happened to me before."

Seth looked him over and said, "His wings, they're smaller than before. Much too small for the size of his body."

Jimmy went to get a closer look, as did Melissa, Fox, and Bumpy. "You're right, Seth. His wings have shrunk," said Jimmy.

"But what'll we do?" said Seth. "Those giants will be up here in no time, and we're stuck. They will probably throw us down to the bottom of the canyon."

"That's my brother for ya," said Melissa. "His first concern is for himself and nothing for our friend, who is obviously in distress."

Seth responded, "Who? Dauber? That's not true! If we can't make it out of here, neither can he. We are all equally doomed!"

Fox yapped nervously as she ran from the edge and back to Dauber. "They are fast, those pesky giants."

"What's that thing you brought back with you?" asked Seth.

"It's a boat. A flat-bottomed boat," answered Jimmy.

"Great, that's really useful out here in the desert."

"The man on the other side of the shadow said to bring it. I don't really know why. Reckon I should have asked, but we were in a hurry, and he seemed a little overwhelmed with all the questions."

Melissa said, "Guys, Fox is right. Those giants are fast and they look really angry. We need to figure something out. And quick."

They began looking for any possible way of escape. Seth lifted the boat up and looked underneath, as if it might sprout wings or something. Jimmy went to the side of the canyon wall in hopes they had missed something, like a door or passageway, but there was nothing. Melissa simply walked back and forth on the ledge, biting her fingernails. Fox followed closely behind her, wagging her tail nervously.

Melissa snapped her fingers and exclaimed. "I've got it. Of course. We just jump back over the shadow, all of us together." But when she looked towards the monolith, her face turned as pale as a ghost. "The shadow, it's gone. There is no shadow. What happened to the shadow?"

"The sun has moved. Try jumping all around it," said Seth.

"Where?" responded Melissa.

"Anywhere, everywhere," answered Jimmy.

Fox was the first to jump. She ran all around the monolith jumping up and down back and forth. All of the others joined her, except for Dauber who was still flapping his wings that seemed to have shrunk even more.

The jumping only resulted in three out-of-breath humans, a hopelessly determined fox, and a leaf trying to dodge all four of them. There was no way off or out. They were indeed trapped.

Jimmy and Seth, breathing heavily, sat with their backs against the tall skinny pillar. They were in deep thought. Melissa made several attempts to stop Fox from jumping. But Fox thought she was playing a game of dodge, so she continued to jump around Melissa long after the others gave up. She forgot all about the original reason they began jumping in the first place; she was having too much fun playing with her friend.

"Look!" exclaimed Seth as he pointed at Dauber.

Dauber had shrunk considerably since they last inspected his wings. And not just his wings had shrunk, but his entire body. It seemed as though Dauber might be returning to his original size.

Dauber did not care what size he was as long as his wings could carry him. He never thought he would want to be small again, but if it meant he could fly, he welcomed the demotion. Actually, he found being gigantic had its own set of problems. He did not like the fact that he could be seen coming from miles away. There were benefits to being small, he realized. But he did wish his friend Sticky could have seen him. He sorely missed his friend back home in the woods of Garland County.

"Maybe we should throw the boat down onto the giants, knock them off the wall," said Seth.

"What good would that do, young feller?" said Bumpy, who was monitoring the situation closer than anyone. "There are hundreds of them giants clawing their way up here."

Melissa had finally managed to catch Fox. She patted her on the head as they stood close to the edge, continuing to watch the onslaught of zealous giants.

"We don't need that cage anymore," said Melissa. "Let's push it over the edge. At least it'll slow them down."

Jimmy and Seth looked at each other as if to say, "Why didn't we think of that?" Without saying a word, they jumped to their feet and rushed over to the cage. With Melissa and Dauber's help, they pushed it to the very edge of the plateau. They would wait until the giants got a little closer before pushing it over. They wanted to knock as many of them down as possible. It might not save them, but it would surely be satisfying to see the enemy suffer a little.

Bumpy positioned himself so he could relay the giants' progress to the others who were waiting behind the cage, ready to push on his command.

Jimmy used the time to think about what Propo had said. He wondered why God chose to use them for such an important task. Why choose him and a couple of inexperienced kids, one of whom did not even believe in God, and the other who only had a simple understanding of the Gospel? There must be a good reason, he thought, and he hoped he would live to find out what it was.

Bumpy floated over to the battalion of four who were waiting patiently to take out as many marauders as possible. "It's time. If we are lucky and it hits just right, we might take out hundreds of them."

Melissa quickly responded, "Forget about luck, I pray that God will defeat our enemies by using their own trap to thwart them all. Dear God, may this cage hit precisely in the right spot to knock all of the giants off this canyon wall. Amen!"

"On the count of three, we push," said Jimmy. "Ready?"

Melissa and Seth nodded. Dauber moved his legs in the dirt like a bull ready to charge. When Jimmy finished counting to three, they all heaved and pushed with all of their might. Watching the large cage, which had only hours earlier held them captive, fall towards the giants was surreal. It felt like they were all part of a medieval battle atop a castle wall. Melissa crossed her fingers for luck, something Bumpy would bring up later, as he did not believe in luck. Seth held his breath and Jimmy gritted his teeth. It was their only hope for a reprieve.

In a matter of seconds, it took out one, two and then three giants. Melissa raised her arms in triumph and Fox jumped with joy. Then they watched in horror as their only weapon of defense hit a small outcropping. The wood broke apart and bounced clear of all of the remaining giants. It was a failure. It was only a matter of minutes before they would be faced with a deadly invasion.

Seth scowled, "A lot of good that prayer did, Melissa."

"It's not over yet," she said.

"It pretty much is."

Dauber walked over to Seth and said, "Never lose hope, Seth. Never."

"Yeah, right. You're one to talk, you can't even fly anymore."

Jimmy spoke up in Dauber's defense, "You do realize that Dauber still has his legs and grippers. He could have crawled up and out of this canyon faster than any giant."

"Then why don't we all jump on him and go," said Seth.

"He's shrunk too much," said Jimmy.

Melissa patted Dauber on the head and said, "You should go now, Dauber. Get out of here before it's too late."

"Never. It's what Jimmy said. I believe it too. There is nothing greater than a friend who would lay down his life for another. I know you all would do the same for me," said Dauber.

Fox pawed at Melissa and said, "I hear something. Do you hear it too?"

"Yeah, I hear the sound of a bunch of grunting, surly giants slobbering their way up here," said Seth.

"I hear it," said Dauber to Fox.

It was not long before they all heard *and* saw it. They looked to the north, up the canyon from which they came, dumbfounded. No one said a word. They just stood, frozen.

It was amazing.

The wall of water gushed towards them, filling the canyon from one side to the other. There was no time to speak or move—all they could do was watch in awe. Other than the sounds of water rushing towards them, the sound of screams and groans could be heard from the enemy below. The water was powerful. Nothing could stop its wrath. The Mara people did not stand a chance. The water swept them off the side of the canyon wall as if they were bugs on a sheet of ice.

Fox watched with curiosity as the giants slipped underneath the water, never to be seen again. She watched one after another go under, thinking that surely a few of them must have had enough strength or skill to surface again. Could they not even tread water? But it did not happen. The current quickly and forcefully whisked the enemy away.

Jimmy noticed that a few of the more normal-sized Mara people were able to float on top of the water for a few moments, but eventually they all succumbed to the current and were dragged down to their ultimate death. Even though they were the same people that only hours before tried to burn him alive, he felt sad as he watched their arms flail, reaching futilely for something solid to hold onto.

After the water completely filled the canyon, wiping away any signs of the giants and the Mara people, it crested just a few inches lower than the surprised victors. In a matter of seconds, all the noisy chaos turned into a peaceful gurgling river. Jimmy looked out across the water and then back at the boat resting only a few feet away. Melissa hugged Fox, who took the opportunity to lick Melissa all over her face.

Bumpy took in the new surroundings. What was once a water-deprived land now had enough water to supply the entire realm. He floated just high enough above the new river to allow his stem to dip below the waterline.

Seth stood with his arms crossed, shaking his head in disbelief. Dauber looked over at Seth and said, "Never again doubt the strength of faith, especially when that faith rests in the very one that gave you breath. We all have a purpose, and just because some of us might not know what ours is doesn't mean we should discourage those that do."

"What? I get it. God saved us, again. But why make us sweat it out, that's all I'm saying."

Melissa rolled her eyes and said, "Oh, boy! I never thought a dirt dauber would be smarter than my own brother. No offense, Dauber."

"None taken," he said.

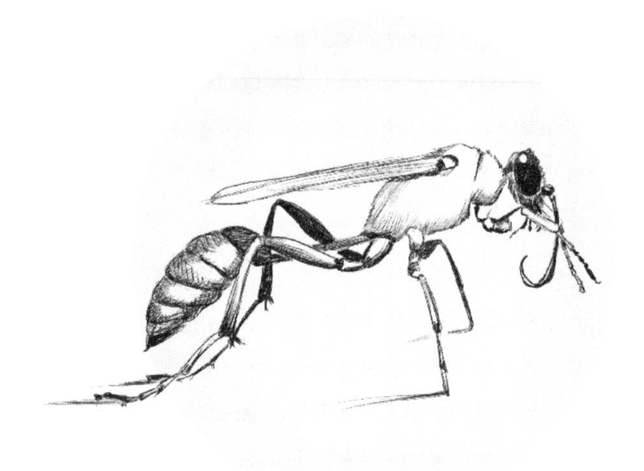

Chapter 30

TRANSITIONS

With no oars to row, the travelers were at the will of the river's current, which was fortunately going in the direction of their destination, the Lake of Entitlement. There were no signs of giants or any other Mara people. Not knowing how to swim was certainly a disadvantage.

After all of the stress and trauma, things now seemed remarkably serene. Melissa stretched out in the sun, which really only amounted to sitting in the middle of the boat between Seth and Jimmy. Her legs dangled over the edge of the boat and her back was propped up against the opposite side. Fox was curled in a tight ball napping in Melissa's lap.

Dauber, who was now the size of a bread loaf, managed to position himself on the edge of the boat next to Melissa's legs. No one said anything, but they found Dauber to be oddly intimidating and rather ugly in his current form. His stinger seemed much more ominous in the cramped quarters. Whenever he moved, even the tiniest bit, everyone would flinch. Luckily Dauber did not pick up on their apprehension, sparing any hurt feelings.

Bumpy amused himself on the tranquil journey by floating in and around the boat. There was not much of a breeze so he chose not to wander too far off. He found that there were more currents of air at the rear where Seth sat holding tightly onto his backpack.

Melissa had asked to borrow Seth's pack so she could cushion her back from the hard, unforgiving wood, but he seemed aggressively opposed to the idea. She was too tired to argue. No one had yet noticed, but the backpack seemed to have attained an increasing significance with Seth. He too could have used it as a cushion, but there he sat cradling it more like a baby.

With all that was going on around them, Seth could never be too careful. He had kept his treasure safe so it would make it back home. He occasionally looked inside, only to quickly zip it back up again. This had become a habit only he was aware of, and he would never again let the pack out of his sight—at least not willingly.

As Bumpy was floating around, he innocently and unknowingly brushed the side of Seth's hand. Seth instinctively flinched, knocking Bumpy away from him. "Oh, no, I'm sorry Bumpy, I wasn't paying attention. Are you okay?"

After regaining his composure Bumpy responded, "I think so, and it's not your fault, partner. I shouldn't have been so careless."

Melissa noticed something fall on Fox's nose. She picked it off and brought it up to her face for a closer look. It was small, brown, and shaped like the state of Idaho. "Oh, no," she said.

"What is it?" asked Jimmy.

"I think it's a piece of Bumpy," she said.

Fox looked up and tilted her head quizzically.

"No!" exclaimed Seth. "I'm sorry Bumpy. When I flinched, I must have broken off a piece of you!"

Bumpy floated over to look at his latest missing membrane and sighed, "Oh, well. It's really quite inevitable for a leaf like me. I'm so dry."

"Why don't you take a dip in the water," suggested Melissa.

"I'm afraid that might be worse. I could get a case of the mildews."

"We should be more careful, and you should not float around as much, Bumpy," said Jimmy.

"Don't y'all worry none about me. There's nothing happening that hasn't happened to a gazillion of my kind before me. It's just the natural course of things."

No one was quite sure if Bumpy was as unaffected by his slow deterioration as he professed, so no one pressed further with any more questions or comments. Melissa found herself amazed at the fact that Bumpy even had a life at all. She felt honored that she got to spend this time with an actual talking, living leaf. It was nothing short of miraculous, and she relished every moment of their time together. Her affection for all living things and all of God's creations was at an all-time high. All of her senses had been elevated. She was more aware and more sensitive to her surroundings than she ever thought possible.

"Hey, y'all. I think we have company," said Jimmy.

"Where?" asked Seth, who sat up on his knees.

"Out in the water, about two hundred feet to the left," said Jimmy.

Melissa quickly moved her legs so that they were no longer dangling over the side. "What'll we do? We don't have anything to defend ourselves with."

Dauber flapped his wings, but still could not get enough lift to go anywhere. He pouted and said nothing as he slowly crawled off the lip of the boat to safety inside. Fox joined Jimmy at the front of the boat, looked out over the water, and said, "I'm sure it's friendly. I've found that things in water are usually one of two things, and I certainly suppose they could be both things too."

"And what are those two things?" asked Melissa after waiting a few seconds for Fox to complete her thought.

"Friendly or tasty, of course. I would not like to think them friendly *and* tasty, but that is certainly a possibility, is it not?"

Melissa shook her head, somewhat disgusted. "I thought foxes were vegetarians?"

"Are vegetarians nice or tasty?" asked Fox.

"A mixture of both, I'm sure," said Jimmy, laughing. He looked back out over the water. "I don't see anything now. Maybe it was the water playing tricks on my eyes."

"No, there were two big fat blobby things swimming quite fast under the water. I saw them myself," said Fox.

"Great, all we need are killer blobby things to overturn our boat," said Seth, holding on even more tightly to his treasure. "I certainly hope *they're* vegetarians."

"If this river hasn't had water in it for hundreds or thousands of years, what in the world could be swimming in it now?" asked Melissa.

As if on cue, the two blobby swimmers, also known as Mackenzie and McClanahan, speedily raced towards the boaters. They leaped over them in an amazing display of grace and agility. Mackenzie could be heard giggling when she was directly overhead. Their entry back into the water would have been scored at least a nine by an Olympic jury. Bumpy, however, would have given them no more than a five as he was the unfortunate recipient of the few drops of water that would have kept them from a perfect score.

"It's the beavers!" exclaimed Melissa.

"Who?" inquired Fox. She and Dauber were the only ones not to have met the artistic duo.

"They are the ones that led us to the other side of the dam," answered Melissa. "You will love them, Fox."

"Beavers are nice, see. Nice and tasty, I was right," said Fox.

Mackenzie and McClanahan rested on their backs as they circled the boat. Dauber, realizing it was now safe, climbed back up on the edge of the boat to get a better look at the beavers. He was a little embarrassed at having sought refuge, something very unlike him, but he had never been so vulnerable before. He was born to fly, and this was the first time in his life he was unable to do so. He felt sure the others understood. The truth is, no one even noticed.

"I see you learned how to swim," said Jimmy.

"We didn't have much choice," said Mackenzie." Our gallery held the water back for a while, but it slowly seeped through. It was more water-worthy than we could have imagined, right, Mac?"

"Yes, dear," McClanahan answered. He paddled in place with half his body above the water as he added, "It wasn't until the water reached the workshop that our home started breaking apart. It wasn't long after that when the water completely overcame us."

"Oh, no. What happened to all of your lovely art?" asked Melissa.

Mackenzie paddled up to Melissa and gently rested her front feet on the boat to steady herself. "Gone. All of it. Years of creating and curating washed away in an instant. We tried to save it. Yes, we did. I had McClanahan moving everything to the upper level, anything that could be moved, of course, but it was all for naught."

"I'm so sorry," said Melissa.

"Not to worry," said McClanahan. "We love to build. I haven't felt so refreshed in decades. I'm not sure if it's the cool water or the thought of all the possibilities of creating new works. But this time we will make sure our home will withstand anything that comes at it."

"Imagine that, a beaver building a water-worthy structure," said Seth.

"Build, build, build, yes we will," said Mackenzie. "We just need to get some materials and decide on a style. Exciting times are these."

Melissa said, "Why don't you come with us to the Lake of Entitlement? There are lots of trees there. Plenty of material for making your new home. Just stay out of the Land of Indulgences, and you should have no problem at all."

"I think that's a great idea, and we could use all the help we can get," said Jimmy.

Mackenzie called out to McClanahan, who was still wading on the other side of the boat. "What do you think, Mac?"

"I think that you should stop calling me Mac for starters."

"Really? It's never bothered you before."

"It has always bothered me."

"Well, isn't that something. You think you know a person," said Mackenzie. "If I promise not to call you Mac, can we go with our friends to the Lake of Entitlement?"

"That wasn't a condition ongoing, but since you offered, yes. Let's see where the current takes us. I'm all in."

That was perhaps the most relaxing time any of them had had since entering through the Water Gate. The current carried the boat passengers and the beavers towards their destination without any effort at all. It gave everyone time to enjoy themselves. Seth taught Dauber and Bumpy a new song which was hardly distinguishable with all of them attempting to sing at the same time without bothering to listen to one another. Melissa and Fox alternated between swimming with the beavers and drying out in the sun.

Not that there were any onlookers, but had there been, they would have heard a lot of laughter and seen a lot of splashing on the river that day. Jimmy, however, did not take part in the festivities. He spent his time floating down the river in deep thought. Jimmy appreciated the respite because he knew there was a lot left to do on this journey. If indeed they were the ones to spread the gospel in this world, they had their work cut out for them. But he was not worried. He was excited. Not many people know what their purpose is at any given moment. Jimmy, for the first time in a long time, knew exactly what he was supposed to do. True, he may not have known exactly how it was to be done, but he knew that would work itself out later.

Chapter 31

WILLOW

"Wow, this is incredible," said Jimmy. "I've never seen such an expansive tree before. It's like a self-contained ecosystem under here."

"This is a willow tree? Like the one in Grandma and Uncle Henry's yard?" asked Seth.

Melissa said, "Other than being a lot bigger, she looks the same to me. Her leaves are the same size and shape."

Fox stopped in the midst of sniffing a big white mushroom and yapped, "I love Willow. There is no other tree like Willow here or there. And I have been acquainted with lots of trees."

Melissa patted Fox on the head and nodded in agreement. "No truer words have ever been spoken. The last time Fox and I were here, Willow saved our lives—risking her own in the process."

"She sounds incredible. Can't wait to meet her. So where to now and how much farther?" asked Seth.

"We just follow the white mushrooms along the root path. It

shouldn't be too much farther. And by the way, Willow already knows we're here. Right, Bumpy?"

Bumpy was resting contentedly in the pouch around Fox's neck. He lifted his head to speak, "Absolutely rootin' tootin' she does. Can't you folks hear these leaves chattering up a storm? They would have told her the second we left the boat at the water's edge. I've never heard so much banter in all my life. I thought living in an oak tree was lively, but this is like nothing I've ever witnessed."

"I don't hear anything," said Seth.

"Rustling, I believe your people call it. The rustling of the leaves," said Bumpy.

"Okay, well, if that's leaf banter, then I guess there is a lot of it, like you said." As Seth looked up at the leaves, he tripped over one of Willow's roots and fell face-first to the ground. No one noticed the large pearl that slipped out of Seth's backpack. It speedily rolled on the ground until it came to rest under one of the larger mushrooms.

Jimmy helped Seth back up and said, "Are you alright?" Seth nodded, obviously embarrassed but physically unscathed. Jimmy continued, "Well, let's follow the mushrooms and keep our eyes and ears open, shall we?"

It was not hard to be quiet. The sound of the leaves was unlike the rustling of leaves back home. Here they sounded more like lullabies sung by whispering fairies. It was beautiful, soothing, and magical. Jimmy appreciated the sound leaves made in his world just as much as this one. There were many days he would lie under the trees in a hammock and fall asleep to the sound of the leaves rustling in the wind. One thing he appreciated more here, though, was the lack of mosquitoes.

Fox, in her excitement to see Willow again, darted in and around her human companions as they followed the path under the branches. She had forgotten how beautiful it was under the safe arms of her friend, Willow. The light filtered down through her limbs to create a warm yellow light as if from a burning fireplace. The hanging foliage rippled like a waterfall.

Seth could not help but notice all the mushrooms and the silly expressions on their faces—even though they did not exactly have faces per se. The fungi were silent and he did not know if they had the ability to talk or think like most of the other life in this world. But they seemed to be looking at him with amusement after his fall, or so he thought. Seth would have toppled a few of them by knocking their heads off, but he knew they served an important purpose by marking the path to the center of the tree, where Melissa said that they would find Willow.

The mushrooms steadily decreased in number as they got closer to the center of the tree. The dirt was richer and softer. It was like walking on air. The large curvy roots, which barely topped the surface at the outskirts of the tree, were now almost waist high and created a clear unmistakable path. The only way off the path would be to climb over the roots.

"Look!" exclaimed Melissa, pointing towards the ground.

A strange creature that looked to be a cross between a shrew and a June bug quickly devoured a fallen leaf and just as quickly pooped out a little brown ball from its rear.

"Never go barefoot in Willow's house," said Melissa.

"Such is the cycle of life," said Jimmy.

"Easy for you to say," said Bumpy, "that wasn't your relative."

"You better stay tight in your little cubby hole, my friend," said Seth. "I wouldn't want you to become the poop beneath our feet."

The little creature looked up in Bumpy's direction and sniffed the air. It scuttled towards Fox, who instinctively jumped back. The small creature quickly darted up and over one of the nearby roots. Bumpy sank deeper into his pouch and would not be seen again until they met Willow.

They continued down the path for a few more minutes. The roots gradually receded back into the ground until there was only a wide-open space surrounding the trunk of the tree.

"This is amazing," said Seth. "Imagine if we had a place like this to hide under when we were kids."

"Yes, I would not even need to dig a burrow," said Fox. "I could raise my pups right here."

"What pups?" asked Seth.

"Future pups, of course. But that's neither here nor there. Where's Willow?"

A soft-spoken voice came from somewhere near the trunk of the tree. Melissa and Fox knew immediately that it was Willow.

"I've been with you since you came under my branches, dear beautiful crimson one."

Fox stood up on her hind feet and yapped as her front feet pawed at the air. Willow sweetly laughed.

"Where is she?" asked Seth looking around.

"I'm here. This is all of me … leaves, limbs, and trunk."

"Oh. So, where's your face or your eyes?"

Willow laughed gently and said to Seth, "Even if the rocks cried out for His glory, they would need no face to do so. No eyes are necessary to declare His greatness. The Creator gives life in the way He sees, not the way we see. I am different than your kind, this is true. But we all live to serve the One who loves His creation."

"All I wanted to know is where I should look when speaking to you," said Seth.

Willow's leaves started to move all at once. And somehow, using a combination of refracting light and her leaves and limbs, she was able to create a sort of face complete with eyes, mouth, and nose. "How is this, brother to Melissa?"

"Wow, that's amazing," said Jimmy.

"You never did that for Fox and me," said Melissa.

"You did not need to see me as you see others. Your faith was strong even then, but I sense it is so much stronger now."

"Thank you, Willow," said Melissa. "A lot has happened since Fox and I were here last. I've been reading the Bible and asking lots of questions."

Willow looked down at Fox and said, "How have you been, beautiful little girl?"

Fox rubbed her nose and cheeks on Willows trunk. "It's been so much fun traveling with my friends. Here is not like where we live. Animals and humans don't speak to one another, and most of the time we are scared of each other."

"Yes, this world is indeed different. It's nice to meet you, brother of Melissa. Rumors told that you were supposed to have been here with your sister the time before. But something happened and what could have been was not. But you are here now and that is good."

"Thanks, yeah, I got a little sidetracked last time. But here I am. Ready to fulfill my destiny," said Seth.

"Willow, this is our friend Jimmy. He's been teaching us lots of stuff about God and the Bible," said Melissa.

"Yes, Jimmy. So young to know so much. You have been to our world before too, have you not?" asked Willow.

"I have. It was years ago. When I was a little younger than Melissa. I'm afraid I wasn't even sure it was all real until we all arrived here yesterday … was it yesterday?"

"And where is your brave flying friend?" asked Willow.

"Dauber?" asked Melissa. "He stayed back at the boat. I think he's a little uncomfortable with his size. He's really supposed to be small, but then he got really big—"

"That's an understatement," interjected Seth.

Melissa continued, "Gigantic. Yes, really, really big. But now he's been shrinking and he's sorta the size of a shoe. Which is still really big for a dirt dauber, but a lot smaller than he was. Anyway, I think he just feels awkward right now."

"The living waters will do that. One drink and the whole being changes. If he grew it was because his heart was bigger than his body could contain. The changes ebb and flow just like the river itself. Your flying friend will be fine. Those around here are quite fond of Dauber—is that what you call him?"

"Yes, Dauber," said Melissa.

"How does anyone know about Dauber?" asked Seth.

"Word spreads quickly here. And there are many words being spread about all of you. Not all of it true, unfortunately," said Willow.

"What exactly are they saying about us?" asked Seth.

"Do you mean what are they saying about *you*, Seth?" asked Jimmy with a grin.

"Yeah, me, you … all of us. We're a team, right?"

Willow spoke, "Don't worry about the rumors of others. Do what you know is right, and whether or not the rumors are true will matter less than the good you do."

"We need to find the Library of Truth," said Jimmy. "We were told that you would know the way."

"And who would have told you that? They think I know everything. While it is true that I have been around longer than most, and I do indeed know a lot, I do not know everything," insisted Willow.

"But you do know where the library is, right?" asked Melissa.

"I know where I have been told the library is. My roots go wider than they go deep, but I am, after all, a tree. I am limited in my reach."

"Then what are we supposed to do?" asked Seth. "We can't just go blindly in search of something not knowing if it's really there or not."

"No, you should not go blindly into anything. Let me look into the matter and I will return shortly. Take some time to rest while I seek the answer to your question. I'm sure you will find it very relaxing here." Willow's face disappeared as the leaves and branches returned to their normal state of hanging.

"Well, that was abrupt. What do we do now?" asked Seth.

"Like she said, relax! Watch this," said Melissa. She kicked off her shoes, stretched her arms up into the air, and yawned. The others watched with curiosity as she lay down on the ground.

"Look!" exclaimed Fox.

Above Melissa's body, branches began stretching downwards like long thin fingers. Melissa motioned for the boys to stay back—indicating everything was okay. Jimmy and Seth stood frozen, watching in awe. One by one the branches moved under Melissa. They seemed to be weaving themselves together.

Fox nervously jumped up and down while sniffing and pawing at the limbs. But they paid her no mind and continued to creep underneath Melissa's body. Melissa patted her belly, signaling Fox to come join her. Fox obliged by climbing on top of Melissa and stretching out. Fox's nose rested right under Melissa's chin.

The men continued to watch as the branches lifted Fox and Melissa off the ground. It was not long before the two girls sat swinging in what could only be compared to a hammock.

Melissa giggled and said, "Now this is what I call relaxing. Come on you two, give it a try."

Jimmy shrugged his shoulders as if to say, "Why not." He lay on the ground not far from Melissa and Fox. Seth watched as the whole process repeated itself.

"That's awesome," said Seth, "but I think I'll go look around for a bit. I don't trust vines creeping around my body." The truth was, Seth was slightly panicked as he had just discovered the pearl was missing form his pack.

"Suit yourself, Bro. Just don't go out from under the branches. You do not want to find yourself on the other side of the Land of Indulgences. Trust me."

"I won't go far," said Seth.

Seth turned to find the path from which they entered. It was hard to differentiate because everything looked very similar. He had to go back to the spot where he fell. That's where he must have lost the giant pearl. His backpack had not been out of his sight since they left the beaver's dam. He correctly assumed the pearl had rolled out of his pack when he hit the ground.

Melissa and Jimmy's voices became fainter the further Seth walked. He was not even sure he was on the right path. Where were those darned mushrooms now? He could not remember if there were mushrooms in the exact spot where he fell. If he was going to find the jewel, he had no choice but to continue walking and hope for a little luck.

When he was at the table of illusions, he managed to get many gold pieces and emeralds, but there was only one pearl. This was the biggest jewel he had ever seen. Something about the pearl was mesmerizing. It had to be worth millions.

Losing something as valuable as the pearl might not have been so bad if he still had the other treasure. Athaliah had bargained with him to give her the other valuables in exchange for the secret of smuggling illusions out of this world into another. He thought it a fair trade at the time, but now he had nothing to show for it.

From the time Seth was five years old, his mom and dad sent him off to spend a week or two at one of her brother's farms. When he was younger it was all fun and games exploring the wide-open pastures, barns, ponds, and surrounding woods. But when he got older, he worked alongside his uncles and cousins bailing hay, picking peaches, and mending barbed wire fences, among a myriad of other farm chores like building chicken coupes and chopping wood. Farm life was hard. Working was hard.

Whenever possible, Seth would sneak off to the one uncle's house who did not make him work. They said Uncle Halbert went crazy from the war and had to live on government handouts. But he never seemed crazy to Seth. He just seemed very eccentric. This particular uncle had eleven children and they were as poor as anyone he ever knew. Their only bathroom was an outhouse.

Seth loved playing with Uncle Halbert's kids, and because they rarely had chores, they had more free time to give Seth lots of attention. He always knew they were poor—with five beds in one room, no kitchen to speak of, and no air conditioning in the hot, humid southern summers—

but it was not until he got older that he truly saw the effect that poverty had on his cousins.

Several died very young due to improper health care, and only the younger ones got a decent education. Some of the other relatives felt sorry for them, but not Seth. He had too much respect for them. They survived a hard childhood without much help from anyone. As it was, they taught Seth how to drive when he was only fourteen. They taught him how to chew tobacco, and how to have fun without any of the things money could buy.

Even so, Seth never wanted to be poor like his "crazy" uncle, or work so hard he had to wake up before dawn every single day of his life. He was content to go to college and have a normal job. But he never dreamed he could be as rich as this.

He had to find that pearl.

The world under Willow's branches seemed endless. The further away he got from the trunk, the more convoluted and confusing it became. If he could find the mushrooms, he felt sure he could trace his steps back to the spot where he lost the jewel.

Part of him wished he never even saw the treasure on the table when they first entered this world. He knew he had become consumed with the idea of how so much money could change his life. That much money would not only change his life but also the lives of his family and everyone he was close to. Who in their right mind would not be consumed with such an opportunity? Or so that's what he kept repeating to himself in between imagining how he would spend his newfound wealth.

He also knew that he was not getting along very well with his family at the moment, and maybe being filthy rich would help him gain a little respect. His dad would not have to work so hard. Schools would be paid for, no more bills. He could even build his grandmother her own house so she would not have to live with his Uncle Henry. During the last twenty-four hours, he had convinced himself that this jewel could solve all of his problems.

All he had to do was find it and do what Athaliah told him to do, and his life would be set. But how could he simply lose something that valuable in the first place?

He was so deep in thought that he almost stepped on a little mushroom sitting all by itself. This mushroom looked different than the other ones. It had a sweet demeanor and almost seemed lonely. Seth was not really happy with himself for attaching human feelings to a plant that didn't even talk or have a face. This world had a way of making a person look at everything differently. It was as if everything was alive and had purpose, even something as lowly as a mushroom.

Seth sat down next to the mushroom and asked, "Where are your friends? The ones that lined the path into this place?"

But there was no answer. Seth felt silly. But it did not stop him from continuing.

"Why are you here all by yourself? Don't you have any friends or family?"

Still no answer.

"Don't feel so bad. Friends and family are not all they're cracked up to be. Still, it does seem pretty lonely here all by yourself."

Seth pulled his knees up to his chest and wrapped his arms around them. If the leaves could talk, like Bumpy said, then they would be able to tell him where his jewel was. One of them had to have seen something, and they should be able to lead him to it.

"Hi, leaves. My name is Seth. I know you have probably been watching me and my friends. I even have a friend like you. He's a leaf, too. Listen, would you mind too terribly if I asked for your help? I lost something pretty valuable, and I would love to get it back. It's a round shiny ball. Have you seen it?"

He waited for an answer but none came. Not so much as a ripple or rustle.

"Geesh! I could have helped so many people with that money. I could have changed a lot of lives for the better." he said angrily.

The branches began to move, and when Seth looked up, he saw the face of Willow. He wondered if she had been following him the whole time. He watched as a branch came down and tapped on the ground twice. After a few seconds, a small creature came running towards Willow and her branch. Willow said something, Seth could not understand the language, but before he knew it, the creature turned its rear towards Seth and pooped. The creature then took its hind legs and kicked the ball of poop towards Seth, who instinctively scooted backward, away from the foul excretion.

"This is what you have been looking for, is it not?" asked Willow.

Seth looked more closely at the object before him, and although it was covered in dust and dirt and who knows what else, he could distinguish the unmistakable shimmer of a pearl. He reached out and grabbed the object and cleaned it off with his shirttail. It shined just as bright as before. It was his gem. It was beautiful.

"Yes. Thank you, Willow. I don't know what to say."

"It's against my better judgment to see that back in your possession, brother of Melissa."

"How did you know I even had it, let alone lost it?"

"Look how you are shaking."

Seth looked at his hands and noticed they were indeed trembling. He quickly shoved them in his pockets, along with the gem.

"Your sister and her crimson friend are the only two creatures ever to have survived the Land of Indulgences. She, like you, was consumed with desire. Her whole body, her entire being, burned with the lust of power and possibilities. But she chose life and truth over the lie."

"What does that have to do with me?"

"We shall see. There are those that have faith in you. Your sister is one. And I must rely on the prophecies that speak deeper than my roots. They tell of your kind bringing light into our world. I don't know what this jewel means to you, or to the prophecy, but it is not for me to keep it from you. You must decide your own fate."

"I thought God decided one's fate."

"Yes, well, perhaps. Or perhaps he allows us to choose. What you must do is choose the path that leads towards wisdom. You cannot bring light into this world unless you first fear the very Creator Himself—that is the beginning of wisdom."

"I'll choose the best path, if I can tell which path that is."

Willow rustled her leaves and moved from one side of Seth to the other. He followed her with his eyes until he had to turn his body. What she spoke next caused all of the leaves in the tree to chatter and chime. "Don't you know who you are, young man?"

"What do you mean?"

"You are a child of the most high," she said. All of the leaves instantly stopped moving and ceased making noise as she continued, "You were knit together by the Creator himself. He always knew you would be. You were known even before you knew yourself."

"What if I choose the wrong way?"

"Truth and love always remain. All are loved by the Creator, even those that reject Him. No matter the way you take, you will forever be loved. But be careful, choosing the wrong path can erase all memory of that love. It is my belief that not knowing you are loved is the darkest of lies."

"I did not steal this. It was there for the taking. I don't see this as some turning point in my eternity."

"Then why are you trembling? Why have your thoughts not departed from the possession?"

"Are you kidding me? You obviously know nothing of my world." Seth brought the jewel out of his pocket and held it in front of him. "This thing could make everyone's life better. Money is essential where I come from. You cannot survive without it."

"Why have you hidden this from your companions? They seem to know nothing of it."

"I haven't hidden it, exactly. I just haven't told them about it yet."

"I have word that Athaliah has told you how to get the treasure back into your world. I'm not sure if what she has said is true. She is very creative and clever, but not always trustworthy."

"What would you have me do with it?"

"That is the correct question, as it is not a matter of what gets done with the treasure but rather what you do with the treasure."

"Sounds a bit cliché."

Willow rustled her leaves and a breeze blew dirt from off the ground. "You are flesh. Without the Word you would still be dust. Your world, not unlike ours, was spoken into existence. The Word became flesh. But it only became in your world. There is but one Creator, one Word. Your people have the testimony of truth through that Word. My people hunger for lack of knowledge."

"If God is who he says he is, then wouldn't all beings have the same advantage no matter where they are?"

"The skies declare the glory in both worlds. There is no excuse for any of us. I know there is a God because His glory exists all around me and even in me. But there are those that would lead others astray. They lie. We need the Word in this world too."

"But why?"

"Knowing is only part of the truth. Living the truth is the other."

"I don't know what that even means, but what does any of this have to do with me? How is this my problem?"

"I suppose it is not your problem at all. Unless you make it so."

"I have enough problems, and besides, I don't even know if I believe in this one God anyway."

"I only have this to offer you, Seth. A word of my own. There is truth, and I know you like truth. Therefore, whether or not you believe the truth should not matter—if it is indeed true."

"I'm only in my first year of college. I haven't taken any philosophy classes yet. So, sorry, but that's way over my head."

"Please, say farewell to your companions for me. You will not see me again. Brother to Melissa, please remember these words: It's not what you take out of the world that will help you find answers. It is what you leave in the world that matters."

"But wait, we came here for answers. We don't know where to go next. How to get home. Melissa thought you would know the way."

"The others know the way already. It's only you that is still lost."

"Okay, fine. I'm the idiot. It's my fault we are lost. Whatever. Just please tell me where to go next."

"You are not strong enough to make it through the Land of Indulgences. But you will do well going over it."

"The only one that can fly is Dauber, and he's not big enough to carry us anymore."

Willow said, "The beavers work fast. Follow the leaf from your world to the place you have come to find."

Seth shook his head in frustration. "The beavers?" Seth had no idea what the beavers had to do with any of this.

Willow continued, "Many blessings, brother to Melissa. I pray your journey here leads you home and back again. Remember, it's what you leave, not what you take." The leaves rustled and the image of Willow disappeared. Seth looked up and all around to see if she might still be there, but she was gone.

Seth took the jewel out of his pocket and polished it with his shirttail. He admired his lost-and-found again treasure, but it did not seem to have the same luster as before. Perhaps the creature left some stain on it, he thought. He hoped the pearl was not tainted as he rubbed it once more before securing it safely in his backpack.

Fox startled Seth and almost knocked him over by jumping on him excitedly. He regained his composure, quickly zipping up the backpack. He scratched Fox on the neck and asked, "Where is everyone else?"

"Where have you been?" asked Melissa, coming around a cluster of low hanging branches. She was followed by Jimmy.

"Where is Bumpy?" asked Seth.

"He's still lounging in his pouch," said Jimmy.

Seth looked over at Fox, who was now a few paces further away. She was still wearing the carrier around her neck.

"Come on, we need to hurry," said Jimmy as he followed after Melissa and Fox.

"Why the rush?" asked Seth who followed along behind the others.

"Dauber said the lake is rising," said Jimmy.

Melissa added, "Very quickly."

"We need to get to the boat."

"Oh, the beavers, they must have built a real dam this time. Where's Dauber?" asked Seth.

"He's back to his normal size. And he can fly again," said Jimmy.

Seth did not ask any more questions. He figured he would have plenty of time for questions once they were out in the open. He was sure they would have a few questions for him as well. He worried about how much to tell them, but maybe Willow had already filled them in. If they knew what Willow knew and he was not forthcoming, they might never trust him again. Seth was double-minded. For now, he would simply follow the others and figure the rest out later.

Chapter 32

NOT OF THIS WORLD

Bethany and Patrick sat on the back deck watching a new crop of leaves fall from the trees. Bethany sipped hot tea and Patrick finished off his last bit of coffee while flipping through a ten-year-old Better Homes and Garden magazine. As much as he disliked Azora, he did enjoy the reprieve of being transported back in time to a simpler life.

There was a nip in the late afternoon air, indicating that fall had finally arrived. Bethany said, "I'm going to get a sweater, would you like me to bring you anything?"

"No thanks, hon. I'm good."

Bethany went inside, leaving the door slightly ajar. Patrick assumed she did not want to alert Azora to their whereabouts with the sound of doors opening and closing. He thought it odd that his mother-in-law was not already out with them. Their visits to the country were always short, and he could not remember a time when Azora did not suck up every moment of their time. Especially if they were outside.

He looked out over the back yard, admiring the natural beauty of the trees. He often thought about moving to this part of the country, knowing that was what Bethany would like, but his work had never really allowed for it. Maybe someday, he thought.

Bethany returned wearing a dark orange wool sweater. He remembered it from last winter. It was too big and hung way past her hips. He always resisted the urge to tell her that she reminded him of a pumpkin when she wore it. After twenty years of marriage, he had learned that there was none more sensitive than his wife. She took everything to heart.

He sat the out-of-date periodical and empty coffee cup down and stood up. Bethany asked, "Where are you going?"

"Right here," he said as he walked up behind his wife and began massaging her shoulders.

"Aww, thank you sweetheart. That feels so good. But maybe I should be massaging you after all that work you did for my brother."

"It was nothing, really. Such a tiny bathroom."

"Still, it was very nice of you."

Patrick continued rubbing his wife's shoulders as he changed the subject, "I can't remember the last time we were alone."

Bethany did not respond as she took a few steps towards the house. "Mom seems to have aged so much in the last couple of years. She's slowing down."

"I walked past the bedroom earlier and she was still there, sitting on the edge of her twin bed staring at the plant. It was weird. Did you see her?"

"Yes. I asked her if she needed anything and she just sort of grunted. Didn't even look up."

"I hope she's feeling alright."

"I'm sure she's fine. Did the kids say what time they would be back?"

"Jimmy said they would be gone all day but back before nightfall."

Neither of them talked about the subject that was on both of their minds—the topic that had been the cause of several arguments between them the last few months. Seth had gone from being the brightest student at his high school to nearly dropping out of college. His confidence had eroded just as fast as his grades. Patrick seemed to think it was normal first-year college stuff and would work itself out, but Bethany was not convinced.

Patrick was more concerned about Melissa's sudden religious conversion. She seemed consumed with all things biblical, and he had visions of her running off to some kibbutz in a faraway land. Bethany reminded him that Melissa had always been impressionable and changed with the seasons. But they both agreed that her current preoccupation seemed different.

Their quiet, peaceful moment together was suddenly interrupted by a loud scream from Azora's bedroom. Without saying a word, they gave each other a concerned look before bolting into the house. Patrick was first as he rounded the dining room table, hitting his knee in the process and cursing loud enough to be heard over Azora, who was now yelling out for her daughter to come quickly.

By the time Bethany made it to the bedroom, Patrick was standing next to her mother with his hand gently under her arm, as if he had just picked her up off the floor. As it turned out, he was just holding her steady, she had not fallen. Azora was standing over the plant with one hand over her mouth. She was mumbling something unintelligible. But what surprised Bethany the most was that her mother was not protesting Patrick's chivalry.

Patrick looked back at his wife standing in the doorway and shrugged his shoulders. He had no clue as to what had just happened.

Bethany walked around to the other side of the plant so she could face her mother before speaking. She said, "Mom, are you alright? What happened?"

Azora did not look up but kept staring at the plant. She continued to mumble softly.

"Mom? What is it? You're starting to get me really worried."

Azora placed her hand on Patrick's shoulder as she moved towards a small wooden chair in the corner of the room. Patrick knew it must be something serious if she was accepting his help. After catching her breath, she looked at her son-in-law and then turned to her daughter. "Don't you see it?"

Bethany responded, "See what?"

"It sprouted a third leaf. It only had two when we brought it in here a little while ago. Now it has three," Azora said.

"Are you sure? Maybe we just missed it? It's so small," said Patrick.

Azora maneuvered in the chair in such a way that forced Patrick to remove his hand from her shoulder. He was not aware that she had come back to her senses and was irritated by his helpful gesture, but Bethany definitely noticed.

Bethany said, "So it grew a third leaf. Is that such a big deal?"

"I know of no plant that can grow that fast," said Azora. "That stuff the koala bears eat grows fast, but not even it grows this fast."

"I don't know. Maybe we just didn't see it before," said Bethany. "Maybe the leaves were stuck together or something."

Patrick offered, "I tell you what, why don't we all just sit here and watch the plant with you. If it grew one leaf that fast maybe it'll grow another one, and we can all be witnesses."

Bethany shot Patrick a frustrated look, but he did not notice. He too was now staring at the mystery plant. She said, "Fine, I'll go grab a chair out of the kitchen and my tea. Would you like some tea, Mom?"

Without looking up, still transfixed on the emergence of another leaf, she answered, "Yes, tea. That would be nice, dear."

Patrick eased over to the side of the small twin bed and sat down. "Would you mind making another pot of coffee too, dear?"

"Oh sure, why not. Anything else?" asked Bethany from the doorway. When no one answered, she turned and walked out. It occurred to her on the way to the kitchen that this was the first time in a very long time that her mother and husband had voluntarily done anything together. It might be an odd activity, to say the least, but it was at least progress.

Chapter 33
The Cleansing

The Land of Indulgences was a fertile land that yielded bountiful crops. The trees and plants offered the most delectable fruits imaginable. The strawberries were the size of small watermelons and tasted as sweet as honey. The peaches were always perfectly ripe and firm. There were many strange and exotic edibles that only existed in this world.

Unfortunately, very few had ever tasted the fruits of the orchard and lived to tell about it. In fact, Melissa may have been the only one. Once you enter the enchanted land and partake of its offerings, you become forever trapped, unable to escape the temptations. Melissa, with the help of Fox and Willow, was cunning enough to survive the spell of the enchanted orchard.

Willow sat on a small knoll near the edge of the Lake of Entitlement. The Land of Indulgences was directly downhill from there. It was obvious why the ground was so rich with nutrients. When water was plentiful, hundreds or thousands of years ago, the rivers and creeks deposited fertile soil in the land.

The Land of Indulgences was nothing more than a continuation of the Lake of Entitlement. The travelers from the other world only discovered this when they stepped out from underneath the protective covering of the enormous Willow tree. Water surrounded them. The trees of the orchard were slowly being enveloped by the same waters that defeated the Mara people.

"How did this happen?" asked Melissa.

"The beavers. That's what Willow said," answered Seth.

"When did she tell you that? Did you talk to Willow?"

"Just briefly, yes. She told me that we needed to go over the Land of Indulgences. I didn't understand what she meant at first, now it makes sense," said Seth.

"Look, there's the boat," said Jimmy, pointing.

The boat had lodged itself right next to Willow, where the rising water met her lowest hanging branches. It was either luck or divine intervention, because without it, they would have had to swim.

Jimmy moved towards the boat and said, "Come on everyone. The water is rising pretty quickly."

Melissa said, "Wait a minute. What about Willow? If the water keeps rising, she is going to go under with all of the other trees here. We can't let that happen."

Fox yapped, "What'll we do, what'll we do?"

"Nothing," said Seth. "There's nothing we can do."

"There must be. If the beavers did this, we can ask them to tear down their dam. Or we can go find it and do it ourselves," said Melissa.

"Seth is right. There is nothing we can do. We don't have oars to row, and even if we did, we have no idea where the beavers are," said Jimmy.

"I'm not going anywhere!" exclaimed Melissa. "I'm not just leaving my friend here to drown."

"Something tells me that Willow was not surprised by all of this," said Jimmy, "but either way, you can't stay here or *you* definitely will drown."

Seth put a hand on his sister's shoulder and said, "I think Willow knew this was going to happen. I think she even maybe wanted it to. I can't be sure, but she told me that the way to where we are going is over the Land of Indulgences, and the only way over the land is on the water, it seems. She even told me that Bumpy would lead us all the way there."

Bumpy stuck his head out of the pouch and said, "Yes, I can smell it. I know where we must go."

Bumpy floated up and out of his protective pouch. Melissa was the first to notice that he had a new injury. "Oh, no. When did that happen, Bumpy?"

"When did what happen?" asked Bumpy.

"That hole, right there," she said as she pointed.

Dauber, who up until now had been out exploring on his own, did a quick flyby to inspect his friend the leaf. "A little larger and I could fly right through you," he said.

"Oh, great. Well that there must be why it's so hard to get lift. The air is blowing right through me. How am I supposed to lead the way without optimum flying capabilities? This is just downright unwarrantable."

"We can help, Bumpy. Have no fear," said Jimmy.

"I could even help you fly, if need be," added Dauber.

"A leaf must freely flow without any influence other than the wind to be sure of the direction he must go. But have no worries, I'm still able, even if I have to sputter all the way there."

"Where is there?" yapped Fox.

"There is the place where the sacred scrolls are kept in this world. They are made of my kind, from trees. It only makes sense that I should be welcomed there. This place has been calling me to it ever since we arrived. But we were not close enough until now," said Bumpy.

"It's the Library of Truth that Propo spoke about. But what about the twelve? I thought we were supposed to go there with the twelve?" asked Melissa.

Jimmy answered, "No. Propo said he will try to find the twelve, but we must carry on. We are the twelve, at least for now."

Seth dipped his fingers into the water to see how cold it was and said, "How can we be the twelve? Counting Fox, Dauber and Bumpy, there are only six of us."

Jimmy said, "We are part of the twelve, I think. If we so choose. I think this world needs us."

"Our own world needs us," countered Seth. "This place isn't any worse than where we come from. Don't you think we should worry about our own kind first?"

"At least they listen to us in this world. Just because we help this world doesn't mean we stop helping ours," said Melissa. "We can do both."

"Good luck with that. We don't even know how to help our world, let alone this one. We are just a few average people, what effect could we have?"

"We will never know if we don't get in the boat and move," said Jimmy. "Let's see where Bumpy takes us and we can decide what to do from there."

"I like floating in the boat. Much better than swimming," said Fox. "And what's more, if we don't do what we came here for, why did we come at all? It's true I like all of you, and what fun it has been to travel about with my bestest human friend and her companions. But even a little ol' fox like me has a reason to be."

"And what would that be?" asked Seth.

Fox joyfully scurried over to Seth and placed her muzzle under his hand. He had no choice but to pat her head. She said, "I don't know exactly precisely, but that won't stop me from doing it."

"Very well said," said Melissa.

"But she didn't say anything," said Seth.

"Sure, she did," added Jimmy.

"I'll tell you this," said Melissa. "She is the only one around here that has nothing but good things to say. No matter what happens she is ready and willing. That's enough for me."

"I second that," said Jimmy.

Fox was still nuzzling Seth, weaving in and out of his legs. "She is impossibly optimistic, I'll give you that," said Seth. He sat on the ground and gave Fox a good rub down.

Seth looked at Bumpy and asked, "Do you think you can find this place with the scrolls?"

"I can find it just as surely as the sun rises!" said Bumpy.

"Well, no one can say that Bumpy doesn't know his purpose," said Seth.

The water had risen another several inches while they stood on Willow's mound, discussing their next move. The Land of Indulgences was almost completely underwater. The tops of many trees were still visible but it would not be long before they disappeared. Willow, of course, would be the last to succumb.

Everyone but Melissa quickly jumped into the boat. Melissa

hesitated—she had hoped to say goodbye to Willow in private. But sadly, Willow did not speak. Fox consoled Melissa while Jimmy gently insisted that they get moving. He wanted to make sure they were too far away to see Willow swallowed up by the deadly flood.

While drifting away from Willow, over the orchard, Melissa could not stop looking back at the tree that risked everything to save a confused girl from another world. Melissa hoped that she could be as brave and wise as her friend the tree someday. When Willow was completely out of sight, Melissa bowed her head to say a silent prayer that God would protect the tree that she had come to admire so much.

"For there is hope for a tree, if it be cut down, that it will sprout again, and that its shoots will not cease," Jimmy said.

Melissa looked up and said, "How did you know what I was praying about?"

"I didn't. But it was a safe guess."

"Nice. Is it from the Bible?" she asked.

Jimmy nodded. "Yes, it's in Job. I don't remember exactly where. Talk about a man that had a lot of troubles."

"And a lot of faith," added Seth.

"You've read Job?" asked Melissa.

"Parts of it. But everyone knows how Job got the short end of the stick. You don't have to read the Bible to know that."

The small boat seemed a lot roomier now that Dauber was back to his normal size. Everyone was relieved that there was no longer a giant stinger mere inches away from their every move. Dauber, in fact, was so small he found a quiet place hidden under the bow in which to rest. He was sure there would be lots of flying and scouting to do once they landed on dry ground. He would need to be well-rested and in excellent superhero form.

Bumpy, although looking quite ragged, managed to float just above the boat. He was not as graceful as he once was. His movements were sometimes jerky and erratic, but he was up to the task at hand. There was really nothing anyone could do to steer the boat, but at least Bumpy could confirm they were headed in the right direction.

Jimmy, knowing that they were at the whims of the current, wanted Bumpy to save his strength for land. Once on foot, they would need him to find the Library of Truth. However, Bumpy was too excited to sit still. Jimmy understood as he too was eager to begin his newfound mission of spreading the Good News to the people of this world. The only thing concerning Jimmy at the moment was that he had to first figure out a way to share the essential message of salvation with Seth.

Seth doubted everything. Yet he was chosen for this journey just like the rest of them. This both perplexed and annoyed Jimmy. Why would God not just have picked people who already believed? Why leave such an important task in the hands of a skeptic? What if Seth never came around? What if Seth caused more harm than good?

And then there was Melissa. She believed but she did not have a solid foundation. How could she help lead a world without the Word into understanding of the truth when she herself was so young in the faith?

Along the way, Jimmy utilized the time to talk about faith. He recited the Lord's Prayer and then pointed out that it was a prime example of how to relate to the Creator whenever people prayed. Jimmy said that they should welcome the Creator into their hearts. They should ask for basic needs like food and shelter, and for forgiveness of transgressions. Nothing they had not heard in church.

Jimmy also spoke about the Apostle Paul. He explained how one of the greatest writers of the Bible once persecuted and even killed believers. Paul was brought up knowing the Word, but knowing and understanding were entirely different things. His knowledge of the truth did not translate to his understanding of it. This was very confusing for Fox who became so overwhelmed that she decided to curl up and take a nap in Seth's lap.

Even though Melissa was a little jealous that Fox was taking a liking to her brother, she thought it was cute to see him petting her so lovingly. She had not seen her brother so calm in months.

The boat drifted onward with Bumpy floating above. They rested as Jimmy recited Bible verses from memory and told Bible stories. Seth knew that much of what Jimmy had to say was directed towards him. He did not mind. In fact, he hoped that one day he would believe fully in something greater than himself. He was not opposed to believing, but like always, he just needed answers.

Chapter 34
The Storm

Clouds had sneaked in and covered the sky, blocking out much of the light. Then, without warning, came the rain. It was a torrential downpour. Bumpy had reluctantly taken cover in the pouch around Fox's neck and Dauber remained dry under the bow of the boat, which was now getting inundated. When Jimmy noticed his feet were underwater, he hollered for everyone to start scooping it out with their bare hands.

If the storm did not let up, or if they did not find land soon, the boat would sink. They could not keep ahead of the water.

Fox was cold and began to shiver, but Bumpy was in danger of further disintegration as the rainwater started to penetrate his pouch. Things were not looking good for the travelers. Even if they found land, they would need to find shelter until the storm passed. They were in an unknown land with few friends and no safe place to wait out the storm.

Melissa, like Fox, was shivering. The water was not that cold, but the rain and wind chilled her to the bone. Even though Jimmy knew that using their hands to scoop out the water would not do much to slow down the inevitable, he knew it would help keep Melissa and Seth's minds off the cold. The constant movement might also help keep them warm until they found cover.

Everyone had become exhausted to the point of collapse. Even Jimmy, with all his faith, could not understand why God would keep putting obstacles in their path. Was it not enough that they were far away from home in a strange and unwelcoming land? He thought that nothing could be worse than the giants, but now he was not so sure. How does one fight or outrun a storm?

Jimmy looked all around but could not see land. It did not mean that land was not nearby; it simply meant that the storm had obscured his view. Land could be to the right or the left or straight ahead. But how could they know? Not that it mattered much anyway, as they had no way to steer.

The boat kept drifting and the rain kept pounding them. It seemed like it had been going on for days, but in actuality had not been more than a couple of hours. Even the ever-optimistic Fox was too busy fidgeting to offer any words of encouragement. Animals could always find shelter from the elements back home. It was odd to be stuck out in the rain, but Seth was warm and he leaned over her just enough to block the worst of it. So perhaps, in a way, she had found a bit of shelter, she thought.

Melissa and Seth had never experienced such misery. Melissa had always loved playing in the rain as a child, but she was always able to run back inside if she got cold or scared. Not here. She was stuck with no options. Seth too was surprised at just how uncomfortable it was. It made him appreciate how good he had it back home.

Jimmy was the only one still attempting to bail out the water when they felt a thump. They had finally hit land. Seth lifted the shivering fox up and out of the boat. She shook her body to fling off the water from her fur, which was quickly replaced with drops from the sky.

Jimmy took Melissa's hand to help her remain steady as she stepped onto land. She stood in place, rubbing her arms in a futile attempt to keep warm. As cold as she was, she could not help but think of how bad her long blonde hair must have looked. It was flat and clumped together like overcooked spaghetti that had been sitting out too long. She wished Jimmy was not there to see her in such an unflattering state.

Seth took up his backpack and surveyed the situation. The dirt was very muddy and walking would be difficult. This place had not seen rain in so long, and there was the definite danger of mudslides. They would need to be careful.

Jimmy, knowing that insects find it difficult to traverse in the rain, stuck his arm under the bow of the boat and said, "Dauber, if you can hear me, crawl on my hand." Dauber happily complied. Jimmy took his arm out and turned his hand over, slightly cupping it so Dauber would be sheltered from the fusillade falling from above. It was quite a thing, Jimmy thought, that Dauber would be so trusting in such a precarious position. One wrong move by Jimmy and Dauber would be crushed.

There, soaking wet in the nonstop rain, Jimmy considered the blessings all about him. Seeing Melissa grow in her faith was inspirational. Watching Seth struggle and seek answers reminded him of himself not so many years ago. Meeting animals and insects that could talk was more miraculous than anything. He was actually becoming friends with a fox and a dirt dauber. It was nothing short of amazing, he thought. He was excited to see what God had in store for them next, and he was also somewhat ashamed at questioning God's plan only minutes earlier.

"Jimmy. Jimmy! Are you with us?" Seth yelled.

Jimmy snapped out of his deep thought and responded, "Yes, right here, what's up?"

"Melissa and I think we saw a light. Over there," Seth said as he pointed.

"How far do you think it is?"

"It can't be too far if we can see it through all this rain and haze."

"But it's so wet," said Melissa. "We can't walk there. I can't even lift my feet. They're so heavy with mud!"

Fox began yapping, "Over this way! There's a trail, and a good trail at that."

The others joined Fox who had trotted a little south of where the boat ran aground. Sure enough, there was a trail. It was about five feet wide and lined with cobblestone as far as they could see.

The rain once again let up and it was now only sprinkling.

"It must lead to something," said Seth.

"Of course. Maybe to the light you guys saw," said Jimmy.

"It seems odd to have this perfectly manicured path out in the middle of nowhere," said Seth.

Jimmy nodded, "I agree, very strange."

"Could be worse. I say we go investigate," said Melissa.

Fox hopped over to Melissa and said, "I'm worried about Bumpy. He's awful wet. Yes, he is. And he hasn't been saying much lately."

Melissa said, "We have no choice. We've got to find shelter and a place to dry out and get warm. I'm concerned about Bumpy, too."

"Well, we're off to see the wizard it seems," said Seth.

"Wizard? What's a wizard?" asked Fox.

"He's just kidding, Fox. Besides, Seth, this road isn't even yellow," said Melissa.

"A wizard is a man with special powers. But I personally don't believe in wizards," said Jimmy matter-of-factly.

"But you believe in Jesus, a man that supposedly walked on water," said Seth.

"Speaking of walking, shall we?" Jimmy extended his arm for the ladies to go first and then he put his free hand and arm, the one not carrying Bumpy, over Seth's shoulder. "Jesus is God and God is all-powerful. Even if ever there was a wizard, perhaps even a wonderful wizard, no wizard could stand up to God."

"Maybe there are lots of wizards and your God is just one of them," said Seth.

Jimmy laughed and recounted the story of how a pharaoh, who enslaved the Israelites in Egypt, called upon all the magicians of the land to outdo the God of Israel. And even though they were somehow able to turn staffs into snakes, it was nothing more than a parlor trick. Moses, the messenger of God, threw down his staff and the Pharaoh watched in dismay as Moses' staff devoured the magician's snakes.

Jimmy would have told more of the story from Exodus, but the rain resumed. There was no time to casually walk, so they had to run. Everyone put their heads down and focused on the path before them. Fox ran ahead of the rest, not because she was faster—which she was—but because she wanted to make sure the path was safe.

Fortunately, it did not take long for them to find from where the mysterious light emanated. As soon as Fox started yapping, they looked up to see a huge castle-like building. From their vantage point it had four turrets, but it did not appear to be a castle built for defense. Each turret had multiple stained-glass windows at least twelve feet high and four feet wide. Although they were high enough to avoid the random invader, it would never hold up to an army.

There was also a moat, with an old-fashioned drawbridge. It was doubtful the bridge had ever been raised as it was lined with full-grown trees in large planters. There were also colorful vines with blooming flowers of purple, red, and gold hanging off the sides touching the water below. No conventional vehicles, if any ever existed here, could cross because of all the trees.

The castle itself was made of beautiful marble that was primarily grey with veins of burgundy. The windows were odd, varying in size and shape, but all were uniform in that they contained stained glass. The roof looked like it was made of solid gold, but it was hard to tell with all the rain.

Before anyone had the time to evaluate whether or not they should knock on the large wooden doors, Fox had already crossed the bridge and was sniffing around the steps leading up to the entry. Melissa tried to call her back as quietly as she could, but Jimmy signaled that they should cross the bridge.

As Jimmy walked across, he was surprised to see that the roots of the trees had penetrated their containers and protruded through to the ground below. The castle must have been at least a few hundred years old, but it looked to be in pristine condition—at least from what could be ascertained at first glance.

Fox ran to greet the others as they crossed over the moat. "This place is beautiful. Not a foul scent to be found. Nor a pleasing one, I should add. But that's neither here nor there, I suppose." Fox was very excited. The others were not sure why. Perhaps her investigative efforts had given her a second wind.

"Well, did you knock on the door yet, Fox?" asked Jimmy.

"Oh, no. I wouldn't and I couldn't. The knocker is much too high for me to reach," replied Fox.

"That's okay," said Jimmy. "Best to have us all together. We don't want them to see only one of us and then surprise them with a whole brood." He turned to the others and said, "Shall we?"

They ascended the steps up to the castle door and spent a few seconds making themselves look as presentable as possible. Melissa ran her fingers through her hair, but it was useless as there were quite a few tangles. Seth knocked the heels of his shoes against the edge of the porch to knock off any remaining mud. Jimmy wiped the water off his arms. Fox, at first perplexed by the grooming of the humans, finally caught on to what they were doing and shook and twisted until her fur was almost dry, much to the chagrin of the others who were now as wet as before. When Fox was done with her own special method of grooming, she looked up to see the others scowling at her.

"What?" Fox innocently asked.

"Never you mind. Go ahead and knock, Jimmy," said Melissa.

"Yuck, who knew foxes smelled so bad. Just add water!" exclaimed Seth.

Fox, appalled at Seth's comment, shook one more time for good measure. She happened to know that there was no better smell than a fox freshly bathed in the falling rain.

Jimmy took the large brass knocker in his hand and struck it. It was loud and otherworldly. According to the short amount of time it took for someone to answer the door, it was apparent that they were seen long before they crossed the moat.

The door at first appeared to open all on its own, as there was no one behind it. But upon closer inspection, they spied four fingers slightly above the door handle.

"Hello? Is anyone there?" asked Jimmy.

There was no answer. The fingers slowly slid back behind the other side of the door, leaving the door partially agape.

"Should we go in?" asked Melissa.

"I don't know about the rest of you, but I'm not going in until I'm invited," said Seth.

But by the time he finished his sentence, Fox had already put her front paws on the door and pushed it all the way open. They could hear footsteps scampering away, but still no welcome.

"Hello," said Melissa as she leaned her head over the threshold of the door, but still not stepping foot inside. She turned to the others behind her and whispered, "I think it must be a child."

"What'll we do?" asked Seth.

"I have an idea," said Jimmy. He lifted up his hand, where Dauber still rested, and whispered something that no one except Dauber could hear.

Before anyone had time to ask what Jimmy had said, Dauber flew into the castle.

"Do you think it's safe for him in there?" asked Melissa.

"Dauber can take care of himself," Jimmy assured her.

Dauber was excited to finally be doing something productive once again. His kind was used to working and being useful. Plus, Jimmy's hand was not the most suitable accommodations. More than once he tightened his grip a little too much for Dauber's comfort. It had been a while since he was able to fly freely in a nice dry place—as a normal-sized dauber, no less.

The first thing Dauber noticed upon entering was the sterility of the place. There were not the usual suspects found in most homes. No spider webs or signs of any insects at all. A dirt dauber would starve here.

He quickly flew from the entryway into what should have been the living room. The dimly lit room relied on what little light penetrated the stained-glass windows and a large fireplace, which was hot and crackling. There was a rather extravagant chair sitting in the middle of the room. Dauber did not know much about decorating and had not been in a castle before, but even he thought it odd to have one giant chair sitting in a room all by itself. The chair was lined with red velvet and shiny jewels all around the edges of the back and seat. It faced the fireplace and looked hardly used.

Dauber flew into an adjoining room. There he found a beautiful ornate table with twelve high-backed wooden chairs. He was quickly distracted when he heard noises coming from an adjacent room, so he skipped his customary thorough search and flew through the large archway. He found himself in a dark corridor with many doors. Doors as far as his eyes could see.

The music was emanating from behind a pair of large double doors located a few yards down to his right. He landed on one of the doorknobs but his grippers were not able to hold onto the shiny slick surface. He made another attempt to land on the knob, knowing he could have simply landed on the wood to which the knob was attached. Dauber was nothing if not stubborn. His second attempt was no more successful than the first, but instead of sliding all the way off, he grabbed the door with his left legs and the knob with his right legs. As far as he was concerned, the knob lost. He had never seen a more beautifully polished object in all his life. Even in the dim light, it sparkled like a thousand shimmering waterfalls.

He was tempted to enter the room with the unusual music via the keyhole of the beautiful sparkling doorknob, but thought better of it. The whole place was a little unsettling. He chose to peer through the keyhole to assess the room beyond.

He could not believe his large compound eyes. Dauber wished that Sticky could see this! He saw a harp, a piano, all kinds of stringed instruments, and lots of strange-looking contraptions he had never seen before. All of them were making music. But Dauber found it highly off-putting that there was no one playing the instruments. They were all moving on their own.

Just when he was ready to fly back and tell the others what he had seen, a large glass container came down on him so fast he had no time to escape. Before he knew it, he was trapped. He could not believe it. He was caught off guard. He was so mad at himself that he did not have time to contemplate his fate.

He flew around the glass container looking for a way of escape. There was nothing. He was at the mercy of his captor. He looked out, attempting to see who or what had him in their grip. It was hard to get a good look. Something obviously had him in their hand and was haphazardly carrying him to another location. When the bumpy ride stopped a few seconds later, the container was set down with a hard thud and then there was a loud clap of wood. Everything went dark.

Dauber could not hear or see anything. He was helpless. But he was not concerned for himself; he desperately wanted to warn his friends. Something was amiss in the perfect castle with the stained-glass windows and tree-lined drawbridge. How could he have been so careless? As he hung under the lid of his prison cell, he vowed to sting whoever it was that had imprisoned him. They would not get away with this—of that he was sure.

The others were led inside by a charming little boy no more than six years of age. He said his dad was busy but would be down to join them just as soon as he was finished with whatever he was doing. The boy, small for his age, had short red hair that was parted in a dapper style that looked straight out of the 1950s. He wore a long-sleeved white oxford with suspenders attached to gray trousers. He walked briskly for a boy on crutches. He must have been born that way and thus quite accustomed to being physically challenged.

"What happened to your leg?" asked Melissa.

The boy replied, "Both legs, you might ask. It was just a little accident. Dad says I'll be better when I'm better."

The others gave each other a look but no one ventured to pry further.

Immediately after walking to the end of the long foyer, they turned left down another long ornate hallway. There were many paintings hanging on the walls, and frescoes, similar to those by Michelangelo, painted across the ceiling. It looked like a museum. Jimmy would have liked to have had more time to examine the artwork but the little boy with the crutches was on a mission, so it seemed. When he finally chose a door after they had passed several along the way, he opened it and then waited outside until everyone entered. They all thought he was well-mannered for such a young person.

"This is one of my father's favorite rooms," said the little boy. "He designed it himself."

Melissa found the room to be gaudy and garish. She looked around and tried to hide her displeasure. Seth, on the other hand, just blurted out his distaste for the décor, which was quickly followed by an elbow in the ribs from Jimmy.

"What?" said Seth.

Jimmy and Melissa gave him a look and Seth rolled his eyes in acknowledgment of the faux pas. Fox was in complete agreement with Seth and would have said so herself had she not been so preoccupied with the mittens on her feet. It was very hard to walk on the smooth floors with her paws covered with cloth. Humans were used to walking with things covering their feet. The place looked sanitary, sure, but not so much that Fox should have to don socks. Foxes are known for their cleanliness. How dare anyone think otherwise, thought Fox.

"Have a seat, please," said the boy. "I will soon be serving some exquisite drinks and nibbles for the guests. But it's much easier to do so when they are seated." The boy hobbled out of the room without saying another word. They assumed it was to get the treats.

Melissa found it hard to contain a giggle. The boy was odd, to say the least. It was a good thing he was adorable, she thought, because otherwise the whole shtick would be downright creepy.

She sunk down in a chair with overly wide wooden armrests that was reminiscent of mid-century style. She thought the immodestly large chair was beautiful with its cream-colored cloth and lacy red velvet pattern. She was not exactly sure what mid-century was, but the furniture looked familiar to her. It reminded her of the old '50s television shows she used to watch with her mom when she would stay home sick from school.

Jimmy loved anything antique, and he too admired the furnishings. He was taken aback at how such a foreign world as this could contain things so familiar from his own world. He wondered if the owner of the castle had visited their world. The coincidence, he thought, would be too great otherwise.

They all sat facing a large desk. Fox and Bumpy, who was still tucked away in his pouch, sat on the cold wood floor between Seth and Melissa. Fox did not try jumping into Melissa's lap for fear of slipping with those awful socks on her paws. She could not wait to take them off. Instead, she sat on the floor and surveyed the room. There were no other doors except the one they entered from. This room had no windows. No alternate routes of escape, surmised Fox. It was a natural inclination for her kind to always be aware of their surroundings, just in case things turned ugly.

The boy returned with a tray holding three cups and a steaming pot. The awkwardness of the sight was too much for Melissa. He held his crutch under his arm with one hand and the tray with the other. The teapot and cups slid from one side of the tray to the other, but the boy managed to keep it all from falling. It was as if he had had lots of practice. Although she was able to contain her laughter moments earlier, she let out a chuckle that could not be disguised as anything else. This did not faze the boy, but it did get a stern look from Jimmy and a quizzical glance from Fox.

They all assumed the hot pot was full of tea. It was not until Seth poured a cup and confirmed after tasting that it was not. "Hot apple cider?" he guessed. It was delicious, but no one else was brave enough to take a drink, even though they each were served and held onto a cup of their own. Melissa thought it smelled delicious but had learned not to trust good smelling things in this world.

While the young boy passed around the warm drinks and made small talk, he seemed particularly interested in Fox and directed most of his banter towards her. Jimmy took the opportunity to assess the situation. He was quite annoyed at himself for trusting the boy so completely as to follow him into a strange house like this. He knew better. But yet there he was. Taking treats from a stranger. Just the thought of his carelessness was making him angry.

"Excuse me," said Jimmy to the boy. "We have a friend that we think might have come in ahead of us. He's not quite the size of that copper-looking thing on the desk there. Oh, and he can fly. Have you seen him, by chance?"

Seth and Melissa wondered why Jimmy chose to bring up Dauber at that moment. It seemed an odd time. But they did not say anything.

"A flying markel?" asked the boy.

"Say what?" asked Jimmy.

The boy lifted up the object Jimmy pointed at, which was a small coin. "You said your friend is a flying markel? I did not know markels could fly, but it makes good sense they could. They seemed to have all just up and flown away, as we don't see them at all anymore."

"I'm so confused. What is a markel?" asked Seth.

"It used to be what the inhabitants traded with. The more markels one had the more things one could get."

"Oh, it's a coin. Money," said Melissa.

"No, our friend is not a markel. He is a dirt dauber. But he is small, like a markel. He came inside and he should be around somewhere. Have you seen him?" asked Jimmy.

The boy tilted his head back and forth in a strange manner and answered flatly, "No."

He was not a good liar.

Jimmy was quickly losing his patience and demanded, "Where is your father? If he is too busy, we can come back later. We simply were hoping for a little shelter from the storm, but perhaps that was a bad idea. Maybe we should be going."

"But it's still raining outside, and we don't even know where we are," said Seth.

"Great, Seth," said Melissa. "Way to hold your cards."

They all turned to the door when they heard a man's voice.

"Let us cut to the chase, as they say in your world," said the man. "We all know why you are here."

He was a tall, formidable-looking young man in his thirties. He was very handsome; some might even say beautiful. Melissa actually had to remind herself to breathe as her awe had stopped all of her bodily functions. Even Seth and Jimmy would admit that the man was definitely a sight to behold. They had never seen anyone like him before.

The debonair gentleman walked past the speechless visitors and seated himself behind the desk. It was obvious he gained pleasure in their reactions. He relished the moment. He picked up a nail file and ran it across his ring finger, just once. It was this that broke his spell over Melissa. She had never before seen a man file his fingernail with such flair. She was all in favor of nice grooming habits, but she found the manner in which it was done a bit pretentious.

Melissa was the first one to speak. "My name is Melissa. This is my brother Seth and our friend Jimmy. The fox is also our friend and, well, we call her Fox."

The man interrupted Melissa, "And somewhere near is a very interesting companion of yours—"

Before the man could finish, Melissa said, "You mean Bumpy?"

"Is that what you call this creature?" The man opened a drawer and pulled out a jar containing Dauber. Dauber clung to the side, looking unbearably mad. He slowly slipped from the side of the glass to the bottom. He was yelling something. Fox could see his mouth move, but no one could hear him through the glass.

Melissa was about to tell the man Dauber's correct name, but Jimmy waved her off and spoke up instead, "Yes, he is our friend. Would you release him, please?"

"Perhaps, but first allow me to introduce myself. I am Master Harmon. The owner and creator of this place."

"People call you Master Harmon?" Seth asked incredulously.

"Some. You may call me Harmon, if you like."

"I like," said Seth.

"Your reputation precedes you, young man."

"Really?"

Harmon laughed and turned to speak to Melissa. "And you? I see you brought reinforcements back with you." He glanced at Jimmy.

"Do I know you?" asked Melissa.

He smiled wryly and said, "Of course you do. You all know me. This is my world, and I'm everywhere here."

Jimmy responded, "I don't recall seeing you on our journey. Would you mind explaining what you mean?'

"Yes, I would." Harmon stood up and walked over to the boy who was standing next to the door. "What are you doing," he said in a stern voice. "Go and get our guests something to eat, immediately!" He turned back towards the guests. "He's a nosey little runt. He just wants to hear and see everything that goes on."

Melissa turned in her chair to face Harmon straight on. "Is that how you treat your child? That's mean. He's just a little boy and he's curious, that's all."

"Fools speak of things they know not of. That boy is over five hundred years old. And the only reason he can walk is because I patched him up. He is glad to be in my servitude, as he owes me for much. He will always owe me."

"He looks and acts like a boy, so as far as I am concerned that's exactly what he is," said Melissa.

"I'm surprised you made it this far. It boggles the mind how such feeble souls as yourselves can even breathe on your own. But be as it may, I am not here to discuss my servant."

"Then what are you here to discuss?" asked Jimmy.

Harmon returned to his seat behind the desk and sat. "You are here to find something that does not exist. The Library of Truth is a fairytale. A myth. If you continue on in your pursuit of it, you will become exactly what you seek. Nothing. You will disappear and become nothing more than a passing conversation of the liars and conformers you have met during your travels here. And they too will eventually forget you ever were."

The boy entered with the same serving tray as before. But rather than allowing him to fumble his way to the desk, Melissa immediately got up to help him. She took the tray from his hands and walked it over to the desk herself. She sat it down right in front of Master Harmon. She then took her seat, staring steely-eyed at her host.

The boy had never before experienced such kindness. As simple as it might have seemed to an onlooker, it was a grand gesture in the eyes of a boy unaccustomed to even the most mundane politeness. Unfortunately, he could not show emotion or gratitude as he was fearful of his master's fury for allowing the girl to usurp his authority. Instead, he slunk quietly to the corner, where it was darkest and he would least likely be noticed until called upon again.

Seth, aware of his sister's knack of pushing people's buttons, quickly spoke up, "Excuse me, Master Harmon. I've got to pee like nobody's business. Could you please tell me where a bathroom is?"

Harmon snapped his fingers and the servant boy scuttled out from his dark corner towards his master. "Escort this guest to a lavatory, immediately."

"Yes, sir." He looked at Seth and said, "Follow me."

The boy could have taken a direct route to the door but instead opted to walk close to Melissa. He paused briefly as he passed her. He inhaled deeply. He also brushed her arm with the back of his hand. He could not help himself. He was enamored. Melissa thought it was so sweet that her eyes watered with tears of both sorrow for the boy's situation and joy at his charming innocence.

Harmon raised his voice and resisted the urge to stand. "What on earth are you doing! You little sniveling imbecile. Get out of here, now!"

"Yes, yes, of course. Please follow me to the bathroom, sir," said the boy as he quickly walked, crutch in hand, to the door.

"Lavatory. You call it what I call it. Lavatory," screeched Harmon.

The others were quite shocked at how quickly such a seemingly composed man could lose his temper over such trivial matters.

Seth, glad to be leaving the presence of the uncomfortable host, walked out of the room following the boy on his crutch.

The boy nervously chattered on his way out of the room. "Yes, of course, sir, lavatory. A lavatory it is. Yes, yes, yes, whatever you say it is, it is …"

After Seth and the 500-year-old boy left the room, Jimmy took the jar holding Dauber and unscrewed the lid. "I think it's about time he got some fresh air, don't you?"

Without waiting for a response, Melissa said, "I think we are capable of determining whether or not the Library of Truth is real or not. And I for one will not take the word of someone who traps harmless creatures in jars."

"How was I to know he was harmless? An uninvited intruder? One can't be too careful in this world. Small things can have large consequences."

Dauber was now out and flying about. He took a couple of quick flybys perilously close to Harmon's head. Harmon did not bother to deflect him with his hand, but he did look extremely irritated. Fox, sensing the tension, whimpered just enough to get Dauber's attention. Dauber flew down and landed on the pouch where Bumpy was quietly tucked out of sight.

While the people discussed the Library of Truth, Dauber thought he would have a private conversation with Bumpy. He obviously did not trust Harmon and he thought it best to devise a getaway plan in case things went awry. Bumpy, as he found out, was in complete agreement.

"There are many paths from my castle and you are quite welcome to take any of them," Harmon was saying. "But I would not be a very good host if I did not at the very least warn you of the storm that is coming."

Jimmy responded, "The storm is the reason we came to your castle in the first place. We were seeking refuge until it passed."

Harmon laughed loudly and said, "The storm I am referring to does not drop water from the sky or blow wind from the west. The storm that is coming is a clash of ideas. You might think of it as more of a battle between the way that things are and the way things might be."

"I don't get it. Why don't you just speak plainly," said Melissa.

"You have tainted this world. You and those with you have brought a pox upon the land. You should have been sterilized in the beginning, but that was not to be."

Jimmy was becoming increasingly uncomfortable with the conversation, but he maintained a good poker face. "Sterilized?"

"Perhaps neutralized would be a better word. I feel your concern, Jimmy. But unfortunately, you need not fear me. I cannot harm you, as much as I might wish that I could."

Melissa got up from her chair and leaned over the desk. "I know we've met before, even if I can't exactly recall when or where, but you don't scare me."

"I know child. You are a strong-willed one, this I know. And of course you have met me. I'm everywhere in this world. It is my world, after all."

Jimmy stood next to Melissa and said, "Look, what's the point of all this?"

Harmon responded, "If you don't know the point, why are you here?"

Melissa interjected, "You obviously know more than we do. So stop toying with us. The storm is your doing. And it led us right here to your doorstep, didn't it?"

"You're getting wiser by each journey. Too bad you won't be taking another. I might not be able to harm you in the conventional ways you are familiar with, but heed my warning. I need not do anything to create the pit into which you will most certainly fall. All I need do is whisper …" All at once they heard a thousand murmurings coming from everywhere. Little beams of ghost-like lights emanated in bursts all around them. Fox whimpered and crawled under Melissa's chair. Jimmy waved his hand as if trying to swat flies. Melissa did her best to not show any sign of concern.

"A nice parlor trick, Master Harmon. But I know the God I serve and He will not fail us, ever," said Jimmy.

Harmon laughed and said, "Your God is not here. Haven't you figured that out, yet? Now, listen closely because this offer will only come once. If you refuse, you are on your own."

"That's okay, we'll take our chances," said Melissa.

"Don't you think you should at the very least hear what a wonderful offer it is?" said Harmon.

"No. I don't need to hear it."

Seth, who had just stepped back into the room with the boy, quickly spoke up, "I for one would like to hear what you have to say, Master Harmon."

Melissa shook her head in disagreement and looked at Jimmy for back up, but he ignored her and gave a reassuring nod in Seth's direction.

"I offer you two paths. One leading back to your world, which I promise will be free of any impediments. But once you take it, you will never be able to return here."

Jimmy asked, "And the other path?"

"Ah, that one is quite splendid indeed. It is the path to glory, beauty, riches, and great power. You are free to come and go as you wish from this world to yours and you will be made kings and queens to rule over any province you choose."

The little boy, now back cowering in his corner, grumbled at the offer his master had just made. It was obvious to all in the room that the promise had been made before and perhaps not quite kept.

Melissa, in an effort to divert Harmon's attention from the boy's overt disapproval of his master's malintent, stood up and placed herself so as to block the boy from Harmon's direct line of sight. "We will not consider any offer you have and we will take our chances out in the storm," she said.

Jimmy stood, walked over to Melissa's side, and said in agreement,

"Thank you for the hospitality, but we will be leaving now."

"The other in your party has not yet spoken," said Harmon.

Seth responded, "Actually, there are a few of us that have not responded, but I'll speak for all of them, as I'm sure they would agree. We are together. We came together and we will be leaving together. Right Fox? Dauber? Bumpy?"

Fox yapped as she made her way to Jimmy and Melissa from under the chair. Dauber did a quick flyby around Harmon's head and then returned to land on Seth's shoulder. Bumpy stayed safely tucked away in his pouch and said nothing.

Harmon froze and looked perplexed as he said, "Dauber? Is there another here?"

"Dauber is the one that flew by your head."

"Who then is Bumpy?" he asked.

Jimmy took Melissa by the hand and began walking towards Seth and the door, "What does it matter who's who. We are leaving and you will never see any of us again."

Harmon waved his hand and the door slammed shut. He motioned towards the boy who then placed himself between the visitors and their only means of escape.

Harmon walked out from behind the desk for the first time. He walked over to Jimmy and looked down upon him. It was like Harmon had all of a sudden gotten taller. Jimmy, slightly over six feet tall, was sure he matched him in height, but now the host was towering over his guest with a most menacing look. Jimmy pulled Melissa behind him and they took a step back, away from Harmon. Fox growled but also retreated.

Seth took his backpack off and knelt down by the boy. He fumbled around inside the pack, looking for something. He had a chance, now that Harmon was preoccupied with the others, to whisper to the boy for help. "I know you don't like this man. Can you help us out of here?"

The boy, not once daring to look at Seth should his master notice, responded, "I have no choice but to obey the Master. His will is my will, I cannot help you."

"I don't believe that," said Seth. He took several gold coins out of his pack and placed them on the ground in front of the boy.

"What would you have me do?"

"I'm beginning to realize that Bumpy is of far more importance on this journey than I first realized. And if your master finds out who, or what, Bumpy is, he will do all in his power to keep us here. Or worse."

The private conversation between the boy and Seth was cut short when Harmon yelled in a loud voice, "Show me who the other is. No one enters or leaves my house without first meeting the Master." Harmon raised his hand and twirled his finger, causing a wind to blow. The wind pushed them and kept them from backing up any further. If it were blowing any harder it would have pushed them to the other end of the room.

Fox, realizing the danger, quickly darted out to nip Harmon's heel. She had taken the awful socks off of her paws earlier just in case such a moment arose. But she miscalculated Harmon's awareness of her actions. He noticed the socks lying on the floor and was ready for her. Without taking his eyes off of Jimmy, he kicked Fox so hard that she flew up into the air.

Dauber, fulfilling his vow to get revenge on his captor, had already begun a first-line assault of his own. He flew at unprecedented speed towards the evil monster with the intent to inflict as much pain and diversion as possible. Dauber had never assumed a defensive assault before. He was both shocked and pleased at his preparedness. It was like he had the power in him his whole life and he was finally realizing his full potential. There was no training for this, he thought. He just knew what to do.

The air pushed him even faster. Too fast, unfortunately. Dauber did not count on Fox being hurled into the air at the exact same moment. There was no time to adjust to the large ball of fur rushing towards him. He collided with Fox and they both hit the wall hard. Fox laid on the ground, not moving. Dauber was nowhere to be seen.

Seth attempted to help Fox, but the boy took his crutch and blocked Seth's path. The crutch turned into a sword. Seth stopped in his tracks. The boy no longer looked like a charming little crippled kid; now he looked like a short, fat, craggy, five-hundred-year-old man. But his expression belied his appearance. Seth noticed a hint of sympathy in the now-yellow-eyed servant.

"Show me the one you are hiding," yelled Harmon.

Both Jimmy and Melissa were aware that their only exit was blocked. Not that it mattered much anyway, because Harmon seemed to have power beyond their understanding or ability to challenge. They were at a loss as to what to do next. Seth, too, was at a loss. He dared not take a step with the deadly sword staring him down.

It was Bumpy who made the next move. Bumpy knew his friends were in trouble, and he had to do something. He had already eased himself halfway out of the pouch before Fox was hurled across the room. While Fox was in the air, he caught the wind that was blowing and used it to propel himself up towards the ceiling.

Evidently, Harmon had lost his focus and the wind he stirred up moments earlier was now petering out in all different directions. It was exactly the kind of wind Bumpy preferred. He could use it to fly any way he wished by simply turning his body at the right angle. His first destination was to fly by Harmon for a formal introduction. "How nice to make your acquaintance," he said as he sped by.

Harmon, shocked to see Bumpy, had to catch his breath before futilely grasping for the fluttering leaf. Harmon knew the prophecy that told of a leaf that would usher the Word back into this world. Harmon's power would be greatly diminished if they found the Library of Truth. He must stop them at all costs. Propo had warned them about Harmon, but the warning was not enough to keep them from falling into his trap.

The others did not know what to think. There was no time. They had no choice but to watch helplessly as it all happened.

After Bumpy introduced himself, he went from high above everyone's head to cascading unpredictably in all directions, making it impossible for Harmon to grab hold of him. He then made it down to the floor and slid like a hockey puck on ice.

As Bumpy got closer to the door, Harmon shouted at the sword-wielding slave, "Stop him, you useless fool!"

The old man took his sword and lunged at Bumpy but missed badly. He tried again and struck the floor hard. He attempted to lift the sword yet again, but it was stuck in the wood floor. In the time it took him to free his sword, Fox had shaken off her brutal blow and quickly raced back to help her friend, the leaf.

Bumpy had made it to the door and Fox was not far behind. The old man raised his sword for one last reprise. There was no doubt in anyone's mind that, short of a miracle, the sword was about to deal a fatal blow. Bumpy was surely a goner. Melissa covered her eyes in horror. Seth grimaced and Jimmy clenched his fists. There was nothing they could do to help their friend. They were too far away and the sword too quick.

But as swift as swords may be, foxes are perhaps even swifter. Fox had jumped in the air milliseconds before the arm of the wannabe executioner made its move. She was not only fast, but she had the skill to predict the motions of her prey. She was endowed with many gifts and she would use them even at the risk of her own life to defend her friends.

Melissa moved her hands from her eyes just in time to see Fox bite down on the arm of the once polite and gentle boy. No one saw it coming. The craggy old man shrieked in pain as he dropped his weapon and tried in vain to shake Fox from his wrist.

Seth, Jimmy, and Melissa instinctively moved closer to the door. They were so busy watching Fox that they totally lost sight of Bumpy. It was not until they had to cover their ears due to Harmon's screams that they realized Bumpy was gone. Bumpy had slid right through the crack under the door.

It was as if Harmon was caught in a spell of some sort. He lost all interest in everything but a torn, little leaf. It was like no one else existed any longer. Before they knew it, Harmon had opened the door to follow after Bumpy. They all stood there confused, trying to figure out exactly what had just happened. But the door stood wide open and they would not tarry long in taking advantage of their host's carelessness.

"Come on, let's go!" yelled Seth.

"Wait," said Melissa. Fox was still gripping the wrist of the servant, who had now reverted back to his original form of a crippled boy. "Fox, you can let go of him now." But Fox would not let go. She growled between her teeth, still clenching the boy. She shook her head from side to side. The boy cried out in pain.

Jimmy walked over to Fox and stroked her fur. "It's okay. You can let him go. We must leave now." Fox reluctantly released her grip but stood guard near her friends in case the boy made another move. But the sword was once more a crutch, and its wielder a harmless servant boy.

Melissa moved her hand towards the boy's wrist. "May I?" He nodded yes and she took his arm to inspect the damage.

"Careful, Sis. He's not some harmless crippled kid. We all saw what he can do."

"He won't hurt me. Will you?"

The boy closed his eyes and sniffled as he shook his head no.

Melissa smiled. She ruffled his hair with her free hand and then turned to look at his wound. "It's not so bad."

Seth, growing impatient, said, "Come on Melissa. We have to go."

"Just one second, Seth." Melissa ripped a small strip of cloth from her shirttail and gently wrapped it over the boy's wound.

Seth turned to Jimmy for help. "Will you tell her to get a move on. What is she doing?"

Jimmy responded. "She's doing something amazing."

"Seriously? You people need your heads examined. We need to get out of here before Harmon comes back."

Before anyone could respond to Seth's pleas for escape, the boy whispered to Melissa, "Why would you help me? I am your enemy."

"I've been reading a book that says we should love and pray for our enemies. Besides, I don't think you mean us any harm. At least not right now."

The boy looked up at her, then at Jimmy. He glanced over at Seth eagerly waiting by the door, and then over to Fox still standing guard by Melissa's side. He looked back at Melissa with tears welling up in his eyes and said, "You should be more careful. Some here would take advantage of your good nature."

"But you aren't," she said.

"I've never experienced such kindness ever before."

"Won't you come with us?" she asked.

"I'm not sure that's such a good idea," said Jimmy.

"I second that," said Seth.

The boy said, "They are right. My nature is mixed at best. I am a servant to the one from which you flee. But I can tell you a secret, a parting gift that may help you get to the Library of Truth."

"So, it does exist?" asked Jimmy.

"Of that I am not sure. Someone like me would never be privy to that knowledge. But we here have all heard rumors."

Seth impatiently interrupted, "So what's the secret? We really need to get a move on."

The boy looked at Seth as he said, "The portrait I pointed out to you on the way to the lavatory, do you remember it?"

"Sure, it was huge," said Seth.

"That's where you must go. That's the only reason this place is here. To hide the door. I'm not supposed to even know of it myself, but as my master says, I am quite the nosey one."

Melissa, without saying another word, lightly kissed the boy on the cheek. And it was this that made his teardrops turn into sobs. The boy held Melissa's hand and said, "I hope I will see you again someday. But your brother is right, you must hurry. Master Harmon will not be long."

Melissa responded, "But what of our friend, the leaf? We can't leave him behind."

"I will see to it that he also makes it through the painting. That is my promise to you. Once through, my master cannot follow," said the boy. "My master has made other attempts to stop all of you, but you have thwarted him every time. Even as powerful as he is, he cannot be everywhere at once. He does not know all. But beware, he takes many forms and you will likely see him again."

Fox looked up at Melissa and said, "How can we trust this one? He has proven deceptive. He even outfoxed a fox, I'd say."

Jimmy responded, "We have no choice, Fox. We have to trust him. I for one pray he will live up to this promise he has made."

"What is a pray?" asked the boy.

"We pray to our Creator. We ask him things, and we give thanks for His blessings," said Melissa.

"But mostly we ask him for things," said Seth.

"He is your creator, too," said Jimmy. "And you can pray to Him anytime you wish. He knows you very well and He loves you."

The boy, still sitting on the ground nursing his wound, looked up at Melissa with the most innocent eyes she had ever seen. "Is this true? What they say?"

"Yes, it is very true. Not everyone believes it to be so, but He has planted himself in the heart of all of his creation and he has left his word for us to learn."

"What is his word?" asked the boy. He was becoming more and more curious about that which they spoke, so much so that he had forgotten all about the pain in his arm.

Jimmy answered, "His word is written down in scripture for all to read. The word teaches us history, genealogy, archeology, prophecy, and most importantly, salvation."

Seth, growing more impatient by the minute, stuck his head outside the door and back again. "So far the coast is clear. I don't know for how much longer." He looked back at the boy and said, "Not everyone believes in God. It takes a lot more than a little chat before a harried escape to get faith. If you don't mind, you can follow up on your own time? Deal?"

"But we don't have any word here. Is that why you are trying to find the Library of Truth?" asked the boy.

"Yes, exactly. Everyone should be able to read and study about God," said Melissa.

Jimmy added, "But even without it, you can pray and ask that He reveal Himself to you. Pray to know who your Creator is. He will answer. His love knows no bounds."

"But I am unworthy. I've done so much wrong serving my master all these years. There is no way such a one could love me."

Seth yelled impatiently, "Let's get out of here, y'all. We don't have time for this."

Ignoring Seth, Jimmy said, "You are exactly the one he loves. The one who needs Him most. We promise to try our best to leave you the Word. If the Library of Truth is real and we succeed, promise us you will read about the one who loves you."

The boy was now standing. "I promise. I want to know this love you speak of. But I'm afraid your brother is right. You must go." He walked with them to the door, limping badly with the crutch in hand. "The master is near."

Melissa knelt down one last time beside the boy. "What's your name?"

"I don't think I've ever had one. If I did, I do not remember."

"We shall call you Malchus," said Jimmy. He motioned for Melissa to come next to him. "Melissa and I are going to pray for you, is that okay?"

"I welcome pray," he said.

Jimmy bowed his head and laid his hands on Malchus. Melissa followed. He prayed, "Lord, God, we pray that you would reveal yourself to Malchus. He knows he has fallen short and is unworthy. But what he does not know is your saving grace. We pray he comes to know you in your fullest and we pray we can leave your word here for everyone in this world to discover your truths—"

Melissa interjected, "And Lord we pray that you would heal this lonely boy here. We pray in the name of Jesus that you would straighten his leg so he would never need a crutch again."

Together they ended, "Amen."

"He's here. Go," Malchus said in a hushed tone. He stood and watched as they all quickly rushed out the door. Seth turned to the right and they ran towards the portrait that Malchus had pointed out to him earlier. Melissa looked back as she ran but the door had closed and she could not wave one last goodbye.

At the very beginning of their meeting, Malchus was not sure if he would tell them about the door to the legendary library. He had never before told any visitor the secret of the castle. Revealing such a secret might cost him his life, after all. But there was something about these people that made him want to take a risk, so he made sure to point out the portrait to Seth just in case his instincts turned out correct. He was glad he did.

The travelers left, not knowing if their healing prayer worked. And so, they would never know unless or until they returned to see for themselves. But what they did know was that Dauber got his revenge. Seconds before Jimmy stepped through the secret passageway, he heard Harmon's deafening scream that reminded him of the times he himself had been stung. And though no one could see, as he was now small again, the smile on Dauber's face as he himself passed through the secret door was bigger than it had ever been before.

Chapter 35

The Path

The portrait had led them outside to the middle of an open space about half the size of a football field. Fortunately, Malchus had kept his promise by leading Bumpy to the painting and a quick escape from Harmon. Malchus did not tell them why Harmon could not follow them through the painting. Harmon was very powerful, but he had limits. One of his limits was the inability to venture near the Library of Truth.

They were all together again, and they were safe, for now.

Looking out in all directions was like looking through a prism or a kaleidoscope. Everything was slowly spinning around them as they remained stationary. In every direction was a unique path. Each one of the paths revolved all the way around the visitors until it vanished. Eventually each path would repeat, circle around again, and start the whole process over—or so it seemed.

The constant motion disoriented and confused everyone but Bumpy. Bumpy was accustomed to the spinning. When he hung on his tree back home, the wind would often twist and turn his body to the point of breaking his stem. He did eventually snap off when his time came in the fall, a perilous season for all leaves.

Jimmy had an idea that would block out the nausea-inducing surroundings. Everyone placed their arms over one another's shoulders much the same as a football team in a huddle. Dauber, Fox, and Bumpy moved to the center.

They had to think.

"By what I can see, the trails repeat. They come and they go, but they repeat." said Jimmy.

"Yes, I noticed the repetition too. There are a set number of paths. One must be the right one," said Seth.

Melissa responded, "So how do we choose?"

"I think I know," Seth continued, "but only because the little Jekyll and

Hyde really took a liking to you, sis.'

"What do you mean?"

"He gave me another clue. When he showed me the portrait, he made a comment about the trail in the woods. The painting was just a bunch of trees."

"And?" Jimmy asked impatiently. It was the first time Jimmy had showed any sign of annoyance. The journey was beginning to fatigue him. Being the oldest, his sense of responsibility for the others weighed heavily upon him.

"Well, there *wasn't* a trail in the painting. There was just a grove of trees. I thought it was odd at the time, but I chalked it up to the kid being strange."

"What are you saying?" asked Melissa.

"I think we avoid the trails and paths," said Seth.

"So? Are you suggesting we go back the way we came? I for one would rather not go back into that place," said Melissa.

"No. We look for the path that isn't a path," said Seth.

Jimmy looked up from the circle and out at the revolving choices. He said, "That would make sense. It's not obvious. Like so many other things here. But I don't see anything that is not a path." Jimmy sighed and Melissa thought she noticed a small frown.

"It'll be alright, Jimmy," she said. "We are all in this together. You don't have to have all of the answers."

Jimmy forced a smile and nodded.

Seth snapped his fingers and said, "We follow Bumpy. He will know which way to go."

Bumpy rose up higher so that everyone could see him better. They were all taken aback at how their friend looked. He was tattered and torn and barely resembled the leaf that emerged from the jar at the lake. Seth reached out and placed him in his hand. Bumpy took the opportunity to rest as he laid flat in Seth's palm. He did not budge.

Seth lifted Bumpy closer to his face. "Bumpy? Are you okay?"

They all watched with bated breath, expecting Bumpy to leap into the air. But instead, he just curled up a little, lifted what appeared to be his head, and said, "I'm a bit worn out but otherwise hunky-dory."

"We know how you feel, old buddy," said Jimmy.

"I also don't want to get caught up in some random current out there. That's all."

Bumpy's statement was partly true. He did not want a sudden wind to carry him through one of the paths without his friends close behind. What he did not tell them was how terrible he really felt. He was as weak as a monarch butterfly on its last day of migration.

"We were kind of hoping you would know where to go from here," said Seth.

Bumpy looked at Seth and said, "Lift me up as high as you can and keep a tight hold of my stem."

Everyone backed up a bit to allow Seth more room to lift his arms. Seth lifted Bumpy up into the air and held him there. It was all Bumpy could do to straighten his body. He needed more rest, but this was not the time. There was still so much work to be done. He stretched his spine as tall as it would go and he looked out at what the others had been talking about.

Bumpy saw the same thing as everyone else. While they remained stationary on their small bit of dirt, the world around them moved. While the others had mentioned seeing about twenty different paths, Bumpy figured there were many more, too many to count. It was as if there was a conveyer belt of choices with no rhyme or reason to the order in which they came. Very little distinguished one path from another.

Bumpy continued to examine the possibilities as they slowly rotated around. One path had brown cobblestones with charming little flowers in between. A few others had bricks with bushes along the sides. There were some that resembled wooden boardwalks. In others Bumpy could see houses and buildings. He noticed a pasture full of creatures resembling cows in one. But most were plain old dirt trails with varying degrees of vegetation. None of them had trees. All of them had blue skies. None of them pointed directly to the Library of Truth.

Seth lowered Bumpy back down and everyone huddled together, waiting for Bumpy to speak.

"Other than a few embellishments, the paths are all pretty much the same," said Bumpy matter-of-factly.

"And?" asked Melissa.

"Take any one of them you wish," said Bumpy. "It matters not the path you take, but rather the choices you make while following it."

Seth interrupted, "But what about the clue the boy gave me? There was no path in the painting."

Jimmy responded, "There is always a path to take, Seth. Even when you can't see it. Bumpy's right. We can't change what we've done to get here, all we can do is continue on and try to make the best choices possible from now on."

"Ugh! That makes no sense. Then what's the point of a bunch of different choices if it doesn't matter which one we take!" exclaimed Seth.

Bumpy turned towards Seth and said, "No one said it doesn't matter which path we take, only that we hope we have prepared ourselves for what lies on the way and that we make the wisest choices we are capable of. The rest is in God's hands, you might say."

"No, *you* might say," said Seth. "I say we analyze the situation and narrow down the possibilities."

Bumpy slipped out of Seth's hand and floated directly in front of his face, "You worry too much, young man. It's time to exercise faith. Every one of us is here for a reason. Some have prepared for the journey more than others. But regardless, you all have gifts." Bumpy, with somewhat of a struggle, lifted up higher into the air. "Follow me."

Before anyone had time to object, Bumpy floated down a path with a cobblestone walkway. He had never before seen little flowers so neatly growing between stones placed just so. The cobblestones were light brown with purple and orange flowers growing between them. He wished all paths were so beautiful.

And although the chosen path was moving, there was plenty of time for each one of the other travelers to step onto the cobblestone path before it disappeared. They made it without any problem at all. It was refreshing to be back in a place where the world around them remained stationary. It was also a relief that it did not appear to be a trap.

Once they were all accounted for, they headed down the path. Seth took hold of Bumpy and gently held him as they walked. There was hardly time to discuss their surroundings before Fox noticed a large, odd-shaped object obstructing their way. She yapped as she ran ahead.

When the others finally caught up with her, Fox was digging up the dirt at the base of a half-buried airplane. The plane looked ancient and it appeared to have crashed. Most of it was intact except for the right wing which was on the ground a few feet south of the fuselage.

The plane was small—it probably could have carried no more than four passengers at a time. The wheels were buried in the ground. Jimmy looked at some of the numbers that had not eroded by time. He said it was a Piper PA-14 built sometime in the 1950s. It was from their world.

Jimmy dug the bottom of the cockpit door free and worked his way inside. After a few minutes of looking around, he discovered something that should not have been in the cockpit of a plane. He yelled out to the others, "Hey y'all. The cockpit has been gutted. But I found a trap door under where the pilot seat would have been. Come take a look."

One by one they all peeked into the open trap door. There were steps leading down, and although it was a tight fit through the opening, the area below appeared to be clean and well lit.

The vote was unanimous. There was no hesitation. They would of course go down and investigate. Each one of them took their turn. It was a short descent. Jimmy went first, followed by Melissa and the rest.

At the bottom of the steps, underneath the plane, was a large cavern. In the cavern was another door, but much more conventional than the one they just stepped through. This door was large enough to fit the plane that was resting up above them. There were two symbols on the large hangar door. One was obviously a cross and the other appeared to be an open book.

Melissa walked over to the door and ran her fingers over the symbolic engravings. Jimmy knocked on the wood with his fist, but no one answered. Fox sniffed around at the bottom of the closed door while Dauber examined the top.

Bumpy was the first to speak. "It's the Library of Truth. I reckon of this we can be sure."

Melissa, still running her fingers over the engraving on the door, looked to Jimmy and Dauber and asked, "Do you think this symbol is supposed to represent the Bible?"

"Could be," said Jimmy.

"Of course, it is," said Seth.

Melissa, more to herself than anyone else, recited a verse she had memorized a few weeks earlier, "This book of law shall not depart out of thy mouth; but thou shall meditate therein day and night, that though mayest observe to do according to all that is written therein: for then thou shall make thy way prosperous, and then thou shalt have good success." Melissa had purposefully used the King James Version when she memorized verses. Partly because she enjoyed the way it sounded, but mostly because she thought it would impress her brother.

Moments after she finished with her recitation of the Old English scripture, the large door opened. Dauber quickly buzzed in and back out again. "The coast is clear," he said right before he darted in for the second time.

Bumpy was the next to enter. He was followed by Seth, Melissa, Fox, and then Jimmy. The door closed in much the same fashion as it had opened—slowly and methodically. As they looked ahead of them into the large cavernous room, they saw many shelves. All were empty. There was no end in sight, just a continuous row of shelves as far as the eye could see both to the right and to the left. It was odd. Who makes a room full of shelves to store nothing at all?

It was a beautiful place, however. The shelves were made of the finest of woods and polished to perfection. They were clean, not even a speck of dust could be seen resting on the sheer surfaces.

Soft light poured in through stained glass windows. Where the windows led to was anyone's guess, as they assumed they were still underground. But that was a question for later. There was too much other stuff to figure out first.

Just as Jimmy was about to take another step, a long tube dropped from the ceiling and began to quietly suck the dirt and debris off his shoes. It then stopped and tapped on his foot. Jimmy understood that it wanted to vacuum the soles of his feet. Once done to satisfaction, the tube continued to clean Jimmy's pants and then moved to the top of his head. Melissa giggled. His hair was sticking straight up as it was being suctioned. He quickly batted the suction tube away from his head and combed his hair back down with his fingers.

When it was Fox's turn to be cleaned, she cooed the whole time. A fox coo could only be compared to a cross between a puppy's howl and a morning dove's whistle. She could not help herself. It felt so good.

Melissa tried to dodge out of the way when another suction tube made its way to her head. She did not like anything touching her hair, but the floating vacuum would not give her a pass. When it was over, Melissa scanned the room for a mirror.

By the time it was Seth's turn, he knew the routine and obliged without hesitation.

The vacuum seemed confused when it reared up in front of Dauber. Likewise, Dauber knew that while it might have been safe for the others, he should avoid it at all costs. Dauber buzzed to the left and the suction followed. Dauber buzzed up, down, and all around, but the device finally caught up and sucked Dauber right up through the tube. Melissa's eyes opened wide and she stifled her shock by placing her hands over her mouth. Fox yapped and tried to grab the floating suction cup with her two front paws.

"Hey, you sucked our friend up!" shouted Seth. "You can't do that, let him out!" But the suction tube just simply recoiled overhead and disappeared.

"What are we going to do?" asked Melissa.

"How in the world should I know?" responded Seth.

"Don't worry, I'm sure Dauber is okay. We will find him. First, let's figure out where we are," said Jimmy. Jimmy had gotten a second wind. His instincts told him that they were exactly where they should be, and they were very close to accomplishing something amazing.

"Well, isn't it obvious? We are in a library. Even I know that," said Fox.

"How would you know what a library is?" asked Jimmy.

"That's neither here nor there, but I know."

"Yes, the little fox is correct. This is a library of sorts," said a voice in the distance. Everyone looked as a man came walking closer to them. But the closer he got the more they realized he was no ordinary man, and he was not really walking. This man had wings, and while his feet seemed to touch the ground, he more or less glided across the floor as his large beautiful wings gently waved through the air. Truth be told, the man—or angel, as it were—was quite imposing. He was taller than both Seth and Jimmy, and very athletic. Had it not been for the slowness of his gait and the gentleness of his voice, everyone would have taken a few steps back.

"Oh, my. You are most beautiful," said the angel to Bumpy. "I am quite honored to meet you." The angel did a slight bow in front of the leaf.

Bumpy said, "Really? If you think I'm all that now, you should have seen me a few weeks ago. May I ask where exactly we are?"

The angel reached out his hand towards Bumpy and said, "We have never been graced with one such as you. It would be my wish to show you our home, if you would allow me the honor."

"I think we would like that," said Bumpy, who allowed the angel to take hold of him.

"Come," he looked at the rest of the group and continued, "Follow me, but please do not touch. This place was created in ancient items. It is valued almost as much as the Ark itself."

"The Ark?" asked Jimmy.

"The Ark of the Covenant," replied the angel.

"Yeah, I ain't touchin' anything in here," said Seth. "If I recall my movie trivia, folks died touching the Ark of the Covenant."

"Well, if you would start reading the Bible instead of watching so many movies, you would know why the Ark of the Covenant is so important," said Melissa.

They followed the angel until he came to a shelf that was much more ornate than the ones they saw near the entrance. The wooden shelves were trimmed in 24 karat gold leaf. When the light hit it, it sparkled and glowed.

"These shelves were reserved for some of the first-ever vessels containing the Word."

"The Word?" asked Fox.

"Yes, the Word of the one you know so very well, sweet creature. The Word of the Creator."

"Why are all of the shelves empty?" asked Jimmy.

The angel replied, "In the days of old, there were scrolls and vessels passed down by many generations. Some that were never even opened. But each and every book, scroll, paper, and fragment was special and served a purpose in the kingdom. Many of them were kept safe in this very place."

"Where are they now?" asked Seth.

"They were erased," he answered.

Jimmy took the small Bible from his back pocket, opened it, and showed it to the angel. "Like this one?"

The angel nodded, "The Word was vanquished from every realm thousands of years ago. The land and its inhabitants have been in a state of entropy ever since."

Seth looked at his sister and said, "Entropy is the same thing as molecular disorder. In other words, everything is dying."

Melissa rolled her eyes at Seth, but truthfully, she was thankful for his arrogance because she had no clue what the angel was talking about.

The angel nodded at Seth and added, "The trees have all died, there is very little water, every living organism has been affected. But worst of all, the spirit of each life in this world has been drained of truth. Love, peace, honor, all the virtues have almost disappeared entirely."

"Doesn't sound too different from our world," said Seth.

Melissa looked puzzled as she asked, "If the Word is gone, then why save this place—the Library of Truth? And why keep it so clean and pristine?"

The angel smiled and took a deep breath before answering, "Hope, my dear. Hope."

"Hope in what?" she asked.

"In *you,* of course." The angel looked at each one of them. "And you, and you, and you, and you. We have been anticipating the arrival of the carriers, and here you are."

"Carriers?" asked Jimmy.

"Yes, you have already brought much more than you know to our land. But there is more to come. The people need the Word and you will bring the Word back."

"But how? My own Bible was erased when we arrived. It's empty," said Jimmy.

"Can the Holy Spirit be erased?" The angel looked directly at Jimmy as he continued, "The whispering has already begun, the waters flowing, the trees growing, but I must warn you. There has been a cost. I'm afraid your own world has been affected by what you have done here. The evil one is not pleased, and he will act ruthlessly to stop you. I am not sure how it spread to your world, and thus, I do not know how to help you defeat it. All I can do is warn you."

"Great. No good deed goes unpunished," said Seth.

Jimmy shook his head in frustration and said, "There must be a way to defeat it. This is the Library of Truth and you're an angel. If you don't know how to defeat it, who would? It's not fair that we have jeopardized our world for the sake of yours. There must be something we can do."

"There is a way. Of this, I am sure. Continue to fight the good fight both here and there. I have faith the one who sent you will honor your efforts." said the angel.

"May I ask you what your name is, sir?" asked Melissa.

"You may call me Apotropos," said the angel.

"I hate to interrupt you, Apotropos, but I'm very worried about our friend Dauber. Will he be okay?"

"Yes, he is just fine. An unfortunate mistake, our overzealous helper vented him back out from whence you came. He will be waiting when you are finished here," said Apotropos. "Follow me, please."

Apotropos turned and everyone followed. It was not long before they entered an empty passageway free of shelves. What began as a straight corridor soon became a complicated maze. There was no way anyone would know which way to go unless they had it memorized.

Along the way, the angel answered questions. He explained how the Holy Spirit inspired the Bible and that there was plenty of evidence of its authenticity to quiet even the loudest of skeptics if they only took the time to thoroughly investigate. He knew about the Dead Sea Scrolls in their world. He explained how that after thousands of years, the words of the Bible had remained unchanged. He and Jimmy had a great conversation about how the Bible was always correct when it addressed science, archeology, as well as prophecy. He said his world once scoffed at the validity of the Word of God to the point that it literally disappeared.

Suddenly a beautiful shofar with a golden mouthpiece appeared a few feet in front of them. It was perfect timing since all of the turns were starting to make Melissa dizzy. The ram's horn was floating in the air by itself. It began to blow as if announcing their arrival. Then a trumpet appeared, also floating in the air. Then a third and a fourth horn joined on the opposite side and they all began playing together. After walking past the horns, they came to a door. The angel stepped to the left and faced the visitors.

"I do not know who heard the horns. I myself do not hear them. But this next passageway is only for those that are called and announced. Let this be fair warning. No one has ever entered that did not hear the music. I'm not even sure it would even be possible. The anthem is this: 'And your ears shall hear a word behind you, saying, "This is the way, walk in it."' I, angel Apotropos declare unless you have heard the shofar and its trumpets, do not enter this gate or I cannot promise you will return."

Everyone froze in silence. No one knew what to make of the decree. Melissa looked at Seth to see if he might have heard anything, but if he did, he was not giving it away. Jimmy was also stone-faced. It was obvious Fox heard nothing as she became distracted by her own tail. Melissa was the first to speak.

"Perhaps none of us are meant to go in."

"I highly doubt that young girl. The prophets told of your coming and now you are all here," said the angel.

Still, no one owned up to having heard the horns. Either fear had captured their imaginations, or perhaps Melissa was right, and no one had been called.

"The door would not stand open if someone was not announced," assured the angel.

"I heard it," said Bumpy.

"Very well, you may enter," said the angel.

Seth stepped out from behind Jimmy and Melissa, "Wait, I heard it too." The last thing Seth wanted to do was to go into a strange place in this strange world alone. The last time that happened it was a very frightening experience. But at least with Bumpy he knew he had a trusted friend.

"Very well, you, too, may enter," declared the angel. "Are there any others?"

No one else stepped forward. It appeared that Bumpy and Seth would be going on this part of the journey without the others. They had no idea what to expect.

"May I ask a question before we go?" asked Bumpy.

"You may, but you mustn't tarry, the door has a mind of its own," said the angel.

"Why was I not cleaned like the rest of my friends here?"

"You embody that which should already be here. Your essence is what this place was created to protect. You see, this place was intended for the most sacred sayings of the very creation itself. It was your kind that collected the rays of the sun, that nourished the very base of what holds the truth. Your kind accepted the life that was given and then gave it back to all those who were willing to hear."

"I reckon I don't fully understand all those words, nor do I feel worthy of such a great honor, but I thank you for it nonetheless," said Bumpy.

"It is we that thank you," said the angel. "I will not see you again. Remember that to understand the ending you must know the beginning. Many spend their lives looking for the meaning of the last book. But the answers are all available before it even begins. Now you must go."

Seth hugged his sister and patted Fox on the head. He shook Jimmy's hand and said, "If anything happens, please take care of my sister and make sure she gets back home."

Jimmy responded, "We don't plan on going anywhere without you. Do what it is you have to do and come back. We started this together and we will finish together."

Seth nodded.

Bumpy floated over Fox's head, teasing her. She swiped at him but missed. "We'll be back in a jiffy, y'all." Bumpy entered the grand door followed closely by Seth. The door closed behind them.

Chapter 36

A Thousand Leaves

As soon as Seth stepped over the threshold, he found himself in a dark place with flames surrounding him. But it was not hot. It was surreal. He looked out and all around him were people. Not recognizable faces, but regular people like back home. Seth greeted them by saying his name and the crowd burst into applause. For some reason, Seth was not surprised. He reacted to the moment as if it were routine. He smiled at the crowd and they cheered. They adored him.

He felt wonderful. Elated. He had often dreamed of becoming someone famous, and now he knew what it felt like to be loved and admired for being so important. The feelings of elation were magnified beyond anything he could have imagined possible. It was like a drug.

He introduced himself again to the same applause. The people erupted. It felt good. Not as good as the first time, but still good. Then he did it again and again and again. It was as if he were a puppet on strings caught in a time warp. He could not help himself. He kept repeating the same motions. Controlled by his own desires, he could not stop the cycle. The adulation suddenly made him feel sick. He panicked because it would not stop. He kept introducing himself and the crowd kept cheering. No one was there to help him. He had the fame he had secretly dreamed of, but all of a sudden it horrified him. It was hollow. But he could not stop.

He could not even look to the left or to the right. He knew he was alone. He knew there was no one to save him. There was no reason to even try. Again, he introduced himself to the people in the flames and they cheered. He closed his eyes as tight as they would go and he thought to himself, "God, please help me."

He opened his eyes and the first thing he saw was Bumpy. Before he could say a word, he dropped to his knees and heaved. He had not eaten in quite some time so nothing came out of his mouth, but he kept heaving. He wished there was something inside of him that could be expelled, but there was not. The dry heaves were necessary and involuntary but not very satisfying.

"What's wrong there, fella?" asked Bumpy.

"Didn't you see it? Weren't you here? There?"

"Where? We just stepped through the door."

"Yeah, a couple of minutes ago. What happened to you?"

"I've been right next to you the whole time, ol' chap. We walked right in and you dropped to your knees sweatin' like a pine tree in a forest fire."

"I was just …" Seth was at a loss for words and did not quite know how to explain what had just happened to him. Neither was he sure it was important any longer. He stood up, looked around, and said, "Where are we?"

"Did you hear the horns blow?" asked Bumpy.

"Of course, why?"

"I didn't."

"Bumpy, that's crazy! Why would you go through the door? The angel said you would never be able to leave."

Bumpy ignored the question and said, "Look around, there are all kinds of books and scrolls and papers in here."

Seth walked to a table. It reminded him of something, but he wasn't sure what. On the table were all kinds of books. Most were bound in leather, but some were wrapped in unfamiliar material. He opened one of them and it was blank. He unrolled a scroll and it was also devoid of any script.

"They're all blank," he said. "Empty pages waiting for an author."

Seth walked over to Bumpy. Now that Bumpy was perfectly still he noticed the wretched condition he was in. The beautiful tan leaf he had met only a couple of days before now looked a sickly shade of grey. Almost half of his body was nothing more than a membrane—holes connected by brittle veins. How could they have been so careless? He was just a leaf. Seth was mad at himself for not taking better care of his friend.

"I'm so sorry, Bumpy."

"For what?"

"You look … You're so … You don't look so good."

"Oh that. Don't you worry none. It's the normal life of a leaf like me."

"But we should have carried you. We could have sheltered you from the rain and the wind."

"Are you kiddin' me? That's what we leaves live for. To feel the wind blow so we can touch one another. And when the rain falls it cleanses us so we can breathe better. And no other leaf I know of has ever gotten to lead an ensemble like you folks into another world. It's been a blast. Look at me, Seth. I'm talking to a human. I played with a fox. I mean, wow! That's a miracle. Most of us just hang up high watching the world pass by. We look down at everyone living their lives until it's time for us to return to our roots."

"But how much longer can you survive. You're almost just a bunch of veins."

"Lift me up, my friend."

Seth complied by gently lifting Bumpy's stem and then sliding his other hand under his body. Seth did not want to show any signs of sadness so he put on a brave face. "What do we do now?"

"Look at where I was resting."

Seth looked down and said, "I don't see anything any more unusual than all the other stuff in here."

"Look more closely."

Seth shrugged his shoulders and bent down to more closely examine the exact spot where Bumpy had been lying down. That's when he noticed it. It was very faint, but it was there. And he could not be certain, but it seemed like it was getting darker.

Bumpy lifted up his head and in a whisper, as that was all he could really manage, said, "Do you see it?" Three distinct words, *In the beginning*, had appeared underneath Bumpy while he was resting, and more letters and words were slowly appearing as well.

"I do. Did you do that?"

"No. It wasn't just me. I think it was us. All of us. Maybe I was the catalyst, but this is exactly as it should be."

"Do you think it will continue? That more letters and words will appear?"

"Of course. It's why we were meant to come."

Seth carefully lifted Bumpy up to his face by his stem and said, "So we can go now. We can go home?"

"Yes, you can go home."

"Great! Let's go tell the others."

"But I won't be going with you. This is the last stop for me."

"Don't be silly. You are coming back with us."

"You and I both know better. Maybe I could have lasted a few more weeks back home, but like Fox would say, 'That's neither here nor there.' I can think of no better place to be laid to rest. But I need to ask you one last favor."

Seth knew that Bumpy was right. There was nothing that could be done for him. He did not have much time left before he totally disintegrated. "You name it. Anything you want."

"If my touching one page caused that letter to appear, imagine what would happen if I could touch them all."

"I guess you have the rest of your life to work on it," said Seth.

Bumpy chuckled a bit. "No, I don't have enough energy left to move, and even if there were a breeze in here to catch—it would flow right through me. But I know how we could do it together."

"How?" asked Seth.

"The minute I left my tree, my life was over. It was the Holy Spirit that breathed more into me and allowed me to be here with you. What I ask you to do is not as extreme as it may seem."

"And that is?"

"It's nothing you haven't done many times before. Just take me in your hands and crumple me up into as many tiny pieces as you can. Then throw me into the air so I can do the work of a thousand leaves."

Seth shook his head vigorously. He was angry. He tried not to show his disdain, but he gritted his teeth and pursed his lips. How could anyone ask another soul to do something so egregious to a friend was beyond his comprehension. He froze, still holding Bumpy in his hand. He tried to regain his composure before addressing the request before him.

As Seth struggled to muster up the strength to speak, Bumpy said, "What would you have me do? Slowly rot and decay here all by myself? I can't leave with you, even if I wanted to. I knew the rules before I went through that door. I have a chance to be a part of something meaningful in this world. I could have been just another leaf that fell off a tree. But if you do what I ask, I'll be a leaf who helped a world see the truth."

Seth thought about what Bumpy said and he reluctantly agreed. They exchanged a few more words and even prayed together. It was the first prayer that ever really meant anything to Seth. It was the first prayer of his that he believed God heard. Seth did not know why at the time, but right there, sitting on the floor of the Library of Truth, Seth asked Jesus Christ into his heart. There was no more denying that God existed. No more denying the reality of a creator.

If the scriptures about creation and the creator threatened some in this world so much that they would hide them from the people, they must be powerful. Seth would not take the Bible for granted any longer. When he got home, in honor of Bumpy, he would join his sister in reading and studying the Word of God. He would no longer take the Bible for granted, and he would do all he could to make sure those in this world had the same opportunity.

Saying goodbye to such an odd and amazing friend as Bumpy was hard enough, but to actually hold such an amazing miracle in your hand and then feel it turn to powder was heartbreaking. It did not matter if it was the best or right thing to do. It did not matter if he was honoring a last request. What mattered was that his friend was gone and he would never see him again.

After he crushed the leaf into as many tiny pieces as possible, Seth stood on the table with all the blank books, opened his palms, and blew as hard as he could. It was as if Bumpy had turned to gold dust. Just as he left Seth's hand, a breeze lifted him up and sent his tiny particles in every direction. Tiny flecks of gold leaf sparkled in the light as they drifted back down on history.

Seth was grateful that he was alone with the books and scrolls. There was no one to hear him cry. He lost all control as the tears streamed down his face. He couldn't catch his breath. He was both shocked and a little embarrassed at his reaction. He had only known the little talking leaf for a few days. It was not like they were family. But there was something about Bumpy that had changed Seth forever. And Seth knew that there would never be another Bumpy. Ever.

Chapter 37

HITHER, THITHER, AND YON

The trip back to their world was uneventful. Well, as uneventful as traveling between worlds could be. For those never having lived such a miracle, it would have been the pinnacle of experiences. But not for the chosen three: Melissa, Seth, and Jimmy. They were bonafide wanderers in the supernatural realm. And in time they would become experts in traversing between worlds.

Seth was none too happy to have given up his prized pearl. It was the pearl he had carefully guarded since taking it from the table of illusions. Willow told him there would be a gatekeeper that could lead them home if he was willing to leave his illusions behind. He did not know exactly what she meant at the time, but when he met the groveling, greedy boat helmsman, he figured it out. Seth convinced the old man might use the pearl to buy a new boat. But by the looks of his overflowing treasure box, raggedy attire, and dilapidated ferryboat, it appeared that he would rather save than spend his earnings.

The gatekeeper was also their lone crewman. As he rowed them out to the spot where they first entered the otherworld, the man did not say a word. He pointed and grunted, which was enough. According to Apotropos, the angel from the Library of Truth, he was from the realm of Suolumne—the home of a strange assortment of hoarders and collectors of antiquities. Jimmy noticed that before they got on the boat, the ferryman eyed the belt given to him by Propo. He was not sure if this was because he admired and wished to acquire it, or if it was a symbol of trust, as Propo had mentioned. Jimmy did not ask.

After traversing the foggy waterway, the ferryman stopped abruptly and pointed. It was obvious to everyone that the Water Gate was below the surface. They were back where they had started at the far end of the Lake of Entitlement on the outskirts of the Dead Woods. Everything was slowly reconnecting via rivers and streams. They wondered what the ferryman did before the Lake of Entitlement was replenished. This world was indeed changing, but the natives had not seen anything yet.

One by one they all dove into the warm, calm water. Melissa went first. She trusted Willow and Apotropos, who had assured them it would be safe. When they came up for air, only seconds later, the water was shockingly cold. They were home again—exactly where they had capsized on Lake Ouachita. Jimmy's canoe was resting safely on the shore. The sun warmed them as they rowed back to where the pickup was parked. According to the position of the sun, Jimmy figured it was around 3 p.m.

The siblings were relieved to find out that they had only been gone a few hours. Jimmy's phone, which he left in the glove compartment of the truck, confirmed it was the same day. They would not have to explain their absence, and they were quite sure their parents had not called the authorities to form a search party. The only thing lost was Melissa's backpack, which fell in the water at the beginning of their journey. Other than that, it was just an uneventful cruise on the lake as far as anyone else was concerned.

After they loaded the canoe in the bed of the truck, it dawned on Jimmy why none of them had gotten hungry while they were gone. It seemed as though days had passed, but in physical reality, it had only been a short time. At least that was his theory.

Before she stepped into the pickup, Melissa looked back through the woods towards the cove. It was not just Seth's pearl that they had left behind. She had hoped that Fox and Dauber would change their minds and follow them back. Dauber's lifespan was at its end, but beyond the Water Gate, in the other world, he had renewed strength and energy. He did not know how much longer he might have if he came back, so he decided to stay in the other world. He would spend his days looking for the eleven. And if he found them, he would help spread the good news of the Word to the Five Realms of Here.

When Dauber asked Fox to send his love to Wanda and Sticky, she declined. She too would be staying behind. She felt she should help Dauber. And since she had no kids or family, she explained that it was the logical choice. Melissa was not surprised. If there was anything she knew about Fox, it was her unbridled loyalty to others.

Everyone had a feeling they would see each other again. Their mission was not complete. They would be traveling back to the other world. It was only a matter of when and how. Even so, there were still tears while bidding farewell. Fox even accused Seth of sniffling, which he blamed on allergies.

It was not until they turned onto the main road that Melissa had an epiphany. She excitedly shared her revelation with Jimmy and Seth that she had not lost her memory. She remembered everything, unlike the last time she had traveled to the Five Realms of Here. Everything they experienced in the other world actually happened, and they all remembered it.

Seth was surprised he hadn't realized it before Melissa mentioned it, but then again, he was preoccupied with a lot of new revelations of his own. He now believed that there must be a God. In a way, his journey was just beginning and he had a lot to learn. He knew life would be very different now. He wondered how he was going to share the news with his dad. He wondered what his reaction would be. Melissa was proud of her brother for opening his heart and mind to God. She looked forward to learning more with her brother by her side.

On the drive back to the Fray house, they all made a vow not to share their experience with anyone. They would keep it just amongst themselves for the time being. Besides, it was highly unlikely anyone would believe them anyway. Both Melissa and Seth were grateful that Jimmy was with them. They found comfort in their newly formed camaraderie.

There was something that none of them would find comfort in, however. Upon returning to the house, Azora seemed very different. She did not even come out to greet them when they returned. She did not say goodbye to Jimmy when he left. When Melissa asked her mom what was wrong, she simply said that Azora was not feeling well.

The fact was, Azora barely left her room the rest of the night or the next day. As the family packed to head back home, Azora sat in her room staring at that plant, which by morning had sprouted yet another leaf and was at least another half-inch higher. When Melissa mentioned the oddity to Jimmy, he said he would look into it. He also said he would check in on Azora to make sure she was okay.

When it was time for them to leave, Azora finally came out of her bedroom. Bethany had never seen her mom looking so disheveled, but she attributed it to her age and the busyness of the holiday. Azora was always dressed early in the morning when she had guests in the house, but now she was still in her robe. Patrick rather enjoyed this new side of his mother-in-law. She was not paying him any attention.

They all walked outside and said their goodbyes in the front yard. Patrick and Seth had already loaded up the van so there was nothing left to do but give the customary hugs and small talk. Everything was as normal as any other farewell until Seth noticed the old hickory tree.

Seth stood next to the tree with his hand on the trunk. "Grandma, what's up with the tree? I didn't know it had died?"

Azora walked over to Seth. "Why there's not a thing wrong with this tree. What are you talkin' about?"

Patrick pointed up to a big mass on one of the lower limbs. "I hadn't noticed, but if it's not dead yet, it will be soon. That looks like canker rot to me."

"That wasn't there last week. That Ratcliffe has done something to my tree!" exclaimed Azora.

Bethany put a reassuring hand on her mother's shoulder and said, "Mom, I don't think anyone could purposefully give a tree a disease."

Azora rebuffed her daughter's gesture and walked towards the neighbor's house, pointing her finger and shouting, "You don't know that man. He's evil. You heard him. He was just here complaining about the hickory nuts in his yard. I'll get him for this. I promise you, I'll get him."

Melissa caught up to her grandmother and took her hand. It seemed to calm her down. "Grandma, I'm sure the tree will be okay. We can have

Jimmy look at it. Maybe there's some kind of treatment for it or something."

Azora walked back over to the Hickory tree and looked it up and down. She frowned and looked over at Patrick, "Your dad's right. If it's not dead, it will be soon. The bark is already starting to peel off. I loved this tree."

"Maybe you can plant another hickory here," said Seth.

"No, once the disease is in the ground, it'll spread to any hickory in a hundred yards of here."

Bethany said, "Next time we come for a visit we'll help you find another tree for the front yard, Mom. It'll be alright."

"I already have another tree. It's sittin' there in my bedroom. And with any luck it'll grow to be a hundred feet tall with big leaves to blow in his yard and roots to clog his pipes and big hard spiky hard-shelled nuts to rain on his garden," said Azora wryly.

"Uh, if it does all that to his yard, imagine what it would do this one," said Patrick.

"Nobody asked you," said Azora. She looked down at her clothes and exclaimed, "What am I still doing in this robe? I got chores to do and calls to make. I'll see y'all in spring? Is that right? Spring goes hand in hand with the resurrection, did you know that, Patrick?"

"And she's back. It's been a pleasure seeing you again after all these years, Azora," said Patrick.

Everyone said their final goodbyes and hugged, including Patrick and Azora, which surprised Bethany. It seemed, to her at least, that progress had been made in their relationship. She thought that Patrick might even return with them on their next visit.

Right before they backed out of the driveway, Seth jumped out of the car and ran up to his grandmother. He held a small piece of wood. It was the gift given to him by the beavers. He asked his grandmother if she knew what kind of wood it was. She held it close to her face and ran her fingers along the grain, but did not have an answer for him. He hugged her goodbye again.

As Seth walked back to the car he stared at the object in his hands. He had no idea what it was or what to do with it. He reached for the car door with one hand and proceeded to put the beaver's gift back into his pocket when out of nowhere a huge bird came straight for him. The bird's wingspan must have been at least eight feet. He raised his hand to deflect the attack. The bird screeched and retreated, but succeeded in knocking the wood spike out of his hand.

Seth paid no attention to the wood piece lying on the ground because he was so taken aback by the boldness of the wild animal. He had never been attacked by a bird before. It was not until it came back that he noticed what had happened. The bird was headed straight for it. The bird was not after Seth at all, but rather the beaver's handmade gift. He did not have time to think so he just made a dive for it. He grabbed it mere seconds before the claws of the bird laid hold.

With the beaver's gift in hand, Seth quickly got into the van. He was breathing heavily and had gotten his pants dirty from landing on the hard ground, but to his surprise, none of his family had even noticed the scuffle.

He nudged his sister and pointed towards the hickory tree. They both watched in awe as a flock of large black birds swarmed the tree right above where their grandmother stood. The birds broke off limb after limb as if it were made of straw. His sister suggested that maybe the birds needed nesting material. But it was fall; egg-laying season was over. And besides, as far as he knew, only eagles used such large tree limbs for nesting. No, something was wrong, and they had to plan a trip back soon to find out what it was.

The last thing they saw before turning the corner was their grandmother standing underneath her beloved hickory tree as a swarm of blackbirds dismantled it piece by piece. The sight was eerie, to say the least. Both Melissa and Seth recalled what they were told by several of the creatures in the other world. There was a war brewing and the answers were in the Word. They both knew there was more work to do, more information to obtain, and more than likely another trip to the Five Realms of Here. This time it was Seth who led the prayer. He grabbed his sister's hand and petitioned the Creator. He didn't care that his dad was watching from the rearview mirror. He was not ashamed, because he knew there was power in prayer and in the Word.

Afterword

Thank you for reading *A Leaf of Faith*. If you enjoyed this book, you would be a huge help by leaving a review on Amazon, Goodreads, and sharing on social media. Reviews are very powerful for authors and will help to let others know about the series.

The first book in the *Messengers and Thieves* series, *Where the Garden Begins*, and the third and final book in the series, *Roots and Branches: The Battle for Here*, are both available on Amazon and other online retailers. Other books, plays, and music by J. Suthern Hicks:

Plays:

Turtle Tears:
A Play in Two Acts

Home, Hearth, and Oreos:
A One Act Play

Children's Books:

Charlie and Chocolate's Purrfect Prayer

Charlie and Chocolate's Furry Forgiveness

Music:

Time to Change:
An Eleven Song Album Performed by Seven Years

To get alerts on new releases please follow: facebook.com/jsuthernhicks and Instagram.com/jsuthernhicks.

The author can be contacted directly by emailing to Humbleentertainment@yahoo.com.